Easter Hair Hunt

Nancy J. Cohen

Published by Orange Grove Press
Printed in the United State of America

Digital ISBN 13: 978-0-9997932-6-8
Print ISBN 13: 978-0-9997932-7-5
Edited by Deni Dietz at Stray Cat Productions
Cover Design by Boulevard Photografica
Digital Layout by www.formatting4U.com
Cover Copy by BlurbWriter.com

This is a work of fiction. Names, characters, places, and incidents either are the product of the author's imagination or are used fictitiously, and any resemblance to actual persons, business establishments, events or locales is entirely coincidental.

Chapter One

"I don't see Blinky anywhere, do you?" Marla Vail asked her best friend, Tally Riggs. They stood on the rear terrace of Tremayne Manor, a historic mansion privately owned but open to the public for special events and guided tours. A wide expanse of lawn faced them.

"She seems to have disappeared," Tally replied. "Where were you supposed to meet her?"

"Blinky told me to wait here after her appearance as the Easter bunny." Bonnie Morris, also known as Blinky, had hired Marla to fix her hair for a fundraiser luncheon that followed the children's Easter egg hunt. Blinky was a customer at Marla's salon as well as a friend.

Tally rocked the stroller holding her nineteen-month old son, Luke, who sat happily playing with a squeaky toy. Marla had figured the duo needed an outing, so she'd invited Tally to join her. After her husband's death, Tally was struggling to raise Luke on her own.

Marla shaded her eyes from the sun and peered at the manicured grounds in front of them. A few stragglers, children who hadn't heeded the call to rejoin their parents, ran about shrieking and hollering as they sought to collect more Easter eggs hidden in the grass.

What could be delaying her client? Tardiness was not a habit where Blinky was concerned. The woman was never late for an appointment. If anything cracked her reserve, she blinked a mile-a-minute. Hence her nickname, that she told even strangers to call her.

"Do you think Blinky needs help getting out of her costume? It did look awfully bulky," Marla said. "I can't imagine what else might be keeping her."

Tally gave Marla a reassuring smile. "Don't worry; she'll turn up. There's still a half-hour until the meal starts. How about if I search inside the house and you check the yard? Blinky might have strayed off the beaten path and gotten lost." Tally pointed toward a row of hedges that bordered the formal gardens. Tall, shady trees edged the rear of the property.

"You're right. She wouldn't want the kids to see her remove the costume, although it's more likely she's changing clothes inside the house."

"Would you rather we switch places? You don't want to fall in your condition."

Marla patted her baby bump. "Now you're sounding like Dalton. Don't coddle me because I'm seven months pregnant." Nonetheless, her back hurt more lately and the added weight made her feel clumsy. She'd better watch her footing.

She had just started down the marble stairs when Lacey Tremayne—their hostess and the estate's owner—called, "Marla, are you free for a few minutes?"

"I suppose. What's up?" Marla asked, turning toward the woman.

Lacey wore her blond hair swept into a chignon. A diamond necklace circled her neck. Her eyes mirrored the blue from her tea-length gown and held a friendly expression. As she drew closer, Marla caught a whiff of expensive perfume.

"I see you're heading out for some fresh air. Would you mind gathering the eggs left in the field? I don't want them hiding in the grass to muck up our gardener's mower. The last of the children are coming in now, and my house staff is busy preparing for the luncheon."

"Sure, I can do that."

Lacey's gaze lowered to Marla's belly. "Are you even able to bend over? If not, I could ask our head gardener. He's working in the greenhouse today. We've given the rest of his crew the weekend off to be with their families."

"I'll be fine," Marla said, accepting the basket the woman offered. She couldn't very well refuse the lady of the house, who'd been kind enough to invite her to stay for the luncheon.

Worried about Blinky, she hastened down the steps and then paused, wondering which way to go first. Would her client have headed toward the formal gardens with cultivated hedges, cascading fountains and geometric flower beds? She wouldn't have gone to the café. Maybe she had ventured farther out on the lawn by the trees.

Deciding to search the level ground first, Marla roamed across the grass, glad she'd worn low-heeled pumps instead of sandals. She had on a dressy top over comfortable black pants, which made walking outside easier.

The Tremayne estate bordered the northern edge of Broward County in Southeast Florida. She'd never heard of it until now or she would have visited sooner. Her husband enjoyed touring historical houses as well as nature parks. Dalton would like the mansion with its museum-quality collections and extensive gardens.

Her cross-body purse bounced with each step. Today's March weather had brought sunny skies and balmy breezes, but it could also bring a quick rain shower. She hurried forward.

A sweet scent cloyed the air as she approached the end of the field, picking up a leftover egg here and there. Thankfully, the ground was dry, and her shoes barely left any impression. She hurried toward a cluster of seagrape trees, eager for the shade. Being heavier these days, she overheated easily and had to pace herself.

As she dodged the broad leaves on overhanging branches, a glint caught her attention. What was that? A piece of metal reflecting the sunlight?

Oh, it's another egg, she realized as she got closer. She picked it up and turned it over in her hand. *That's weird.* This was not a child's plastic toy like the others she'd retrieved. The egg she held appeared to be a real treasure, or else a fancy replica. Lines of rose-cut diamonds set in gold quartered its ruby enameled surface. Or were those crystals? Surely, this exquisite piece wasn't meant to be lying in the grass. Someone must have dropped it by mistake.

A central seam split the surface. Did the thing open? She tried to pry it apart without any success. There must be a trick to it. Maybe pushing on the top gem would trigger the release.

Just then the sun exposed a flash of white among the shrubbery. She stepped over for a closer look. As she parted the branches, a gasp escaped her lips.

Dear Lord. Lying face-down on the ground was the missing Easter bunny, still in full costume.

"Blinky, are you all right?" Marla called. She stuck the jeweled egg in her pocket and dropped her basket on the grass.

The figure didn't move a muscle. Had Blinky fainted? Maybe she couldn't breathe in that outfit.

Marla fought an urge to remove the headpiece, because that would entail dragging her friend into the clearing. She shouldn't exert herself that way.

How could she help? A zipper ran down the back of the costume. No indication of movement was present. Was Blinky breathing at all?

Maybe she could loosen the headpiece and feel for a pulse at the neck. But as she leaned nearer, her breath hitched. A blotch of red congealed on the ground beneath the body.

Marla's heart thudded in her chest. *Is that blood? You'd better not touch anything. Call for help.*

She whipped out her cell phone and dialed nine-one-one. After giving the relevant information, she rang off and called Tally.

"I'm out on the lawn," she said. "I found Blinky. She's still in her costume and lying unresponsive on the ground."

"Holy smokes! What's wrong with her?"

"I'm not sure. I've called for the medics, and the police should be arriving." Marla hesitated to mention her other observations. She shouldn't say anything until the first responder confirmed her suspicions.

"Did you notify Dalton?"

"Not yet. I'd like to get a better assessment of Blinky's condition first." Marla thought of her husband, happily at home, relaxing on this Saturday afternoon, along with his teenage daughter, Brianna. Tomorrow was the proper Easter holiday when they were hosting a family dinner.

Sirens sounded in the distance. "You can tell Mrs. Tremayne," she added, "but don't let people come out on the lawn. We need to keep the place clear."

Turmoil erupted as the authorities pulled into the driveway. Marla waved her arms until they spotted her on the lawn. The paramedics approached, carrying their equipment, while Marla snagged the police officer who was first on the scene.

"Hi, I'm the one who called for help," she mentioned, pointing to the figure on the ground. "I didn't want to touch anything, or I might have felt for a pulse."

"You did right to call us, ma'am." He took one look at the crimson blotch and yanked out his radio. He moved aside to make some calls she couldn't overhear.

The medics withdrew the prone woman from the bushes. They unzipped her furry white suit and turned her over. Marla had been right in that the headpiece could be removed separately. But as they lifted the bunny head away, she cried out in stunned surprise.

It wasn't Blinky.

A man's face greeted her. And from the stranger's dilated, fixed pupils, he wouldn't be telling them his identity any time soon. Her gaze swept downward, noting a bloody gash in the costume's midsection.

Blinky had disappeared, leaving a dead guy in her wake.

Her shock notwithstanding, Marla had enough presence of mind to snap a couple of quick photos with her cell phone. Maybe it would help in identifying this man.

"Ma'am, I'll have to ask you to put away your phone and step aside," said the police officer. "We need to secure the scene. Can you tell me what happened?"

She stuffed the mobile device inside her purse. "My name is Marla Vail. I was picking up stray toy Easter eggs after a children's egg hunt. I'm a guest at the manor. My friend had been dressed up as the bunny, but now she's missing. I don't know how this man got her costume."

"Why do you look familiar to me?"

"We've probably met at a social event. I'm married to Detective Dalton Vail."

The officer's face split into a grin. "Of course. I'm Henry Matson." They shook hands. "I've heard about your exploits, Mrs. Vail."

"No doubt," she murmured. She could imagine the look on Dalton's face when he was informed about her involvement in yet another case.

She didn't have to wait long to see him in person.

"Marla, I got a call you were here," his concerned voice said from behind, as she was relating what she knew to Officer Matson. Dalton had arrived along with the backup team. "The boys tipped me off when they heard your name on dispatch. What's going on?"

Marla whirled to greet her husband. Reassurance flowed through her like warm honey at his familiar countenance. "Sorry I didn't notify you. I thought Blinky might have fainted, but it wasn't her in the costume at all. I've never seen this man before."

"Whoa, slow down. Are you all right?" His glance dropped to her belly.

"I'm fine, thanks. Physically, at least." She'd started to tremble. Maybe his arrival had triggered her reaction. She hadn't allowed herself to think about the body lying there until now.

A lock of peppery hair spilled onto his forehead. He ignored it, withdrawing a notebook and pen from his pocket. "Henry, I'll take over the interview," he told the first responder.

Before he could begin, one of the medics signaled him over. "Detective Vail, you should see this." They'd partially removed the costume, confirming a slash wound in the victim's body.

"Has he been stabbed?" she asked in a raspy tone. Her throat had gone dry.

Dalton flashed her a look of exasperation. "Marla, the M.E. is on his way. He'll determine the cause of death. Please stand back so my men can do their work."

While he gave orders, Marla made another quick call to Tally, suggesting her friend go home with Luke. She could catch a ride later, or else Dalton would give her a lift.

"Mrs. Tremayne wanted to come outside, but I told her you had things under control. She's needed as hostess for the luncheon," Tally said.

"The person in the costume is dead," Marla confided in a hushed tone. "And it isn't Blinky. It's a man I've never seen before. Has Blinky turned up inside the house, by any chance? Did you see if she's among the lunch guests?"

"No, she's not. How did this person die?"

"It looks as though he was stabbed and then thrown under the bushes."

"That's awful. How would he have ended up in Blinky's costume?"

"Good question. I'm worried about her, but I haven't searched everywhere. She might be over by the formal gardens. Maybe she got lost on the trails, as you'd suggested."

Tally drew in a sharp intake of air. "You don't think *she* did this, do you?"

"I doubt Blinky could have managed to toss the man's body under the shrubbery. But why give her costume to someone else and then vanish? Hang on. I'm coming up to the house."

She informed Dalton of her plans and then tromped across the grass to the mansion dominating the landscape. The white-columned structure had originated as a winter home for the wealthy Tremayne family, who'd made their early fortune in Florida railroads and later in road barricades.

Luke was in his stroller, squirming restlessly. He'd probably sensed the tension in the air. Lacey Tremayne had come outdoors and stood alongside Tally on the rear terrace. Her forehead creased as she rubbed a hand over her face.

"I can't believe this has happened in the middle of our holiday event. What am I to tell my guests? They're wondering why the police and rescue vehicles are here. However can I explain this to them?"

"Say a staff member collapsed," Marla suggested. "Would you know this person?" She displayed the photo on her cell phone.

"Good heavens. That's Paolo, our head gardener. He looks…"

"Yes, I'm afraid so. You can positively identify him?" She'd have to tell Dalton this news.

Lacey nodded, her complexion pale. "Is that the bunny suit he's wearing? What is *he* doing in it? And what happened to Blinky?"

"Your guess is as good as mine." Marla shoved her hand into a pants pocket, where her fingers encountered an oval object. "Omigosh, I forgot about this. It was lying on the ground near Paolo." She held out the jeweled egg to their hostess.

Lacey's jaw gaped. "That's one of the eggs from our collection. I can't imagine how it got outside." She plucked the egg from Marla's fingers.

"What do you mean? It belongs in the house?"

"Come with me and I'll show you."

Marla addressed Tally. "I know you want to stay, but Luke is restless. The little guy needs a nap. It's been a long morning." The child's fussy cries confirmed her assessment.

Tally's concerned gaze swept over her son. "I don't want to leave you alone."

"I'll be okay. Dalton is here if I need him. Go ahead. We'll catch up later."

They said their farewells, and Marla hustled to follow Mrs. Tremayne inside the house.

Marla had only gotten a quick glimpse of the interior at her arrival. The entry hall at the front had faux stone walls, a crystal chandelier, and a grand staircase leading to the second level. Portraits of famous Russian royalty adorned the walls. Marla had gotten a kick out of it, since her own heritage went back to Russian aristocracy before the Revolution.

Voices rose in laughter from the dining room as Marla followed Lacey through a series of rooms. The guests appeared to be ignoring the turmoil outside. Then again, the action was happening back toward the tree line, so it might not be visible from their window view.

"I wish I'd taken the guided tour of your house," Marla said as they passed into a room containing built-in, lighted display cases holding fancy porcelain dinnerware.

Lacey halted to regard her with a proud smile. "My husband's grandmother became interested in Imperial art when she visited Moscow and St. Petersburg. Many of these pieces come from dessert services used by Catherine the Great. They bear the insignia of Russia's most elite orders. The Queen would give dinners each year to honor the people who'd earned knighthoods."

"These little cups are cute," Marla said, examining a set emblazoned with silver stars.

"Those are my favorites. The ice cups were used for

sorbets and custards, and I have a fondness for gelato. But come, I must see if this egg is truly from our collection."

They passed through several rooms that would befit a palace with their ornate furnishings and valuable artifacts. Marla wondered why more security measures weren't evident. She'd noticed the guard patrolling the interior, and each room had video monitors, but what about motion detectors and infrared lasers like she'd seen in movies?

Lacey headed directly to a tabletop display case in the center of one room. "Oh, my Lord," she said, staring in disbelief.

"What is it?" Marla peered at a label that said the items in the case were made by Carl Fabergé, the famous jeweler commissioned by Russian royalty to make precious works of art. Three jeweled eggs rested on individual stands inside the glass case.

Uh-oh. One of them didn't look right.

"This Fabergé egg belongs in that spot." Lacey pointed a shaky finger at the case. "Someone must have stolen it and substituted a fake one in its place."

Lacey was correct. Those crystals glued onto the egg's scarlet surface had a dull tint. At a glance, it might pass muster, but not when tour groups came through and people got a good look.

Marla's stomach sank as she realized what this meant. The theft must have been planned for today while Lacey's attention was diverted. Somebody had prepared to steal the valued treasure by obtaining a substitute to take its place.

Had this same person also attacked the gardener? If so, it meant someone in the house might be a thief and a murderer.

Chapter Two

"Aside from the twenty guests at your luncheon, who else was present in the house today?" Dalton asked Mrs. Tremayne, who sat in the library being interviewed. He'd allowed Marla to remain, in case she picked up nuances he missed.

After replacing the treasured egg where it belonged, Lacey had rejoined her guests. Marla had accompanied her since her husband was occupied examining the crime scene. She may have lost her appetite earlier, but the crab and avocado salad brought it back in full force.

"The kitchen staff was on duty," Lacey replied, clasping her hands together. "We'd hired extra catering help, so they were here, too. Heather, our head docent, had the day off because we weren't conducting tours today. And Sarah, our gift shop manager, left after the egg hunt."

"I'll need the names and addresses of everyone on your guest list as well as the staff members present. How about outside?"

"Other than Paolo, you mean? Our café manager, Michelle Stringer, came in to meet some suppliers, although the restaurant was closed for the holiday weekend. It's a private concession."

Marla half-listened as she scanned the wood paneling and cozy fireplace. The marble mantelpiece held a set of tall brass candlesticks that reminded her of the classic Clue game. You could easily brain someone with one of those heavy objects.

Floor-to-ceiling bookshelves lined the walls, where the musty odor of books mingled with the fresh scent of lemon oil. Her gaze rested on a plush armchair. It tempted her to relax and escape reality with a good book.

Especially when the real world outside included murder. Dalton suspected that was the case, which the medical examiner would confirm. But how had the head gardener ended up in the bunny suit, and where had Blinky gone?

Concern for her client made her bite her lower lip. Something was wrong in this place. She could sense it. Lacey seemed more upset by the near-theft of her precious egg than the fact that her gardener was dead and Blinky was missing.

The estate's owner had unlocked the display case with a key she wore around her neck and replaced the fake egg with the real one.

"This key opens all the cases," Lacey had admitted. "It's old-fashioned, I know, but we have enough security otherwise. Or at least, I thought we did until today."

"Maybe the video footage will show more," Marla suggested. She had neglected to mention the incident with the egg to Dalton and knew he'd be annoyed she had tampered with evidence.

Lacey outed her first. "I can't imagine how Paolo got hold of the egg," she said, brushing a straggling hair off her face. "Maybe he was responsible for the other missing items as well."

Dalton tilted his head. "Excuse me?"

"Oh, didn't your wife tell you? Marla found one of our priceless Fabergé eggs out on the lawn near where she discovered… you know. A fake egg had been substituted for the real one in the display case, which was still locked, by the way." Lacey's brow furrowed, as though she'd just realized this fact for the first time.

Dalton shot Marla a reproachful glance, no doubt because she should have mentioned this nugget earlier. She ignored him and asked Lacey who else had a key.

"Daniel, my son, has one. So does Rick Eaton, our security chief."

Dalton tensed, his pen poised over his notebook. "Is Eaton present, or is he off today?"

"Rick has the weekend off. And before you ask, Daniel made sure he had other things to do to keep himself occupied. My son doesn't like these house parties. He says we shouldn't invite riffraff into our home. His attitude isn't very charitable."

She spoke of her son in a disparaging tone, Marla noted. "How many security people are on duty?" she asked.

"Three people are on the team. Normally, two of them patrol the house. One covers the upstairs while another person stays down here. The third patrols the perimeter. We gave two of them the day off for today, though, since we're not doing tours."

Dalton's eyes scrunched in the way they did when he was applying logic. "Let me see if I've got this straight. This morning, the kids and their parents were here. Most of them have left by now."

"That's correct. People buy tickets to the Easter egg hunt and then separately for the formal luncheon, which is for adults only. Thank you again for letting me finish lunch with my guests. They paid enough to dine with me and deserved my full attention. People like to visit with the aristocracy, so to speak."

Marla hid a cough behind her hand. Dalton let the remark pass, considering his next question while she squirmed in her armchair. Her back had begun to hurt, and her hand inadvertently settled over her belly. He must have noticed because his lips pursed.

"Marla, why don't you go home? You look tired. I'll catch up to you later." He turned to the hostess. "We're having our family over for Easter dinner tomorrow. I told my wife it would be easier for us all to go out, but she insisted."

Lacey gave Marla a polite smile. “How far along are you?”

“I’m seven months. I shouldn’t have eaten so much, but your meal was delicious. Thanks again for including me.”

“My pleasure. It’s too bad your friend Tally couldn’t stay, but she’d brought her son along.”

“I know. Blinky would have sat next to me. I can’t imagine where she’s gone. How did Paolo end up in her costume?” She gave Dalton an alarmed glance as a sudden thought occurred to her. “Have you searched the grounds? Maybe whoever stabbed Paolo got to her first.”

Lacey clapped a hand over her heart. “Stabbed, you say? Why didn’t you tell me this before, Detective?”

“We won’t know for sure how he died until the medical examiner officially determines the cause of death, ma’am. I’d appreciate it if you didn’t share this information.”

“Of course not. How horrifying. Poor Paolo.” Lacey shook her head, her face sorrowful.

“My men are searching for Blinky. Hopefully, we’ll find her alive and well. Maybe she witnessed what happened and ran off scared,” he suggested in a calming tone.

After she’d switched costumes with the guy? Marla thought. Had she been forced to do so, or had it been a deliberate act on her part? Maybe she’d observed the thief in action. He caught her spying and went after her. She did a costume switch, hoping he’d chase Paolo instead. But that didn’t make any sense. It wouldn’t explain Blinky’s continued absence.

“You’d mentioned other missing items besides the egg,” she told the lady of the house. “What did you mean?”

Lacey glanced at the room’s entrance and lowered her voice. “Other artifacts have disappeared. Small things that might not be noticed right away, but still valuable. I’ve told Rick to be more vigilant, but he hasn’t detected anything. Nor have the video cameras picked up any unusual sightings.”

"I'll want copies of all recent footage," Dalton said, his brows drawing together at this latest revelation. "And a list of these missing objects. We should probably see if we can get any prints off the eggs that were touched and the display case handle."

"You're not getting black dust on my treasures, Detective. I'd rather you focus on finding Blinky and the person who killed my gardener."

"Have you told anyone else about the thefts?" Marla asked.

"Only my son. He says it's good because it reduces the clutter. I'm afraid my offspring doesn't appreciate history the way I do. I've been thinking I should donate the house and its contents to the historical society instead of leaving it to him. Daniel will sell the house and squander his inheritance if he's my sole heir."

Marla was surprised by her statement. Had Connor Tremayne left nothing to his son when he died? "The money from the tours must help pay for maintenance," she said, curious about the estate's finances. "I assume a place like this requires constant work."

"That's why I initiated the guided tours. Our admission fees go toward restoration." Lacey gave her a wan smile. "Things were falling apart when dear Connor married me. He had a brilliant mind, but he couldn't see his nose in front of his face when it came to common sense. I consider myself the estate's custodian. It's my greatest wish to see this house and its contents preserved for future generations to enjoy."

So who had brought the money into the marriage? Had Lacey wed her husband to gain a fortune? Or had she been the one to provide needed funds for renovations, much like the cash-poor noblemen did in England when they wed American heiresses?

A sudden notion gave her pause. Could Lacey have orchestrated the theft of the valuable egg in order to collect insurance? Maybe the lady of the manor needed more money than she let on. Dalton should examine the estate accounts if he thought it might relate to his case.

So many questions, and she lacked the energy to pursue the answers. Blinky's disappearance bothered her the most, but she couldn't deal with it now.

Pressing a hand to her lower back, she rose. "I can't sit any longer. Please excuse me, but I need to go home. Dalton, you can get my formal statement later."

He leapt from his chair. "I'll give you a ride."

"No, don't bother. You have other people to interview."

"Call Brie to come and get you then. She's doing homework and will be glad for the excuse to take a break." His teenage daughter, a junior in high school, had her driver's license.

"Okay. Brianna can use my car since Tally picked me up earlier." Marla turned to Mrs. Tremayne, who'd also risen. "I'm sorry my visit got cut short. I would have loved to see more of your house. I'll have to come back under better circumstances."

"It's been a pleasure meeting you, dear. I can see why Blinky raves about you so much. I hope you'll pay us another visit soon."

Marla handed her a business card. "Can you please notify me if Blinky turns up? I'm really worried about her."

"Of course. This is all so troubling. I'm beginning to get a headache."

Marla waggled her eyebrows at Dalton as she took her leave. He'd have his work cut out for him interviewing the staff and then following up with the guests who were there that day.

Brianna arrived about a half hour after Marla's call for pickup. "I can't believe you found another dead body," she told Marla during the drive home. The teen focused on driving, her gaze straight ahead. "You said he was stabbed?"

"He had a bloody gash in his midsection, so it looks that way."

"Did Dad find the murder weapon?"

"Actually, he didn't mention it. The killer could have dropped it in the bushes." Would the size or shape of the wound fit a thin knife or a wider one, like a sword from the mansion's collections? Then again, the weapon could have been a kitchen knife or even a gardening tool, considering the victim's identity. Or it might be a personal blade belonging to the killer. Why else would the culprit have removed it?

Without the weapon, they wouldn't get any answers until the M.E.'s report came in.

"I'm more concerned about my client who's missing," she told her stepdaughter. "When I last saw her, Blinky was wearing the bunny costume. How did the gardener come to be wearing it? And where has Blinky gone? I hope your father can locate her."

Brianna's brow creased. "Now he'll want to work tomorrow. I've set the table for Easter dinner as you asked, but there's still a lot to do before company comes."

"He's already picked up the ham, and I'll be making a lamb roast. We should be okay as long as he shows up in time for dinner. His parents would be grievously sorry if he couldn't make it." When on a fresh case, Dalton often worked long hours. She expected him to go into the office tomorrow, but hopefully only in the morning. He'd want to interview people, but they would be busy with the holiday, too.

****

As Sunday rolled around, Marla's prediction came true. Dalton left early to get caught up on paperwork. Marla started preparing the leg of lamb to put into the slow cooker. Kate—Dalton's mom—had bought the pot for her as a holiday gift. She said Marla would be super busy once the baby arrived, and putting in a meal to simmer all day might be helpful.

As per the recipe she'd found, Marla cut slits into the

meat and inserted sprigs of rosemary and garlic cloves. After drizzling olive oil over the roast, she placed it into the slow cooker. Next she squeezed cut halves of lemon over the top and dropped the rinds into the pot. With the temperature on low, she set the timer for eight hours.

She considered what to do next. A spinach salad would start off the main meal. That was Dalton's domain. He'd put all the ingredients together when he got home. Rosemary red potatoes and fresh asparagus were the accompaniments, but she wouldn't fix those until later.

She'd come across a recipe online for acorn squash slices and had asked Dalton to bring home some squashes so she could try it. The recipe used herbs, not brown sugar or maple syrup, so it should be healthier with fewer calories. She figured they couldn't have enough side dishes, and this occasion gave her the excuse to try something new.

Marla's mother, Anita, was bringing a carrot cake for dessert, while Dalton's parents, Kate and John, were bringing wine. Brianna had called dibs on making garlic cheese biscuits.

Soon the house was filled with delicious aromas. Brianna, after segregating the ingredients she would use later, went to her room to finish her homework. Marla assembled the stuffed mushrooms and chili dip she'd serve for appetizers and refrigerated them to bake later.

Weary of working in the kitchen and wanting some fresh air, she took the dogs for a walk. Spooks strained on his leash. The cream-colored poodle had spied a squirrel, his favorite prey. Lucky, a golden retriever, prowled the sidewalk with her nose sniffing the ground.

The day had turned out temperate and sunny. Marla waved hello to Susan Feinberg a couple of doors down. Susan, a friend and neighbor as well as a client at Marla's salon, was the same age as Marla. She had two school-age children and baked the best brownies on the block.

"You look nice," Susan commented while her kids fumbled over a basketball. Her son won the skirmish with his younger sister and tossed the ball into a portable weighted net. "Are you going out for a holiday dinner?"

"Our families are coming over," Marla said. "I did my hair and makeup. I'll change into something nicer later." Susan already knew that Marla was Jewish and Dalton was Catholic. Although neither was very religious, they'd made the decision early in their two-year-old marriage to honor their respective traditions.

"How many people are you having?" Susan asked.

"Dalton's parents are coming, along with my mother and her boyfriend. We're also expecting my brother and his family, which will be nice since we haven't seen each other in a while. That makes eleven of us altogether." *Twelve, if you count the baby growing inside me.*

Marla rubbed her belly, feeling a kick in response. She smiled inwardly, her heart swelling with love for the child joined to her. It was still difficult to conceive that she and Dalton were expecting a baby boy. Marla hadn't wanted kids of her own until recently, and now at thirty-nine, she hoped there wouldn't be any complications.

"We should go to lunch," Susan suggested. "I see you at the salon when you do my hair and around the neighborhood, but we haven't had a good schmooze in some time."

"I know, and I could use your advice. Dalton wants to buy baby furniture, but I'm afraid to tempt fate. Things could still happen, if you know what I mean."

Susan gave her a bemused glance. "Things can always happen, Marla. You can't think that way. It's fun to go shopping to furnish your nursery. Better now than later, when you'll have a hundred other things to do. Call me this week, and we'll set a date to get together."

As Marla continued along the sidewalk, she mused over the pending changes in her life. Hopefully, Dalton's parents wouldn't pressure her about furnishing the baby's room. She heard enough on that topic from her own mother. Maybe she could steer the conversation to their latest case rather than personal issues. Ma's boyfriend, Reed, got a kick out of her sleuthing. The former literature professor enjoyed a challenge.

Speaking of challenges, she gave Dalton one in the kitchen that afternoon. He'd come home from work with the acorn squashes she'd requested. Occupied with retrieving serving platters, Marla asked him to stick a squash in the microwave for five minutes. Once softened, she could slice it and save the baking part for later.

She'd lined up her serving dishes and was drying dishes by the sink when a loud popping noise sounded from behind. She whipped around just as the microwave door burst open. With a shriek, she leapt back. That thing might have cracked her on the head if she'd been nearby.

Her heart pounding, she dropped her dish towel and rushed over to cancel the programming. Steam billowed from the interior. Her pulse calmed as she regarded the mangled mess inside the oven. Thank goodness no one had stood within range of that door.

"How long did you put this in for?" she asked Dalton, who'd hurried over from his perch in front of the TV. He gaped at the microwave unit, his astonished expression diminishing her ire.

"Fifteen minutes."

"I said five minutes, not fifteen. No wonder it exploded. You should have pricked the skin to let air escape. It's a good thing we have more squash to cook."

Brianna wandered into the room. "What did you do, Dad?"

He pointed to his chest. "Hey, why does everybody blame me? How am I supposed to know about these things? At least nobody was hurt."

"It's okay, hon." Marla sidled closer and kissed him. "I'll

clean it up, and no one will be the wiser. That is, if the microwave isn't broken."

The only thing broken was Dalton's pride. He slinked off to the family room to watch TV, while Brianna and Marla discussed baking times for their respective dishes and the order for oven usage. Coordinating a holiday meal took advance planning.

All went smoothly when their families arrived. Kate and John brought two bottles of wine. Dalton chilled the white and left out the red. Anita and Reed contributed carrot cake as expected, along with a package of decorated sugar cookies. Marla's brother, Michael, and his wife, Charlene, brought homemade guacamole and corn chips.

They made small talk during the first hour. Marla enjoyed chatting with Jacob and Rebecca. Her nephew and niece seemed to get bigger every time she saw them. Jacob, nine years old, had dark hair and expressive eyes that would make him a stunner to the ladies when he hit his later teens. His sister, who would turn six in June, was a girly girl who loved to dress in sparkly clothes and watch Disney princess movies.

Their parents seemed to be avoiding each other. Michael and Charlene added to the conversation but kept their distance. Nobody else seemed to notice the strain between them, so Marla didn't say anything. Perhaps she was misinterpreting.

"I saw something on the news about an incident at Tremayne Manor," Reed said in a dignified tone befitting a retired university professor. His jacket and tie came from old habits, while the other men had dressed casually.

Seated at the dinner table, Reed dug into a bite of his spinach salad. He sat between Anita and John to Marla's right. Kate was next to John, with Brianna squeezed in on his right. Michael and his family sat opposite them.

Dalton, heading the table at the other end, raised his eyebrows. "Marla stumbled across a dead body on the Tremayne estate," he remarked as though it were a daily occurrence.

All eyes turned to stare at her.

Anita's mouth pursed. "Don't you have enough to do getting ready for a baby without being involved in another murder? What were you doing there anyway?"

Marla chewed and swallowed a fresh strawberry. "My client, nicknamed Blinky, was dressed as the Easter bunny for the egg hunt. She'd hired me to do her hair before the fundraiser luncheon that followed. When I went to find her, Blinky had vanished. In her place was Paolo, the head gardener."

"You mean, they'd switched places? And that man ended up dead?"

Marla broke a cheese biscuit in two and slathered butter on one half. "Yes, but that's not all. Somebody had dropped a valuable Fabergé egg on the grass near the body. It belonged to a collection in the house."

"Curiouser and curiouser," Reed said, quoting *Alice's Adventures in Wonderland.* "The house was built by the Tremayne family, who wanted a winter residence in Florida. When Connor's grandmother traveled to Moscow and Saint Petersburg, she fell in love with their palaces. She began collecting art from the Imperial Russian era. Her husband hired architects to add lighted display cases throughout their house to showcase her acquisitions."

"Have you seen the place?" Marla asked him. "It's like a treasure museum more so than a lived-in residence."

Reed nodded, lifting his water glass. "Tremayne Manor and Whitehall in Palm Beach are my local favorites, along with Vizcaya in Miami. Hmm, maybe I should run guided tours of historic houses in the tri-county region."

Anita beamed at him. "That's a terrific idea. It'll give you something to do after—" she broke off, her face flushing. "Oh, heck. I was going to save this announcement until after dinner, but I almost spilled the beans anyway. Reed and I have decided to get married."

"What?" Marla half rose from her chair. Wasn't this too quick? It seemed as though they'd only just met. And yet, Ma and Reed had cruised together and appeared with each other at all their recent family events. She forced a pleased smile to her face. "Congratulations are in order. Let's raise a toast, everyone!"

"That's fantastic, Ma." Michael got up and kissed Anita and shook Reed's hand.

Marla heard Charlene's quiet snort. What was going on there?

"This is wonderful news," Kate added. She and John clinked glasses with each other in tribute to the engagement.

Marla glanced at her mother's hand. Anita didn't wear a diamond ring to signify her status. Had the proposal just taken place? "Will you be planning a wedding?" she asked, her throat tight.

"We'll set a date after you have the baby. We don't want to rain on your parade."

"So will Reed move into your house? His condo would be too small for both of you."

Anita gave her an excited grin. "We're going to sell our places and move into a senior community in Boynton Beach."

"What? You're moving away?" It wasn't that far, but considering how Marla had expected to rely upon Ma when she had the baby, they might as well be going to the next planet.

"Oh, come on. We'll be less than an hour or so from you. Besides, we'll be closer to Reed's son and his wife, whom you've never met."

"Hey, what about us?" Michael said, reaching for his wine glass.

"We'll be nearer to Boca than we are now. Your children can see us more often."

Marla fell silent. She should be happy for her mother, and yet, she couldn't help feeling a sense of loss.

"I'm excited for you," Brianna said, picking up the slack.

"Now I'll have an excuse to get a new dress. Reed, does this mean we'll get to meet your family?"

He had two sons from a previous marriage. With his extended family, their holiday dinners would get larger. Marla wasn't sure how she felt about losing their sense of intimacy. She'd have enough to contend with once the baby arrived and had counted on her mother's full attention. This change would disrupt everything.

Feeling as though she'd been gob-smacked, she rose to deliver the next course.

"We're thinking of holding an engagement party," Reed replied. "We'll let you know the plans when we're ready. You can meet my kids then." He turned to Dalton. "I hope you'll be finished with this case soon with all the family events in the works."

"Me, too." Dalton stood to help Marla collect the empty salad bowls.

"Speaking of momentous occasions, I want to do a baby shower for you," Ma said, once Marla and Dalton were seated again. "How about the Saturday before Passover?"

Marla consulted her cell phone calendar. "I'm free that day. I'll reserve the date. Nicole's bachelorette party isn't until the following weekend, so she'll be able to come."

"Great, then I'll start looking into venues. All the brides with June weddings will have booked the popular places, so we can't waste time. How about Tremayne Manor? You have connections there."

"Are you kidding? I just found a dead body on their grounds. Plus, I'm worried about Blinky. Maybe I should talk to her neighbors to see if anyone's heard from her. You wouldn't mind, would you?" she asked her husband.

He nodded. "Go ahead. We'll be busy interviewing everyone from the estate. Just be careful not to paint a target on your back. You're responsible for two people now, and your safety comes first."

Chapter Three

The best way for Marla to avoid thinking about all the changes to come was to keep busy. And so on Monday morning, she ran a bunch of errands before driving to Blinky's house to look for clues to the woman's absence. Her time was limited since she had an appointment at the veterinarian's office later for the dogs.

Blinky lived in an upscale gated community in a subsection of Palm Haven. Typical of southeastern Florida enclaves, the development boasted manicured lawns, flowering hibiscus and shady live oaks. Marla loved the queen palms, their graceful fronds swaying in the breeze. Tropical foliage always brought her a sense of calm.

She searched for Blinky's address, which she'd obtained from her client files. As she approached the two-story Mediterranean-style house, she noted the absence of any cars in the driveway. Wide hurricane impact windows stared back at her from the sand-painted façade as she emerged from her parked car and stepped toward the front porch. A sweet scent perfumed the warm spring air.

Storm season was only a couple of months away, and with it came humidity and averages in the nineties. She should be enjoying this weather before the baby came and it turned too broiling hot to go outside. Instead, she might be on a fool's errand, doing what should be Dalton's business. But so far his colleagues had failed to locate her missing friend.

Marla rang the doorbell, listening for a response from inside. Nothing. She rapped on the cherry-stained door with the same results. Now what?

Hoping neighbors weren't watching, she loped around the house, thinking Blinky might be lounging on the patio out back. That was unlikely, considering she'd have notified Marla when she came home. So it didn't come as a surprise that no one occupied the chairs on the screened-in porch. Clear water glistened in a rectangular pool with nary a ripple in sight.

The kitchen appeared dark inside, and so did the garage when Marla made her way around to that side of the house. She peeked in a window, observing the empty space inside. Was Blinky's car still parked at the Tremayne estate? She called her husband to ask, telling him she'd found no one at home.

"Her vehicle hasn't moved. It's parked at Mrs. Tremayne's place," he confirmed.

"I'll speak to Blinky's neighbors. They might know where she could be hiding."

"Be careful what you say. Her disappearance may be linked to the murder case. We're focusing our investigation on Tremayne Manor right now, but eventually, we'll broaden our scope."

Marla viewed the silent street. "Maybe I should let your department handle it. I don't want to sabotage your efforts. Besides, Blinky might surprise us by turning up with an innocent excuse. It's only been a couple of days. What else have you learned?"

"She didn't go in to work today. People in her office are puzzled by her lack of communication. They say it's unusual for her. Nor has she been in contact with her son or daughter, both of whom live out of town. They wanted to fly in, but I told them to hang tight until we have more information."

"Do you think they're telling the truth?" she asked, remembering that Blinky's real name was Bonnie Morris. She was a widow with two grown kids. How frightening for them if their mother was truly missing. Or were they aware of her location?

"I didn't hear any nuances in their tone to suggest either one was lying," Dalton replied. "Hey, aren't you supposed to take the dogs to the vet today?"

"Yes, but the appointment isn't until two. I have the morning free." Mondays were her day off during the week. She patted her belly as the baby kicked, as though to say, *Not for long, Mom. Soon your time will be mine.*

"My men are interviewing the estate's gardening crew this morning," Dalton told her. "None of them were present on Saturday, but they might know something about Paolo that's relevant."

"You can't be certain he was the intended target. It might have been Blinky. I couldn't tell who it was in that costume. Hold on, I'm getting another call."

"Marla? It's Lacey Tremayne," the woman's tremulous voice said on the other end. "I'd like to see you again if you have time."

"Sure. What's it about?" Marla's pulse accelerated. Had Lacey found something related to Blinky's absence? Or was she merely making a friendly overture?

"I've been doing some checking around, and I hear you're good at solving crimes. I'd like to talk to you regarding the thefts we've been having."

A flash of disappointment swept through her. She'd hoped it was news about her friend. "I'm actually free right now if you want me to come over," Marla offered.

"That would be great. Have you heard anything about Blinky?"

"Sorry, no. I was hoping she might have called you."

"Her car is still parked where she left it on Saturday. That can't be a good sign. But we'll continue this discussion once you're here."

Marla switched back to Dalton and informed him about her plans.

"Let me know if you learn anything interesting," he said before ringing off.

After she arrived at Tremayne Manor, Lacey invited her into the French Drawing Room. Lacey ordered refreshments from a maid as Marla seated herself on a fancy armchair. She noted the set of porcelain dinnerware in a display case, the oil paintings on the walls, and the figurines on a marble mantelpiece. A crystal chandelier provided overhead illumination, but Marla preferred the softer lighting from lamps placed around the room. Floor-to-ceiling windows overlooked the rear garden.

She waited for Lacey to start their conversation. Lemon oil fragrance drifted her way along with the heavy scent of lilies from a fresh bouquet on a table. Did the gardeners provide cut flowers from the gardens? Wait, hadn't Paolo been working in the greenhouse the day he was killed?

She'd have to ask Dalton if he'd checked the place. Maybe that was where Paolo and Blinky had exchanged the bunny costume.

Lacey distracted her with small talk before the maid returned. "Is this your first baby?" she asked with a pleasant smile. She wore a comfortable slacks set with yellow gold jewelry.

"Yes, it is. We're very excited. Dalton wants to buy furniture for the nursery, but I'm superstitious in that regard. I'd rather wait until it's nearly time."

"I hear you. It was the same for us. Will you be having a baby shower?"

"My mother wants to host one for me."

"You work in a salon, don't you? The staff might be planning a surprise party."

Marla didn't explain that she owned the salon and day spa. "You could be right. Then again, my mom will probably invite the staff to her event."

"Ah, here comes Ginny with our tea."

Marla picked up a delicate bone china cup and took a sip of fragrant jasmine tea. After the maid left, she resumed their conversation. "Do you just have the one child?" she asked.

Lacey chewed and swallowed a bite from a lemon poppy seed scone. "When we married, Connor didn't want children. He liked to travel and live a jet set lifestyle. But I was younger and didn't feel fulfilled. Eventually, I convinced Connor to expand the family but with only one child. I stopped taking birth control pills, and a year later, Daniel arrived. We might have been better off had I listened to my husband."

"What do you mean?" Marla put her teacup down on a side table.

Lacey cast a glance toward the doorway and lowered her voice. "Daniel always gave us problems. He was a spoiled child who wasn't happy with anything. I think he was troublesome because Connor didn't pay him enough attention."

"Some men get jealous over a firstborn son." Or so Marla had heard from a few of her clients.

"You're right. Daniel stunted his lifestyle. I wanted to be home to raise our son. Connor resented having to make any adjustments. I think he regretted his behavior in the end. That day when he went out on his yacht, he said, 'Take care of our son.' It was an odd thing for him to say, but I couldn't ask him about it. He never returned from that trip."

"I'm sorry," Marla said, wanting to learn more about the circumstances of her husband's death but too polite to pry.

"He concerns me, you know," Lacey continued, her head bent. She wore her wavy hair down today, and curtains of it shaded her expression.

"Who? You mean Daniel?"

"It's the reason why I haven't told anyone about the items missing from the house. I'm afraid my son might be the one taking them."

Marla stared at her. "Why would you think that?"

Lacey met her gaze with sad eyes. "I don't know him very

well anymore. He's secretive and keeps to himself. What I do know is that he's a whiz at computers and could tamper with the security feed if it suited his purpose. He doesn't need money. He gets an adequate allowance. So I don't know what he would hope to gain."

"I appreciate you confiding in me, Lacey. This doesn't mean Daniel is the thief, especially because he doesn't have a viable motive. It could turn out to be someone else."

"Yes, and that's what I'm hoping. I want you to investigate. The cops don't care about petty theft when they're dealing with a murder and a missing person. Will you help me identify the crook? If not my son, it has to be somebody intimate with the house. I trust my staff, but we do have temporary help sometimes, and people come and go here all the time on the tours. You'll have your work cut out for you. I'll pay you, of course."

Marla waved a hand. "That's not necessary. I help my husband with his cases all the time. This could be part of the same investigation." She had a hunch they were related. It couldn't be a coincidence that a Fabergé egg had been stolen from Lacey's collection and ended up outside by the dead body.

A shadow appeared out the window, and she spotted a masked figure scooting past. She leapt from her seat. "Did you see that?"

Lacey gave a snort of dismissal. "Oh, don't mind him. That's Karl, our beekeeper. He always goes around in his protective gear. Says it protects him from the hives, although he's nowhere near them when he's in the vicinity of the house. Maybe he's spraying today. He's also our exterminator."

"You have your own beekeeper?" Spraying for pests would account for the mask if he wasn't near the bees. Otherwise, anyone could be wearing that outfit.

"It was Sarah's idea," Lacey replied. "She's our gift shop manager. She thought it would be a boon to sales to sell our own labeled honey. It's been a huge success. But never mind

Karl. He mostly keeps to himself out by his shed, and we rarely interact." Her gaze turned wistful. "He does vaguely remind me of someone, though. It must be the way he walks. Anyway, that's irrelevant. Where will you start your inquiries?"

Marla pursed her lips. "If it's okay with you, I'd like to talk to your neighbors to make sure these thefts are confined to your house alone. We want to be certain there's not a broader scheme going on here."

Lacey rose and smoothed her pants. "Let me know what you need, Marla. My resources are at your disposal. And if Blinky shows her head anywhere, I expect you'll notify me immediately."

"Yes, of course." They shook hands, then Lacey led her to the door. Once outside, Marla glanced at her watch. She had time to speak to a few neighbors before rushing home for lunch and taking the dogs to the vet.

She didn't hit pay dirt until the third house, a two-story structure with stone turrets and a second-floor balcony. It was farther down the road from the Tremayne estate, which had its own private lane. All the houses here were so spread out that Marla had to drive from place to place.

"I love the manor," said the occupant, a brunette whose makeup and dressy clothes indicated she might be about to go out. "My name is Julie Sprinkle, by the way."

"I'm Marla Vail and a friend of Lacey's. My husband is the detective investigating the incident from the other day."

"You mean, the murder." Julie put her hands to her face. "How awful! And weird, too. I heard the fellow had on a bunny costume when he was killed."

"There had been an Easter egg hunt for the kids. Did you know the victim? I understand he was the head gardener. Maybe he did other lawns in the area."

"I doubt he'd have time. Tremayne Manor employs a full-time gardening staff. They're kept busy maintaining the landscaping. I'm so envious of their formal gardens."

I need to explore the grounds, Marla resolved. She hadn't gone beyond the house or the rear lawn to date. "Lacey gave me permission to mention that a few items have gone missing from her house. Have you noticed anything similar? We're wondering if somebody is targeting the neighborhood or if it's just her place."

Julie frowned, still poised in the doorway. "They let in the public for tours at that house. What else do you expect? I gather Mrs. Tremayne needs the money to maintain the place, but all kinds of people can gain access that way."

"Guests still have to pay an admission fee," Marla noted. "And they have guards patrolling each level during tour hours."

Julie's lips pursed. "Obviously, security needs to be beefed up if things are being taken. One solution would be for Lacey to donate the house to the historical society. Then it would become their problem. She and her son could still live there, but the responsibility wouldn't be on their shoulders anymore. The treasures inside belong in a museum anyway."

"Lacey had mentioned that idea to me, but how would Daniel feel about losing his inheritance? I imagine after Lacey, the property goes to him."

"That depends on how Connor left things. If the property is in a trust, Lacey might be acting as trustee rather than owning the house outright. You'd think Connor would have made provisions for his son that way. Otherwise, what if she remarries? Her new husband could inherit the estate."

"Good points." She should ask Dalton to look into the estate documents. Meanwhile, she might have a chat with the son to sound him out on things. "As far as you know, have any other thefts occurred in this community?" she asked for confirmation.

"Not that I've heard. I keep in touch with people on our neighborhood app, and we usually share the news if there's a problem."

"Okay, thanks. I appreciate your information." Marla handed over a business card. "If you remember anything else, please give me a call."

Julie's face brightened. "You own the Cut 'N Dye Salon and Day Spa? I've been thinking of getting bronze highlights. What do you think?" She ruffled her medium brown hair styled in a cute bob.

"They'd look great on you. Stop by when you can. We give a discount to new customers."

Marla strode away, pleased with herself. She'd gained information and possibly a new client all in one swoop. It appeared the thefts were limited to Tremayne Manor after all. Dalton could verify this by checking the police reports for the area.

She touched base with him at home before taking their two dogs to the veterinary office. "Thanks for the update," he said after she'd related her news. He didn't offer anything in return, and Marla had to hang up since time was short.

At the vet's, the technician called for Lucky and Spooks to come inside. The poodle shivered as Marla placed him on the treatment table. Visiting the doctor was not his favorite activity. Lucky sniffed the edges of the room, her tail down, until it was her turn. The golden retriever took two people to hoist her onto the table.

Dr. Nelson pronounced the animals to be in good shape, administered their shots, and renewed their prescriptions. She gave them each a pat for good behavior.

Marla proceeded to the checkout desk where she bought a new supply of heartworm medication, anti-tick pills, and eye drops for Spooks. The bill tabulated to several hundred dollars. Dogs cost as much as people to go to the doctor's, she reflected during the drive home.

She offered each pet a treat in the kitchen and let them out into the fenced backyard. Then she considered what to do for the rest of the day. A nap might be in order. This morning's activities had tired her, and she needed to conserve her energy. But right after she'd let the dogs back inside, the phone rang.

"Marla, are you busy?" Ma asked in her singsong voice.

"I was just going to take a nap. What is it?"

"I'd like you to come over and tell me what things you want to keep. If I'm going to move in with Reed, I have to get rid of stuff. We've enough furniture between the two of us, but I can't take all my *tchotchkes*. I need help sorting through them."

Marla's temples throbbed. "Right now? I've been out all day and was hoping for some downtime to relax."

"All right," Anita said, her voice softening. "We can make a date for another afternoon. I suppose I'm being selfish in wanting more time with you."

A wave of guilt washed over Marla. "What about Michael? He could help you pack."

"Your brother said he'd come on Sunday. His wife won't be able to make it." Anita clucked her tongue. "Charlene has some kind of work event the next day that requires preparation."

"Is everything okay between the two of them? I sensed some tension at our dinner yesterday."

"Michael said she's been under pressure at work. I'll ask him more about it when he comes over."

"Let's check our calendars for a date when you and I can get together. I'd rather visit you when I have more energy." Marla would rather not go there at all, but she did want to have a say in how Ma disposed of her goods.

"We also need to talk about your baby shower, and I want to show you the plans for the place we're buying in Boynton Beach."

"I'll look forward to it," Marla said without any enthusiasm. She hung up and stretched out on the family room sofa. More comfortable lying down, she dialed Tally at her dress shop.

"Hi, have you got a minute? I wanted to give you an update," she told her friend.

"I was going to text you later," Tally said. "Has Blinky shown up yet?"

"I'm afraid not." Marla brought her up to date on events.

"I spoke to one of Lacey's neighbors. The woman hadn't heard about any other thefts in the area. It appears the thief is only operating at the manor."

One person missing, another one dead, plus stolen heirlooms. How did these tie in together? Or did they?

"Did you speak to any of the staff?" Tally asked.

"I don't want to step on Dalton's toes until he finishes his interviews. Lacey seemed concerned about her son. She said he has the skills to tamper with the video surveillance. He also possesses a key to the display cases."

"What would be his motive? To make money selling these things to a buyer?"

"Lacey said he gets a generous allowance. Daniel could be afraid his mother will gift the house to the historical society, and he's getting his cut this way. Or else he's taking the items he wants to keep before she donates everything."

"Those could be possible reasons." Tally spoke to someone at her shop and then resumed their conversation. "You might also consider who needs money desperately enough to steal from the estate. That could apply to the property's finances and not only the artifacts."

Leave it to Tally to come up with a new angle. Marla knew she could count on her best friend to have a fresh perspective.

"I'm always glad when I review a case with you," she said. "You've a different way of looking at things. It seems logical that the thief most likely is a staff member. Dalton is checking into everyone's background."

"Then let's hope he discovers the crook as well as the killer. Keep me informed, will you?" After a few more parting words, Tally rang off.

Chapter Four

Marla couldn't do anything further on the case until later in the week. Meanwhile, she told Nicole what was going on during a break at work on Tuesday morning.

"No way, girlfriend," said the cinnamon-skinned stylist with an astonished expression. "You went to an Easter egg hunt and turned up a dead body along with a Fabergé egg? That would only happen to you."

"I know. How am I so lucky?" Marla stacked foils for her next appointment, ignoring the background music from the speakers and the splash of water from the shampoo sinks.

Nicole cleaned her counter with a lemon-scented spray. "What do you suppose has happened to Blinky?"

Marla shrugged. "I haven't a clue, and her disappearance gnaws at me. Why would she give her costume to someone else? None of it makes any sense."

"She could have had any number of reasons to run away, especially if she saw the gardener being murdered."

"What if she was the intended target?" Marla suggested. "Blinky might have convinced the gardener to put on her bunny suit, maybe even paid him. Then while the killer went after him as the decoy, she vanished. But that would assume Blinky knew the guilty party and was desperate to avoid him."

"Has Dalton turned up anything on her background check? Could she have had secrets from her past that returned to pose a threat?"

"Not to my knowledge. The other option is that the gardener spotted the thief through the window and got caught spying. He requested Blinky give him her bunny outfit so he could disguise himself. The thief might have been someone he recognized from the household. Otherwise, why wouldn't he have gone directly to Lacey to report what he'd seen?"

Nicole paused with her cleaning cloth in hand. "If you find the person who stole the egg, you might find your murderer. What's your plan?"

Marla placed the foils on her wheeled roundabout. "Blinky's children haven't heard from her, nor have her colleagues at work. Her car is still parked at Tremayne Manor. I spoke to a neighbor. The lady said no one else has reported any break-ins, so it appears the thief's range is limited to the manor house. Lacey confessed to some misgivings about her son. I need to speak to him. If I wait a few more days, Dalton will have time to interview the guy first. His team has been questioning the gardeners and other estate staff."

Nicole gave her a shrewd glance. "Lots of folks must work on the estate. I've never gone on their tour. Maybe I'll ask Kevin if he wants to visit the place."

Marla smiled at the mention of Nicole's fiancé. "Is Kevin getting nervous with your wedding only two months away?"

Her friends had gotten engaged in November on their trip to Atlantis in the Bahamas. Marla hoped she could make their Memorial Day wedding, but it was awfully close to her due date.

"He's excited and can't wait for the big day. We still have to do our food tasting and decide on the cake. Kevin likes the yellow cake with chocolate mousse in the middle, but I love the vanilla cake with raspberry cream."

"Why don't you order both? You can do half of one and half of the other."

"That's an idea. It's too bad you can't come along on my bachelorette party. You make things seem so easy."

Tired of standing on her feet, Marla sank into her salon chair. "I'd love to go to New Orleans but not when I'm pregnant. You'll have a blast."

"Any progress in setting up your nursery?" Nicole asked with a twinkle in her eye.

Visions of baby items spun through her head. "We've picked out a changing table that converts into a dresser when the child is older, but it costs over two thousand dollars. The stroller we like is nearly one thousand, and car seats are another major purchase. I didn't realize things were so expensive."

"Wait until you have to save for the kid's college fund. Have you registered for gifts yet?"

Marla mentioned a popular superstore. "By the way, did you remind Kevin about our double date after work on Saturday?" she inquired, keeping her expression neutral.

She'd planned a surprise bridal shower for Nicole. Kevin was supposed to drop her off at the restaurant. Presumably he'd go to park the car and then would turn up, along with Dalton, in time for dessert.

"It's on my calendar. I can't believe I'm getting married and you're having a baby." Nicole shook her head. She wore her straightened hair to her shoulders and would curl it with extensions for her wedding.

"Tell me about it," Marla drawled. Between baby and bridal showers, planning a nursery or planning a wedding, plus everyday work, neither one of them had much spare time.

Robyn, the receptionist, waved from the front desk. Marla's customer had arrived.

She stood to retrieve her client. "I'll swing by Tremayne Manor on Thursday morning to see if I can talk to Lacey's son. Then if Dalton is done interviewing the staff, I can proceed in that direction. We need to find Blinky as fast as possible so we can put this to rest."

Nicole checked her wristwatch with an annoyed frown. "My client is late again. That woman never shows up on time.

By the way, how's Tally? Didn't she go with you to the Easter egg hunt? Her son must have enjoyed himself."

"Luke was a bit young for the festivities, but he had a good time scooting around on the grass. Tally loves being back at work. Combining a dress boutique and bistro was a brilliant idea. I told you she sells clothes only for social occasions now. Customers linger over snacks or have a light lunch while they try on evening gowns. I don't know where Tally finds the energy. Luke is a handful at home, but he seems happy at the day care center."

"It can't be easy being a single mom. Soon you'll be chasing after a little one like that. You'll be digging him out of scrapes instead of digging for clues on the next murder case."

"That's what Dalton hopes, but I'm not so sure I want to give up my activities in that regard. I help people find closure. And it brings Dalton home quicker when he solves his cases."

"Then good luck with your interviews. Maybe Blinky will turn up in the interim."

"You said it. If not, I hope she's somewhere safe." *But even if she was, wouldn't she have notified me?*

Occupied with her clients, Marla didn't notice Robyn coming up behind her until the receptionist poked her on the arm.

"Hey, Marla. There's a guy up front who says he needs a haircut. He insists on coming to your chair. I can fit him in between your three o'clock and three forty-five appointment, if that works for you. The first one is a touch-up, so you'll have about a half-hour while the color processes."

Marla glanced at the wall clock. "Sure, you can add him. Is it someone I know?"

"I don't think so. He said his mother recommended you. His name is Daniel Tremayne."

Marla almost dropped her comb. "That's unexpected, as well as convenient. I've wanted to talk to him. Please ask if he doesn't mind waiting fifteen minutes."

She spared a surreptitious glance toward the front of the shop. A lanky young man paced in obvious discomfort from the scowl on his face. His posture slumped, which didn't help his overall unkempt appearance. He wore a loose tee-shirt over a pair of scruffy jeans.

Why wouldn't he have gone to a barbershop or one of those chain places that charged less money?

Maybe Lacey had sent him here on purpose. But then, how did she get him to agree? Or did he come because he had something to relate regarding his mother?

After she'd finished her current client, she walked over to greet him. "Hi, I'm Marla. It's great to meet you," she said, shaking his hand. "Come on over to my chair, and we'll see what we can do for you today."

Marla seated him at her station and ruffled his limp strands of mud-brown hair. "What did you have in mind?"

He appraised her in the mirror. "My hair is too long. I need a trim, but don't cut it too short. I need to maintain my image."

As what? A spoiled, rich boy? Marla couldn't read him but sensed he had more to say.

"How about if we lift it this much?" she said, demonstrating. Her gaze drifted to the tattoos on his upper arms, then she zeroed in on his fingernails. He kept them clean and clipped short.

"That'll work," he replied in a noncommittal tone.

She sent him to get shampooed. While he was gone, she mulled over the purpose for his visit. He didn't keep her in the dark for long.

"My mother wanted me to check out your place," he said as Marla fastened a cape around his neck and replaced the wet towel with a dry one. "Mom likes her current hairdresser, but she's looking for a salon with spa services. I'll bring her a copy of your menu and prices."

Is that the only reason you're here? she wondered.

"We'd love to have her join our client list," Marla said in a smooth tone. "How is she doing? I'm sorry for how things turned out this past weekend."

Daniel's mouth flattened. "She's upset because that police detective keeps coming around to ask questions."

Marla squeezed the shears in her hand. "That detective happens to be my husband. I was there that day but I didn't see you around, either at the hunt or the charity luncheon."

"Are you kidding? No way was I going to show my face to that crowd of shrieking kids and snotty women."

"Don't the tours and special events bring in needed funds? A historic house like yours must require constant maintenance."

"You're damn right. Heather, our head docent, says my mom should donate the place to the historical society. Then they'd be responsible for the upkeep."

"Is your mother considering that option? With the proper legal agreement, I imagine you and your mom could continue to live there after transferring ownership. Or is the property in a trust? If so, the terms might dictate a beneficiary."

"The deed is in my mother's name. My dad transferred title to her years ago. By rights it should be mine next, not that anyone cares."

"What would you do if you inherited it? I don't know if I'd want a property that extensive. The taxes and insurance must be astronomical."

He gave her a morose stare. "I have an idea that would bring in money, but in a different way."

Marla lifted a strand of his hair and clipped off a half-inch. Her hands moved automatically while she spoke. "Have you discussed this proposal with your mother?"

"She and I don't agree on things. She'd never understand."

A ripple of emotion crossed his face, but Marla couldn't decipher it. She thought about what he'd said. Why would his father have deeded the property to Lacey instead of putting it into a family trust? And why wouldn't Lacey leave the property to her son rather than the historical society? Was she afraid Daniel wouldn't appreciate their legacy?

Maybe Dalton could get to the root of these issues. The estate documents should help to clarify things.

She finished the cut and picked up the blow-dryer. As she dried his hair, she wondered what questions to ask next. Had Daniel really come at Lacey's request, or had he meant to speak to her for reasons of his own?

"What kind of work do you do, Daniel?" she asked in a friendly, conversational tone, after she'd laid the blow-dryer down. She shaped his hair with her comb, parting it on the natural side.

His brows lifted as he watched her movements in the mirror. "I'm in cyber security. I work from my home office for an online tech firm. The company pays well, and the job allows me to have a flexible schedule."

"Don't you miss the company of working with other people?"

"You sound like my mother. She nags me to go out and meet chicks. She needs to worry about her own affairs, not mine."

So why don't you have a girlfriend? Do you have any friends at all? And why do you still live at home? Can't you afford a place of your own?

"Your mother mentioned to me that items in the house have gone missing. What do you think about the thefts?" she asked him with a glance at her watch. She needed to finish up before her next customer arrived.

He scowled at her. "If you invite members of the public to invade our house, you're taking a risk. Mom is fond of all the crap in the place, but I'd sell the stuff if it belonged to me."

"I understand you have a key to the display cases."

"Hey, don't look at me. Maybe you should talk to Bruno."

"The maintenance man? Why him?"

"He has a chip on his shoulder about rich people. I don't know why he stays on, but he says it's because his family has always worked for ours."

"How about Rick, the security chief? He's in charge of protecting the house's contents."

"I don't think he'll be staying on forever. But I've said enough. Are we almost done?"

Marla put down her comb, secretly pleased at the satisfied look on his face as he assessed her work. "Sure. Is there anything else you want to mention before you go?"

He stood and took off his cape, tossing it onto the seat. "Yeah, there is one more thing. I don't have access to our business's financial records, but your husband might be able to obtain them. Just saying, you know?"

Not really. What are you implying? Is there someone at home you don't trust?

A sudden realization hit her. Lacey would have had to register the house and gardens as a business to conduct public tours.

"I hear you," she told Daniel. "And I appreciate your visit today. I hope you like the way your hair turned out."

As Daniel left and Marla cleaned her station, she wondered if he truly suspected someone of tampering with estate finances. Or had he meant to deflect suspicion from himself? If so, he'd mentioned the head docent, the security chief, and the maintenance man as potential people of interest. He had also raised more questions than he had answered. Who did run the business aspects of the estate? Was his mother the sole person in charge?

And again, why had Connor Tremayne transferred the deed to his wife instead of putting the property into a trust? Moreover, who else was on his side of the family? Could there be cousins or other relatives that he didn't want to inherit?

She shook her head. Dalton would have to deal with the

possibilities. And what did any of this stuff have to do with Blinky? Why was her friend still missing?

It wasn't until she'd sent her next client to the shampoo chair that she thought of another question she should have asked Daniel. If he'd been working in his home office the day of the Easter egg hunt, had he seen anything noteworthy out the window?

She told Dalton about their conversation later when she had a break. She'd gone into the back storeroom to use her cell phone in private and to grab a water bottle from their supply. Her wistful glance fell upon the staff's coffee maker. She missed drinking coffee while pregnant.

"The son works for an online tech company that provides cyber security to large corporations," Dalton confirmed when she'd concluded her tale.

"If he's so good with computers, why doesn't he design a program to monitor the priceless relics in the house?"

"You said he called the stuff crap. Evidently he doesn't place any value on the items."

"Maybe he's full of bluster because he doesn't own them. Did you check the provisions in his father's will?"

"Yes, that much is public record. Connor left his personal possessions and assets to Lacey."

"And nothing to his son? Not even his watch or other jewelry? That's very odd. It makes me wonder about their relationship."

"We didn't talk about his dad in my initial interview. I mainly focused on his knowledge of the gardener and what he observed that day. Daniel claimed to be in his home office at work during the afternoon. The room has a window that overlooks the rear lawn. He'd put his ear buds in to listen to music once the kids started screaming outside."

"How about when the cops showed up?" Marla asked, wondering if his desk faced the window or the door.

"He didn't notice the commotion. As for the dead guy,

Daniel had no quarrels with the gardener. He caught him yelling at the exterminator a couple of times for trampling on the plants, but otherwise, Paolo seemed to get along with everyone."

"According to Daniel, the property belongs to Lacey."

"That's right. Connor transferred title to her ten years ago. It's almost as if he could foresee the boating accident that killed him two years later."

"It's still strange he didn't arrange for the property to pass to his son," Marla commented. "How was it handed down from his parents?"

"It was in a revocable trust. When Connor's father died and he became the trustee, he had the power to change the provisions."

"Maybe Lacey had some hold over him that caused him to sign over the property. And then he ends up dead. Maybe you should look closer into the incident with his yacht."

"That's not my concern right now. I need to finish my interviews with the staff at the estate."

"Any word on Blinky? The longer she's missing, the more I fear something terrible has happened to her."

"Her case is being handled by another department. They've promised to let me know if anything develops. Listen, I have to go. We'll catch up later."

"Wait, there's something else." But he'd already hung up. Darn, she had wanted to suggest he look into the estate's business records.

She completed her work for the rest of the day with a heavy heart. Blinky's disappearance weighed on her. What else could she do to find her friend?

It was all so complicated. They had three mysteries to solve—the murder, the thefts, and the missing person.

The baby kicked. As she rubbed her belly, Marla thought of one more item to add to the list. She and Dalton still needed to agree on a name for their son.

Chapter Five

Marla and Dalton debated baby names on the way to their appointment at the obstetrician's office on Wednesday morning. She wasn't in a good mood, not being allowed to eat before a scheduled glucose test that hadn't sounded pleasant.

"I don't know why you aren't considering the names I've suggested," Marla said. She'd wanted to pick a name that started with an 'R' after her father, Robert. "Richard Howard Vail has a nice ring to it."

"Richard is too common. I don't like Ralph, Roger, or Roy either. We could put my Uncle Harry's name first."

His mother had lost a younger brother who'd died as a child. Kate would be honored for them to remember him this way. But Marla felt adamant that her father's memory should come first. Dalton could choose the middle name for his side. They'd both liked Howard but couldn't agree on a first name.

"We're here, so this discussion is over for now. Let me get the door for you," Dalton said.

In the doctor's treatment room, Marla was given a bottle of sugar water to drink. While waiting for her blood to be drawn one hour later, she went for an ultrasound. She grimaced at the baby's curled-up breech position. His knees almost reached his head.

"I hope he turns around before I give birth," she groused, her temples throbbing. She was starving, and drinking the concentrated sugar water hadn't helped.

"Now that you're officially starting your third trimester, you'll feel lots more movement," the doctor said with a sage look in her eyes. "The baby has time to present in a head-first position. You'll probably feel it when he repositions himself."

After Marla got her blood drawn—the lab tech took four vials—she and Dalton both received Dtap vaccines. She made her next appointment for three weeks later.

Drained by the ordeal, she scarfed down the egg white and avocado sandwich Dalton bought at a fast-food restaurant before taking her home. He left right away for his office.

After freshening up, Marla headed to the salon. She yearned to stay home and rest but didn't have that luxury, and the next day would be just as busy. Thursdays were her late day at work, but she had plans for the morning. She'd booked the ten o'clock tour at Tremayne Manor and made a lunch reservation at the café.

****

Promptly at nine-thirty on Thursday, Marla approached the gift shop located at the side of the manor house. She had to collect her ticket there, so that would be her first stop.

The store resided in what must have been a porch back in the day. Likely it had been enclosed around the time the house opened to the public. Door chimes jingled as she pushed open the door indicated for ticket sales.

A pleasant citrus scent entered her nose as she stepped inside. Colorful displays offered museum-quality gifts, gardening tools, fancy stationery, jewelry, Florida souvenirs and toys. Marla couldn't resist the temptation to browse. Maybe Dalton would like that fancy magnifying glass or a book on Russian antiquities. She could always use a new spoon rest for their kitchen.

"Hello, may I help you?" asked the lady at the cash register. Her voice held a slight nasal twang. She stood about two inches shorter than Marla and had friendly honey-colored eyes. Marla liked how she wore her auburn hair in a shoulder-length wavy style.

"I made a reservation for the ten o'clock tour, and I'm here to pick up my ticket. My name is Marla Vail." Marla withdrew a credit card from her wallet as she approached the counter.

"I'm Sarah O'Malley, the store manager." After processing the payment, Sarah handed the card back to Marla along with a printed ticket and a receipt.

"I was here the day of the Easter egg hunt. How sad that such a pleasant event turned into a nightmare." Marla glanced around, noting an inner door that must lead into the house. No other customers were present.

Sarah's face blanched. "We were open for a few hours while the kids were here with their parents, but then we closed once the luncheon started. I saw the police cars and rescue van in the driveway when I left, but I figured one of the guests had taken ill. Poor Lacey is still upset."

"So am I." Marla lowered her voice and leaned closer. "My friend, Blinky, is missing. She was playing the Easter bunny."

"I heard about her. It's frightening. One person is dead and another is missing. I'll offer a prayer for your friend's safe return."

"Thanks. The more days that pass, the more afraid I am for her well-being."

"What do you think happened?" Sarah shuffled a collection of folded fans on the counter.

Maybe I should get one of those for my purse. It could be useful in the heat, Marla thought. "I'm hoping Blinky ran away scared rather than the worse alternative. Have you heard any scuttlebutt among the household staff?"

Sarah lifted her long nose in the air. Her taut features and thin lips reminded Marla of the wicked witch in *Wizard of Oz.* "I don't gossip, if that's what you're asking."

"I'm married to the police detective on the case," Marla

admitted. "Any clues that might help us find Blinky would be appreciated." She gestured toward the gardening corner with its decorative tools, packaged seeds, yard signs and statues. "Were you acquainted with the gardener who died? Maybe he had some input into your selections, since that's his department."

"Since I'm the sole buyer for the store, Lacey lets me order whatever I think is appropriate. I rarely speak to the outdoor staff." She said it in a snotty manner, as though consorting with the other hired help was beneath her station.

"Lacey mentioned it was your idea to bring in a beekeeper," Marla told her. "She said your honey sales were through the roof."

Marla's statement elicited a smile. "That's true. I figured private label honey would do well on our shelves. I'm thinking we should offer jams and jellies next."

"Does the café lady use any of your products in her restaurant?" Marla asked, thinking they could sell the stuff in two places and garner more sales.

"Michelle runs the place as an independent concession, so we don't cross over with any of our merchandise."

"I have a lunch reservation there. I'm looking forward to eating by the formal gardens."

"You'll love it. The setting is delightful."

"Is that near where the beekeeper has his hives? I don't want to worry about bees or wasps if I sit outside."

Sarah's hands stilled. "They won't be a problem. The honeybee hives are well away from populated areas."

"How did you meet the beekeeper? That's an unusual occupation."

"We met at a local park where he was giving a lecture. Karl does our bug spraying as well. You won't find any wasp nests, ant hills or spider webs near the house when he's around."

"I can see why it's a full-time job," Marla conceded. "He'd have to maintain the lawns and garden paths so they're safe for visitors, in addition to treating the house."

"His services are very valuable to the estate."

And to you? Marla wondered. The woman spoke with an unusual amount of pride regarding the place's exterminator. "Tell me, if you decide to sell private label jams, do you plan to take up canning? Where would you get the fruit? Or would you buy the product and apply your own labels? I notice you stock other gourmet foods, like hot sauces, olive oils and vinegar."

"Those are locally sourced items. They're popular with tourists. We wouldn't have any problem getting jars of jam to label from a local farm if we decide to pursue that avenue."

Marla leaned against the counter. "Were you here from the start, when the house first opened to visitors? Or did you come on board after the shop was established?"

Sarah rearranged a collection of glass paperweights by the cash register. "I've been working for the Tremaynes for fifteen years. It seems like a lifetime since I started as a maid. It was my idea to establish the gift shop. Things are so different now."

"How about the tour leader?" Marla asked, hoping to get the scoop on another staff member. "Was she also employed here before Lacey turned the place into a business?"

Sarah glanced at a pair of women who'd come inside to browse. Her mouth set in a firm line as she returned her attention to Marla. "Heather is in charge of tour groups. She sets the schedule and does the training for our other docents. Doesn't your husband know all this? What has he learned about the case?"

"He doesn't share his findings." Marla tapped her chin. "I'm confused on one point. Was opening the house for tours an idea that Lacey conceived on her own, or did it come from someone else?"

Sarah glowered at her. "Lacey came up with the idea of showcasing the place to the public. Connor died and didn't leave her enough to manage the estate. That fool. I told him… I mean, he didn't do enough to provide for his family. He should have settled things before his accident."

"So Lacey needed money?"

"Listen, luv, if you owned a place this big, you'd need money to maintain it, too. Opening the house for tours and catered social events was a brilliant move on Lacey's part."

"I gather you enjoy managing the shop?"

"It's gratifying to see my ideas put into practice. Our most popular items are the reproductions of Russian artifacts on display inside the house. Maybe you'd like to buy a pair of those hand-painted enameled candlesticks as a gift? Or perhaps you'd like one of our nesting dolls? Visitors love them."

"I'll look around more after the tour. I'd better get going. Thanks for talking to me. I appreciate your insights into the house's history."

Marla turned away, then appeared to hesitate. She spun around to face the shopkeeper. "Oh, one more thing. Lacey mentioned she'd been unable to locate some of the artifacts in the house. You haven't had any items disappear from your inventory, have you?"

"Not that I've noticed," Sarah said in a guarded tone.

"Would you say her business is doing well?"

"It's been a lucrative enterprise."

Marla tilted her head. "I suppose you manage the records for the gift shop. Do you report the revenue directly to Lacey? Or to her accountant?"

Sarah's gaze chilled. "You're awfully curious about our affairs. Did your husband send you to interrogate us?"

"Lacey personally asked me to make inquiries," Marla said as the inner door opened, and a woman announced the pending start of the tour. Her pulse quickened. She only had a few minutes left to conclude this interview. "Here's my card. Please give me a call if you think of anything that might help locate my friend."

Sarah took the card and perused it. "You own a hair salon? What do you plan to do after the baby is born?"

"I'll take the first few months off, then we might hire a nanny. Do you have any children?"

A pained expression entered Sarah's eyes. "No, I don't. I've never been married." Her face brightened. "But the store keeps me busy, so I'm happy. I've a gift show to attend next month in Savannah, and I get to travel abroad twice a year to find new items for the shop. I love what I do. Now you'd better hurry, or you'll miss the start of the tour."

"Thanks. I'm glad we had a chance to chat." Marla turned away, wishing they could talk more. Sarah hadn't responded to her comment about the shop's financial records, not that it mattered right now.

Then again, if someone was stealing artifacts to sell, that person's motive had to be a need for money. She doubted anybody would take them in such a subtle manner out of spite.

However, Dalton had taught her to examine all the possibilities. Maybe Lacey had an enemy who held a grudge against her. Taking her valued treasures would certainly cause her distress, even if those items had originally belonged to her husband's family. Maybe the thief wasn't concerned so much with the money as with getting even.

Marla rubbed a hand over her face. If she hadn't found the Fabergé egg by the dead gardener, she might have assumed the murder and the thefts were unrelated. But then Lacey wouldn't have confessed to the missing items from her collection and started Marla down this path. And how did Blinky fit in? Had she been in the wrong place at the wrong time?

Dalton's people were combing the woods for clues. She hoped their search would come up empty. If they didn't find a body or evidence of foul play, Blinky might still be alive and hiding out somewhere.

She cast aside her thoughts as the tour began. Learning more about the house's history might help in her investigation.

Heather Wishbone, the tour guide, appeared to be in her early sixties and married, judging from the diamond band on her finger. She wore her bleached blond hair in a feathery layered bob and crimson lipstick on her wide mouth. The lip color matched her nail polish.

Her put-together look was complete with a pink floral-tiered chiffon dress that outlined her slender figure. Marla figured she must go to the gym to work out, or else she didn't eat much. Her creamy complexion showed few signs of aging as well.

I feel like a tank in comparison. When the baby comes, I'll have to do something to lose this extra weight. Now that I'm in my third trimester, it'll only get worse.

Marla focused on the woman's opening spiel, distracted by her rapid-fire delivery. Heather was saying how Thomas Tremayne originally built the house as a winter residence for his family. He added display cases later to showcase his wife's collection of decorative arts from eighteenth-century France and Imperial Russia. Their daughter added the formal gardens and greenhouse.

"Connor Tremayne, the man's grandson and an only child, meant to continue the family legacy," their guide explained. "He fell in love with a woman who appreciated art as much as he did. Lacey, an heiress in her own right, grew up in Palm Beach."

That answers my question about who brought money into the marriage, Marla thought. Both partners came from wealthy backgrounds.

"Theirs was a marriage made in heaven," Heather stated. "Well, until it wasn't."

She said this last statement in a low undertone, but Marla caught it. *What does that mean?* She lost the opportunity to ask as the head docent led the group from the entry hall into the French Drawing Room.

"Observe the blue Sèvres porcelain in those glass cases," Heather said, continuing with a litany of the objects on display. "Mounted over the fireplace is a portrait of the

Duchess of Parma, Louis XV's eldest daughter. I love the details on her gown."

Marla only half-listened as the crowd moved away. She trailed them into the Russian Porcelain Room while wondering how to get Heather alone to question her. Then they entered the section where Marla had seen the Fabergé eggs. She had to listen to this part.

"The Treasure Room contains over four hundred items, including icons and chalices from the Russian Orthodox Church, works by Carl Fabergé, and a selection of gold boxes that were popular accessories in that era."

Marla raised her hand. "I've seen only one security guard downstairs as well as video monitors. That doesn't seem like enough precautions. Shouldn't these things be in a vault instead of out in the open like this?"

"We don't advertise all of our security features, dear." After describing a number of the items on display, Heather led the way into the library. The wood paneling made from Florida pine, soft lamp lighting, and plush seating arrangements invited readers to snatch a book off a shelf and sit for hours.

Marla winced, remembering her earlier visit there. She'd sat in on Dalton's interview with Lacey right after the charity luncheon the day of the murder.

"Note the exquisite roll-top desk in that corner," Heather said, pointing. "It's decorated with wood veneers, mother-of-pearl, gilt bronze and ivory. The piece was crafted in Germany in the 1700s. The dainty handles on the writing implements are crafted from wood and inlaid with mother-of-pearl."

"Does the desk have hidden compartments?" a balding man in his sixties asked. "My uncle used to have one of those, and he showed me how to open the secret panels."

"Yes, and how about the house?" another woman inserted. "Any hidden passageways?"

Heather lifted an imperious eyebrow. "The walls of this house aren't thick enough to conceal any tunnels. As for the desk, I imagine it has its secrets."

Marla inhaled a musty scent reminiscent of the public libraries where she'd spent time during school. She peered at row after row of volumes that stretched to the ceiling. The wide range of reading material offered a broad selection to suit anyone's taste.

She missed what Heather was saying about the books, because a stocky man in a security uniform had entered the room. He stood by the doorway, arms folded at his chest. This was the same guard she'd seen roaming the first floor earlier.

As long as the tour group was occupied, she sidled over to stand beside him.

"Hi, you must have Heather's talk memorized by now. Have you worked at the manor for a long time?" she asked with a friendly smile. "This place could be a museum. I can't believe Lacey actually lives here."

"I've been working at the house since the days when Connor Tremayne was still alive," the man said with a nod. "They used to throw some glitzy parties back then. Now, not much happens except for the tours and special events." He gave her a quick onceover. "Haven't I seen you before?"

"Lacey invited me for tea the other day. I'd never toured the rest of the house, so I signed up for the one today. I'm looking forward to exploring the gardens afterward. My name is Marla Vail. And you are?"

His flinty eyes narrowed. The slate gray color of his brows didn't match his military-cut black hair. She could tell from the lighter roots that he darkened it. "I'm Rick Eaton, chief of security. How come your name sounds familiar?"

"I'm married to the police detective investigating the gardener's death. That was a shocker. Too bad you weren't on duty that day."

He stiffened. "Mrs. Tremayne said I could take the day

off. Most of the guests would be outside, except during the luncheon. It wasn't necessary for my whole team to be here."

"How many of you are there?" She kept her voice low so as not to draw attention their way.

"Me, Ed, and Claire. What, you have something against females as security guards?" he said in response to Marla's pensive glance. "We're an equal opportunity employer."

"No, it's great. I'm all for gender equality. I realized it must have been Ed here that day."

"He didn't want to intimidate the kids joining the Easter egg hunt, so he mostly patrolled the house. Poor fella felt terrible about what happened. He's fairly new to the job."

Marla glanced at Heather, who'd moved to a portable bar where she was describing the crystal decanter to the crowd. It might only be a few more moments before the tour moved on.

"Did Ed fail to notice a Fabergé egg was missing?" she said to Rick. "I assume Lacey told you what transpired that day."

He gave a glum nod. "We don't look inside every case each time we enter a room. Besides, that particular one was still locked when Lacey discovered the substitution. Since nothing had been broken, it wouldn't have triggered an alarm."

"She told me only three people have keys to the display cases—you, Lacey, and her son."

His brow furrowed. "That's true. Lacey wouldn't let the cops dust for prints. It would have been a mess to clean."

"Speaking of cleaning, who dusts all these things? I'd be scared to death of knocking an item over and breaking it."

"The housekeeping staff takes care of that chore. They're very careful."

"Sarah from the gift shop told me she'd started here as a maid," Marla commented. "Did you know her back then?"

The security chief snorted. "Sarah loved working in the big house. Said she'd be mistress of her own someday. Didn't happen, did it?"

"No, but she got promoted. Managing the gift shop has to be better than polishing silver and dusting all these *tchotchkes*. Do the maids open the locked cases to dust the items inside? I know the wine goblets at my house get murky in our glass-fronted cabinet. They need a good rinsing on occasion."

"Mrs. Tremayne won't let anyone touch the objects under glass."

"Not even her son? Is it true he has no interest in them? It's part of his family's legacy."

"Is it? You should talk to Bruno on the topic. Or better still, go enjoy the tour and mind your own business. You know what they say about the curious cat."

Chapter Six

Heather led the group into the oak-paneled dining room and launched into her next spiel. She described the French furnishings, the crystal chandeliers, the statuettes on the marble mantelpiece, and the hunting scenes depicted on the wall paintings.

Marla stared at the long rectangular table set for twenty. It was covered with a white damask tablecloth and set with bone china dishware, crystal wine glasses, and silver utensils from the house's collections. How did people see each other across the table over those polished candelabras and floral centerpieces?

She imagined herself dining there, with servants offering course after course of gourmet delicacies. Never mind that she wouldn't have anything suitable in her wardrobe for a formal dinner. She'd feel awkward just figuring out which fork to use for each course or how to eat a shrimp without using her fingers.

True, she'd dined here during the charity luncheon following the Easter egg hunt, but the table settings hadn't been anywhere near this fancy. That event was reminiscent of a normal meal in a restaurant, albeit with uniformed catering staff serving the food. They'd only had three courses, and the salad had already been plated when she'd found her seat. Nor had any elaborate flowers or silver candlesticks been obstructing her view. This scene looked like something out of a period TV show.

"The floral arrangements come from our own flower gardens and greenhouse on the property," Heather said, while members of the group milled around admiring the room's accoutrements.

"Who's going to be in charge of yard work now that Paolo is gone?" Marla sidled up to ask.

Heather gave her a stern glance. "That's for Lacey to decide. It's horrible what happened to him. I can't understand how the man ended up in a bunny costume. The whole thing is bizarre."

"Having a murder on the grounds doesn't seem to have kept the tourists away."

"On the contrary, our reservations for the week are sold out." Heather sighed, her eyes sad. "Someone will have to replace those flowers when they wilt. Paolo used to take loving care of the cut blooms."

"Did he do the actual arrangements?"

"Oh, no. Paolo didn't come inside the house. Mrs. Docket, the housekeeper, is talented in that way. She loves doing the florals."

"Mrs. Docket? I don't recall meeting anyone by that name."

"She's had time off and missed all the excitement. I believe Lacey called to fill her in on things."

Did Dalton know about this person? Lacey hadn't mentioned a housekeeper once in their conversations. Her mind recalled the locked display cases. Wouldn't the housekeeper be privy to a key? Evidently not, if Lacey had only given one to her security chief and to her son. But why give one to Daniel when she clearly didn't trust him?

"You had a nice chat with Rick earlier," the head docent remarked, while her charges read the explanatory signs posted around the room.

"Yes, apparently he's been on the staff since Connor's time. It must have been a glorious era between the family's travels to collect art and the fancy dinner parties they held on the estate. I can't imagine what it must have been like to live here then."

"Lacey always was a consummate hostess, but she'd been trained to run a household," Heather said with a fond smile. "Now she gets to host her charity luncheons instead. It's good for Lacey to channel her energies that way."

Marla gave the tour leader a curious glance. "I understand she came from a wealthy Palm Beach family. How did she and Connor meet?"

Heather's eyebrows lifted. "That's an interesting story. Connor had gone with his parents to one of their yacht club functions. He always did love boating. His family often sailed down the Intracoastal on weekends. Lacey enjoyed painting as a hobby, and an artist she admired was doing a charity auction at the club. She came along as a guest of a friend. Lacey and Connor bid against each other. They met at lunch afterward, and the rest is history."

"If I may ask, how did Connor die? I heard it was a boating accident. He must have been accomplished at the helm, or whatever you call it."

Marla and Dalton had meant to take boating lessons but had never gotten around to it. Not that they could afford to own a boat or spare the time to go sailing, but it would be a safety measure. She shuddered at the memory of being trapped on board a yacht one time with a killer. She'd been lucky to survive that incident unscathed, especially since she'd had no idea how to steer the vessel once she had subdued her attacker. Fortunately, the Coast Guard arrived before she got far from shore.

Heather glanced at the doorway and pursed her lips. "Nobody really knows exactly what happened the day Connor disappeared. It was a stormy afternoon, and he'd been intending to sail to the Keys. Lacey had a fondness for Key lime pie, and they had a favorite store where they bought pies to put in the freezer. I think he meant to surprise her for her birthday. Then the storm came. His boat was found abandoned near Key Largo. No trace of him was ever found."

"Did he provide for his wife? Lacey would have been accustomed to a certain standard of living."

"He left enough for her personal needs, but not to maintain a place this size. She'd used up most of her own savings for renovations. I applied for the job of docent when I heard about the opening. I've always loved historic houses."

"Do you live nearby? Actually, where does the staff sleep at night?"

Heather spread her hands. "People go home. We live in modern times. The former servants' quarters now act as storage space or administrative offices. The servant's hall was converted into one of our galleries." She glanced at her wristwatch. "Excuse me, we have to get moving. The tour needs to end by eleven-thirty."

Marla didn't have time to dwell on their conversation, because the kitchen caught her fancy. The commercial refrigeration unit, walk-in freezer, industrial stove, sinks and work counters were perfect for large catered events. Their group had to view things from a roped-off area because the kitchen was in use by the cook. The tempting aroma of roasting meat drifted their way as the head docent pointed out a dumbwaiter leading to the second floor.

Next they entered the French Porcelain Room, where Heather paused to describe the various items adorning the walls. Marla's eyes glazed over as she described a set of blue and gold dishes and rambled on about their history. Who could carry that soup tureen into the dining room? They must have used a cart to wheel the platters and heavy trays in there, unless they employed servers with strong arms.

Had Dalton interviewed the catering staff from the Easter luncheon? It made sense to bring in temporary workers for special events. Possibly they'd worked there before and knew some of the permanent help. If so, who coordinated their activities? She'd guess the housekeeper had that role, unless Lacey preferred to be personally involved.

She paid half-attention when they went upstairs and toured the sample bedrooms. A closed door at the end led to the owner's suites, which were closed to the group. That must be where Lacey and Daniel lived, Marla presumed. The other rooms were furnished in French style befitting an earlier era.

Marla gawked at the silver and royal blue dressing room that was larger than her master bedroom at home. You could dine in there, conduct business, and visit with friends. The closet held an assortment of clothing and accessories suitable to a lady of fashion, including hats that would be fun to try on.

Ladies in those days passed on their gowns to the next generation instead of tossing them into the donation pile. She eyed a couple of mannequins dressed in ball gowns with tiaras on their heads. The figures reminded her that Lacey must have worn jewelry to their parties. What had she done with her baubles after her husband died? Did she keep them in a safety deposit box at the bank, or had she sold them for extra cash? Lacey hadn't said the thief was interested in her personal items, only the home's artifacts. How did she insure the place with so many valuables?

Marla shook off her confusing web of questions and focused on the rest of the tour. Once it concluded, the group members were left on their own to view the grounds and formal gardens. She glanced at her watch. She'd timed the excursion perfectly as it was now lunch hour.

"I enjoyed the tour," she told Heather before the older woman left to prepare for the next group. "It's too bad Mrs. Docket isn't here so I could meet her. When does she return?"

"Next Monday. We're pretty much a smoothly oiled machine, though. Everyone knows their roles, and we're cross-trained in case we have to pitch in elsewhere."

Tired of standing, Marla shifted her feet. Her back ached and that wicker chair on the rear terrace looked inviting. But she had to move on for her lunch reservation.

"I imagine the household maintenance is totally separate

from the business of running the tours and charity events. Does Lacey manage everything on her own?" she asked in a last-ditch attempt to acquire information.

Heather's face cracked into a smile. "Heck, no. The café is an independent concession. Sarah handles the gift shop. She does the ticket sales for our tours, so she's responsible for this revenue along with her store's accounts. That leaves the special events. Lacey manages the luncheons, unless it's a big affair, in which case she'll hire an event planner. She's pretty good at these things herself, having been brought up planning elegant soirees and parties."

The docent's eyes scrunched. "It's too bad she doesn't bring her son into the fold. I'd bet he would be a whiz at bookkeeping, but she doesn't trust him to have her best interests at heart. They're at odds with each other over the eventual disposition of the estate."

"What does Daniel suggest doing with the place?" Marla asked, thrilled to be getting some answers.

"That's something he hasn't shared with any of us, but you can be sure it wouldn't involve Lacey's treasures. He's made his opinions known about the museum pieces. That's why Lacey should consider donating the house to the historical society while she holds the reins. It's the best solution if she means to preserve her husband's legacy. Now please excuse me. I have to start the next tour. I can't be late, or… never mind. I'm glad you could join us. I love talking about the house and its history."

She sped off toward the foyer, leaving Marla in her wake.

Marla's thoughts jumbled as she dug her sunglasses from her purse and headed down the rear terrace stairs and toward the café. She looked forward to exploring the gardens after lunch, although taking a nap was looking even better. The baby kicked, giving emphasis to her notion.

Hey, my son. We're learning a lot today. Let's see what the restaurant lady has to say.

She took a table outside overlooking a cluster of pink azalea bushes. Beyond stretched the formal gardens, with geometric beds of flowers and manicured hedges. Grateful to be seated, she studied the menu and chose a tomato stuffed with curried chicken salad for her entrée.

"Is Michelle working today?" she asked the waitress, whose name tag read Kim. The young woman wore a green logo shirt and a pair of black pants. Marla liked the bun that kept her hair neatly off her face.

"Yes, Michelle is inside. Did you want to speak to her, ma'am?"

"I have some questions to ask, if you could tell her I'm here." Marla placed her order and sat back to enjoy the ambiance. A wasp flitted past, making her think of the bug guy. It was his job to destroy wasp nests and spider webs to keep the area safe for guests. Never mind the mosquitoes in the summer.

You won't find me sitting outside then unless it's by the screened-in pool.

She patted her belly. She and Dalton would have another focus this year at that season.

After the waitress delivered her lemonade, she settled back to wait for her food as well as a conversation with the café manager. Her wait extended until after she'd finished her meal.

"What can I do for you?" a woman said from behind in a strong Southern accent. She came into view, striking Marla with her dark beauty. She had ebony hair, chocolate-brown eyes, and caramel skin. Her hair, styled in a short bob, complemented her facial contours. From the hint of gray at her temples, Marla would put her age in the forties.

"Hi, I'm Marla Vail, a friend of Lacey's. I was unfortunate enough to find Paolo the day he… you know."

"How horrible. And you being pregnant! I hope the trauma didn't hurt the baby."

"It's not my first… I mean, I've been in this situation before. My husband is the detective assigned to the case. Lacey asked me to get involved since I've helped solve some of his cases."

"Is that so?" Michelle plopped onto the opposite seat and swiped a hand over her face. "I couldn't believe it when I heard the news. Poor Paolo. He always had a big grin and a friendly word for me when he came by."

"I understand your restaurant was closed for the day, but you were here to meet some suppliers?" Marla asked for clarification.

Michelle gave a vehement nod. "I needed to review my order with the fish purveyor. I haven't been happy with the quality of their product lately or their claims about the source. I've decided to switch vendors."

"So you do all the buying for the café?"

"Buying, sourcing, cooking, and managing," Michelle said with a proud grin.

"Those are big shoes to fill." Marla swirled her finger on her water glass, watching the pattern on the condensation. "So you're more than just the manager."

"Actually, I'm the chef. I know this place is small, but it's a start. I grabbed the opportunity when the chance came. I used to cater parties for the Tremaynes back in the day. When I heard Lacey meant to open a café on the grounds as part of her new business venture, I applied for the job."

"You've had formal training?"

"I've been through culinary school. With my Creole heritage, how can I not like to cook?" Michelle spread her hands as though this inference were common knowledge.

"I'm surprised you haven't opened a place in town. Why stay here, where you're lucky to get noticed?"

"It builds my credentials. Besides, I don't have the money to open a big restaurant. Nor do I want to climb the rungs at someone else's establishment. This suits me for now.

I'm essentially my own boss since we're an independent concession."

"How many other people work here?"

"You've met Kim, our waitress. On busy days, Matt comes in to help. But you didn't come here to talk about me. What is it you really want to know?"

"If your restaurant functions independently, what does the Tremayne estate get out of it?" Marla asked, getting to the point. Sweat broke out on her brow. Maybe she should have chosen a seat indoors in the air-conditioning. Being pregnant made her more sensitive to the heat.

"We pay the estate a percentage of our revenue."

"So it's not a flat rate, like a monthly rent?" Marla thought of her salon. Her stylists paid a percentage as well, rather than renting their chairs.

Michelle's brow folded. "A static rent would have been more difficult, considering how the summer months are usually slower. This way is fair."

It's only fair if you're accurate in your bookkeeping, Marla thought. "Do you interact much with the other members of the household?"

"Lacey will come by for a cup of coffee and a chat in the morning sometimes before we open. Our hours run from eleven to five, although we close at three during the summer. You can book a formal afternoon tea if you wish, and we do group events such as baby showers."

Marla heard the suggestive note in her voice. "So you're saying Lacey likes an early conversation before anyone else arrives?" she asked, ignoring the last remark. "What do you talk about, if you can tell me without betraying any confidences?"

"We discuss our businesses and how to publicize our efforts. It's too bad she can't ask her son to help, but that boy stays locked in his room most of the day."

"Does he ever come by for a meal?"

"Nah, although I've seen Daniel meet a friend over by

the greenhouse. It's odd, considering how he doesn't seem to care about the gardens. He always appears to argue with this guy. The funny thing is that I've seen the security chief talking to this fellow, too."

"Really? And this person isn't on the staff, like one of the gardeners?"

"He's nobody that I've ever met. Sometimes the workers bring their friends or family around to see the place. Lacey is pretty lenient in that regard. She figures if they're impressed, they'll tell others and it will draw in more customers. But this man comes alone. He gives me the creeps the way he skulks around the place."

Marla spied an ant crawling along the table. She grabbed her paper napkin and squashed it. "Can you describe him?"

"He's tall and lanky but always wears a hoodie, so I can't see his features. I have a feeling that the less I know, the better. Next time I see him, I'm going inside for sure."

"Are you certain it's a man?"

"I've seen his shoes. No woman would be caught dead in those ugly things."

"Did you happen to see him on the grounds the day Paolo died?"

Michelle's gaze chilled. "I saw nothing. Now if you'll excuse me, I have to get back to my kitchen."

"Wait, I'd like to bring my husband a gift. What do you suggest I might buy him in the shop? He likes plants, so I'm thinking along the lines of a gardening tool."

"Bless your heart, aren't you a thoughtful one. I'm sure Sarah can give you some ideas."

"She's been working here a while, hasn't she? Did you know Connor when he was still alive?"

Michelle, who'd half-risen to leave, sat again. "As I said earlier, I catered parties in the early days. So yes, I knew Connor. He enjoyed mingling with his guests and appreciated fine cuisine."

Marla wanted to keep her talking longer, so she appealed to the woman's ego. "What would you consider to be your specialty dish?"

"I make a mean gumbo. My mama in N'Awlins made it and her mother before then. It's a recipe passed down through the generations to the women in my family."

"Do you still have relatives there? If so, what keeps you in Florida?"

Michelle's teeth flashed white in a broad smile. "My husband is an orderly at the hospital and he likes his job. His steady paycheck is especially important because… well, we're stuck here for now."

"Oh, I didn't realize you were married. You don't wear a ring."

"It would get in the way when I'm cooking. Now I really do have to be on my way." The café manager nodded toward a couple of tables that had been filled.

"I'm sorry to have kept you so long, but I've enjoyed our talk. I love speaking to other businesswomen. It's interesting to hear people's backgrounds and goals." She offered Michelle a business card.

"You're a salon owner? That's good to know."

"Stop by if you need a trim. We give a discount to new clients. Otherwise, I hope you'll contact me if you have any further information relevant to my husband's case."

"I've probably said enough already." Michelle gave a furtive glance toward the garden. "Please don't repeat what we've discussed. There may be a snake in the swamp, and we can't be sure where it will strike next."

Chapter Seven

Marla arrived at work on Thursday afternoon just as her first client walked in the door. She didn't have time to discuss her latest findings with anyone until a break came at five. Nicole and the others were getting ready to leave, but Marla had to stay until she'd finished her last customer around eight.

I really have to cut back on my hours, she thought, dropping into her chair to ease the ache in her back.

"Are you all right?" Nicole asked, noting Marla's grimace of discomfort.

"I feel like a whale, and I still have two more months to go." She rubbed her belly.

"Having a healthy child will be worth the wait." Nicole, who had finished cleaning her station, took her purse from its drawer. She cast Marla a concerned glance. "I hope you didn't spend the morning running around town chasing after suspects."

Marla bent her head, soft waves of hair veiling her face. "I took the tour this morning at Tremayne Manor. The art collections are amazing. I'd like to go back with Dalton when he's finished this case. He hasn't had the chance to appreciate the place as a visitor. Unfortunately, we've still had no word from Blinky."

Nicole leaned against her counter. The doorbells chimed as the other stylists left, waving their goodbyes. "Has Dalton checked her credit cards to see if there have been any recent charges? Or her bank accounts for withdrawals?"

"Good points. I'll have to ask him. He's likely done his due diligence in that regard, but we haven't talked about it. At least I got to speak to some of the staff members at the manor house."

"Oh yeah? What did you learn?" Nicole's eyes sparked at the idea of juicy gossip.

"Sarah O'Malley, the gift shop lady, does her own buying for the store. Apparently, Lacey gives her leeway to do whatever she wants."

"So she keeps the financial records? Who gets her reports?"

Marla shrugged. "I have no idea. When I mentioned bookkeeping, Sarah changed the subject. I meant to go back and ask her about it after lunch but I forgot."

"It would be interesting to learn if she submits her files to Lacey or to an accountant," Nicole said. "Who manages the business end of the estate?"

"Lacey is in charge. She must have filed for a business license when she conceived of the idea for the tours. Michelle, the café lady, also runs her own show. She pays a percentage of her restaurant income to the estate."

"What about zoning? Wouldn't it have to be mixed use for residential and commercial?"

"You're right. And if so, how was Lacey able to get it changed?" Marla rubbed her temples. "I just want Blinky to turn up unharmed, then Dalton can solve the rest."

"Sure, girlfriend, like you're going to sit idly by when there's a crime involved. Who else did you speak to at the mansion?"

"I chatted up the tour director. I'd like to age as well as Heather Wishbone. Her roots could use a touch-up, but she dresses stylishly and keeps her weight in check. She's passionate about history, which is why she took the job as head docent. According to Heather, Lacey and Connor met at a luncheon following a charity art event at a yacht club. Connor had loved boating."

A memory surfaced, and she frowned at the thought. Hadn't Heather said Lacey enjoyed painting? Was it a hobby she still pursued?

Filing the question away for her next visit, she reviewed her conversation with the tour guide. "Connor went sailing to the Keys one day before Lacey's birthday to buy some of her favorite Key lime pies. A storm blew up. Later, his boat was found abandoned near Key Largo. No trace was found of his body."

"That must have been a difficult time for Lacey and her son," Nicole said, a sympathetic look on her face. "Did her husband leave enough money for them to be comfortable?"

"Lacey needed cash to maintain the house. She came up with the idea of opening the place to the public. You have to admit, it's a brilliant way to make money to preserve her husband's legacy while sharing museum-quality artifacts with people who enjoy them. Lacey added the extra wing and gazebo for special catered events, which was another clever move on her part."

"She should open a bed-and-breakfast in that place. People would pay money to stay there."

"Not with so many treasures openly displayed. Their security chief confirmed that, besides himself, only Daniel and Lacey have keys to the locked cases. That strikes me as odd, considering how Daniel doesn't value the stuff like his mom."

She envisioned the young man meeting the person in the hoodie Michelle had mentioned. Could Daniel be the thief, stealing the objects and then selling them to this stranger? She shared her theory with Nicole.

"It's possible, although didn't you say Michelle had seen Rick, the security chief, meeting with this man, too? Maybe the three of them are working together."

"That would explain a lot of things," Marla said. "Daniel steals the items. Rick looks the other way. The guy in a hoodie pays them both off. I hate thinking ill of Daniel. It would hurt his mother if he turns out to be the thief."

"Maybe he resents the fact that his father didn't leave the property to him," Nicole suggested.

"If so, who has Lacey named as beneficiary in her trust? She's considering donating the house to the historical society. If she were to die today, who would inherit it?"

Nicole jabbed a finger in the air. "Maybe Lacey meant for her son to be her heir, but she's having second thoughts because of his disrespectful attitude. But let's talk instead about the Fabergé egg that was stolen. How do you think it ended up lying in the grass next to the dead gardener?"

"I wish I knew. Maybe Paolo saw the thief in action and ran after him. They wrestled over the egg and the crook stabbed Paolo in the shuffle. The thief fled, leaving the egg behind."

"Would the gardener have had time to change into the bunny costume in this scenario?"

"Probably not." Marla crossed and uncrossed her legs, seeking a comfortable position. She yearned to kick off her shoes and lie down. "I should go back on Monday and talk to the housekeeper. Mrs. Docket has been off for the week, and she might be able to shed light on her fellow staff members. Dalton's team has been interviewing the gardeners. I wonder if that includes the beekeeper who's also the exterminator for the house."

"Maybe he saw something the day Paolo was killed."

"I haven't spoken to the guy. You and Kevin should take the tour, Nicole. The grounds are beautiful, too. I walked through them fairly quickly, but I'd like to go back with Dalton to truly enjoy the formal gardens. I haven't gone inside the greenhouse yet, either."

With a shiver, she remembered another experience in a conservatory where she'd been trapped with a killer. She'd rather wait to go inside this one until Dalton could accompany her.

"Has the murder weapon been found?" Nicole asked, slinging her purse strap over one shoulder. "You'd said Paolo had been stabbed. Was the wound from a knife or a gardening tool?"

"Dalton hasn't told me, but he must have the autopsy report by now." With a sense of revulsion, she remembered the blood beneath the body. That meant Paolo was still alive when he'd been stabbed, right? He couldn't have been poisoned first, for example. That wouldn't have left him with the wits to change outfits.

"My guess is Paolo saw the thief through the window and recognized him or her," Marla said. "Afraid he'd been spotted, he nabbed Blinky and convinced her to give him the bunny costume as a disguise. But that wouldn't explain why Blinky is still missing, unless she'd witnessed the murder. If that's the case, why hasn't she come forward? I can't shake the feeling that something terrible has happened to her."

A thoughtful expression entered Nicole's eyes. "Or else Paolo was the thief. He slipped inside the house when everyone was distracted, switched the eggs, and ran off with the jeweled piece. He took the costume from Blinky to aid in his escape."

Marla wrinkled her brow. "That doesn't make sense. Who killed him then, and why? And how would he unlock the display case to steal the egg?"

"As I said, Rick and Paolo could have been working together. Maybe Paolo tried to double-cross the guy in the hoodie. This fellow might be their fence. He stabbed Paolo, who dropped the egg. The killer ran off without retrieving it."

Marla mulled over her friend's ideas. "If you think about it, the buyer for the egg must be a private collector. This means the fence would need connections in the art world. As for Rick being involved, he was off for the weekend. He would have had to leave the display case open beforehand." She rubbed a hand over her face. "What concerns me is that we're no closer to finding Blinky. All I want is to discover what happened to her."

Marla pushed aside her concerns when her next client walked in. Nicole left, offering to discuss things further in the morning.

By the time Marla got home that night, she wanted only to collapse in bed after a late dinner. She was too tired to talk to Dalton about the case. He looked beat as well, so she put off the topic until the next morning.

"I need to tell you what I learned at Tremayne Manor yesterday," she said after breakfast.

"Go ahead." Dalton, seated at the kitchen table, put down his pen. He liked to do the daily crossword puzzle in the newspaper and subscribed to the print edition. Brianna had already left for school. They'd taken the dogs out. Now he lingered with a cup of coffee, while Marla sniffed the brewed aroma with longing. She couldn't wait until she could drink caffeinated beverages again.

Plopping into the opposite seat, she related what the people at Tremayne Manor had shared with her.

"Interesting about the guy in the hoodie," Dalton said, his brow furrowing. "I hadn't heard about him before. So the son meets this person on occasion, and so does the security chief?"

"Michelle, the café manager, said there may be a snake in the swamp. Do you think she meant one of them?"

Dalton spread his hands. "Who knows? I'd like to find this person and question him. Was he there the day of the murder?"

"If so, nobody has reported him. Speaking of bodies, did you get the autopsy results?"

"Yes, I did. Without getting too technical, the stab wound is what killed the gardener. He died from a hemothorax due to penetration of the right lung. The wound's two sharp edges indicate a dagger or double-edged blade as the murder weapon, while abrasions at the edge suggest a hilt mark. White synthetic fibers were also present. They're a match for the bunny costume."

"That's it? This doesn't narrow down the possibilities too much."

"No, but it pretty much eliminates the tools in the greenhouse."

"What about the beekeeper's shed?"

"I only got a quick look inside when I interviewed the fellow. All he wanted to talk about was his hives. He was fooling with a swarm box, and I didn't care to get too close."

Marla had no idea what that meant, but it was beside the point. "Did Karl see anything the day Paolo was killed? I believe he was on the premises."

"Nope, he'd been dealing with a nuke. Not a bomb, but a nucleus thing where the bees, who have left another hive, go to reestablish themselves. I'm not explaining it well, but bees aren't my thing." He gave a visible shudder.

"No way. You're afraid of honeybees?"

His mouth curved down. "Those nasties pack a mean sting. And don't ever get me started on wasps. If we get nests around here, we're calling our own exterminator."

"Karl has the perfect excuse to sneak around the house while spraying the exterior."

"So do a lot of other people, like the security staff. Now that you've told me there's a housekeeper, I'm wondering why she doesn't have a key to the display cases instead of Daniel Tremayne. Why does the kid need one?"

Marla tilted her head. "I've wondered the same thing. Maybe Lacey, despite her misgivings, still trusts him more than anyone else. Those items are part of his family heritage. Although when I mentioned this to Rick, he said I should talk to Bruno, the maintenance man. Have you interviewed him? He's another person with access to the house and grounds. He probably has his own stash of tools somewhere."

"They're likely to be found in the truck he drives to work each day. Most of these people don't live at Tremayne Manor. Your question raises a valid point, though. I wonder where their vehicles were parked on the day of the egg hunt."

Marla's pulse accelerated. "You don't think Blinky borrowed one of them, do you? Did anyone report a missing car or truck?"

"Not really. If she did take a staff member's vehicle, she'd need a key. That meant she would have had the owner's cooperation." He pulled out his notebook and scribbled a note to himself.

"Have you checked Blinky's credit card statements and bank accounts to look for unusual activity?"

"Her credit cards haven't been used since the day of her disappearance. There's been no activity on her bank accounts, either." His voice held a hint of irritation.

He must be frustrated by their lack of progress, Marla surmised, worry gnawing at her for her friend's safety. "How about the catering staff hired for that day? Did you talk to them?"

"They were occupied inside the house and stuck mostly to the kitchen."

"It's possible Lacey uses the same company for special events if she likes their services. Did anyone wander off to chat with the permanent staff? Or take a long break during the morning's set-up for the luncheon?"

He pushed the newspaper across the table and stood. "My team has viewed the video surveillance. Nobody acted suspicious. As for the feed from the treasure room, there's a time jump, making me suspect a segment might have been edited out."

"Can your tech guys recover it?" she asked, thinking how Daniel was a computer expert.

"We'll see. Either the culprit was one of the three people with a key, or someone else has a duplicate."

"That's easy for the handyman to do. How much time does he spend at the place, anyway? He can't fix pipes and toilets all day."

"Bruno has experience in construction. He does a lot of the renovations and also maintains the outdoor structures. He'll pitch in with the yard guys when needed, too, helping to mulch the plants and prune the trees."

"He's a versatile fellow. Where was he the day of the murder?"

Dalton lifted his car keys from the set of hooks by the garage door. "Bruno had been working on the gazebo out by the formal gardens. The roof needed repair. They do a lot of weddings there."

"I don't suppose anyone could verify his alibi? Other than Paolo being in the greenhouse, the rest of the gardening staff was off duty that day."

"You're right, and the beekeeper was in his shed for most of the afternoon."

Marla shook her head. "It's odd that no one saw anything. Either that, or they're covering for each other. But why, and how does Blinky figure into things?"

"You worry about our son," Dalton said, pointing to her belly with a stern look on his face, "and let me deal with this case. It's not good for the baby for you to be stressed."

"I can't help it, not when my friend is missing. Maybe I should dig into her relationships to see if there's a connection to anybody at the house. If Blinky was the one running scared, then she'd likely instigated the costume exchange with Paolo. The killer might have gone after him and stabbed the wrong person. Blinky went into hiding, knowing he'd realize his mistake soon enough."

"It's a viable theory. We still haven't found the rest of the costume. If we do, that might provide more clues regarding your friend's disappearance."

"Huh? What do you mean?"

"Didn't you notice the victim's hands and feet weren't covered by the bunny outfit?"

Marla slapped a hand to her cheek. "Omigosh. I never thought about it, but you're right."

"Blinky and Paolo may have been in a hurry to do the costume exchange. He didn't bother to put on the mittens or paws. They would have impeded his movements, in any case."

"Good point." She mulled over this revelation. What did it mean that the missing costume parts hadn't turned up? If Dalton's team found them, would they find Blinky?

"How about your background checks into the estate's personnel?" she asked. "Assuming the thief is selling the items he's stolen, has anyone received income from an unknown source?"

Dalton's eyes narrowed, flinty specs in his irises. "We did learn something interesting from our research. Paolo the gardener had been convicted for stealing people's mail and altering their personal checks. He spent time in prison for mail theft and check fraud. It appears our victim was guilty of a felony."

Chapter Eight

"Maybe Paolo was the thief who stole the Fabergé egg," Marla said to Nicole later at work in the salon. They stood by their stations, waiting for their next customers to walk in. Sounds of water splashing and hair dryers whirring in the background provided a sense of comfort. "He may have passed off the goods he'd stolen to a fence he met in jail. That would be the man in the hoodie. Their deal went sour, and this person stabbed Paolo."

"Or, Paolo caught the crook in action and confronted him," Nicole countered. "The guy—or lady thief—struggled with him over the egg, and Paolo ended up getting stabbed."

Marla frowned at her. "That doesn't explain why Paolo would have changed into the bunny suit. Perhaps the bad guy, in the midst of his thievery, spied Paolo out the window. The pair exchanged glances. Paolo recognized the thief. Realizing his danger, he ran off to don a disguise."

"The guy saw Blinky hand off the outfit to the gardener and chased after him," Nicole said, picking up the thread. "They scuffled, and the crook stabbed Paolo. But then, why did Blinky run away? Did she witness the crime?"

"She might have been afraid the killer would come after her next. The murderer couldn't take the risk that Paolo had revealed his identity to Blinky."

"We've already been over these possibilities," Nicole reminded her.

"I know, but we might think of something we'd overlooked."

The front doorbells chimed. "Here comes my two o'clock," Nicole said with a sympathetic glance in Marla's direction. "Try to relax, girlfriend. It's not good for the baby for you to be stressed. It's bad enough that you're on your feet all day."

Marla put a hand to the small of her back. "Tell me about it. Hey, don't forget our dinner date with the guys tomorrow night. I'm hoping you'll fill me in on wedding details."

"There isn't much to relate. We're on schedule with all the vendors. We've selected the menu and decided on the wedding cake. We'll do the yellow cake with chocolate mousse that Kevin liked. Better to let your man have the small wins so we can have the bigger ones, right?"

"I'd agree with you there."

"I can't believe we're getting gifts already. How about you?"

"It's too early. We have to add things to the registry before my mother's party invites go out. I need to do more research first. The choices are overwhelming." Marla almost clapped her hands in anticipation of the surprise bridal shower she had planned for Nicole.

Her mood quelled when thoughts of Blinky surfaced along with her fears about what might have happened to her. It must be related to the theft, since the dead man was found in the vicinity of the Fabergé egg. Were those things really so valuable?

She asked Dalton about it that night, but he seemed to be in a pensive mood and wasn't forthcoming with a helpful response. So she focused instead on drawing his mind away from work to more pleasurable activities.

Saturday morning before work, she sat at the computer. Dalton had left the house with Brianna to run some errands. She squinted at the screen as she read how Carl Fabergé was born in 1846 in St. Petersburg, Russia. He gained recognition as a brilliant designer and was awarded a gold medal in 1882 at an exhibit in Moscow. This led to his being appointed jeweler to the Imperial Russian court.

Czar Alexander III initiated the custom of presenting his wife with a Fabergé egg each Easter. The first of the fifty eggs created was called the Hen Egg. His son, Nicholas II, continued the tradition by giving an egg to both his mother and his wife.

The Russian Revolution of 1917 put an end to the royal family along with Fabergé's studios. He fled to Switzerland, where he died in 1920.

Only forty-three of the fifty eggs survived. The Queen of England owned three of them as part of the Royal Collection. Most of the rest were either in Russian or American museums. They were highly valued because of their rarity and uniqueness.

But how much are they worth? Marla pondered, scrolling through the links after she asked this question in a search window.

She found some examples that indicated they ranged in value from five million to thirty million dollars. The Winter Egg had sold to a collector in 1994 for five-point-five million. The Coronation Egg was worth twenty million, and the Rothschild Egg was valued at eighteen-point-five million dollars. The value depended on the egg's design, its age, and other factors.

A collector would need to have very deep pockets to own one of them, Marla thought. And what was the point when you hid your treasures away in a private vault, sharing them only with a select few? The money could be better spent helping people.

But that was merely her opinion, and people had been keeping private collections forever. It brought to mind that someone wanted the egg Lacey Tremayne owned. Why else would that particular one have been stolen?

She studied a photo of the Rosebud egg. It truly was a beautiful piece of art. This was the first jeweled egg that Emperor Nicholas II had given to his wife, Empress Alexandra Feodorovna. Crafted from multi-colored gold, it was covered with translucent red enamel on a wave-patterned guilloché field and quartered by lines of rose-cut diamonds. Diamond-set Cupid's arrows symbolizing love decorated the egg. At its apex was a miniature portrait of the young emperor under a table-cut diamond. Its base held the date under another diamond.

Wait, what's this? As Marla continued to read the description of the Rosebud Egg and scrolled farther to regard the next photo, her jaw gaped.

The egg opened to reveal a hinged yellow and green enamel rosebud inside a cream velvet lining. This rosebud further symbolized the love between the emperor and the empress. The bud in turn contained two surprises, a diamond-set miniature replica of the Imperial crown, representing Alexandra's new life as empress, and a ruby pendant. These items were lost and their present whereabouts unknown.

Moreover, every egg opened to contain a tiny surprise. Marla's eyes bulged as she learned that these might include watches, miniature portraits, and jeweled pendants that could be worth more than half of the egg's value.

Did Lacey know what the stolen egg hid inside? Maybe the thief hadn't been after the egg at all but the surprise secreted there.

Whoa, that was a new idea. Marla shut down her browser and stared at the icons on her monitor screen. Should she call Lacey and ask for more details, or go over there in person? She glanced at her watch and cursed. She'd be late for work if she didn't leave immediately.

Shoving her chair back, she rose, turned off the monitor, and grabbed her purse. She would have to deal with this question another time.

She'd meant to talk to the housekeeper at Lacey's place on Monday. She could kill two birds with one stone by interviewing Lacey again, too.

As she walked out the kitchen door into the garage, she bit her lower lip. Too much time had passed since Blinky's disappearance. Today was exactly one week. Unless she'd initiated the vanishing act herself, Blinky's chances for survival lessened with each day. But what else could Marla do to find her if the police couldn't even trace her movements?

They'd searched the woods surrounding the estate and hadn't found a body. That might be reassuring, but there were other ways to hide a corpse. Marla shuddered at the notion. Had the cops thoroughly explored the estate grounds, greenhouse, and sheds? She'd only casually strolled through the gardens and hadn't seen everything. They'd been more extensive than expected.

Perhaps there was a body of water nearby where a body could be dumped. Florida had abundant lakes and canals, with alligators on the prowl. It wouldn't take long for evidence to be consumed. The police would have to scour the bottom of any nearby pond for bits and pieces.

Dalton had said Blinky's cell phone hadn't been used since the day of her disappearance. Her last position put her at Tremayne Manor. The phone, which hadn't been found in her parked car, appeared to be turned off. Nothing stood out from the woman's phone records either.

As Marla drove to work, she refocused her attention on happier events for the baby's sake. Nicole's bridal shower was that evening, and she needed to call the restaurant to confirm their arrangements.

She and Dalton were supposed to meet Nicole and Kevin there for their alleged double date at six-thirty. Marla planned to arrive an hour early to set out the centerpieces and party favors, confer with the staff, and greet the guests who came at six. According to their plan, Kevin would drop Nicole off and urge her to go inside while he parked the car. He'd leave and come back with Dalton at eight in time for dessert.

Events transpired smoothly later that evening. Nicole walked into the private dining room and stopped with a stunned expression when she observed the crowd gathered there. Marla hoped she'd invited the people who mattered. Kevin had helped her determine the guest list. She'd included a mixture of salon staff, friends, and family members.

"Oh. My. God. What's everyone doing here?" Nicole gaped at them, then her gaze snagged Marla's. "You're responsible, aren't you? And where's Dalton? Don't tell me the guys knew about this."

Wearing a big grin, Marla shuffled forward and steered her toward an older woman with nutmeg skin and stark white hair. "Look who's joined us."

"Mama!" Nicole shrieked, rushing forward. A series of hugs followed, next to her cousin who'd accompanied her mother, to her bridesmaids, and to the rest of the company.

Once they'd settled down, the staff served dinner. Marla dodged the inevitable questions about her baby. She held her belly, wishing she would get the birth over with and yet relishing these last few months of freedom. Having a child changed your life forever. Was she up to the task? How did Nicole feel about having children? With a start, she realized she'd never asked.

"Kevin and Dalton will be showing up later for dessert," she said across the horseshoe-shaped table arrangement. Nicole sat at the head seat along with her mother and cousin. The bridesmaids flanked them. Marla sat off to the side along with their salon staff, while Nicole's friends occupied the other end. The white tablecloths held red napkins, the two colors reflected in the floral centerpieces Marla had brought.

"Kevin never said a word. He's good at keeping secrets," Nicole said with a wink.

Like the people at Tremayne Manor, Marla thought. She

couldn't wait until Monday to question Lacey about the surprise inside the Fabergé egg. She'd told Dalton about it, but he had seemed distracted. Besides, he was focused on a murderer, not a mere thief.

"How's the search for Blinky coming?" Nicole asked in an aside to Marla while opening presents. She made the proper exclamation of awe and gratitude at the marble cheese slab and cutting knife in her hands before setting it aside.

Kevin and Dalton had arrived. They'd shared in the cake Marla had brought and were hustling the unwrapped gifts into Kevin's car. Marla glanced at the door, not wanting Dalton to think she was discussing a case during Nicole's special event. Nonetheless, she answered the question.

"Not well. There's still no trace of her."

"Is that Bonnie Morris you're talking about?" called Kathy, one of Nicole's friends standing within earshot. "I heard she's missing."

"Do you know her?" Marla asked, her senses sharpening. She left Nicole to her gifts and strode over to the woman, who wore a fire-engine red top with silver trim and matching hoop earrings.

"I sure do. Blinky and I met at a meeting for Female Entrepreneurs of Tomorrow. The Broward County branch holds our annual recognition luncheon at Tremayne Manor. Blinky impressed me as an energetic and goal-driven woman."

"That sounds like a worthy organization," Marla said. "I haven't heard of it before."

"We're businesswomen who mentor prospective female business owners."

"Is that so? I own a hair salon and day spa." Marla passed over one of her cards.

"Oh, you're in Palm Haven? You should check out our group. I run an online travel agency," Kathy explained, digging into her purse for one of her own cards. "I'd started out as an agent at a local office, but it wasn't profitable like in the old days. So I got on board with technology and bought a company still in its infancy. We've expanded to worldwide operations."

"That's awesome. Where is your office located?"

"We're downtown near Las Olas. Fort Lauderdale is a magnet for the Latin American market. Most of our staff is bilingual. We get some walk-ins, but we don't advertise. Well, not in print anyway. Blinky manages our online campaign, or at least she did until she went missing. Oh gosh, I hope she turns up soon."

"Me, too. The longer she's gone, the more worried I am for her safety."

They fell into a morose silence. Marla changed the topic to a lighter subject to get the woman talking again. "How did you and Nicole become friends?" she asked.

Kathy's mouth curved upward, and the skin crinkled beside her eyes. "We met when Nicole was dating Eddie. Our guys belonged to a group that sponsored a soccer team for boys. I got to talking about my hair, and Nicole confessed she was a stylist. I already had a regular hairdresser, but I took her advice and changed my style. I still wear it that way and love it." Kathy fluffed her chin-length bob.

"It does look great on you. I'm surprised we never met before. I used to go to barbecues at Eddie's house in those days."

"I travel a lot for my business, or at least I did back then." Kathy wagged her ring finger that sported a gold band. "Once I had kids, I stayed home a lot more."

"Oh? How old are they? I'm about to have my first, although my husband has a teenage daughter. It's a second marriage for both of us," she explained.

They veered into a discussion about children until Marla noted Nicole was almost finished unwrapping her gifts. Soon everyone who hadn't already left would depart. Dalton was aiming pointed glances her way. She needed to conclude this conversation.

“Tell me, is your women’s entrepreneur organization where Blinky met Lacey?” she asked. “I’d wondered how Blinky ended up being the Easter bunny at Tremayne Manor.”

Kathy’s eyes widened. “Oh, you don’t know? Blinky’s advertising firm, Bonview Enterprises, promotes the manor’s tours and catering facilities. Lacey hired them when she started her business. I guess she didn’t mind the scandal that almost brought Blinky’s company to an end.”

Chapter Nine

"Did you know about this so-called scandal?" Marla asked her husband during the drive home. She couldn't help her accusatory tone, thinking he might have withheld information.

A frown creased Dalton's brow as he stared forward, gripping the steering wheel. "Yes, but I considered it irrelevant to the current situation."

"Kathy said Blinky's company screwed up by missing a deadline. Their client's competitor took the lead and made the client lose an important customer. They couldn't make up the loss and went into bankruptcy. That's a pretty big error."

"And it happened years ago. If somebody bore a grudge that long, he'd have acted on it before today."

"Maybe a fresh opportunity arose to get even. Does anyone at the manor have a relationship to that other company? Did you even look that closely into Blinky's background?"

His lips thinned. "Marla, you know another department is handling Blinky's case. I can't tell them what to do."

"No, but you can make suggestions. Blinky's disappearance, the thefts at the estate, and the murder are likely connected. It doesn't help that they're being handled by different departments. Are you cross-communicating about the data you discover?"

"When we think it's important, yes we are. Why don't you let me manage my own case?"

"Sure, you do that. But I mean to ask Lacey about the surprise inside the stolen egg. And if the housekeeper happens to be there on Monday, I'll interview her as well. She wasn't there the day of the murder, but she might know something about the gardener."

The lines bracketing his mouth deepened. "I can't stop you from visiting a friend. Just be careful not to reveal anything about my investigation."

"Don't worry about me. I'm the voice of discretion." She supposed she should cut him some slack. He was good at his job, and if he thought an item was relevant, he'd pursue it.

"Let's talk about something more pleasant," Dalton suggested. "We should take Brianna to breakfast tomorrow before the hospital tour. She's been yearning for chocolate chip pancakes."

"Will we have enough time to drop her off at home? The tour starts at ten."

"We can eat earlier, if she'll get up. She might prefer to sleep in."

Marla clasped her hands in her lap. "I'm nervous about the tour. It'll make everything seem more real to see the delivery suite. They have a mock-up room they show to visitors."

Dalton's face lost its color. "That's wonderful. I can't wait."

"You've already been through this once before. You shouldn't be squeamish."

"I'm not. It makes me more worried for you, though. Childbirth still comes with risks."

"I'll be fine." Seriously, was it going to be her role to reassure him? "It'll be good to get this weight off. I have to watch my salt intake more and try to get in a brief rest period each day when I can put my feet up. I'm feeling more tired, too."

"Are you taking your vitamins? Maybe a dose of iron

will strengthen you. I'll grill steaks tomorrow night. If you want, invite Anita and Reed over to join us."

"I'd rather have a quiet evening. I'm meeting Ma on Monday to plan the baby shower. She said we should create a registry at a second store so people will have more options. You and I still need to pick stuff for the gift list. We could get that done later tomorrow."

They'd already selected furniture for the nursery. Marla had asked her friends about practical items such as breast feeding accessories, diapers, and other basic supplies. It was a whole new world, and Marla wished she could focus on baby care without so many distractions.

Her mother had offered to buy the expensive bureau that doubled as a changing table. Dalton's mom had called dibs on the crib. That took care of their major expenses, aside from the strollers and car seats. Speaking of Kate, Marla had promised to call her mother-in-law. Kate had offered to co-host the shower with Anita. Their guest list kept growing, and if they wanted to receive gifts for things they really needed, she and Dalton had to spend time at the baby store.

They headed there on Sunday afternoon following the hospital tour. At the registry desk, Marla obtained an electronic scanner to record their selections. They stood by in dazed confusion at the array of choices. Overhead signs divided the store into sections.

"I hope someone buys the crib mattress for us," Marla said as they entered the bedding area. "It's nearly three hundred dollars. We should add a couple of sheet sets. Look for ones with gray or blue designs to match our color scheme."

"This is cool." Dalton indicated a fitted sheet depicting popular cartoon cars. She could tell he was excited by the way his pitch elevated.

"That's twin size. You'll have to wait until the baby is older." She smiled at his passion for cars, something he'd carried over to the miniature car collection in his office. Maybe she'd find him a related item for his next birthday. "Here are sheets with elephants or giraffes. We could do an animal theme."

"You can choose. It doesn't matter to me." He rubbed a finger around his collar. "I don't remember so many decisions when Pam and I had Brianna."

"That was seventeen years ago. Things have changed since then."

"Yes, they've gotten more complicated."

"It helps that you're here with me to make these decisions," she said with a tender smile.

His gaze smoldered. "Always. Let's finish up this section and move on."

Marla stared at the colorful mobiles, wall decals, and diaper stackers. Did they need a sound machine shaped like an owl or a nightlight that changed colors?

She made several choices while Dalton wandered off. The car seat and stroller sections overwhelmed her. Fortunately, she had friends who'd given birth and who could advise her on the essentials. It was incredible how much stuff you needed for a baby. At least when you had a second kid, you could reuse everything, especially the clothing.

Dalton had discovered the section on health and safety. Marla let him study the baby monitors and electrical outlet protectors while she strolled toward the bath care corner.

I should bring Ma here. She'd love to pick out things with me. It would be as much a learning experience for her mother as it was for Marla.

****

This idea evaporated from her mind on Monday when she saw Anita. Marla had spent time earlier getting caught up on emails and balancing the ledgers for the salon. She'd also looked up more items for the baby registry, checking reviews online. It was a time-consuming process.

A quick call to Lacey confirmed she would be home that afternoon. Marla intended to go over there after lunch at her mother's house.

Anita greeted her inside the foyer of her one-story home. Marla's eyes widened in surprise. "What's this? You've packed all these boxes already?" She indicated the stacked cartons lining the hallway.

"Michael was here yesterday. He helped me sort through things. You can look to see what you might want to keep. I haven't put away any of the good stuff yet."

Marla glanced at the expensive figurines, tea pot collections, and Asian art works that served no purpose except to collect dust. "I wish I had more room in my house, but we have too much clutter already. You're not getting rid of everything, are you?"

Good God, she realized, *I sound like Daniel Tremayne who doesn't appreciate his family's heirlooms. Is this what my child will say to me someday?*

A sense of loss assailed her, for each generation that gave way to the next. Why bother collecting anything in life when it all got discarded in the end?

"I'm keeping some of my furniture and knickknacks, but not many," Anita said with a frown. "Reed and I are both past due going through our households and seeing what we don't need anymore. Although we're moving into a bigger place, it has an open design, so we'll lose the living room."

Marla didn't care for the modern housing designs. Well, with one exception. "Your kitchen will be huge. That's a bonus."

"True; we'll enjoy entertaining there. Reed and I will make new friends and have a busy life together. I'm lucky to get the chance at my age."

"You're too young for senior living."

"We're moving to an active fifty-five and over community. Better to make the move now than later, when it would become more difficult. It's exciting but also stressful. We'll have to uproot ourselves and start all over again. But there will come a day when we can't drive far, and this development has enough amenities so it's self-contained."

Anita served lunch, and Marla swallowed a bite of tuna salad sandwich. "I thought you'd want to be closer when I had children," she said after taking a sip of lemonade. "Instead, you're moving farther away." She couldn't help her feeling of abandonment. Having a baby was a major step in her life. She wanted her mother there.

"I'll be as far away as a phone call. We'll be around for the important events and to watch our grandchildren grow."

"But how will I know what to do? You're supposed to teach me."

"Don't worry. I'll be there during the first few weeks when you need me the most. You'll be a wonderful mother. Call your brother and ask him for advice."

"Sure, Ma." *Like I need another chore on my to-do list.* "Did he say anything to you about Charlene when he was here yesterday?"

"His wife is restless. She's not getting the promotion she'd hoped for, and if she stays at this school, it might never come her way. She'd have to change districts, but then her commute would be longer."

"I'd have thought she would be counting down the days to retirement rather than wanting more responsibility as a principal. Do you think they'll move?"

"Michael can't go anywhere. His business is located in Boca Raton. But he also considers his work to be more important than his wife's career. He needs to support her goals."

"Charlene could look into private schools to see if they have an opening."

"Oh, yeah? You tell her. I have to be careful what I say to my daughter-in-law these days. It's like walking on eggshells around her. She's extremely sensitive, and I can easily offend her. I hope she isn't thinking of leaving your brother and moving back north."

"That would be awful. What would happen to the children?" Marla's stomach sank. If Charlene left, her brother would be devastated. Or had things progressed to the point where it would be a relief to him?

"I'll give Michael a call," she promised.

"Thanks, I'm sure he'd appreciate it. Now let's talk about more pleasant things," Anita said, stacking their dirty dishes for later removal to the kitchen. "Once the baby shower invitations go out, you'll be getting gifts. Have you added a second store to your registry?"

"Yes, we opened a new account." She mentioned the name of the place. "I spoke to my friend Justine about bottles. She recommended some brands but said I shouldn't get too many until we see which type the baby likes better. I've added these items plus an electric bottle warmer to the list."

"That's good. I've booked a room at the country club for the shower. We can bring our own cake, and I thought we'd supply the champagne, too. The corkage fee is reasonable, and it'll save us money to do it that way." Anita clapped her hands. "I'm so excited. Kate and I have been conferring over centerpieces and party favors."

Marla tilted her head. "What about your engagement party? Didn't you mention having one so we can meet Reed's family?"

"Yes, but when can we fit it in? Your schedule is so busy."

"How about early May? That would work for me." They studied the calendar and chose a date.

Anita's eyebrows drew together. "We'll have to find a venue. My house is a mess with boxes all over, and it won't hold as many people as we'll want to invite."

“Let me know if I can help you find a place.” Marla stood and took their empty plates into the kitchen.

“Where are you headed from here?” Anita asked, rising to join her. She proceeded to wash the dishes in the sink while Marla finished clearing the table.

“I’m stopping by Tremayne Manor to talk to Lacey. There’s something I need to ask her.”

Anita wagged her finger. “You be careful, *bubeleh.* I don’t like you messing with murderers in your condition. The people in that house could be dangerous.”

Tell me something I don’t know. “It’s broad daylight. Nothing will happen, and what I learn might be important to Dalton’s case.”

****

Tours were in progress when Marla arrived at the mansion. She parked in the public lot and entered through the gift shop entrance where visitors bought tickets. A few ladies milled around inside the store to browse the wares. Marla marched straight to the inner door that led into the house. On the other side, she paused to text Lacey that she’d arrived.

Following instructions, Marla found a door in the hall labeled “for staff only” and discovered a servant’s staircase to the second level. The family’s suites took up this entire side, which was closed to the public. It couldn’t be easy staying hidden during the weekdays when tours were active, but then Lacey often came down to greet guests.

Lacey met Marla with a smile and led her into a private parlor. Unlike the rooms preserved from an earlier era, this décor was contemporary with wood accents. A set of large windows made it bright and airy as did the sunny yellow and warm brown throw pillows on the camel sofa. A silver tea service rested on a coffee table along with a platter of iced petit fours.

"Would you care for a cup of tea?" Lacey offered as Marla sat on the couch.

"Sure, thanks," Marla said to be polite. She couldn't help reaching for one of the confectionary desserts. The sugary taste made her smack her lips.

Once they were past idle chitchat, Marla got to the point of her visit. "I've been reading up on Fabergé eggs and learned that each one contained a surprise. I assume you knew this? What was inside the egg that was nearly stolen?"

Lacey plucked at an imaginary speck on her chiffon palazzo pants that she wore with a matching top. "It held a ruby pendant, but that was lost years ago."

"Could anything else have been hidden inside more recently?" Marla suggested. "When was the last time you opened it?"

"I checked it that same day you returned it. Nothing was inside. Before then, I'd only looked when Connor was here. I had no reason to inspect it otherwise since the original surprise was gone. Why? Are you thinking the thief might have been after something inside the egg, rather than the actual egg itself?" Lacey looked shocked by the idea.

"It would explain why the egg had been discarded."

"The thief may simply have dropped it during his scuffle with Paolo and ran off without realizing he'd left it behind. Or someone spooked him, and he high-tailed it out of there before he could retrieve it."

"You mean, when Blinky came upon them, and he had to deal with her."

Lacey's face paled. "Oh, my word. Have you heard from her? I'm afraid to ask what your husband might have discovered."

Marla let her gaze flit around the room, alighting on the various figurines and framed family photographs. Connor appeared to be a handsome man except for a rather broad nose.

"Another department is handling the missing person case. They've come up empty. Nobody has a clue as to Blinky's whereabouts. I did learn how the two of you were connected. You'd hired her firm to advertise your estate."

"That's right. We were introduced at a meeting for an organization that supports women business leaders. You might want to join. You'd qualify as a salon owner."

"I'll think about it. This past weekend, I ran into one of their members at a bridal shower for my friend. This lady mentioned a scandal involving Blinky that nearly derailed her company."

Lacey stood to pace the room, hands folded behind her back. "That happened right before I started our tours. Blinky wasn't actually responsible. One of her account executives missed a deadline, and it was critically important to their client. The client sued for return of fees plus damages, since it caused them to go into bankruptcy. But they'd been on the rocks beforehand, so they couldn't pass the sole blame onto Bonview Enterprises."

"This track record didn't bother you when you were looking for a firm to hire?"

"Blinky assured me she'd handle my account personally. She had a good reputation on her own, and she's kept her word."

"What happened to the other business owner? Did he leave town, or is he still around?"

"Ben Rogers was his name. He'd sold a product that involved cleaning agents for cars. You know how love bugs will mess up your car's front grating and windshield when you drive through Florida during mating season? His chemical solvent could clean off the sticky mess."

"That would be useful. So what happened? Couldn't he sell the stuff regardless of the client he'd lost?"

"His buyer had been a major chain of gas stations. Another competitor edged in and took his spot."

"What about automotive supply stores? They'd snap up a product like that if it worked."

"Nobody wanted to risk signing a contract with Ben Rogers after his reputation soured. He blamed Blinky's company, but no one would listen."

Marla couldn't believe one advertising contract would make such a big difference. The man should have been able to rebound if his product was so unique. "What is Rogers doing now?"

Lacey halted with a shrug. "According to Blinky, he opened an automotive repair center. It did so well that he expanded to branches in other locations. She felt better knowing the man was successful."

"Did the two of them have any further contact?" Marla asked, wondering how closely Blinky had monitored her former customer.

"She offered to give him free advertising to make up for the problems she'd caused him. He turned her down. In fact, I remember her telling me that he was quite nasty about it."

"How so?" Marla took a sip of tepid tea from her cup. She tried to avoid caffeine in her state but couldn't resist an occasional dose.

Lacey plopped into an armchair opposite Marla. "Blinky showed up at Ben's shop unexpectedly one morning. The garage was closed, and no one responded to her knock on the office door. She saw lights on inside and assumed they were getting ready to open for the day. A side door was slightly ajar, so she went inside. Ben was at work on an expensive model car. His mechanics scattered at her arrival."

"I don't imagine he was happy at her turning up that way."

"Ben shouted at her to leave, that she had no business intruding on them. She explained her proposal, which he refused to accept. She got frightened by the menacing look he gave her and left."

"How long ago was this incident?"

"It was fairly recent. I think she needed some work done on her car and didn't want to go to the dealer. Ben's shop had earned good reviews, but she knew he wouldn't be thrilled to see her. She decided to make amends with him first and was disappointed when he didn't give her the chance. Her company could have helped to publicize his franchises."

Is it just me, or does this story sound strange? Marla wondered.

Blinky's firm screwed up and lost Ben Rogers as a client. He reinvented himself and opened a chain of automotive centers. Then more recently, Blinky had car problems and decided he was the person to fix them? Why not approach him sooner and offer to promote his new business? It didn't make sense the way Lacey explained the situation.

"I appreciate the information," she said, rising with a grunt of discomfort. Her hips felt stiff. She'd been sitting for too long.

"I'm glad you came. I just wish you had better news." Lacey stood and smoothed her pants.

Marla perused the titles on the bookshelf after studying the family photos. A collection of thrillers mingled with biographies and celebrity memoirs.

"Who collects stamps?" she asked, pointing to a framed collage.

"Hey, it ain't me," rang a familiar voice from the doorway. Daniel stood there, leaning against the door frame.

How long has he been listening in? A whole slew of new questions popped into Marla's mind as she turned to face the son of the house.

Chapter Ten

"Dad was an avid stamp collector," he said, sauntering inside, hands in his jeans' pockets. "Mom sold most of his stuff. I had no interest in old pieces of paper."

"They weren't worth as much as I'd hoped," Lacey admitted. "Connor loved his stamps. He got fired up about their history and even went to philatelic events. That's what a person who collects stamps is called, a philatelist."

"I'm afraid my knowledge in the field is sorely lacking," Marla responded, silently agreeing with Daniel's opinion.

Lacey paced the carpet. "I did like hearing about the historical aspect. In the early days of mail delivery, a letter's recipient had to pay a fee. Letters were folded and sealed with no envelopes since postage was based on weight. But people tried to cheat by putting a secret code on the outside of the letter, so the receiver could read the message and refuse delivery. The postal service turned to prepaid postage as a way to get paid for their efforts."

"Sealing wax was used on letters," Marla remembered from period movies she'd seen. Noblemen would stamp the melted wax with their signet rings.

"That's correct. Rowland Hill, an English inventor, proposed that mail should go anywhere in Britain for the same rate, a penny per half ounce. The sender would pay for the postage, denoted by a small piece of colored paper on the outside of the letter. The first government-issued stamp, called the Penny Black, was issued in 1840. It was printed in black and had Queen Victoria on the picture."

"When was the first stamp made in the United States?" Marla asked, thinking to repeat this information to Dalton. As a history buff, he'd be interested in early postal service lore.

"The U.S. Postal Service printed its first stamps in 1847," Lacey said, while Daniel leaned against the wall with a bored expression. "We had a five-cent stamp picturing Benjamin Franklin and a ten-cent stamp with George Washington. Most were produced in pre-gummed, non-perforated sheets that clerks had to cut."

"What kind of stamps did Connor collect?"

Lacey spread her hands. "You'd have to ask his pal, Jonas Sommers. I liked learning about the history aspect but not the rest. Jonny is a walking encyclopedia on the topic."

"Did this guy have any interest in buying Connor's collection after he passed? That would have made it easier for you to unload the stuff."

"No, I went through a stamp dealer. Jonny acted oddly at the time. He advised me to hold onto Connor's stamps. But neither Daniel nor I had any interest in them. It's like any collection. You pay a lot to acquire the items and then receive barely anything when you sell them."

She cast her son a disapproving glare. "That's why I'm considering donating this house and its contents to the historical society. The artifacts would be kept intact. People would appreciate them for years to come."

Daniel detached from the wall to approach them. A hank of limp hair obscured his forehead. "This property could be put to better use."

"You mean, you'd sell it to a housing developer who'd raze everything to build condominiums," Lacey retorted.

"Hey, it would make a great golf course, too," Daniel replied with a wicked grin.

Marla gave him a sharp glance. Somehow, she didn't think

he had either of those goals in mind. So what would he do with the property if he inherited it, other than selling the contents he didn't want to keep? Those could just as well be donated to a museum while leaving the rest of the estate intact.

Lacey compressed her mouth. "Was there a reason you came to interrupt our conversation?" she asked in a taut voice.

"I heard you two speaking. It's distracting me from my work."

"Too bad. Why don't you take a break and go for a walk? The exercise would do you good."

"I was wondering how the murder investigation is going." Daniel addressed Marla. "Has your husband reached any conclusions?"

She shook her head. "He doesn't share those details with me. I'm worried about my friend who hasn't shown up yet. You don't have anything to add to the case, do you?"

"Nope. I hope you find her soon. It's not a good omen that she's still missing."

She gave him an assessing glance, wondering if he meant something more. But he kept passing disgruntled looks toward his mother rather than paying attention to her. Perhaps he'd just come here to annoy Lacey. If so, he'd succeeded in his purpose.

Nonetheless, if Marla could get him alone, she'd question him further.

"I'm going back to work," Daniel announced with a scowl. "Keep your voices down so I can concentrate, okay? You're talking so loud that Bruno will hear you. He's doing something to the back stairs to fix the creaking noise."

"Oh, really?" Lacey's face brightened. "I'll have to show him where I think a pipe is leaking in my bathroom. I didn't know he'd be in the house today. When I spoke to him last, he said he had some repairs to do on the greenhouse."

"It must be handy having your own repairman on site," Marla said, sensing an undercurrent to their conversation.

"I'll say. We couldn't get by without him. I certainly can't rely on Daniel to get his hands dirty, can I?"

Daniel wiggled his fingers. "They're my bread and butter, Mother. I can't risk damaging them with menial chores like Brutus does every day."

"It's Bruno, as you well know. And those so-called menial tasks are essential to our well-being. You should be grateful to him. His family has always worked for us, but he could have done something different."

"But he stuck close, didn't he? I don't see you encouraging him to pursue another career."

"That's enough," Lacey snapped. "Go back to your desk and bury yourself there all day. It's what you do best."

Daniel turned on his heel and left without any parting words. Marla cleared her throat at the tense silence that ensued.

"Um, I'd like to speak to the housekeeper if it's okay," she told Lacey. "I know she was off the day Paolo got killed, but Mrs. Docket might know things about him that could be useful." *Not to mention you and the other members of the household*, she thought. The housekeeper could be a gold mine of information.

"Sure, I'll introduce you." Lacey moved toward the door, gesturing for Marla to follow. "I must apologize for my son's rudeness. He's not practiced in the social niceties and has no desire to learn. Things would be more peaceful around here if he moved out, but he seems ensconced for some reason. The boy unnerves me. It's unnatural to spend so much time alone like he does. And when he gets motivated to go out, it's with unsavory types. It scares me."

"What do you mean? Have you met his friends?"

"I've only seen one of them at a distance. He always wears a hoodie and comes by the house alone. He waits near the tree line for Daniel to meet him there. Maybe they're doing something illegal, and Paolo spotted them. It's a terrible thing to say about my son, but I fear for your friend if she's involved."

"I'll share your concerns with my husband, if you don't mind." They'd paused by the door, lowering their voices so the maintenance man couldn't overhear them. "Have you ever peeked at your son's computer to see what he's really doing on it?"

"Certainly not. I respect his privacy, even if he doesn't respect mine."

They headed downstairs via the public staircase as no tour group was presently in view. Maybe Lacey meant to steer her away from Bruno, who was working close by.

Mrs. Docket was seated at a small desk in an alcove off the kitchen when they approached her. The middle-aged lady rose to greet them with an exclamation of pleasure. She wore her tinted golden hair tied into a bun and a black dress over her matronly figure.

"Miz Lacey, how did you know I needed to see you?" she said in a respectful tone. "I've been reviewing the menu for next week's wedding breakfast, and there's a problem getting the kiwi due to a product recall."

"I'm sure we can find a substitute," Lacey said. Her entire countenance softened in the other woman's company. Marla could sense their fondness for each other in their easy manner. "Allow me to introduce Marla Vail. She's a hairstylist and salon owner. Marla was supposed to fix Blinky's hair after she got out of the bunny costume the day of the egg hunt."

Mrs. Docket clapped a hand to her mouth. "Good Heavens. I couldn't believe it when I heard what happened. I'm so sorry."

"I hope there will be nothing to be sorry about when Blinky is found," Marla replied. "I'd like to have a chat with you, if you have time."

The housekeeper glanced at Lacey, who gave a nod of approval. "Right now is good."

"I'll leave you two together, then," Lacey told them. "I want to have a word with Cook while I'm here. We'll talk later about the wedding menu, Arlene." She bustled off toward the kitchen staff.

Why would Lacey employ a cook and two assistants in an industrial-size kitchen? She wasn't responsible for the café. Michelle was chef and manager of that establishment. Maybe they provided meals for the estate's workers. Otherwise, Lacey and Daniel wouldn't need much in the way of food preparation.

She asked the housekeeper these questions, while trying to ignore the mouth-watering aroma of baking bread that permeated the place. At the far end was the roped-off area where the tour groups passed through. It led into the rest of the house in a different direction than Lacey had taken her. Marla wouldn't care to have people gawking at her all day. At least Mrs. Docket's desk was out of view.

"We have a fortieth birthday party here today," Mrs. Docket said. "It's in our smaller reception hall in the catering wing. The guest list isn't too large, so we're handling the meal ourselves."

"You're not using the dining room in the house?" Marla asked, remembering that's where the Easter luncheon had been held.

The housekeeper shook her head. "When more than twenty people are involved, we assign events to one of our reception rooms. Cook can manage the smaller numbers herself. Otherwise, we bring in caterers."

"I attended the charity luncheon the day before Easter. Lacey mentioned she'd hired extra catering help for that event."

Mrs. Docket's eyes narrowed. "Sometimes Cook will ask for added servers or kitchen assistants for special events in the house. Miz Lacey is happy to accommodate her."

"Do you like working for Lacey? Have you been here long?"

"Oh Lord, I'll say. I've worked for the Tremaynes since I

was a gal. Worked my way up from maid. Things were glorious when Connor was alive. Our positions were full-time then. They often had a houseful of guests or held parties several times a week."

"I understand Sarah, the gift shop manager, also worked her way up the rungs in the household."

"Hmph. That girl always had ambitions. She was a fool to think things would go her way."

"How so?" Marla inquired, observing the young women bustling in the kitchen. One of them was stir-frying something with rosemary from the fragrant aroma drifting her way, while another was icing a cake. A hunger pang grabbed her. She'd eaten a substantial breakfast. It must be that greedy bugger inside of her demanding more food.

Mrs. Docket clasped her hands together on her desktop. "Sarah wore her heart on her sleeve, and it fluttered every time Mr. Tremayne walked past. You could see she was sweet on him."

Marla refocused her attention. "Did he notice? Or worse, did Lacey?"

"Heavens, no. Miz Lacey would have kicked the girl out if she'd seen the looks Sarah cast her husband's way. As for Mr. Tremayne, either he ignored the twit or he was subtle about his interests."

"Was he a womanizer?" Marla asked, hoping to gain more insights into family dynamics.

Mrs. Docket fixed her a stern glare. "I'm not one to gossip about my employers, Mrs. Vail."

"I respect that, but one of them is dead. And the other one had a murder occur on her premises. My husband is the homicide detective on the case. I'm sure he'll come by to interview you. He's also doing background checks on all the staff. If you have anything to contribute, you'll need to cough it up sooner or later. In the meantime, you can count on me to be the soul of discretion."

The housekeeper pressed her lips together. “Let me get you a seat. You can’t be comfortable standing for so long.” She led Marla to a small work-table with stools set around it. They both claimed seats. Marla was glad to get the weight off her feet.

Mrs. Docket leaned forward and spoke in a low voice. “If you must know, Mr. Tremayne was fonder of his collections than his wife. Another pretty skirt wouldn’t distract him. When he wasn’t on his boat, he had his nose buried in the house’s history books and artifacts. But the man did have a temper. I was glad he’d kept his swords locked up whenever his son irked him.”

Marla sat up straight. “What swords? I don’t recall seeing any weapons on the tour.”

“They’re not available for public viewing.”

From the woman’s shuttered face, Marla realized she’d have to try another tack. “Tell me, does your kitchen provide meals for the on-site staff during the day? Or do they bring their own lunches from home? And what is your cook’s name, by the way?”

“Joan Craig. She’s a peach. In my opinion, Cook is a better chef than Michelle who runs the café. Have you tried the food there? It’s nowhere near as good as our cook makes. She’s been to culinary school, too, but she doesn’t put on airs about it.”

“Is there rivalry between the two? I’d imagine having two chefs on premises might cause some competition.”

Mrs. Docket waved a hand. “Nah, Michelle only caters to visitors. Cook here does the heavy-lifting. She always has something on hand for the staff. The outside people usually take care of their own meals, but you’ll see the security guys in here a lot.”

“Really? They just pop in for a snack, or do they stay to chat?”

“Ed hovers around Kristina there.” She indicated the

young blonde with a ponytail. "Those two have something brewing, if you ask me. He's polite, at least. When Rick comes in, he orders us around like he's a military commander. The man has been even surlier since the attempted robbery."

"Rick had the weekend off. Do you think he blames himself for not being here when events transpired?"

Mrs. Docket glanced away. "Who knows? But it's no great loss. The valuable egg was returned, thanks to you."

So she knows about my role. Does she know anything about Blinky, as well?

"I found it lying on the ground next to Paolo's body. My friend, Blinky, is still missing from that day. Have you heard any gossip regarding her possible whereabouts?"

"I know she was playing the Easter bunny, and her costume somehow ended up on the gardener's body. That was a horrible ending for the poor man."

"Were you acquainted with him?"

The housekeeper's gaze swung back to Marla. She held a pained expression in her eyes. "Paolo would bring in freshly cut flowers from the greenhouse for me to arrange. He loved his plants. He was a soft-spoken guy who mostly kept out of everyone's way. His gardeners did their work in a discreet manner, so visitors never noticed their labors. He was a good manager and a nice man. I can't imagine who could have hurt him."

"Maybe he saw who was stealing the Fabergé egg through the room's window. The thief noticed Paolo and charged after him. That's my theory."

"Then why would he change into the bunny suit?" Mrs. Docket rubbed a hand over her face. "I'd rather not think about such unpleasantness. It's safer around here if you keep your head down."

"What does that mean?"

Mrs. Docket glanced at her watch with a frown. "It means none of us is safe until the killer is found. I'm sorry about your friend. I hope she turns up okay, but it doesn't bode well for her to have been missing for a week."

"It's more than a week now, and you're right. I fear for her safety. Anything at all you can tell me might be helpful, even if it seems insignificant."

The housekeeper gave a furtive glance toward the kitchen staff, who seemed oblivious to their conversation.

"Not all of us are who we seem to be. That's all I'll stay on the subject, but heed my words. Be careful what you say and to whom you say it, or you could find yourself in danger."

Chapter Eleven

Mrs. Docket frowned at the floor and gave a muttered curse. "Don't tell me we have ants again. Karl just sprayed in here last month."

Marla noted the direction of her glance. It looked as though sugar ants had set a trail. "Does the bug man always do the interior? At our house, he treats the perimeter. That works to keep the insects out except for the occasional palmetto bug," Marla stated.

The housekeeper grimaced. "Usually he stands in the doorway and begs food. That man must pack it away like an elephant. Breakfast, lunch and dinner, the grizzled old coot is there. You'd think he would weigh a ton, but I guess he gets his exercise tromping around the estate."

"He makes the honey for the gift shop, doesn't he? Does your kitchen staff use his product?"

"You can ask Cook yourself." Mrs. Docket hollered at the chef. "Hey, Joan, do you have a minute?" She turned back to Marla. "I'm sorry to cut this short, but I have to get back to work. It's been a pleasure, dearie."

The housekeeper introduced Marla to the woman with a stocky figure and friendly face. The scent of bakery goods accompanied her. Coiled wisps of rust-colored hair escaped a net on her head. She brushed down her apron and regarded Marla with a quizzical smile.

"I was wondering if you used the honey produced on the estate," Marla said. "I saw it for sale at the gift shop."

"Sure, we do. It's a fine product with a high grade and is delicious with our walnut pastry. If you can use honey instead of refined sugar in a recipe, it's a healthier choice."

"Do you have much contact with the beekeeper? Mrs. Docket says he requests meal handouts several times a day."

Joan snorted. "That fellow must inhale the food. But then, he does walk the grounds every day doing his duties, so I suppose it makes him hungry."

"He's not married, is he? Otherwise, you'd think his wife would pack him a lunch and feed him the rest at home."

"I don't ask about his personal life. He's a peculiar sort. With that long white beard, he could pass for Santa Claus, especially if he added extra padding to his bulk. It's his hands, though, which bother me. They don't look like any laborer's hands, nor do they match his supposed age. Too smooth, you understand?"

"My mother is sixty-eight, and she looks like she could be in her fifties except for her white hair. Her hands don't show any wrinkles, either. I really need to meet this man, though." She pointed to the floor. "Mrs. Docket said you need him to spray for ants."

"Mercy, you're right. Those stubborn critters keep coming back even though we store our supplies properly. Sometimes they come in if a tree branch is touching the house. I'll tell…" Her face fell. "I can't tell Paolo anymore, can I? He took care of those things for us."

"Who's acting as head gardener in his place?" Marla asked, adjusting her legs on the stool.

"Lacey hasn't appointed anyone yet. The other fellows don't have his education or experience. They're okay to work the flower beds and pull the weeds and spread the mulch, but not to design the patterns or maintain the greenhouse. Paolo was a gem. He'll be hard to replace."

"Can you think of anyone who might have wanted to harm him?" Marla queried, drumming her fingers on the table to expend her energy.

Joan sank onto the opposite seat. "No, ma'am, unless he'd seen something he shouldn't have. I keep my nose down and my head in my work. It's safer around here that way."

"Mrs. Docket said something similar. What are you implying?"

"It doesn't pay to pry into anyone's business, that's all."

"My friend, Blinky, has been missing since the Easter egg hunt. Have you heard any rumors about what might have happened to her?" The sound of splashing water reached Marla's ears as one of the kitchen assistants washed a load of pots in the sink.

"Sorry, I can't help you there."

"I'm hoping she's holed up somewhere safe while waiting for things to clear, but that won't happen until Paolo's killer is found."

Joan gave a woeful shake of her netted head. "His murder hasn't affected our catering business. We've got bookings through the next six months. This week alone is a birthday party, brunch meeting, and baby shower." She pointed to Marla's bulging belly. "When is your little one going to arrive?"

"My due date is in mid-June. I'm lucky it's before hurricane season ramps up and before the worst of the summer heat."

Joan fanned herself with her hand. "I'll say. It's hot enough around here as it is."

Marla considered how to frame the other questions she wanted answered. "I attended the luncheon after the Easter egg hunt. Lacey said she'd hired extra help for that day. Is it usually the same crew who assists the household staff? I know you bring in an outside caterer for larger parties."

"Yes, we like Abigail's Sugar Angels. She's great to work with and has set menus for all our needs. Her company can provide anything we require."

"Were they here that day?"

"Uh-huh. It was a plated luncheon for twenty, but we also had to prepare snacks for the kids who participated in the hunt, along with their parents. There was a lot going on. When Lacey said some of the staff should take the weekend off to be with their families, I suggested we bring in Abigail's people to assist us."

Dalton had already interviewed the caterers, and Marla didn't care to pursue that angle further. It was easier for her to stick with the staff at the estate.

"Is there anything you would like to add?" she asked, rising. Her body felt stiff. Sitting on a stool hadn't been all that comfortable.

"Nope. I wish you luck, though. Your husband asked us some of these same questions."

Marla took her leave, exiting through the kitchen door to the herb garden outside. The air smelled sweet and fresh compared to the cooking aromas indoors. Adjusting her purse strap across one shoulder, she strode along the gravel path toward a series of sheds in the distance. The afternoon sun beat upon her head, heating her uncovered scalp. She put on sunglasses against the glare and admired the colorful red and pink Pentas along the way.

On her left rose the greenhouse, while on her right began the formal gardens and wooded trail. She wouldn't be so foolish as to head in that direction on her own.

The beekeeper's shack was easily identified by the symbol of a honeybee on the door. Marla rapped on the faded wood exterior. Her knock elicited several crashes and thumping noises from within before the door burst open. A white-bearded gent met her with wary eyes.

"What do you want? This place ain't open to the public, missy."

"I'd hoped to have a few words with you. Karl, is it? I'm a friend of Lacey's. I've met Sarah in the gift shop, and she said it was her idea to start selling estate-labeled honey in the store. It's been a big hit with customers."

The man straightened his shoulders. “That’s true. What you meanin’ to ask me about?”

Marla peered beyond his shoulder. A mess of equipment and tools cluttered the interior, including a body suit with a veiled hat hanging on a hook. Sealed cartons and other supplies littered the floor.

“I’m curious how you got started in the beekeeping business. I imagine it’s unusual for an exterminator to turn that into a hobby. Oh, that reminds me. The kitchen has ants, so they’ll need you to spray in there. The cook said a tree branch might be touching the house, giving them a path inside. Paolo used to trim the trees. It’s sad what happened to him.” She watched Karl’s face for a reaction.

His expression turned impassive. “Poor chap. Things didn’t end well for him.”

“Were you in your shed that day? Maybe you noticed him with the Easter bunny lady.”

“I was busy with my bees. Didn’t see nothing or hear nothing. That’s what I told the cop who questioned me.”

“I’m married to the detective on the case. Is this where you keep your hives?”

“No, they’re farther out in the fields closer to the flowers. My swarm box is here, though.” He indicated a wooden rectangular box on a counter.

“What’s that?”

“It’s what I use to catch swarms,” Karl said, the corners of his mouth turning down at her obvious ignorance. “You bait it with honeycombs and lemongrass oil to attract bees that have left their hive.”

“Why would they leave their home?” Marla knew nothing about the subject. Then again, she avoided stinging insects whenever possible. Even the thought of bees or wasps made her shudder, although they weren’t as bad as spiders.

Karl stroked his beard. “When the bee population gets too large for the hive, their queen exits with about half of the worker bees. The others cluster around outside while their scouts search for a new location. When they've found a place, they return and perform a sort of waggle dance."

He seemed willing to explain but not to invite her inside. Just as well. Marla wouldn't want to be alone with him in his shed.

"O-kay. And then what?" she asked, fascinated despite her aversion to the creatures.

"At the new site, the first bees to arrive will release a pheromone to guide the rest of the bees into the new hive. This pheromone resembles the scent of lemongrass oil. So using this oil in my swarm traps will lure them in. Once I have them, I'll transfer them into a nucleus box. That's where they establish themselves before I transfer them to a new hive."

"And you keep the hives out on the grounds? Isn't it dangerous for visitors with bees swarming around?"

"If you don't bother them, they won't bother you."

"How do you harvest the honey?" She glanced beyond him but didn't notice any bottling equipment. Maybe the jars were in those sealed boxes.

"I use a honey extractor and other tools. It's a whole process. So is beekeeping. It keeps me busy year-round making sure the hives continue to thrive and remain healthy. Did you realize bees can catch diseases? We monitor them for infestations and make sure they get enough food and water during the winter months."

"They eat nectar from flowers, right?" Marla asked. Clearly, she'd pushed the man's hot button by getting him to talk about his passion.

"Actually, the worker bees—who are females—collect nectar and pollen to take back to the hive. The nectar provides carbohydrates. Enzymes in the bees' gut helps to break it down into simple sugars that are stored inside the honeycomb. The constant fanning of the bees' wings causes it to evaporate, creating liquid honey. As for the pollen, it contains proteins and amino acids. The worker bees mix this into a form of bee bread to feed the growing larvae."

"What do the male bees do, if not the main work of the hive? Do they guard the place?"

He snickered at her naïve question. "The sole purpose of the male drones is to mate with a virgin queen from another hive. She'll mate with up to eight drones and uses their sperm for the rest of her five-to-six-year lifespan."

"What happens if the queen dies?"

"A queenless hive can raise a new queen by feeding the larvae only royal jelly. That's a milky secretion produced by worker bees. Some people believe it has health benefits."

"Like honey, right? So yours comes from flowers planted on the estate and not from flowering fruit trees?"

"Correct. We market our wildflower honey."

Marla sought a way to keep him talking. The other people on the estate didn't seem to have much contact with the guy. She'd lucked out by catching him at home, so to speak. Did he actually live here or somewhere else? "How do you harvest it? Don't the bees protest?"

He gave her a scornful glance. "That's what the smoker is for. It makes them docile by masking the alarm pheromone given off by guard bees. I'll collect the honeycomb frames and scrape off the wax cap that bees make to seal off each cell. Then I place the frames in my extractor. It spins the frames and forces the honey from the comb."

"And then what?"

"I'll strain the honey and bottle it."

"Is that what's labeled raw honey?"

"Yep. Raw honey can contain traces of yeast, wax, and pollen. It's useful for combating seasonal allergies. On the other hand, pasteurized honey has been heated and processed to remove impurities."

Marla noticed how his gruff manner of speech had disappeared. "Do you believe the claims about honey's health benefits?" she asked. "I've read that it served as an antibiotic salve in the old days."

"That's right. You can apply it topically to disinfect wounds. It's also a natural cough suppressant, plus honey boosts your immune system and improves brain function. It's much better for you than refined sugar." He pointed to her belly. "Don't feed it to your kid until he's over twelve months old. Honey can contain bacteria that might cause infant botulism leading to paralysis. Even pasteurized honey could contain these spores."

Marla shifted her feet, uncomfortable from standing in place too long. The sun was heating the back of her head, making her wish she'd worn a hat. "If it was Sarah's idea to sell estate-labeled honey in the gift shop, how did you two meet, if you don't mind my asking?"

His eyes narrowed as though he did mind, but he replied nonetheless. "I was working part-time at the plant nursery on Flamingo Road when Sarah came in to look for decorative gardening tools to sell in her shop. She was like a ray of sunshine when she walked into the place."

Did his voice soften at the mention of the gift shop manager? Wait, hadn't Sarah said they'd met when Karl gave a lecture in the park? "How did she learn you had bug-catching skills?" Marla asked, wondering if one of them might be lying.

"We got to chatting, and I mentioned my entomology license. The estate needed an exterminator, so Sarah recommended me to the owner. Lacey took me on full-time. I'd always had an interest in bees, so we got started on our own production when Sarah suggested selling honey in the shop." His brows drew together. "What has Sarah told you about me?"

"Not much other than how your honey is a hit with her customers."

Marla frowned, studying his hair as he stepped into the

sunlight. It was uniformly white, the beard and the thinned hair on his head that he'd brushed back. But his stubble coming in was a darker tint and so were his eyebrows. She remembered the housekeeper's words that not everybody was who they seemed. Did Dalton do a background check on this guy? Had Lacey done one before she'd hired him? Or had she left that job to her security team?

Karl scowled at her. "We're done talking. I'd suggest you stay away from the hives and this shed hereafter. A lady in your condition should be more careful. We wouldn't want you to get stung, would we?"

With those words, he turned and slammed the door in her face.

Chapter Twelve

Marla returned to her Camry in the visitor parking lot and abruptly halted. A note was stuck under her windshield wiper. She scanned the area but didn't see anyone else in the immediate vicinity. Who might have put it there? Surely it wasn't an advertisement like the ones she sometimes found on her car in the supermarket parking lot.

Holding the folded paper by a corner and shaking it open, she squinted at the message. Her blood chilled at the words printed in a bold font.

I'm okay but I need you to stop looking for me.

Marla stared at the message, a shiver racking her spine. Could this be from Blinky? That would mean her friend was hiding out on the estate, unless she'd followed Marla there. Or possibly someone else left the note to throw her off the trail. This folded piece of white computer paper with printed letters could have been typed by anyone.

The visitor parking lot held a number of cars but no signs of movement. If it was Blinky, why here and why now?

It doesn't make sense. She could have contacted me at any time.

Dalton's team might be able to get some prints off this sheet of paper. Marla remembered his explanation of how they lifted latent fingerprints from porous surfaces. They already had her prints in their database to eliminate them. It was worth a try.

She took an evidence bag that he'd put into her glove compartment for occasions such as this and stuck the note inside. Her nape prickled, and she glanced up. Was she being watched?

The windows of the mansion glared back at her, sunlight reflecting from an angle. Or they could have security cameras aimed at the driveway. Actually, where did Rick Eaton and his team monitor the security feed?

She'd ask Dalton about it later. He must have seen the video footage from the attempted robbery. Was there a dedicated room inside the house where Rick observed the goings-on?

For that matter, did Lacey have a safe room where she could go in case of danger?

Tempted to go back inside and ask, Marla hesitated. She really needed to go home and rest for the baby's sake. She'd done enough traipsing around for one day. Besides, her body sagged with fatigue.

As she drove away, she admired the pink and white azalea bushes in bloom, the stately royal palms, and the trees with purple trumpet-shaped flowers along the drive. If only Blinky would turn up safe, she could appreciate the place better.

At home, she received a phone call soon after she'd let the dogs out into the backyard. Her heart raced with alarm when she saw it came from the doctor's office.

"Marla? Hi, this is Sally, Dr. Winthrop's nurse. I don't know if you've seen your lab results on our patient portal, but your iron is a bit low. We'd like you to start taking a supplement."

No wonder I feel tired all the time. "Is that all? Was everything else okay?"

"Yes, all the other results were good. Let us know if you have any questions."

Marla hung up and got busy prepping for dinner. She'd have to buy the iron pills tomorrow.

Once Dalton arrived, she told him the news. He seemed

unfazed by the lab report and went to change into more comfortable clothes. What would happen when the baby came? Their time would telescope into feeding sessions, diaper changes and stroller walks.

She put off discussing the rest of the day's revelations until they lay in bed later. He'd picked up an ecological thriller about the melting icecaps and how they would impact Florida.

"You should read a story about bees," she said. "I spoke to the beekeeper today at Tremayne Manor. He gave me an earful about bee habits and the beekeeping business."

Dalton reached for his bookmark and placed it inside the book, closing it with a grunt. "I got a lecture when I interviewed him, too. The guy seems to know his stuff."

"Did you see his hives? He told me they were out in the fields by the flowers."

"That makes sense, since the bees need the nectar. But no, I didn't spot any hive boxes."

"He has all sorts of equipment inside his shed. I didn't go in, but I got a peek. Don't you think he looks like Santa Claus with his long, white beard?"

"His eyebrows are a darker tint."

"So I noticed. Also, his hair is too uniformly one color. I talked to the housekeeper and the mansion's chef about him. Joan, the cook, said his hands are smoother than his apparent age would warrant."

Dalton glowered at her. "That doesn't mean anything. Your mom looks younger than her age. She barely has any wrinkles."

"According to Joan, Karl begs meals from their kitchen three times a day. Like, how come he never brings his own lunch? Where does he live, anyway?"

"He rents an apartment in the neighborhood. Nobody there has anything adverse to say about him. The man pays his rent on time and keeps a low profile."

"Karl said he met Sarah, the gift shop lady, when he

worked part-time at a plant nursery. She'd told me they had met when he gave a lecture in the park."

His brows lifted. "Now that's an interesting contradiction."

"It could mean one of them is lying. Oh, heck. I forgot to give you the note." Marla lumbered out of bed and down the hall to their home office. She returned holding the paper bag with the message left on her car.

Dalton peeked at the missive and put the bag aside to process the paper at work the next day. "I don't think your friend wrote this message. She would need access to a computer. Plus, to leave this on your car, she'd have to have been on the estate."

"Does Lacey have a safe room in the house? Maybe Blinky is hiding out in there."

"Nope. I already checked. And the security monitors don't show any evidence of her presence. Daniel has the skills to tamper with the recordings, but I don't see the two of them working together."

"Things must be connected somehow. We just can't see the links." Marla remembered another item Mrs. Docket had mentioned. "The housekeeper said Mr. Tremayne kept a sword collection. I didn't notice any swords during the tour."

Dalton's expression brightened. "Really? I haven't seen them, either. Maybe he kept them in a private vault."

"Did you check for hidden passages like at Sugar Crest Plantation Resort?" They'd found a maze of secret passageways at the haunted hotel on Florida's west coast where her family had held its Thanksgiving reunion.

"The house's walls aren't thick enough. What else did you learn while you were there?"

"I asked Lacey what had been the surprise inside the Fabergé egg she'd nearly lost. It had been a ruby pendant, but that's long gone. Then I asked her what she knew about the scandal involving Blinky. Obviously this hadn't deterred Lacey from hiring Blinky's advertising firm."

"What relevance does that have to the case?"

"Maybe something or perhaps none at all. The client who lost his shirt because of her firm's blunder was Ben Rogers. His company had sold cleaning agents for cars to a major chain of gas stations. They lost this client to a competitor when Blinky's company failed to meet their deadline."

Dalton shook his head. "I don't see how missing some ads would lead to a company's downfall."

"It would allow a competitor to jump the gun on a product," she suggested. "We probably don't know all the particulars. Later Ben opened an automotive repair center. When Blinky needed some work done on her car recently, she decided to make amends. She showed up at Ben's place of business and surprised him. He wasn't happy to see her and chased her out."

"The other department that's handling the missing person case sent an officer to speak to Ben Rogers. He denied seeing Blinky in the years since the initial incident."

"Then the man wasn't being truthful. Blinky must have tried to offer him compensation when the brouhaha first happened. Why would she approach him now?"

"To seek atonement, even though the fault for the incident wasn't hers? Supposing they did meet, I don't see how this relates to events at Tremayne Manor," Dalton said.

"If Ben had been seeking revenge, he might have been waiting for the right opportunity. Blinky gave it to him when she showed up at his door."

"So what? He chased her out. That should have been the end of it."

"Not if she'd angered him again."

"Look, why don't you leave the case to me?" He rolled to his side and smoothed his hand over her belly. "Our son wants your full attention."

"He'll have it soon enough. Meanwhile, my Camry seems to have developed an odd rumble," she said, quirking her eyebrows. "I'd better have it checked at the automotive center."

****

Tuesday morning before work, Marla headed over to Ben's repair shop. Located in a commercial section, the car place was squeezed between a pool supply store and a lighting emporium. Marla examined the latter with interest. She hadn't realized this was here, and she'd been thinking of what lamps to get for the baby's room.

Don't get distracted, she told herself. *You're here for a purpose.*

Why was she bothering to chase down this lead, anyway? Was it because the police didn't seem to be getting far in locating Blinky?

Sooner or later, she'd have to put her child's needs first, but that didn't mean she'd neglect her friends. What made her think she'd have to give up this aspect of her life? She could still go to girls' night out and be there when her friends needed her.

As she emerged from her car in the repair place's lot, she felt the baby kick. A flood of love filled her, obliterating thoughts of anything else. Truly her son would become her focus once he was born. But she had a few more months left where she could do some good.

She waddled toward the garage bays, noting they were closed despite a sign on the office door announcing the shop was open. She rapped on the faded wood, listening for sounds from within. Maybe they took appointments only?

A moment later, the door swung wide and a dark-haired fellow in grease-stained coveralls stared at her. "Can I help you?" he said with a Latin accent. Smells of motor oil and chemical solvents accompanied him.

"I'd like to speak to Ben Rogers about a mutual friend," she replied, sticking her foot in the doorway. "Oh, and my car has a rumble. I'd hoped you would check it out to see what's wrong."

The man's glance dropped to her telltale figure, and his eyes widened. "*Si, señora,* wait here please."

Marla craned her neck to peer beyond his shoulder as he moved away. A corridor stretched ahead. To the right, mechanics worked on a shiny black vehicle in the large garage. A few other cars waited for attention in the other bays. Overhead lights glared from above.

An office to the left had a wall of windows facing the hallway. At the end was a closed door. Maybe a restroom? She wrinkled her nose at the thought of having to use it.

A man in a gray uniform shirt and trousers exited the office and strode toward her. He had sandy brown hair and a moustache to go along with a pinched mouth and wary expression.

"I'm Ben Rogers. Who are you?"

"My name is Marla Vail. I'm a friend of Blinky's. I mean, Bonnie Morris. I gather you're aware she's gone missing. My husband is Detective Dalton Vail with the Palm Haven police force. He mentioned that one of their officers spoke to you?"

The crease deepened between his brows. "I told the cop everything I knew, which isn't much."

"I realize Blinky isn't on your favorite people list, but you might know some detail that could help us find her. She's been missing for over a week, and I'm deeply worried about what might have happened." Marla patted her abdomen. "It's not good for me to be stressed in my delicate condition."

His gaze didn't waver. "Carlos said you wanted us to look at your car."

"It has a strange rumble when it's in gear." She handed him her keys, hoping that wouldn't be a mistake. They could trap her here, but Dalton knew where she'd gone. She had promised to call him after her interview.

The man glanced up and down the street before gesturing for her to come inside. He signaled for one of the fellows to come over and tossed him the keys. "Check out her car,

Emilio. She says it has a rumble." His eyebrows waggled with meaning.

The other guy nodded. "Sure, boss. I'm on it."

Marla followed him into the office cluttered with papers, an empty coffee mug, a wilted plant, and several flashlights. For power blackouts? He sat behind his wood desk and indicated a worn leather chair for her to claim.

"Blinky wanted to make amends, you know," she began, crossing and uncrossing her legs. "She had a car issue and came here planning to make you an offer of free advertising for your shop."

Ben's face darkened. "We didn't need her help. She doesn't handle her clients personally like she promises."

"It was unfortunate that the man who handled your account didn't do his job properly. And yes, Blinky should have supervised him better. Things might have turned out differently if she'd been more diligent. But I understand how she'd want to make up for her employee's incompetence."

Ben glanced at the business card Marla presented him. "You own a salon. How would you feel if you paid big bucks to an advertising company, and the chief executive handed your account off to an underling? And that person let you down?"

"I'd be disappointed and wouldn't trust them again, but only if the boss had promised to personally manage my account."

"Exactly. From the way Blinky made her proposal, it sounded as though she would be the lead runner on our ad campaign. But she sloughed it off to an employee who failed at his job."

"That must have been disappointing to Blinky as well. As business owners, we're ultimately responsible for our employees, even if they're independent contractors. Surely she disciplined this person?"

"She fired him. Regardless, I wouldn't do business with her again. You can't trust her to keep her word."

"What happened when she showed up here years later?"

He snorted. "She wasn't welcome. I didn't care what she offered. It was too late."

Could the employee who'd been fired from his position still hold a grudge? Marla wondered. Where was this person now? Dalton's team must have this information. She'd ask him later, but for now, she needed to learn more from this guy.

"It's great that you recovered from the setback and became successful," she said, sweeping her arm in a broad gesture. "You might not have started your chain of automotive centers otherwise."

His lips quirked in a half-smile. "That's true. We're still expanding our franchises. It could have been the best thing that ever happened to me."

"Do you sell the same cleaning solvent you'd produced before? Or has it been superseded by newer products?"

His chest puffed out. "Mine is still the best. It works great on love bugs. We get a slew of cars in here during mating season."

"Wouldn't people just go to a car wash?"

"You need special chemicals to get the sticky bodies off your grill and windshield. Those bugs make a mess. I studied them, you know, to devise my formula. They like grassy habitats. That's why you'll see them when you're driving along the turnpike in the central part of the state, where there's nothing on either side of the road but a flat savanna."

"I've noticed them in the spring and mostly in the afternoons."

"They come out twice a year. May and September are the most popular months. They'll wait until the sun comes up and the air warms before flying. They're searching for nectar and pollen, their main sources of food."

"Are they native to Florida?" Marla asked, curious about the creatures that could cause damage to her car.

"Nope, they arrived here from Central America in the late 1940s," Ben replied with an impatient glance at a wall clock.

Marla shifted her position to ease an ache in her back. "I've seen them at turnpike plazas. They crawl on the gas pumps and concrete posts at the gas station. It's gross."

Ben's mouth curved upward. "Love bugs are attracted to car fumes. These contain a component that smells similar to decayed vegetation. That's where female love bugs lay their eggs."

"I hate how they fly into your windshield and get smashed when you're driving," Marla said with a grimace. "You can hear the splats each time they hit the window. Their mess makes it hard to see, and the windshield wipers only smear the stuff. Why do they fly paired?"

"They're mating. The males and females face in opposite directions and remain paired for about three days. Then the male gets exhausted and dies. After they separate, the female lays her eggs. She doesn't live much longer."

They had a short lifespan, Marla thought with a sense of pity. "Do love bugs secrete something that causes the sticky splatter? My window washer fluid won't clean it off."

"Their bodies are acidic," Ben explained. "You have to deal with it right away, or the residue can damage your paint. Our cleaning solution won't harm your car's finish or strip the wax. We sell it by the gallon if you want a jug. I'd also recommend bug splatter sponges that come five to a box. If you're going on a trip, you might want to add a bug screen that attaches to the front of your car to prevent the bugs from clogging your radiator."

"I suppose you sell that, too? I've heard you should spritz your grill with cooking spray before leaving home during mating season."

Marla noted a shipping manifest on his desk. Some of the packages were addressed to different countries. His operation must have a broader sweep than she'd realized.

“Tell me, do you send your special bug cleaner abroad?” she asked. “I suppose it could be useful in a warm climate like ours where they have these bugs. I’ll tell my friends if they can order it online.”

Ben turned the paper over and slapped his hand atop it. “We do a brisk business wherever these pesky insects find a home.” His glance swept to the window overlooking the garage bays. “Oh look, your vehicle is done. Let’s see what they found.”

From the way he shuffled her from his office, she got the impression her question had startled him. Was cleaning solution the only thing he shipped abroad?

Chapter Thirteen

"Ben seemed eager to get rid of me once I mentioned those shipping manifests," Marla told Nicole later at work. They had a moment free between clients, and Marla had brought the other stylist up to date. She'd already notified Dalton of her discussion.

"Do you think Blinky noticed the same thing? Something wonky could be going on there that made Ben go after her."

"He waited until she was dressed as the Easter bunny for a bunch of kids? That makes no sense."

Nicole gave her a keen glance. "Ben might have followed her. She spotted him, guessed his intent, and ran. She convinced the gardener to put on her outfit and act as a decoy. When she heard the man had been killed, she went into hiding, fearing Ben would find her to finish the job."

"Good theory, but illogical. Why wait until that day to do her in? Nonetheless, I get the feeling more is going on at that shop than Ben wants anyone to realize. Maybe Dalton has news in this regard. He didn't say much when I called him earlier."

"So you're eliminating Ben Rogers as a suspect?"

"Not entirely, but he isn't high on my list."

"Then who is at the top, girlfriend?" Nicole twirled the swivel chair at her station. She'd already cleaned the area and kept glancing at the parking lot through the front window. It wasn't like her next customer to be late.

"It has to be someone who works at Tremayne Manor,"

Marla replied. "I found a warning note left on my car parked there the other day. The beekeeper comes to mind. He skulks around the property in his protective gear. I have to say that he does know his business. I got a whole lecture on beekeeping and the production of honey when I spoke to him."

"What did he do before he got the job there?"

"He has an entomology degree. He met Sarah, the gift shop lady, when she came into a plant nursery where he had a part-time job behind the cash register. But she told me she'd heard him give a lecture in the park."

Nicole tapped her chin. "Hmm, something sounds irregular about those two."

"Tell me about it. I can't see why either one of them would be lying, though. It's not as if there's anything between them. Mrs. Docket, the housekeeper, told me Sarah had a soft spot for Connor Tremayne when he was alive. She'd worked in the house as a maid in those days."

"What about the thefts? Whoever is stealing those items must need money."

Marla, tired of standing, sank into her chair. "Daniel could be taking the items he wants to keep before his mother donates the estate to the historical society."

"Is she considering his wishes at all? And what gives her the right to dispose of her husband's legacy that way? Didn't he leave it in trust for his son?"

"Apparently not. He deeded the place outright to his wife. Maybe he didn't consider Daniel to be a smart money manager. All the kid does is sit in his room all day with his computer for company."

"How do you know what he's doing in there is legit? He could be a hacker or money launderer. Didn't you say he met with a stranger in a hoodie on the estate grounds?"

"That's right. Michelle, the café manager, mentioned this guy. She said Rick, the security chief, has also been seen with this man."

"It would be Rick's job to question any strangers on the premises. Was this hooded man around on the day of the crime?" Nicole brushed a few stray hairs from the chair at her station.

"Nobody has reported seeing him. Rick was off duty that day. And Daniel told my husband he didn't observe anything relevant from his window."

"Didn't you say the café lady was there accepting supplies?"

"Yes, but her restaurant faces the formal gardens. The murder happened over by the trees on the rear lawn. She didn't notice any unusual activity, or so she says."

"Where did the costume exchange occur? Did none of the other gardeners see anything?"

"Paolo was the only one present that day. He had work to do in the greenhouse. Dalton checked it out and didn't find anything significant."

"Regardless of where they switched outfits, it still doesn't explain how Paolo ended up with the Fabergé egg or why Blinky disappeared," Nicole noted.

Not unless one of them took it, Marla thought with sudden clarity. Good God, what if Blinky had been the thief? But then she wouldn't have had access to steal any other items from the house. Someone working inside would have to be in on the deal.

No, that was absurd. It seemed more logical that Paolo was the guilty party. He got spotted in the act and needed a disguise, so he convinced Blinky to give him the costume.

Of course, it was still possible Paolo had caught the thief in action and fled in panic. He accosted Blinky, donned her costume, and… what? Ran smack into the crook outside? The egg got dropped in their struggle? Then the killer would have picked it up, if he'd stolen it in the first place. Unless he got spooked and ran off without it.

Maybe that's when Blinky came upon the scene. The bad guy forgot about the egg in his haste to chase after her. And why did she assume the guilty party was a man? It could just as well be a woman. Had the CSI team recovered any DNA that might indicate the killer's gender?

She shared these ideas with Nicole, before noticing their customers approaching from the parking lot. Marla stood, feeling drained of energy. She needed to put aside these thoughts and concentrate on work.

"How do you know the egg was real?" Nicole asked out of left field. "Maybe the thief dropped it on purpose because he recognized it as a fake."

Marla gawked at her. *What a novel idea.* "Then the murder would have happened for nothing. Why stab Paolo over a worthless substitute?"

"Perhaps there's more than one reproduction in the house," Nicole suggested. "Didn't you say the gift shop sells items that are copies of artifacts?"

"Yes, some of the Russian relics have been reproduced, and I suspect some jewelry as well. That's commonplace for historical houses. Look at all the stuff sold by the Smithsonian museums. They're not selling actual treasures but goods that look like them. Tourists eat them up."

"Maybe Dalton should call in an appraiser to check out the eggs in Lacey's collection," Nicole said.

"He couldn't do that without a warrant, and there's no valid reason to get one. Besides, I'd be more suspicious if Lacey had made an insurance claim, but she hasn't reported anything missing before now."

"It's possible she doesn't know about the substitutions."

"True, but the items she told me were stolen haven't been replaced. Still, you present a valid reason for why the thief might have discarded the Fabergé egg."

Marla's thoughts scattered as she greeted her next client and sent the woman to the shampoo sink. This was all too much to bear. Yearning to focus on her baby, she prayed for Blinky to show up alive and well. Where was her friend? Had she gone to ground somewhere unexpected where nobody could hunt her down?

Surely evidence would have turned up by now if Blinky had been assaulted on the estate. She should check out the greenhouse even though Dalton had already been through there. Maybe she'd notice a tool out of place or a stain that had been overlooked.

A text message popped up on her cell phone, as though she'd conjured a response.

I have something to tell you, Sarah O'Malley, the gift shop manager, wrote. *Can you meet me here at closing?*

Marla glanced at her watch with a grimace. The gift shop closed at five, and she wouldn't be finished with her last client by then. "I can come around six," she wrote back. "What is it about?"

You'll find out. I'll wait here for you. Please come alone.

"Did you learn something about Blinky?"

Not exactly, but... wait, someone just walked into the shop. We'll talk later.

Curiosity tore at Marla through the rest of the day. At five-thirty, she finally finished her last customer. After gathering her purse, she sent both Dalton and Brianna a text that she'd be detoured coming home by a stop at Tremayne Manor, and they should eat dinner without her.

Dalton's call immediately followed. "Why are you going over there? You need to get off your feet and get some rest. Can't your visit wait for another day?"

Her heart warmed to the concern in his tone. "Sarah sent me a text to meet her there. She has something to tell me. It could be relevant to the case."

He gave a resigned sigh. "All right, but I'll join you."

"She told me to come alone. If you show up, it'll destroy her trust. I have to do this by myself."

"Then I'll park down the road. Keep your cell phone on so I can hear what's going on."

She set the alarm and exited the salon. The March winds had picked up, scurrying dead leaves on the asphalt in the parking lot.

Marla gripped the door handle to her Camry. She swept her gaze over the back seat to make sure no one hid there as Dalton had taught her and glanced at the undercarriage for unusual wires or foil. Spotting nothing out of the ordinary, she slid into the driver's seat. The air-conditioning kicked in when she started the engine.

How much would her life change when the baby came? Already she had obligations with the dogs and Brianna and her husband. A baby could totally consume her life. Where did that leave Marla, the business owner and amateur sleuth? Would her identity be erased?

Growth and change were inevitable. It meant taking risks and sometimes jumping head-first into a situation outside your comfort zone. Having a baby was one of those life-changing events. Better to face it as a new adventure than to dodge and hide.

Like Blinky. The thought came unbidden into her mind. Maybe Sarah would shed some light on Blinky's disappearance.

Marla shoved the car into gear, exited the parking lot, and zoomed down the road.

Rush hour traffic impeded her progress so that it took an extra twenty minutes to arrive at Tremayne Manor. The visitor lot was empty when Marla pulled into a space. In the near distance, the majestic house arose in the midst of manicured lawns, shaped shrubbery and planted flower beds. Late afternoon sunlight glinted off its windows and cast a surreal glow over the deserted grounds.

Gravel crunched underfoot as Marla headed toward the ticket entrance at the gift shop. The front door would be locked, the docents gone home for the day. An air of abandonment hovered around the place, like a monument to the past that had outlived its usefulness.

Her vehicle had been the only one in the lot. Where did Sarah park? Or the other staff, for that matter?

Possibly the cook stayed through dinner, or did she leave meals for Lacey and Daniel to heat up for themselves? If so, then she would have left already. Mrs. Docket, the housekeeper, lived off premises like the rest of the staff. That would leave the pair alone in the house, unless they employed security staff for the night hours. More likely, the guards departed once the tours ended and the house was secured.

Marla wouldn't want to live in a place like this if it were her choice. Ghosts from the past might haunt the corridors. Then again, Heather hadn't mentioned any ghost stories associated with the mansion.

As she approached the polished wood door, she cocked her head. Had Sarah left it open for her? The gift shop manager wouldn't keep it ajar like this otherwise, would she?

"Sarah, are you in there? It's me, Marla." No response.

Marla stepped inside, the hairs rising on her nape. The unearthly quiet made her pulse race. Her gaze swept the countertops, display cases, and goods for sale around the shop. All appeared to be properly in place.

Except for the body lying on the floor behind the cash register.

Chapter Fourteen

Marla's breath hitched, and her limbs froze. *No, tell me that's not Sarah.* This couldn't be happening again. And yet, the coppery smell of blood told its own story.

She summoned Dalton before forcing her feet to move forward. Sarah lay face-up, a look of stunned surprise in her glazed eyes. Her red hair splayed on the floor, like an angelic halo. A crimson stain spread on the jade blouse she'd worn over black leggings. It had already started to congeal. This couldn't have occurred too long ago.

Marla's gaze zeroed in on the wound. Had Sarah been shot? Marla didn't see a weapon in the immediate vicinity.

Did that mean the killer was still around? Her heart leapt into her throat. While part of her wanted to kneel at Sarah's side to verify her status, she'd better get out of there *now*.

Covering her mouth with her hand, she turned and sped outside onto the grass. Her stomach heaved, but she suppressed the bile rising in her throat and stumbled toward her Camry. She slid inside, locked the doors and waited for Dalton.

He arrived within minutes. Marla rolled down her window as he approached with a stern look on his face.

"If I'd gotten here sooner, I might have been able to prevent this from happening," she said in a rush of words. Guilt washed over her. She should have come as soon as she'd received the message from Sarah.

"Then you could have ended up in the same condition. Stay here," Dalton ordered. He disappeared inside the shop for a short interval.

When he returned, Marla shut off the engine that she'd kept on for the air-conditioning and emerged from the car.

"Tell me again how you found the woman." Dalton placed a comforting hand on her shoulder.

"The side door to the gift shop was open. I went inside and saw Sarah lying there. She's dead, isn't she? Was she shot? Do you think the killer might still be on the property?"

He stepped back and pulled out his notebook. "Do you know if Mrs. Tremayne is home?"

She noticed he hadn't answered her questions and had reverted to his professional tone.

The sun's descent hit her at an angle that made her fumble for a pair of sunglasses. "I have no idea. You'd think the ruckus we're making would alert Lacey if she's in the house. You could call her or ring the front doorbell."

Maybe the killer went on a rampage and murdered everyone present. Did this person enter the shop through the side door or through the inner door from the house? The latter had been shut when she'd been in the store. She'd assumed it was locked, but perhaps not.

"Why don't you go home?" Dalton said. "You've had a shock, and it's been a long day. I can get your formal statement later." He glanced up as a rescue truck and squad car squealed into the parking lot.

Marla surmised he'd called for backup while inside the shop. She recognized the gleam in his eyes. She'd lose him to his job now. There wasn't any point to her remaining. And better he should be the one to inform Lacey.

She felt his gaze on her back as she drove away. Was someone else watching her departure, tagging her as a threat? Had they overheard Sarah on the phone asking her to stop by and wondering what the woman had already told her?

Her fingers tightened on the steering wheel. Had a similar fate happened to Blinky? Did her friend see something the day of the egg hunt that she shouldn't have and met her death as a result? Dalton's team had scoured the woods and the formal gardens. Had they checked all the work sheds on the property?

She skidded to a halt down the road as an earlier thought surfaced. Where did the staff park when they came to work? The lot at the side of the house was for visitors. In the old days, a chauffeur would drop off the occupants and drive around… to where? Was there another road leading to a detached garage?

She made a U-turn and headed back toward the house. Wait, there it was—a small offshoot through a wooded section. She turned down the nearly hidden lane and followed it to a multi-car garage with another parking lot. Elation left her breathless. Did Dalton know this was here?

The staff must park at this lot during the day. She could see a clear path leading to the employee entrance at the house. This would be perfect for the catering staff as well when they were hired for special events.

Now what? She didn't dare explore the garage on her own. Maybe there was a window where she could peek in to see if any vehicles were present.

She parked and texted Dalton. "I've found a garage behind the house. Can you break away for a few minutes and meet me here? Or have you already learned if Lacey is home?"

No one is answering the doorbell. I've a call in to Lacey, but she hasn't responded. Don't go inside without me. I'll be right there.

He arrived without delay. After reprimanding her for not going home, he accepted her explanation. They strode to the side of the garage and peered in the windows.

"Hey, I didn't notice this room when we searched the place," Dalton said, frowning at a grimy pane near the rear corner.

"You've been here before? Why didn't you mention it?" His words registered. "Wait, are you saying there's a hidden room?" Her heart raced at the idea. Maybe they'd find a clue to Blinky's disappearance.

The garage door was locked, so they tramped over to a side door and used Marla's handy lock picks that she carried in her purse.

"As far as you know, I entered on my own and then summoned you to my side," she said as the lock gave way. She pushed open the door, wrinkling her nose at the chemical smell inside.

Dalton turned on the light. The interior was empty except for a single vehicle. The Prius had seen a few years. "That's Daniel's car," he said. "Either he's at home, or he and his mom went out together."

"Where is the hidden room?" Marla asked, prowling the perimeter. She estimated where the space should be, but a shelving unit stood there. Wait a minute. Could the opening be behind it?

"Dalton, come over here. I think there's a door behind these wire shelves."

Together they managed to swing the shelves outward. Sure enough, a door faced them.

She'd expected to find work tools inside the room they entered, but not the other items. On a countertop rested the furry white hands and feet from a bunny costume.

Marla had never thought about it before, but people dressed up as the Easter bunny at the mall were fully costumed. Otherwise, they'd give themselves away as actors.

"Good Lord, how did these get here?" Dalton said, staring at the items.

She pointed to the bulky feet. "Paolo couldn't run fast if he'd put these on. Plus, I imagine he was in a hurry to change and didn't bother to get fully costumed. Or maybe these mittens and paws were too small for his build. Did this mean

Blinky was in here with him? If so, after she gave him the costume, what was she wearing?"

"Your friend might have had on some lightweight clothing under the bunny suit. I'll take these into evidence. I can't believe we missed this room the first time around."

Marla's spirits fell. She'd hoped to find a clue as to Blinky's whereabouts. "What will you tell people about how we got inside the garage?"

He gave her a crooked grin. "As you suggested, you entered through an unlocked side door and called me when you discovered these items."

"Did you try contacting Daniel? He might be home. If he's buried in his computer programs, he might not have heard the commotion downstairs."

Dalton grunted. "I sent him an email. Figured it might pop up on his screen, but he didn't respond to that message or to my text. Maybe he and his mother are somewhere together and they've turned off their phones."

"You should check the house to make sure nothing bad has happened to them," Marla advised, dread pitting her stomach.

"I know. We don't need a warrant under these circumstances. Steve is handling that job."

"Oh, I hadn't realized Sergeant Peterson was here." Marla knew most of his department members. She'd met them at the police station, at their annual barbecue, or at other social events.

She sagged against a counter. "What information could Sarah have had that led to her death? There's no doubt in my mind that her phone call to me triggered the killer." Marla hoped Lacey and Daniel were somewhere safe having a good time. Lacey would be devastated when she heard about Sarah.

"The gift shop manager might have discovered the thief's identity and threatened him with exposure," Dalton suggested, rubbing a hand across his face. Fatigue lines etched his forehead. How would he manage when the baby kept them up at night?

"I was thinking about the jewelry, candlesticks and other items in the gift shop that are reproductions for visitors to buy," she said. "What if some of the artifacts in the house are fakes as well? You should bring in an appraiser to check the Fabergé eggs. Maybe the reason the killer left it behind wasn't because he got spooked by killing Paolo and inadvertently dropped it. Maybe he tossed it away because he knew it was a fake."

Dalton's brow furrowed. "That's an interesting theory. The gift shop manager may have been part of it. We can check her invoices to see where she purchased her inventory."

"Sarah had to be working with someone if this is true. She wouldn't have had such broad access to the house." A memory floated to the surface, making Marla's temples throb. "I forgot to tell you the docent mentioned Lacey liked to paint as a hobby when Connor was alive. I'd gotten the impression she'd given up the practice but forgot to ask her about it. She might have connections in the art world."

"You're suggesting Lacey could be the one selling items from the house?" Dalton scoffed.

"She'd never claimed the missing items on her insurance. Maybe mentioning them to me was a smokescreen. She could be replacing the house's treasures with reproductions." Marla clapped a hand to her mouth. "Do you think she was working with Sarah in that regard? Lord save me, I can't believe I'm saying this. Is it possible Lacey was involved in her death?"

Dalton's gaze darkened. "I doubt it. Why would Lacey consider donating her house and its contents to the historical museum if she knew the relics weren't real?"

"For the tax deduction? She could hope no one discovered her scheme." Marla swallowed down discomfort over her next question. "How did Sarah die?"

"There appears a stab wound on the victim similar to the

one on Paolo. We'll know more after the M.E.'s report is available."

Marla propped her hands on her hips. "Are you implying the killer stabs these people, removes the blade, and stashes it somewhere? He'd have to wipe it off first. Have you looked for traces of blood elsewhere on the property?"

"Let us do our jobs, will you? You're looking tired. You should go home."

"All right, but call me when you hear from Lacey. I'd like to know she's okay. I don't really believe she's capable of killing anyone. I'm more worried for Blinky. You've searched the entire estate, right? All the work sheds, the greenhouse and the gardens?"

"We've got it covered. We haven't found any suspicious mounds of fresh dirt on the property or other unusual findings."

Marla's throat closed at the images his words conjured. She stepped outside, relishing the late afternoon sunshine and the warm spring air. Dalton followed her out the side door.

She turned toward him. "Do me a favor, and take a look at Sarah's financial accounts. She managed the bookkeeping for the on-site store, and there doesn't appear to be much oversight involved. You could find a paper trail that might prove useful."

"We'll look into it. I'll probably be here late, so don't wait up for me." He gave her a desultory kiss on the mouth, his mind already on the job.

Marla drove home, disturbed by visions of Sarah lying on the floor. She hadn't known the gardener, but she had been acquainted with the gift shop lady. Who would Dalton have to notify about her death? Did she have family in the area? With a jolt, Marla realized she knew very little about the woman's personal life except that she was single.

At home, Marla greeted Brianna with a hug and a brief explanation of events. The teen had a ton of questions, but

Marla wasn't in the mood to respond. Tonight's dinner was leftovers, so she put the dishes out for the girl to help herself and headed into the shower to scrub off the taint of death.

The dogs brought her comfort when she reentered the kitchen. They nudged her ankles, needing her affection. Petting them calmed her nerves.

She really should sit back and let Dalton do the job he did best. *No more,* she promised him silently. *News will surface about Blinky eventually. I have to be patient.*

Nonetheless, her heart leapt with joy when he texted to tell her Lacey had contacted him. She'd gone to a charity benefit, while her son was at a concert. The homeowner had been shocked to hear the news about Sarah.

Relieved their family was safe, Marla turned to mundane tasks. The next day would keep her busy with a full schedule. She was glad to remain at home for now and planned to crawl into bed early.

Wednesday passed by in a blur, and so it wasn't until Thursday morning that Marla thought about Lacey again. She should offer support to the woman and decided to stop by to express her condolences.

En route to Tremayne Manor, she picked up a box of chocolates, unsure of what else might be appropriate. Crime scene tape blocked off the gift shop entrance, and a sign indicated tours were temporarily suspended. Mrs. Docket answered the front doorbell at Marla's summons.

"Mrs. Tremayne isn't seeing visitors," the housekeeper said in a stiff tone.

"I'm here as a friend. I brought something for Lacey. I know she must be upset about Sarah's death."

Mrs. Docket accepted the candy. "I'll see if she's available. Please wait inside the foyer."

While Marla stood by, she examined the faux rock on the walls. If this were a medieval castle, the foyer would hold a display of armaments meant to intimidate enemies. Where had

Connor hidden his swords? And why hadn't he left these personal possessions to his son? Maybe because he knew Daniel wouldn't care about ancient relics. Lacey may have sold them, like she'd sold his stamp collection.

After a few minutes, Mrs. Docket returned and guided her upstairs to the sunny family parlor. "Miz Lacey will be along shortly. Can I bring you a cup of tea or coffee?"

"No, thanks. I'm fine. I have to go in to work myself soon."

"That's right, you own a hair salon. How long do you plan to keep working?" The housekeeper pointed to Marla's belly.

Why did everyone ask that question? "I'll stay as long as I can. Tell me, did Sarah have any concerns the last time you saw her?"

"Not that I recall. Poor thing. I can't believe she's gone." A sorrowful expression crossed Mrs. Docket's face.

"I understand both Lacey and Daniel were out of the house when it happened. Had all the employees gone home?" Marla asked for clarification.

The older woman nodded and smoothed her apron. "We'd closed the public rooms for the day. Cook didn't stay since Miz Lacey was going out."

"Sarah hadn't left yet," Marla reminded her.

"That's true. She'd mentioned something about balancing her budget."

That must have been Sarah's excuse to remain behind and call Marla. But why did Sarah choose to meet her here? They could have met at a coffee shop or anywhere else. Did the gift shop lady have something in particular to show her?

"I don't suppose I could get a peek inside the store?" Marla said. "Whatever Sarah had been working on that day might relate to her death."

"Sorry, there's crime scene tape across the doors. Those detectives are due back today. Once we have clearance to reopen, I can let you in there, but not now."

"I understand. So there's nothing else you can tell me about Sarah? Any tiny thing you might have noticed that could help us find her killer?"

Mrs. Docket gave a vehement shake of her head. "Sorry, ma'am, I have nothing to add. Now I'd better get back to work before Miz Lacey finds me chit-chatting and wasting time."

The housekeeper scurried out. Did she really know nothing, or was she aware of surveillance devices trained on them? Marla looked around the room. Did the security staff monitor the private quarters as well? Or if not them, Daniel might have hidden cameras around the place.

Voices murmured from down the hall. She recognized Lacey's higher-pitched tone and a man's gravelly voice.

"You have to tell them what you've seen, Bruno."

"I'm not reporting a ghost. It's my imagination. Your welfare is what concerns me, dear lady."

"Too bad you weren't here to watch over Sarah. I do appreciate your diligence, though. We couldn't get by without you."

"*We* couldn't… or did you mean *you* can't do without me?" the maintenance man said. "You know how I feel about things."

"Don't start, Bruno. We wouldn't want Daniel to suspect anything."

"Not much gets past that boy. You should listen to his ideas, Lacey."

"I'm not going down that road. This place has too much history to leave it in his slippery hands. He'd sell everything in a heartbeat."

"Maybe, but you should give him a chance."

"Your soft spot makes you vulnerable to his manipulation. Don't let him fool you. He isn't the kid you're imagining. Like, where did he go today? That boy leaves without any explanation and shares nothing about his activities or friends. I don't trust him."

"That's sad. But it doesn't mean you can't trust me. Did you at least look in the room as I asked?"

"Yes, and everything was in its place. So put the ghost to rest."

Footsteps approached while Marla stood by, hoping they wouldn't discover her eavesdropping.

"Please see if you can re-hang that picture in the dining room," Lacey added in a loud tone, clearly not realizing Marla could hear every word they'd spoken. "I don't know why it would loosen all of a sudden. And then let's talk about the gutter outside. One of the gardeners said there's a leak by the kitchen door. We wouldn't want people to get wet once the rainy season starts."

"Of course. I am ever your faithful servant," Bruno stated in a brusque voice.

"I know," Lacey said in a softer tone than Marla believed was warranted. Their relationship hinted at something closer than employer and employee.

Bruno had worked for the family a long time. Why would he stay on when he could probably get a more lucrative position elsewhere with benefits? Was it because he had a fondness for the owner?

She recalled that a couple of people had advised her to speak to the maintenance man. Rick, the security chief, and Daniel, Lacey's son, had both mentioned his name.

Wait a minute. Hadn't Dalton told her that Bruno had been around the day of Paolo's murder? He'd been fixing the gazebo over by the botanical gardens.

Had he also been working late on Tuesday when Sarah was killed?

Chapter Fifteen

"I'm sorry to keep you waiting," Lacey said, breezing into the parlor. "It's been a hectic morning."

"I can imagine. Your entire routine must be disrupted. Please accept my sincere condolences regarding Sarah. I wanted to make sure you were all right." Marla studied the estate owner, who appeared as put together as ever with her hair up in a twist, her makeup applied with an expert touch, and her palazzo pants matched to a flowery top.

Lacey eyed her in return. "I'm told you're the one who found her. What were you doing here after hours?"

"Sarah had something to tell me. Now I'll never know what she meant to say."

Lacey sank into an armchair, and Marla followed suit on a sofa. "I can't even think about replacing her. It's so awful. Your husband said we'll be able to reopen once his team finishes processing the scene, but…" Lacey's voice broke, and a brief silence ensued. After a moment, she continued. "We relied on her talents. She was creative about selecting items for the shop."

"What about the reproductions? I'll bet those are popular with visitors."

Lacey gave a rueful chuckle. "Yes, customers especially like the jewelry. We really couldn't have started this whole venture without Sarah. She was our driving force."

"She started here as a maid, didn't she? Where did she get the knowledge to be a buyer for the store?"

"We all learned the business from the ground up. It wasn't easy after Connor died."

"A lot of your staff was here back then. They must be very loyal."

"Or I pay them well. What is it you want to know, Marla? You're not here just to comfort me, although I appreciate the chocolates. That was a thoughtful gesture. But you're taking time away from your salon to be here."

"I don't go in until one o'clock on Thursdays, so my morning is free." Marla gestured toward the exit. "I heard Bruno's voice from down the hall. We haven't had a chance to chat. Would you mind if I had a word with him?"

"About what?" Lacey's gaze chilled.

"He's familiar with the house and would notice if anything was amiss. You did want me to investigate the thefts, remember?"

A look of relief flitted across Lacey's face. "Of course. He'll be in the dining room fixing one of the pictures."

"You know, it crossed my mind that Sarah had ordered the replicas of artifacts in the house. How do you know the thief wasn't working with her and substituting fakes for the real thing?"

Lacey stared at her. "That's a preposterous idea. Then items wouldn't be missing. They'd appear to be in place."

"It would explain why I found the Fabergé egg discarded on the grass. Maybe you should get some of these things reappraised, like the painting Bruno is fixing. Why would it loosen from the wall all by itself?"

"One of the maids might have dusted it, and the screw wasn't secure. You're searching for ghosts where they don't exist."

Isn't that what Lacey had told Bruno, too? Did the maintenance man suspect the same as Marla? He'd be familiar with the contents in the house as well as the people who worked there. But if he was complaining to Lacey about things, he couldn't be the thief, could he?

Marla rose, anxious to speak to the man. "Who will take over the gift shop management and ticket sales with Sarah gone?" she asked.

Lacey stood to face her. "The poor woman isn't in her grave yet, Marla. I haven't thought about it until now, but I'll probably have to hire outside help."

"You can't promote one of the other maids to her position? Sarah must have seemed very capable when you appointed her to gift store manager."

"Having a shop on premises was Sarah's idea in the first place. Doing the tours and special events gave me a purpose after Connor died. It helped Sarah, too. She'd been here long enough that she grieved for him alongside me."

"Does she have relatives in the area? I'd like to attend her funeral if it's local."

"Sarah was single. She never married. I couldn't understand why she wouldn't go out and meet men, but she said her heart belonged to someone who'd promised to return for her. How sad that she waited in vain. Her parents are elderly, and she has a brother who lives near them in Austin. I suppose they'll bury her there."

Marla wanted to linger and ask more questions, but she didn't dare miss her chance to interview Bruno. She made her excuses and hurried off.

He'd just completed his job in the formal dining room when she entered. The table was as she remembered with the gleaming place settings, fancy candelabra, and lush flower arrangements. Who was bringing Mrs. Docket the cut blooms now that Paolo was gone?

She cleared her throat. "Hi, I'm a friend of Lacey's. My name is Marla Vail. She said I could speak to you about recent events. You might know my husband. He's the detective investigating Paolo's death. I presume he's interviewed you already?"

"That is correct, ma'am." The man wore a plaid shirt

with a pair of belted jeans. An open toolbox lay at his feet. He stooped to close it and secure the latch before straightening to face her.

"How long have you been working for the Tremaynes?" Marla began, absorbing the quiet air without tourists there. The place seemed forlorn, an empty testament to the past. What had Daniel said—that it could be put to better use? What did he really mean?

"I've worked here since my daddy was in charge of maintenance," Bruno replied. "When he died, I took over the job. Connor and I… well, I was only two years older than him. We played together as we grew up. Daddy hoped I'd make something of myself, maybe go to college. I tried, but that path wasn't right for me. So I came back here."

"Had you ever worked in another profession?" she asked, wondering what he'd done in the between years.

He snorted. "I ended up in construction. Learned enough to get my own license. But my dreams of starting my own company fell apart when I came home and met Lacey."

"What do you mean? Wasn't she married to Connor by that time?"

"They were engaged. But a more beautiful woman I'd never seen. I had to stay and maintain the house for her sake. They'd be raising children here, and daddy was getting past his years. I couldn't see them hiring no one else."

"It sounds as though you liked Lacey."

His brows drew together. "Didn't matter if I admired her. She was way out of my class. Connor was a handsome boy, and they made a fine couple. They both shared a lot of interests."

"Did things go well with their marriage?" She leaned an elbow on one of the dining room chairs to relieve some of the weight on her feet.

"For a while." A distant look entered Bruno's eyes. "They traveled and hosted parties at the mansion and added to their collections. Lacey was into art as much as Connor. But he got sidetracked by his passion for boating when she wanted to stay home and paint."

"I heard she'd had an interest in painting. What medium did she favor? Are any of her works on display in the house?"

He waved a hand. "Nah, she never considered her stuff to be good enough to show anyone else. She dabbled in watercolors. It angered her when Connor sailed off on his yacht with friends from the boat club. He started drinking more, and Lacey signed up for classes to learn how to do oils."

"Weren't they supportive of each other's interests?"

"Connor's interests started wandering, if you know what I mean. I tried to counsel him. We'd grown up together and had been close as kids. But things had changed between us. He resented my intrusion and threatened to fire me if I didn't mind my own business. So I became Lacey's friend instead. She needed someone to listen to her."

Were you more than friends? Marla wanted to ask but didn't. "What happened when Daniel was born? Did that draw Lacey and Connor back together?"

"In the beginning. Connor wanted to be a decent father, and he tried his best. I'll give the man credit for that much."

"But then his attention started to wander again?" Marla guessed.

Bruno glanced at a surveillance camera mounted on the wall. He picked up his toolbox and gestured for her to follow him. They ended up outside, at the rear of the house. The scent of freshly cut grass reached her nose. Birds twittered in the distance, and a light breeze wafted their way.

"Connor didn't have a lot of patience," Bruno explained, finding a place under the overhang to stand in the shade. "As Daniel got older, his father was around less and less."

"How did he treat his son? Was he kind toward him?"

Bruno's mouth compressed, and his eyes scrunched. "He was there for the important events, but he wasn't there in terms of loving the child. Connor grew even more distant from his family as time went on."

"But you were there for them? How did Daniel react to his father's indifference?"

"As any child would, he felt it was his fault. It saddened me to watch him shrivel into himself. He didn't make friends easily, and he turned to his electronics for constant company."

"That's sad. But what about your life? Didn't you want to marry and have a family of your own?" she asked, squinting against the sunlight.

He shook his head. "This place is where I belonged; with the house, the history, and the people."

"Daniel doesn't seem to appreciate the house as much as his mother."

"He has other ideas that he won't share with anyone, least of all with Lacey."

"Does he confide in you?" she said, wondering if they had a special bond.

"Nuh-uh. I'm careful to preserve our relationship. He sees me as the hired help, nothing more. That kid just needs someone to listen to him and to straighten him out, but it can't be me."

"What do you know about the items that have gone missing from the house? Lacey asked me to look into it."

Bruno's face washed of emotion. "The thefts started three years ago. I noticed a statue missing from the Russian room. Nobody touches those things except for Mrs. Docket, and she couldn't find the statue anywhere, either. Other small objects began to go missing, too."

"Was there anybody new on the staff at the time that might have access to these areas?"

He shook his head. "Nope. Most of us have been here since Connor's time."

"How about needing money? It's likely the thief is selling the goods."

He gave her a startled glance. "That's around the time Heather's husband got sick, now that I think about it. But our head docent loves the house and values its history. No way would she steal its treasures for personal gain."

"What's the matter with her husband?"

"He has a rare illness that requires expensive medicines, and they're both in that phase before Medicare when health insurance premiums are sky-high."

"I'm sorry to hear this."

"That's why she leaves every day at two o'clock. She has to relieve the caretaker. It's a sad situation."

"Does she have children who can help?"

"They live out of state. Heather manages the best she can. This job gives her a purpose and distracts her from her problems. Don't go bothering her with your questions, you hear?"

Marla appreciated the concern in his voice. It sounded as though Bruno took care of more than the house. "Who else might be hurting for money?"

He snorted. "There probably isn't one among us who couldn't use supplemental income."

Another query about the staff hovered on her tongue, but she'd better not press her luck. She changed tactics instead. "Don't you think it's odd how the video recordings don't show anybody taking these items? Someone must be tampering with the video feed."

"You'd have to ask Rick about that, ma'am. He's in charge of surveillance."

"Maybe so, but Lacey's son is the one with computer skills. He works in cyber security. If anyone knew how to edit files, it would be him. Does he have access to the security room on the team's off hours?"

"It's kept locked. What are you implying? That Daniel is stealing from his own house?"

"He doesn't own the place, nor does he value the treasures same as his mom."

"So you think he's taking things out of spite?" Bruno scoffed.

"Maybe he needs the money and is selling them. He's been spotted on the grounds meeting some guy wearing a hoodie. Have you noticed this stranger?"

"No, ma'am. But you're totally off the mark if you're suspecting Daniel. That boy has his problems, thanks to his father, but he has a good heart."

"You seem to have a lot of faith in Daniel when he doesn't show the same regard for you."

"All that poor boy ever wanted was his father's love. I couldn't ever be a substitute for Connor, no matter how much I..." His voice drifted off, and a wistful look came into his eyes. "I'm here for him if he ever needs a friend. It's my guess he doesn't consider himself worthy of affection. That's a shame, because Daniel has more smarts than his dad ever did. So what if his priorities are different? Some would see this place as a mausoleum rather than a museum."

Marla wondered at the pain in his expression. Where did Bruno fit into this equation? Was it merely his loyalty to the family that fueled his devotion or something more?

"Opening the house for tours was a brilliant idea," she said. "Most of us want to see how the wealthy half live. It's like touring the castles in England. Tell me, how were relations between Lacey and Connor at the time of his death? Was Lacey more relieved than sad over his loss?"

"She grieved for her husband," Bruno replied in a curt tone.

"Did she ever resume her painting? It might have brought her comfort after he died."

"No. She lost interest and gave it up. Now I've said enough. You're better off tending to your own family and leaving ours alone."

She noticed his use of the plural pronoun. "Wait, I understand you were working on the gazebo the day Paolo was killed. Did you see anything suspicious?"

"If I had, I would have told your husband."

"What about that guy in the hoodie? You didn't notice if he was present?"

"I already said I haven't seen this person."

"Rick has also been spotted in his company. Who could the man be if it's someone both Rick and Daniel know?"

"Beats me. Now if you'll excuse me, I have a leaky gutter to fix."

"Were you aware Paolo had served time in jail? He had a history of mail theft and check fraud."

That statement stopped Bruno cold, same as if she'd turned on the water hose and sprayed him down. He turned toward her with a look of incredulity on his face. "Is that true? Paolo seemed like a decent guy. He was a hard worker and loved his plants."

"Perhaps this man in the hoodie was someone he'd met in prison."

"What are you implying? Paolo was stealing the goods and passing them off to this guy? You think the man is a fence?"

"It's possible." *Although if so, how would Paolo have gained access to the house? Maybe Sarah had let him inside through the gift shop entrance.*

"I understand Daniel and his mom were out on Tuesday when Sarah was killed," Marla said. "Had you already left for the day, or were you working late that afternoon?"

"I was out of here by five." He shook his head. "I can't believe Sarah is gone. Paolo and I crossed paths on occasion, but we didn't know each other well. Sarah was a friend. She recognized a kindred soul in me. We both wanted something we couldn't have."

"Such as?" Marla wished he'd blurt out whatever he meant instead of skirting the issue.

"It doesn't matter. None of us have been angels in this life, but now she's one of them in the hereafter. I hope she achieves her dreams there." He switched his attention to Marla. "As for you, I'd keep my nose out of other people's business if you want to stay safe."

He stomped off, while Marla stood staring after him. He'd dropped a few hints but she wasn't sure where they led.

She reentered the quiet house through the kitchen entrance. As she passed the library en route to the front door, she spotted Rick, the security chief, bent over the antique roll-top desk. Pausing in the doorway, she cleared her throat.

Rick jerked upright and spun to face her.

Chapter Sixteen

"What are you doing here?" Rick snapped as he scowled at her.

"I came to offer my condolences to Lacey. Did you find anything interesting in Connor's old desk? It's a beautiful piece of art, isn't it? My husband would love to have one like that."

"I'll bet he wouldn't be happy to see you snooping around here."

"That's supposed to be your job, isn't it? What were you looking for?"

"Just making sure everything is intact. Sometimes visitors put their greasy fingers on the furnishings."

Oh, really? Maybe your greasy fingers are taking things that don't belong to you.

As security chief, it would be easy for Rick to steal small objects that might go unnoticed. Or maybe he knew something about the desk that she didn't. Certainly it warranted a closer examination when no one else was around.

What about security footage? She glanced upward to note a camera mounted on a corner by the ceiling. It was aimed toward a wide angle and might not specifically pick up the desk. Was Rick really checking the placement of items on its surface, or had he been searching the piece?

"Did Connor use this desk, or was it put here for show?" she asked. "There must have been all sorts of interesting stuff left in the drawers. I love that letter opener with the carved bone handle."

He gave her a smug glance as though he knew she was fishing for information. "Lacey wanted the desk moved after her husband passed, because it reminded her too much of the days when he was alive. He'd spent many hours in this chair. But Heather convinced her to keep it in the library where it belonged."

"How about his sword collection? I don't recall seeing any display of weapons on the tour."

"They're in a private vault. Connor knew Lacey wouldn't want to display weaponry among their fine china, porcelain statues, and religious icons. Nobody knows where it's located."

"You'd think he would tell his wife. Then again, none of these objects belonged to her until Connor died, did they?" Marla put a hand to her lower back. Damned ache had started again.

"You're wrong there, Mrs. Vail. Connor signed over the deed to the missus earlier. It all belonged to her."

"Why would he do such a thing? And why not make clearer provisions for his son?" Marla lowered her voice so they wouldn't be overheard in case Daniel had set up hidden microphones around the house.

With his computer skills, he could be monitoring every room aside from the security cameras. But if there were competing devices in an area, wouldn't they produce some kind of feedback or interference? Or maybe he was tapping into the line from Rick's setup instead. She had no knowledge of surveillance technology, but Daniel could be an expert in the field.

Rick compressed his mouth. "Connor should have thought of his other relations, but no, the sonovabitch gave everything to his wife."

"By relations, do you mean Daniel, or did he have an extended family?"

"The rest of his family. His daddy stole everything from them. Like father, like son."

Marla stepped back at the vehemence in his tone. "I'm sorry. I wasn't aware there was bad blood between Connor and his relatives."

"Tell your husband to trace the history of the Tremaynes. He'll see what I mean. Now if you're done here, I'll escort you to the front door."

Marla glanced at her watch. Good heavens, it was past noon. She'd be late for work. Her stomach growled, reminding her she hadn't eaten lunch. It wasn't healthy for the baby for her to skip meals.

She made it to the salon's parking lot in record time. A gnawing feeling in her gut made her stop by Bagel Busters to order a grilled cheese and tomato sandwich. Arnie, the owner and her long-time friend, stood behind the cash register. He wore his customary apron over jeans and a tee shirt. His face broke into a grin at her arrival.

"Marla, where have you been?" he said in his New York accent. "I've been worried about you. You've never stayed away this long. Robyn has been coming to get the platters for the salon, but you usually beat your receptionist to it once or twice a week."

"I haven't had any spare time. Looks like your place is hopping." She nodded at the crowd. Noisy chatter competed with the clang of dishes and the clink of glassware.

He rounded the counter to give her a hug. Then he stepped back to examine her. "*Oy vey*, you're bigger than the last time I saw you. How far along are you now?"

"It'll be thirty weeks on Saturday. I'm officially in my third trimester."

"Jill is excited about the baby shower. She got the email invite yesterday."

"That was fast. It seems as though I just talked to my mother about it. Then again, the shower date is two weeks from this weekend. We probably should have planned it sooner." That was Marla's fault. She hadn't wanted to broach the subject earlier.

Arnie stroked his moustache, suspiciously darker than she remembered. So was his hair, a shoe polish black. She narrowed her eyes. In his mid-forties, he'd already been sporting some gray at his hairline, but it wasn't there anymore.

"What can I do for you?" he asked. "Did you come to say hello, or do you want a table?"

"I need lunch to go." She placed her order then stood by while he rang up another customer's bill. When he was free, Arnie signaled to an employee to watch the register. He took a seat opposite Marla at an empty table.

"How are Dalton and Brianna?" he asked, leaning forward and clasping his hands. "Are they excited about the baby? I'll bet Dalton is over the moon about having a son."

Marla smiled fondly at the memory of their gender reveal party. She and Dalton had learned about their child's sex at the same time as their guests. His face had lit up like a streak of lightning when the edible confetti inside the cake turned out to be blue. She'd asked the doctor's office to reveal the information in a note inside a sealed envelope. She'd given it to the bakery without peeking. Experienced at these occasions, the bakers knew what to do.

"We've been adding items to our registry, but I'm kind of superstitious," she confessed. "Jewish people don't have baby showers by tradition. We have a bris or baby naming afterward when friends bring gifts."

"That's changed. Nobody wants to wait anymore. You need to furnish the nursery ahead of time, and you're far enough along by now."

"You're right. We've already started decorating the baby's room."

He grinned, clearly pleased for her. "Jill can't wait to go shopping at the baby store."

"How are your kids, Arnie? Josh and Lisa are growing up so fast." He'd been widowed when his first wife died in a tragic car accident. When Jillian Barlow met him, she'd fallen for the devoted father and deli owner.

"They're good. I think Josh will be taller than me. He's shooting up like a corn stalk. Maybe he'll go for the basketball team in high school." Arnie waggled his eyebrows, clearly excited by the prospect.

She'd hoped for news that Jill might be pregnant, but either her friend was taking her time or they weren't announcing it. Marla grabbed the salt shaker and twirled it in her fingers. "Despite my efforts to stay away from crime scenes, I've become involved in another murder investigation," she said, staring at a stray mark on the table's surface.

Arnie gaped at her. "No way. In your condition?"

"I'm perfectly capable of normal activity, thank you. But I'm being careful. The head gardener died at Tremayne Manor. Maybe you heard about it on the news?"

"Yes, it happened over Easter weekend right after the egg hunt for the children. What a sorrowful conclusion to a happy event."

"I was there with Bonnie Morris, or Blinky as we know her. She had dressed as the Easter bunny for the kids. I was supposed to fix her hair for a fundraiser luncheon after she'd changed clothes. But she vanished, and I found the Easter bunny outside lying on the grass. The gardener wore the costume. He'd been stabbed."

"She'd changed outfits with the gardener? Why?"

Marla shrugged. "We have lots of theories but not enough answers. Blinky is still missing."

"So a dead guy turns up in her costume and she's gone? You don't think she could have done the deed, do you?"

"Heavens, no. What would be her motive? Besides, Blinky is too straight-laced to commit a crime. I'm worried sick about her. Maybe whoever murdered the gardener snatched her because she witnessed the murder."

Arnie glanced away. "I suppose the cops searched the estate for another body."

"They've found nothing. Nor has Blinky used her credit cards since then or touched her bank accounts. Her cell phone is turned off, and the last known coordinates show Tremayne Manor. It's all very odd."

A waitress stopped by to ask Arnie a question. Once he'd replied, he returned his attention to Marla. "What have you learned so far? Is Dalton on the case?" he asked.

"Dalton is investigating the murders, but another department is handling the missing person situation."

"Wait, did you say *murders*?"

"Yes. The gift shop lady ended up dead in the same manner."

"*Oy gevalt*. I hope you're not messing around at that place. It sounds like a nest of vipers."

"You could be right. Michelle, the café lady, told me there may be a snake in the swamp, and who knows where it will strike next? I've been talking to the Tremayne family and their staff. They're a suspicious bunch. They all have secrets to hide." She gave him a quick rundown of the suspects.

"And none of Blinky's friends or relatives have had any contact with her? What about work colleagues?"

"She owns an advertising firm. I spoke to a disgruntled customer, but their disagreement happened years ago. She'd tried to make amends back then as well as more recently, but he rejected her offers. The guy runs an automotive repair center. He has a somewhat shady air about him but I don't know that it relates to this business." Marla shifted in her chair, impatient to move on. She'd make her first client appointment of the day without a minute to spare.

Arnie drew his brows together. "Okay, let's backtrack a minute. How did your friend end up as the Easter bunny?

Doesn't Tremayne Manor hold an egg hunt every year? Is this a routine thing for Blinky?"

"No, this was her first time. The previous volunteer wasn't available. Luckily, the suit fit Blinky well enough. Lacey Tremayne sponsors the event, and she'd met Blinky at a meeting. They're both members of Female Entrepreneurs of Tomorrow. The charity luncheon at the manor was a fundraiser for this organization."

"That's their only connection?" Arnie asked.

"Blinky's firm advertises the tours and special events at Tremayne Manor. The estate hosts weddings, showers, group meetings and personal celebrations."

Arnie squinted at her. "You're saying Lacey and Blinky are connected through a business relationship, in addition to the volunteer group?"

Marla nodded. "Lacey uses caterers for outside events, but sometimes she'll add extra servers or kitchen assistants for larger parties at the house. She did this for the charity luncheon. Dalton spoke to those people, but they didn't contribute much."

"Who bought tickets to the meal? Were any of the organization's board members present? Are they volunteers, or do some of them get paid?"

Now it was Marla's turn to gawk at Arnie. "I have no idea. We really haven't given this group much thought in terms of the investigation."

"Maybe one of their members had a grudge against Blinky. It might be worth the effort to check them out."

"You could be right. Thanks, Arnie. You've given me a new angle to consider."

A waitress headed their way waving a brown bag. "Here's your lunch, luv. You're looking well."

"Thanks, Ruth." Marla took the bag and rose. "I'd better go. I'm late for work already."

"Be careful, you hear?" Arnie chided. "Your health is more important than these shenanigans."

Marla rolled her eyes on the way to the checkout counter. Why did men treat her like a delicate flower that would wilt at the slightest adversity?

Arnie took his place at the cash register, accepted her payment and handed her a receipt.

She hustled into the salon where her one o'clock highlights was waiting. While the woman's color processed, Marla scarfed down her meal. Her busy schedule didn't provide another lull until five o'clock, when she had a half hour between customers. After waving the other stylists goodbye for the night, she dialed Dalton's number.

"What's up?" he said, answering after three rings.

"I paid a condolence call to Lacey this morning. I'll tell you what I learned, but first, is there anything new on your end that you can share?"

"I need to take a drive to Homestead. There's a place I have to check out. We could go on Sunday, if you'd like to make a day trip out of it." His tone sounded hopeful.

"You'd allow me to come along?"

"There's a farmer's market you'd enjoy. Plus, we could go to the fruit winery while we're in the area. I know you've wanted to visit it."

"I can't drink while I'm pregnant," she reminded him.

"Yes, but you've mentioned this place to me more than once. They have a café and gift shop besides the winery. I hear the brewery section is popular."

"Now I know why you want to go. It sounds like fun. But why the visit?"

Dalton's voice lowered. "When I was chatting with the beekeeper at the Tremayne estate, I noticed some cartons inside his shack. He said they were hive supplies. From the return address, I noted the shipments came from a place called Howard's Honey House in Homestead."

"So what? Are you hoping those people will shed more light on Karl's background?"

"Karl Simmons started working for Lacey a year or so after her husband disappeared on his yacht. I can't find much about him before that time. He did work at the nursery where Sarah claimed she'd met him. And the college does have a graduate by his name who'd earned an entomology degree. But as for what he did in between those events, there's *nada*."

"I think we both agree he's a person of interest, but listen to this," Marla said in an eager tone. "I had a chat with Bruno, the maintenance man at Tremayne Manor. Before my conversation with Lacey, I overheard the two of them together. Lacey told Bruno he should report what he'd seen, and he replied that he's not mentioning a ghost. Then they talked about Daniel. Bruno was awfully defensive of the boy."

"Bruno's family has a solid base with the Tremaynes. Their employment goes back to his grandfather's time."

"That seems to be the case with some of Lacey's other staff members, but it doesn't account for Bruno's attitude. He seems willing to turn a blind eye to anything the kid is doing. It's too bad you can't get a warrant to check Daniel's hard drive. I'd love to know what's on it besides his work-related stuff. What can he possibly do all day in his room?"

"Maybe he's addicted to video games."

An idea dawned. "Maybe he is addicted, but to games of chance." She straightened her spine. "That might account for Daniel meeting the man in the hoodie. What if he needs money to feed an online gambling habit? Either he could be the one selling goods from the house, or he could be borrowing funds."

"That's an intriguing possibility. It's a shame the gardens don't have surveillance cameras."

"I should have asked Rick about it. When I spoke to him, he was particularly vehement about his history with the Tremaynes. Did you check to see if Connor had any other relations? Rick suggested I mention this to you."

"We've been focused on the two victims. While it may

not be a coincidence they both died on the property, we have been looking into their personal backgrounds."

"Rick accused Connor's father of stealing property from his extended family. You should examine the possibility that one of them still holds a grudge."

"Why? You think after all these years, this person may have killed the gardener? That makes no sense."

"You're right, but check into it anyway, will you?" Marla glanced up as the front doorbells chimed. "I have to go. My next client is here."

"Hold on. My mother called. She wanted to know if we plan to baptize the baby."

Marla swallowed, almost choking on her saliva. "What? Have you told her about the bris?"

"She'd prefer we have the circumcision done at the hospital. If we decide to do it at home, shouldn't we honor my family traditions, too?"

"I'm not sure Ma would be happy about a baptism. She's more than eager to contact a *mohel* on our behalf." Marla had already explained that a *mohel* was a person qualified by Jewish law to perform circumcisions. Usually the ceremony, called a bris, was done eight days following the birth. The religious ritual took place in the family's home along with a party.

"If we have the deed done at the hospital, we wouldn't need a bris," Dalton pointed out.

"Then we'd have a baby-naming ceremony instead with the rabbi at our house. I doubt we can do both a baptism and a bris, Dalton. We're going to have to make a choice about our child's religious upbringing."

He gave a heavy sigh. "Let's talk about it after these cases are solved. In the meantime, I have a murderer to catch."

Chapter Seventeen

Sunday dawned bright and dry with a warm breeze. Marla dreaded the summer months when the humidity would drag her down. Hopefully, she'd give birth on time and before the heat intensity brought storms their way.

Brianna joined them for the ride. "Can we stop at Craig Berry Farm?" she asked from the back seat of Dalton's sedan. "Their cinnamon buns are supposed to be the best."

"Didn't you eat enough pancakes for breakfast?" Dalton replied, his eyes focused on the road. They'd taken the turnpike extension to avoid the Miami traffic as they headed south.

"Yes, but I'll be hungry again by the time we get there."

"I want to see the winery," Marla stated. "We can have lunch at their café if we do the farms first. Didn't you also want to visit some farmer's market?" she asked her husband. They'd never visited the Redlands but had heard about the attractions in this rural section of Southeast Florida.

"We have to stop at Robert's Marketplace. They have fresh produce and gourmet food items. Their specialty is fruit-flavored milkshakes," he told his daughter. "And they have a petting zoo in back."

"I'm not a little kid, Dad," Brianna retorted. "Who cares about a bunch of animals? Can I taste the wine if we go to the winery? It must be healthy if it's made from fruit."

"I can't drink either," Marla reminded her, "so your dad

will have to sample for both of us. Their gift shop might have some cute things. Where should we go first?"

Dalton made the decision. "Craig Berry Farm. It might get crowded later on."

Unfortunately, by the time they got there, the line to enter was way too long. Marla had no desire to wait an hour under the broiling sun. Instead, they headed toward Howard's Honey House along winding country roads bordered by shady trees. The state's agricultural roots were evident in the fields of crops stretching into the distance on either side of the road.

A handmade sign for Honey and Beeswax pointed them down a dirt lane toward a shack with some outbuildings. A rusted bicycle sat next to a scrub pine at the makeshift parking lot. Marla got out, gravel crunching underfoot. Tractors and other farm equipment rested under an awning that looked as though it would blow down in a big wind. Saw palmettos dotted the property along with a smattering of pine trees.

The honey house turned out to be a wood hut with a set of steps leading to a shaded front porch. Marla hesitated as she read a sign saying, CAUTION, ACTIVE BEES. She didn't want to risk getting stung in her condition.

"This place has a sort of rural charm," Dalton commented, preceding her up the ramp. He paused to regard the rocking chairs on the porch as though he wouldn't mind parking himself there for a few hours.

Standing near those potted flowering plants wasn't a good idea with bees flitting around. Marla passed her husband, pushed open the screen door, and entered the shop.

Shelves holding jars of honey in varying shapes and sizes drew her attention. One corner held vintage farming equipment. She surveyed the bath salts, natural soaps, dish towels, and honey sticks that were for sale along with packaged honeycombs and honeyed spoons for swirling in a cup of tea. Gift baskets themed in vanilla peppermint, cranberry pomegranate, and cherry almond made her want to reach for her wallet.

I have to buy something. It would be the right thing to do. Maybe it would make up for her snooping, but she also liked to support small business enterprises.

"Good morning," she said in a bright tone to the lady who manned the cash register. A cinnamon scent wafted her way as Brianna examined the jars of honey. Dalton picked up a brochure on the famed local winery before meandering toward the cashier.

"What can I do for you?" the brassy blonde asked. She looked to be in her mid-forties.

"A friend referred us to you. His name is Karl Simmons. I believe you've shipped some supplies his way? We're interested in getting started on beekeeping."

The woman tipped her head in acknowledgment. "Karl is one of our wholesale clients. I'm Beatrice Howard, by the way. You can call me Bea. Appropriate, isn't it?" she said with a snort of laughter. "My husband, Stuart, is out back harvesting our combs."

"What kind of supplies do you send to Karl?" Dalton asked, fingering a honey spoon on the counter. His brow wrinkled as though he couldn't fathom its purpose.

"We sell him our raw honey, and he sticks his own labels on the jars. But you're interested in starting your own hives, yes?"

"We've seen Karl's equipment, and he's explained the process to us," Marla said. "That's what got us interested. He said his hives are located out by the flower beds."

"You'll want to keep your bees near their source of nectar and pollen. Did Karl also mention you can buy a startup kit online these days? We don't sell those here."

"I know. We came to learn about the different varieties of honey."

Beatrice walked around to the display shelves. "The traits differ depending on which blossoms the worker bees select for their source of nectar. Honey color can range from very light to dark amber, with flavor ranging accordingly from mild to bold. Here we produce wildflower, orange blossom, and saw palmetto honey."

"The saw palmetto looks lighter than the others," Marla noted.

"Yes, and it's milder tasting. Orange blossom, as you'd expect, is a sweet honey with a hint of citrus. Our wildflower is a blend of late summer honey. It has a bolder flavor."

"I've read about the use of honey to treat infections." Marla glanced at Dalton. He appeared content to let her take the lead.

"It's long been known honey has antiseptic and antibacterial properties. There's even a type of honey, called Manuka honey, which can prevent a bad kind of bacteria in the gut."

"Do you have tupelo honey? Supposedly, it's the only one that won't crystallize."

"We don't produce it here. Tupelo honey is difficult to harvest, and the trees only grow by the riverbanks in northwest Florida. When you can get it, tupelo honey commands a high price. It's a good example of a single-flower varietal, as opposed to a multi-floral type like our wildflower blend."

"The gift shop at Tremayne Manor seems to do well with their brand," Dalton mentioned, casting Marla a hooded glance telling her to get back on track.

She noted Brianna was filling a shopping basket with items to purchase. This could end up being an expensive trip.

"Karl slaps his own labels on our jars, but so do lots of our other customers," Beatrice admitted. "We do a booming wholesale business, especially with the Florida tourist trade. Everybody wants a jar of souvenir honey. Our stand is off the beaten path, but we're in a great spot for the hives. It doesn't pay to move them closer to town, because then you run into other problems."

"Like what?" Marla asked. Clearly, the woman was happy to talk about her business. They were fairly isolated out here, surrounded by fields of crops and orange groves. But she wanted to hear more about Karl. Did the beekeeper who worked for Lacey Tremayne really keep his own hives? If so, why would he buy cartons of unlabeled jars from this place? Maybe his production didn't keep up with demand.

Bea's husband chose that moment to saunter inside. Stuart Howard's weathered face revealed his lifetime of outdoor activity. He had tattooed forearms, a hoop earring that could have suited a pirate, and a nose that reminded Marla of a cauliflower.

Beatrice did a round of introductions. "Marla and her husband are interested in beekeeping as a hobby. She says Karl Simmons referred them to us."

"Is that so? We sell our honey to Karl. We're not in the business of selling beekeeping kits. You can get those online."

His wife nodded. "That's what I told them. But they might want to supplement their own honey production like Karl if their sales start to soar."

"How much research have you done into the business?" The owner cast his wife a bemused glance, as though they'd encountered rookie hobbyists before.

"We know what we need to get started," Dalton replied.

"You should also know what could threaten your hives. People are responsible for the two most prominent causes of declining bee population—pesticides and habitat loss. Biologists have found more than one hundred and fifty chemical residues in bee pollen."

Marla wrinkled her nose. "That's awful. What can help to improve the situation?"

"Sustainable farming preserves wild habitats and protects the bees. Pesticides and chemical fertilizers are not the only causes of colony collapse, though. Viral pathogens and parasitic mites play a role. But entomologists say no single pathogen or parasite appears to explain the current rate of hive collapse."

"Didn't Karl study entomology in college?" Marla asked Dalton. "Maybe he's continuing his research at Tremayne Manor."

"It's possible," Dalton said. "His knowledge would come in handy to help save the bees, or at least to preserve the ones on the estate."

"Bears seeking honey and bees from other colonies can threaten a hive," Stuart continued. "Mice come inside seeking warmth during the winter. They'll eat through the wax and frames to build a nest. Termites, hornets and wasps are also natural enemies."

"So are spider webs, I would imagine," Marla said with a grimace. "But if the beekeeper can't spray near a hive, how does he prevent these pests from threatening the colonies?" She thought of Karl who acted as beekeeper and exterminator. In a way, it made sense for him to do both jobs since the bug man had to be careful not to kill off his own bees.

"If I have to spray in the vicinity of a hive, I'll drape wet burlap over it to discourage the bees from emerging," Stuart explained with a frown, as though the notion displeased him. "You can also use short-acting pesticides. This way, if you spray at night, by morning any toxins will have dissipated."

"Bees must be sensitive creatures with so many problems," she commented.

"They're like any animals in the wild. Drought, global warming, and air pollution can harm them. But besides these broader issues, bees need to keep their bodies warm. That's why they forage in the summer and stay inside during the winter. Our job is to make sure they have enough food, ventilation, and water, which they use to dissolve crystallized honey."

"How do you go near the hives without getting stung?" Marla asked. "Does the suit fully protect you?"

Stuart gave a harsh chuckle and pointed to his nose. "I learned my lessons the hard way before I got suited up. Bees tend to attack the face of mammals, so your veil is an essential piece of equipment. Bees have carbon dioxide receptors on their antennae. This allows them to detect our exhalations and respond aggressively. It helps protect the hive against bears. Bees can also sense your fear. If you're nervous, you'll breathe more heavily, which the bees can detect. They'll also pick up on shaky hands. You'll want to use your smoker to tranquilize them."

"I read how that's important," Marla said with a nod.

"Do you know how it works? Smoke makes the bees believe there may be a wildfire. This prompts them to eat as much honey as they can prior to a potential move. A full stomach makes them more docile, so they'll have trouble tipping their abdomens up to sting. But more importantly, smoke masks the alarm pheromone given off by guard bees."

"What do you mean?" More and more, this discussion made Marla want to keep her distance from any flowers that wild bees might visit or from any hollow tree trunks that might house them.

"Their alarm pheromone smells like banana candy," Stuart explained. "If you smell bananas in your hive, you need to add another puff of smoke. I'd suggest you don't eat bananas when you're working near the bees."

Or if I'm walking through the woods, Marla thought, keeping her expression neutral.

"That's good advice, thanks." She glanced at Dalton, unsure what to ask next. They hadn't learned a great deal about Karl, just that he bought wholesale jars of honey from the Howards and added his own private label. But so did other businesses. It could be that his supply didn't keep up with demand, and he chose to supplement his product.

The entomology angle was interesting, though. If he was researching causes of declining bee populations, he might be in contact with colleagues from his university days. They'd have to look further into the man's academic credentials. Meanwhile, Dalton should make a more concerted effort to locate his hives over by the flower beds.

She thought of one more question. "Does Karl's order for honey come in on a regular basis? I mean, how does he know how much he'll need based on his hive production?"

"Oh, he doesn't place the orders. Karl visited our place originally, but he leaves the purchasing to his girlfriend. You know, the lady that runs the gift shop at the manor house."

Chapter Eighteen

"Do you mean Sarah?" Marla asked the store's proprietor. "If so, I'm sorry to inform you that she passed away recently."

"What?" Beatrice slapped her hands to her cheeks. "It's not possible. I just spoke to her last week."

"She placed another order? How often did you hear from her?" Marla picked up a plastic-wrapped lemon honey soap from the counter and sniffed it. She widened her eyes in pleasure at the citrus scent. Soaps always made nice gifts. Maybe she'd buy a few of them.

"Sarah would only call with a change from her regular purchase. She added another ten jars this month as sales had been brisk over the Easter holiday. Sorry, why are you so keen on this information?"

"We're investigating two murders that occurred at Tremayne Manor, ma'am." Dalton whipped out his badge, revealing his identity.

"You're not implicating us, I hope?" Stuart asked with a fearful glance. "Our only contact has been through the beekeeper and his lady friend. Are you saying she's one of your victims?"

Dalton's lips thinned. "That's correct. Did you speak to her in person?"

Beatrice bobbed her head. "The poor woman. I can't believe she's gone. Then again, she mentioned something about 'the ungrateful wretch' before she hung up. Do you think she meant Karl? I got the impression Sarah had a thing for him, but her feelings may not have been reciprocated. Anyway, I'll bring up their orders online." She turned to her computer.

After a few minutes of typing, she signaled to Dalton to take a look. He requested a printout of recent months.

While they were occupied, Marla addressed Stuart. "Did Sarah or Karl ever mention my friend, Bonnie Morris? Or a gardener named Paolo?" When he shook his head, she plowed on. "How about Mrs. Tremayne or her son, Daniel?"

He snorted. "I got the feeling from Sarah that Mrs. Tremayne doesn't know what's going on beneath her nose. The gift shop is handled by a manager. The head docent leads the tours. Even the café is run independently. For all her claims about being business savvy, Lacey Tremayne knows how to put on a good party, but her staff runs the show otherwise."

Before Marla could pursue this statement, Brianna carried over a pile of goods for checkout. Marla was glad to support the owners and added a few items herself. Dalton chose a jar of honey mustard and one of barbecue sauce to add to their shopping cart.

Pleased with their haul along with the information they'd gained, Marla made a beeline to the car outside to escape the insects buzzing around the structure.

Hah, a beeline. She'd learned this expression stemmed from the worker bees. When laden with nectar and pollen, they flew the shortest route back to the hive.

During the drive to the winery, she shared her theories with Brianna and Dalton. "Let's review what we've learned from this visit," she suggested, raising her hand to tick off her points finger-by-finger. "Karl is receiving cartons of honey jars to which he applies Tremayne Manor labels. He must have a labeling machine somewhere. Did you notice one in his shed?" she asked Dalton.

His hands on the wheel, he shook his head. "I took in the

equipment at a glance. If one's inside there, I didn't recognize it. I'll check more closely next time."

"It's peculiar how Karl always wears his beekeeping outfit near the house. I suppose it makes sense for him to spray the grounds for pests while being suited up. Otherwise, he'd have to use a face mask."

"The guy who sprays our house doesn't wear one," Brianna piped up from the back seat.

"True, but if he's spraying nests in the trees or under the house's overhang, it's a smart thing to do. I'd add goggles, too, if the stuff could hit my eyes."

"What about the store owner's crack about Sarah having a thing for Karl?" Brianna asked in an innocent tone.

"You were listening?" Marla had thought the teen was busy shopping.

"Do you think I'd miss the juicy details? I learned more about bees than I ever wanted to know."

Marla chuckled. "Me, too. I like honey in my tea, but that's about it. I don't care to be around live bees."

Dalton gave her a bemused glance. "Now you know not to eat bananas before we go for our nature walks. The scent might attract an aggressive response from any worker bees in the area."

"You're so right. But let's get back on track," she said, gazing out the window at the fallow fields beyond. The sun blazed overhead, heating the temperature into the upper seventies. This would be a perfect beach day, and yet here they were cruising the Redlands of Dade County. "It appears Sarah might have liked Karl more than he cared for her. Do you think they had a lover's spat, and he killed her over it?"

"No way," Brianna scoffed. "He'd be killing the goose that laid the golden egg. Sarah obtained the extra jars of honey for him."

"She's the one who sold them in the gift shop," Dalton reminded them. "Besides, how would Paolo's death relate to their relationship?"

Marla gave a weary sigh. “Good question. I found it interesting how Stuart said Lacey’s staff runs the business. It’s true. Sarah sold the tour tickets. Heather conducts the tours and directs the other docents. Michelle manages the café. Lacey’s main role seems to be event planning, which was her forte as a society wife.”

“Does Daniel operate their website?” Brianna queried. “Or is that job the responsibility of Blinky’s advertising firm?”

“We can look online to see if the web designer is listed on their site. Did you find out who oversees the financial accounts?” Marla asked her husband. Her gaze drew comfort from his stalwart figure. His hair had receded more since she’d met him, but he looked distinguished with the silvery strands peppering his black hair.

She touched her own longish waves. When they’d met, her style had been a short bob that hadn’t taken her long to fix in the morning. Now she used a curling iron, although her hair wasn’t as stick straight as Brianna’s.

Her thoughts tumbled like a kaleidoscope and rearranged themselves, focusing on Blinky in her bunny suit. The brunette had wanted her hair combed out after the children’s egg hunt so she would look her best for the fundraiser luncheon.

“Lacey said she compiles the reports from her different sources and sends the spreadsheets to her accountant,” Dalton replied with a glower. “You knew I would check into her business records first thing. I didn’t find any irregularities.”

“Does Lacey trust her managers to be truthful? Any one of them could be skimming their account or ordering supplies with false invoices. Does this apply to the kitchen staff as well?”

“The chef does her own grocery shopping and submits the receipts to Lacey,” he admitted.

Perhaps Lacey truly was naïve. If Marla were in Lacey’s

shoes, she'd micromanage her lead people. But then, she enjoyed taking charge of the business aspects.

Lacey might have been better off sticking to her painting and parties. Too bad she couldn't trust her son. With his computer expertise, he might be good at math. What had Daniel meant when he'd said he had another purpose in mind for the estate, should he inherit it? Would he sell the property to a golf course conglomerate or a housing developer?

Marla shuddered at the thought. No wonder Lacey was considering the historical society as a beneficiary. Preserving the family's legacy would be paramount to her.

Connor's legacy, she corrected herself.

"I meant to ask you about the women's organization where Lacey is a member," she said to Dalton. "Blinky was involved in their group, too. That's how she got roped into playing the Easter bunny. Did you interview any of those people regarding her disappearance?"

"We had a cursory conversation," Dalton replied, his gaze on the road. "The ladies weren't very helpful. I thought I'd told you this before."

Maybe she should talk to these people. The women might open up to her as a female entrepreneur more readily than to a police detective.

Brianna tapped Marla's shoulder from behind. "Hey, we're here. That wasn't too far."

A big sign for Shelley's Winery loomed ahead. Dalton turned in and found a parking space.

"I'm hungry," Marla said. "Let's eat first before doing the tour."

The one-story main building looked inviting with its Colonial Revival style. The columns and shaded portico reminded her of a Napa Valley winery. They approached via a path lined with queen palms and purple flowers. She inhaled the scent of fresh water as they passed a cascading, tiered fountain.

Past a pair of double doors, she paused inside the front entrance to gawk at a display of novelty gift items and wine bottles for sale. The store was mainly to her right, where tour tickets were sold and cartons of wine were available. Straight ahead was the tasting bar, with stools lining a circular wood counter supported by oak barrels. Gleaming glassware hung suspended overhead from branches of a tree sculpture. A couple of patrons sat at the bar beyond a table displaying purse hangars and embroidered dish towels.

"I'll go buy our tour tickets while you get a table," Dalton told her.

Marla veered toward the restaurant to her left. Its plain wood tables were set with utensils and wine glasses. A blackboard above the cash register showed the day's meal specials. As her gaze swept the area, she noted a lovely mural with red flowers and greenery painted on the ceiling. The place impressed her as being from an earlier era, making her wonder when the winery had been built.

She and Brianna took seats and ordered lemonade while waiting for Dalton to join them.

"I'm getting the burger with fried avocado," Brianna announced once he'd arrived and they had a chance to study the menu.

"Me, too. That sounds good," Dalton said.

"It comes with fries. I need something healthier." Marla ordered a platter with grilled chicken, coconut rice, black beans and diced tomatoes. "You know, seeing this food makes me think I should talk to the cook again at Tremayne Manor. She must hear a lot of gossip. Maybe she knows something about Sarah's relationship to Karl."

Dalton jabbed a finger in the air. "Be careful. If you get too nosy, you'll paint a target on your back."

"Don't worry. I'll think of a good excuse for a return visit." The baby kicked, no doubt chastising her for thinking about the case instead of him. A flicker of guilt surfaced. She should be thinking of the child growing inside her more than anything else.

Brianna, sitting next to her, put a hand out to feel the baby's movements. "I can't believe my brother is in there. When are you going to pick a name already?"

"We're still deciding." Marla exchanged a bemused glance with Dalton. Everybody was asking them the same question. They didn't want to jinx things by telling anyone their favorite choices. Nor had they reached an agreement on any one name in particular.

Her mouth watered as the scent of barbecued beef drifted her way from the kitchen. While waiting for their meals, she turned their conversation to the baby registry, the upcoming shower, and the nursery furnishings. Babies were a much pleasanter topic than murder.

Halfway through lunch, Brianna waved a hand. "I have a brilliant idea. Your mom and Reed plan to have an engagement party, right? Have they set a date or picked a place yet?"

"They've decided on May eleventh, but I don't know if Ma has found a venue. Let me text her and see what she says." Marla took a sip of lemonade before typing her message.

"*We're not sure yet. Lots of places are booked already,* Anita responded.

"I'll help look into restaurants with private rooms," she wrote back.

They had Reed's family to consider. His children would be attending the party along with whatever other relatives he invited. It could grow into a large event.

"Brie, what did you have in mind?" she asked, curious to hear the teen's idea.

"Tremayne Manor hosts parties. Why don't you consult them about hiring a room?"

"You mean, pretend as though I want to book an event? That would give me an excuse to consult the cook about the menu. But it would have to be a small enough affair that they wouldn't need to bring in a party planner."

"Either way, you'd have a reason to snoop around. And who knows, maybe they'll have a space available and your mom would like it."

"You girls are too clever for your own good," Dalton said, polishing off his burger. He pushed his plate away. "Look, I think the tour group is gathering. We'd better go."

After he paid the bill, they went outside where a balmy breeze brought warm air scented by spring blossoms. Tropical trees and tall palms dotted a courtyard where they posed for photos. Tiki huts offered picnic tables for visitors who wanted to linger.

Their pony-tailed guide led the group along a shaded boardwalk toward a coral rock waterfall. As they stood by the pond, they viewed large orange Koi fish gliding by in the water.

"Hiram Shelley came here in the mid-nineties," the young woman said. She wore a red tee shirt that sported the winery's logo along with a pair of white Capris and flip-flops. "He'd grown up in New York State and had worked in wineries there as a kid. But he always dreamed of living in Florida. After he moved down, Shelley opened a produce packing house that served the local farming community. Eventually, he bought one hundred acres and started his own fruit-growing business.

"One of his early visitors was a friend and winemaker from New York. This guy noted that blemished or overly ripe fruits were discarded since they wouldn't sell. Why not use these less than perfect fruits to make wine? Shelley opened the winery in 2005. The brewery was added in 2011."

The guide led them to another open area with machinery resting on a concrete slab. "Our wines are made from avocados, lychees, mangos, passion fruit, guava and coconut. Here's where we press the fruit for juice, which is then fermented. The resulting liquid is filtered to remove any remaining solids and bottled in dark bottles to prevent sunlight from penetrating. Since we don't have to age our product, it's a pretty quick process from harvesting to bottling."

At the brewery section in another building, they entered a taproom where Dalton sampled several varieties of fruit-flavored craft beers. A dark, cavernous hall with evening entertainment brought in crowds. Billiards tables sat in front of a well-lit bar. Marla wrinkled her nose. The place smelled like a brewery.

A quick walk-through finished the tour. This included a room lined with wood casks, a control room with steel vats, a big storage area with more machinery, and a room with walls of beer cans reaching toward the ceiling.

At the bar in the gift shop, Dalton chose five wines to taste. Marla allowed herself to take a sip of each one. They couldn't be very strong, right? She liked the Private Reserve, a dry white wine that she could serve with dinner. Brianna tried a sip of Passionate Embrace, a sweet wine made from Passion Fruit. Dalton sampled the Hurricane Twister, but it proved too fruity for his taste.

Their stomachs satisfied and their thirst quenched, they drove on to the next adventure at Robert's Marketplace.

"Brie, here's ten dollars if you want to get one of their tropical fruit milkshakes." Dalton handed over the bill as they strode toward an open-air building from the dusty parking lot. "Also, you can buy food pellets to feed to the animals at their petting zoo."

"I'm too old for that, Dad."

Nonetheless, after browsing in the gourmet food section, Marla and Dalton found his daughter feeding the goats at a rear pen. A giant turtle lumbered toward them, its mouth stretched in a grin that almost looked evil. *Watch it, buddy,* Marla told him mentally. *You should be glad you're cared for here and can't walk across the road to become roadkill. Or worse, end up in someone's turtle soup.* He leered at her as though reading her thoughts.

They made their purchases after Brianna waited fifteen minutes in line to get a Key lime milkshake. They were about to leave when Dalton got a text message. Standing by the exit, he frowned at his phone.

"Damn, I'm going to have to go into work."

"What now?" Marla asked, her pulse accelerating. *Please let it not be another victim.*

"Ben Rogers' garage is under investigation by another agency."

"I'm not surprised. What for?"

"We've had a rash of car thefts in the area recently and have suspected there's a chop shop in the vicinity. It appears Rogers' place is under surveillance."

Marla's blood chilled. "Do you think Blinky got wind of it when she went to see him, and Ben is the one who made her disappear?"

Chapter Nineteen

"Even if Ben Rogers is part of a car theft ring, it doesn't mean he's guilty of abducting Blinky. The two may be completely unrelated," Dalton said during the drive home. He stayed focused on the road, his profile stern as he gazed ahead.

"That man has held a grudge against Blinky forever. I knew there was something off about him when I went to his automotive center." Marla sipped from a bottle of water she'd bought at the fruit stand. She'd been feeling short of breath from the heat by the time they'd piled into the car for the trip home.

"Nonetheless, my bet is still on someone from Tremayne Manor. Otherwise, why would Rogers have killed Paolo the gardener? Or Sarah from the gift shop?"

"He could easily have thought Paolo was Blinky inside the bunny costume. He wouldn't have known they'd switched places. When he realized his mistake, he abducted her. As for Sarah, she might have discovered his identity somehow."

"Hey, he could be the guy in the hoodie," Brianna suggested in a tone way too bright for the sordid topic under discussion.

Really, the girl is starting to become too much like me, Marla thought with a sense of pride along with a touch of dismay. Then again, Brie was much more bookish. Graduate work was in her future for sure.

"If your theory is correct, what was Ben doing on the Tremayne estate? Watching for an opportunity to nab

Blinky?" Marla said with a shake of her head. "That idea doesn't make sense. He could have accosted her anywhere."

"Don't forget the scuttlebutt that Daniel Tremayne and Rick Eaton were meeting this hoodie person on the sly," Dalton added.

Marla watched the scenery whiz by on the turnpike. They'd reentered civilization, passing one neighborhood after another in Dade County as they neared the western edges of Miami.

"One of them could be the thief Lacey wanted me to catch," she proposed. "The man in the hoodie could be acting as a fence to sell the goods. It might have been pure coincidence that Paolo got in his way."

"Didn't you say Rick is security chief at the manor?" Brianna said. "Maybe the three of them are working together."

Marla lifted her brows. "Nicole suggested the same thing. Daniel has a set of keys to the display cases. He steals the objects, and Rick turns a blind eye to his actions. One of them meets the fence outside to hand over the goods and collect payment. Daniel alters the video feed so no one notices anything happened."

"Lacey noted the missing items," the teen pointed out.

Marla turned toward Dalton. "Did you ever get those Fabergé eggs authenticated? If Sarah had reproductions in her gift shop, she may have ordered other pieces as well. She could have been involved along with Daniel or Rick. Her partner turned on her, and she ended up dead."

Dalton snorted. "Why not include the entire staff? Do you really believe Lacey is so naïve that she wouldn't be aware people were ripping her off under her nose? Including her son?"

"She told me she suspected him, remember?"

"Then which one of them took Blinky?" he asked.

Marla spread her hands. "Have you done a thorough search of Ben's garage? Maybe he has a hidden bay where he's holding her captive."

"You've seen too many crime shows on television. They can't have a secret underground lair in South Florida. And what would be the purpose in keeping her alive? Two others have died already."

"I don't know. Maybe I'm foolish for hoping she might be okay."

"The game is up for Ben Rogers either way," Dalton said. "Even if he's not involved in her abduction, he might know something."

Marla sat up straight. "Hey, remember I told you about those shipping manifests in his office? He's sending stuff overseas, and I'll bet it's not his love bug cleaning solution."

"I'll tell the boys in the other department, but they're probably already following a paper trail." He grinned at her, lightening the mood. "Now let's discuss a more important topic. What's for dinner?"

After they got home, Dalton headed into the office, while Brianna went to her room to make plans with her friends for Spring Break the following week.

Marla set to work preparing their evening meal even though she would prefer to lie on the couch in the family room and put her feet up. She'd picked up some fish the day before to make Tilapia Dijon. It took her little time to assemble the ingredients and stick the dish in the oven at four hundred degrees for twenty minutes.

She'd bought pre-made garlic mashed potatoes as an accompaniment, so she only had to put together a salad and pick a vegetable from the freezer. Their microwave did the rest.

Dalton came home a couple of hours later. "I don't think Rogers is our man," he said in a morose tone as he took his seat at the dinner table. Marla served him, having eaten earlier with Brianna. "He may be a crook, but I believe him in regards to Blinky's disappearance. He'd buried the hatchet with her long ago as far as he was concerned."

"So he's a dead end," Marla concluded, sitting across

from Dalton with a weary sigh. It seemed as though their efforts were taking them in circles and getting nowhere. "Are you any closer to identifying Paolo's killer?"

Dalton took a drink of water. "We're looking into his prison record to see who he might have met there. That could provide a lead we can follow. If anyone from Tremayne Manor is guilty, they're covering their tracks well. We have lots of suspicions but can't solidify them."

"What can I do to help?" Marla asked, wondering where she'd get the energy.

"Talk to the cook, like you'd suggested. Servants always know everything about their employers, or at least it used to be that way. I'm going to contact Lacey's attorney about the estate documents. And I'll look into Connor's extended family as you'd suggested."

"Good luck. I have lunch with Ma tomorrow after I run some errands in the morning."

****

Marla made it to the restaurant ten minutes early on Monday to meet her mother. She felt oddly out of sorts. Maybe she was just discouraged over their lack of progress in locating Blinky.

Her thoughts tumbled in another direction. If Blinky was found alive and had been hiding, Marla would kill the woman herself for not notifying anyone.

Shame on you, Marla. If that's the case, Blinky must have had a good reason to disappear.

She shuffled aside thoughts of bad deeds when Ma walked through the doors. Already, the popular diner was busy with the lunch crowd. They got a table in a quiet corner.

"How far along are you now?" Anita asked, peering at Marla over her menu.

"Saturday will be thirty-one weeks. I have another doctor visit coming up. They'll be doing an ultrasound again."

"That's good. Have you and Dalton decided on a name for the child?" Anita hooked a red-painted fingernail at her like a question mark.

"I told you we want to pick a name that starts with an 'R' after Dad, but Dalton and I can't agree on one we both like. Are you all set for the baby shower?" she asked to change the subject.

Anita smiled, crinkling the lines beside her eyes. She didn't have many wrinkles for a woman her age. Reed was getting a treasure by marrying her, but it worked both ways. Marla's mother wore a glow that had nothing to do with her floral top, turquoise pants, or chunky jewelry. Even her short, white hair seemed to gleam under the restaurant's recessed lighting.

"The party favors came in. I almost ordered the blue egg timers that said *Time for Baby*, but I didn't think you'd appreciate the plastic egg casing."

"Good God, no." Marla felt the blood drain from her face as she pictured the colored plastic Easter eggs on the ground at Tremayne Manor. They'd led to her discovery of Paolo's dead body dressed in the bunny suit.

Anita showed her a photo on her phone. "Here's what I ordered instead. Aren't they cute?"

The honeycomb-shaped soaps had *Mommy-to-Bee* on the wrapping. Marla swallowed a lump in her throat at the spelling. *Bees, as in honeybees? You've got to be kidding me.*

"That's great, Ma. Nice choice," she said in a choked tone.

"Oh, and I got the most adorable motherhood advice cards for your guests to fill in." Anita blabbered on about the centerpieces and cake and other details, oblivious to Marla's discomfort.

"How are you doing with RSVPs?" she asked, desperate to erase the image of bees from her mind. Of all themes for her mother to pick, it had to be that one.

"We're still waiting to hear from a few people, but we've made our minimum of twenty-five. It should be a lovely affair. We have to thank my friend, Rita, who belongs to the country club, for sponsoring us."

"Have you thought about where to hold your wedding? I could always ask at Tremayne Manor what dates they have available."

Anita arched her brows. "You weren't interested when I'd mentioned that idea for your baby shower."

"True, but your wedding is some time off."

"We've decided to plan the event for September. That way, your baby will be three months old, and the social season will have started."

Marla nodded her understanding. Over the summer, the snowbirds were absent and residents vacationed in northern climates. Organizations went on hiatus in regards to their meetings. The show season at the performing arts center slowed. And a general miasma descended on the region along with the threat of hurricanes. Tourists returned after Labor Day, when social events swung into action for the fall.

"September is storm season," she reminded her mother. "If you book a place then, be sure to get insurance. When is Rosh Hashanah?"

"September twenty-ninth. So any weekend after Labor Day will work except for that one." Her mother's mouth curved upward. "Did I already ask you to be my matron of honor?"

"No, but I'd be honored. Are you having bridesmaids?" She'd had attendants when she married Dalton, even though it had been a second marriage for both of them. In fact, they had done the whole shebang, albeit not as elaborately as the first time around. Did Ma want the same thing at her age?

"I'll ask Charlene and a few of my cousins to stand with me. But they won't be bridesmaids in the traditional sense. Y'all can wear whatever you want. By the way, did you ever call your brother?"

A guilty flush stole over Marla's face. "Sorry, I've been too busy. Have you heard from him since we last spoke?"

"No, he doesn't respond to my texts or phone messages." Anita sat back as the waitress delivered their meals and refilled their water glasses. She took a bite from her salad with grilled salmon before continuing. "I talked to Charlene. She says things are fine, but I can hear in her voice that they're not. She sounds polite and distant. I hope she doesn't plan on leaving Michael and moving away to achieve her dream of becoming a principal."

"Oh, like you're moving away from me?" Marla couldn't help saying.

A hurt look sprang into Anita's eyes. "You keep hammering me on that point. Reed and I are doing what's best for us at our stage in life. We want to be with people our own age who have the same interests."

"Even if it means living farther from your new grandson?" Marla stabbed the fork into her mouth, gulping down a bite of dilled chicken salad.

"Boynton Beach isn't on another planet. If you need me, I can be here fast enough. You should be happy for us starting a new life together."

"I am," Marla said, blinking away unexpected moisture from her eyes. "But you're my mother. I need you here when I have the baby."

"And as I've said to you before, I'll be around to help you those first few weeks. Once you gain confidence, you'll be able to manage on your own. Reed and I have things we want to do. I'll babysit in a pinch, but you'll have to figure out your own arrangements. Kate and John live in Delray. I know they'd be happy to pitch in."

Marla bent her head to hide the insecurity in her eyes. "Dalton's done this before. I hope he remembers what to do when the time comes."

Anita chuckled. "Changing a diaper is like riding a

bicycle. You don't forget. I have faith in you, *bubeleh.* You'll do fine and will be a great mother."

Marla sipped from her water glass. "I wish Dalton would solve this case so he could focus on our family. It's taking him into the office on weekends."

"Is he any closer to finding the killer?"

"No, and now he has two murders to solve. If it weren't for Blinky, I'd leave the crimes to his team to solve."

"I thought you said another department was handling her disappearing act."

"Her trail seems to have gone cold. I don't know if that's good or bad. Could she still be hiding somewhere, or am I deluding myself in hoping she's okay? Maybe the killer got lucky in stashing her body where nobody thought to look."

"You don't usually give up on a friend," Anita said, wagging a finger at her. "People rarely just vanish."

"That's not true." Marla reminded her mother of a couple of other cases involving young women in the state who'd been abducted and never found. For sure, those girls had been murdered or sold into white slavery. Their cases haunted her to this day. But Blinky's disappearance wasn't a seemingly random act. It had to be related to Paolo's death.

"If Blinky is alive and well and tucked away somewhere safe, you'd think she would have contacted you," Anita remarked, wiping her mouth with a napkin. "She knew you were waiting to do her hair at the Easter egg hunt. You'd worry about her disappearance."

"Who knows, Ma? I only hope she is alive somewhere, in which case she must have her reasons for staying out of touch. Now let's discuss happier topics."

Weddings and parties were a much more pleasant subject and less stressful for her son, who could sense her emotions. He gave a kick in agreement, letting his presence be known. She had to think of his needs first. It would be that way from now until forever.

Didn't her mother deserve a reprieve at this stage in her life? She'd spent her childbearing years raising Marla and Michael. She had been there for Michael's kids as they grew into adorable school age children. And she'd still be around for Marla's son. They were lucky to have her, when other people had lost parents by now.

"Ma, how about if we hold your engagement party at our house?" she offered. "Then you'd only have to get a place for the wedding. It's easier than finding a restaurant with private space that isn't already booked by now." She'd failed to perform that duty as promised. This was an easier solution.

Anita gave her a startled glance. "Don't you have too much to do getting the nursery ready?"

"We're making progress. Besides, we can cater the food, and I'll have plenty of helpers between Brianna and Dalton. Think about it, okay? Meanwhile, I can help you research wedding venues for September."

As Marla left the restaurant, she reflected on their conversation. If only she could close the missing person case and move on. Time would telescope as the baby's due date approached. She needed every spare moment to prepare.

When she reached her car in the restaurant's parking lot, her cell phone played its tune. She glanced at the screen, and her heart flipped.

A text message had come in from Blinky.

Chapter Twenty

Marla read the message. Blinky's words chilled her blood and made her breath come short. She read the text again, praying it was truly from the sender.

Help! I need you to pick me up. Come alone and tell no one. Hurry; I don't have much time.

Marla's fingers shook as she replied, "Where are you?"

Blinky responded with an address Marla didn't recognize.

"On my way. Hang tight," she wrote back.

Could this be a trap? Was the kidnapper setting her up for a snatch? She should at least tell Dalton where she was going.

Marla slid into her car, started the engine, and turned the air-conditioning a few degrees lower. Dalton would insist on accompanying her, but that would take time she might not have. Plus, if Blinky's vanishing act had been deliberate, she shouldn't betray her friend's trust.

But it wasn't safe to drive off to unknown parts without backup. So she wrote a text message to Dalton.

"I've heard from Blinky. She wants me to come and get her but without anyone else." Marla typed in the address. "If you don't hear back from me by three, send in the troops. Fingers crossed that it's good news."

What? Hold on. How do you know the caller ID wasn't spoofed? This could be a trap!

"I know. I'll be careful. I have to take that chance."

Blinky had implied that time was of the essence. Marla programmed in the location on her phone and stuck the device in its cradle. Her tires squealed as she zoomed out of the parking lot and onto the main road. She could reach the place in less than thirty minutes if traffic cooperated.

Her brow creased into a frown. The directions had her heading east toward the Intracoastal and a particular area of town that was unfamiliar to her. How did Blinky end up there? Tremayne Manor was in the opposite direction at the northwest quadrant of Broward County.

As long as Blinky was safe, she could learn the details later.

At Andrews Avenue, she turned south. She followed a winding path while approaching a tributary of the New River. Yachts and sailboats gleamed at a marina as she neared her destination. Before she reached the place, a figure stepped from behind a nearby tree. Blinky, looking disheveled in a pair of baggy pants and an oversized shirt, waved her down.

Marla screeched her car to a halt. She unlocked the doors, and Blinky hopped inside.

"Drive, Marla," the woman said in a tremulous tone. "Take me away from here."

"I told Dalton I was coming to get you. I'd better notify him you're alive and well."

Marla pulled to a halt by the curb and sent Dalton a text message that she had Blinky safe by her side. He could tell the cops looking for her that she'd been found.

She turned to regard Blinky's haggard face, thin frame, and bruised wrists. The woman wore a rumpled man's shirt and belted trousers that looked sizes too big. Blinky kept glancing at the side mirror, clearly anxious about being spotted.

"Where were you all this time?" Marla asked, while considering what questions Dalton would want answered.

Blinky held her stomach, as though trying to stem a tide of emotions. "I was kidnapped and held on a boat called *Beethoven*. I saw the name as I was escaping. It's in that marina."

"Can you tell me who took you?"

Blinky shook her head, her scraggly hair curtaining her expression. "I never saw his face. He always wore a hoodie and a mask."

Marla relayed the information via text and then veered back onto the road. "Do you want me to take you home? You could get cleaned up before we go anywhere else." Blinky looked as though she could use a hot shower and shampoo. Marla knew a good cleansing could help to wash away one's fears.

"No, he'll go there if he discovers I've escaped." Blinky ran a shaky hand across her brow. "I can't believe I got away after all this time. I knew he'd kill me once I finished the job that kept me alive." She blinked repetitively, living up to her nickname.

Marla gave her a startled glance. "You were working for this guy? Doing what?"

"Helping him acquire a piece of property. I have connections in the real estate world. He needed to hide his tracks, so I acted as the principal for him."

"He let you use a computer for these transactions?" Marla gawked at her. Surely Blinky could have found a way to get a message to her friends, or at least her children?

"Only while he was sitting behind me with a gun at my back. I wasn't mistreated. He locked me in the guest suite with enough food and water for the day. Unfortunately, the cabin didn't have a sun roof or any windows that opened. They were smash-proof, too. I tried every means to escape, knowing my time was running out."

"So how did you get free?"

"The man only came by in the evenings. I'd been working on loosening the door hinges. Thankfully, he never noticed. I finally got them to the point where they'd come apart, but I had to wait until I knew he'd left the boat."

Marla decided they were far enough south to get onto I-595 and head west. That would be the quickest route toward their end of town. She turned onto a road that would lead to a ramp.

"Wait. Take me to the airport," Blinky said. "I'll go stay with my son. The man who took me thought I didn't have family because none of my relatives live in the area. That's why he decided I would suit his plans, because nobody would care if I disappeared."

"That's not true. You have friends, and your colleagues were concerned when you didn't show up for work. This guy's plan was what—to buy a piece of property?"

"It's a derelict estate on the northern edge of the county, but it includes acres of farmland and has a lot of potential. I didn't question why he wanted it. The less I knew, the better." Blinky's eyes narrowed. "I'd hoped you would find me sooner. Were you even looking for me?"

"Every spare minute of every day. I was worried sick about you. Dalton said another department was in charge of your missing person case. He's been busy investigating Paolo's death. What happened that day?"

"I don't want to talk about it, okay?" Blinky slid open the compartment between their seats and peered inside at the jumble of tools Marla kept there. "Do you have any water bottles in here? I need a drink. My throat is so dry."

"Sorry, I didn't think to bring any water, but I have a tin of mints."

Blinky found the container and stuffed a couple of peppermint candies into her mouth. "I can't wait to get a decent meal. The lout fed me, but it was fast food or sandwiches most of the time with an occasional hot meal." Her face sagged. "I'm afraid I won't be much help in identifying him. He did a good job of removing any personal items from the cabin."

"What about scents or scars or other clues? The timbre of his voice, for example."

"He spoke through some scary voice thing." She gave a visible shudder. "I wondered why he went to the effort of disguising himself when he planned to kill me anyway."

"Did he? Or would he have run when you'd accomplished the job he set for you?"

"He'd threatened my life numerous times. I believe he meant it, too." She blinked repetitively and clasped her hands together. "I want to leave all this behind until the cops catch the guy."

"You can't just walk away. The police will have questions. You're a person of interest in two murder cases."

"*Two* cases? Who else died?"

"I found Paolo's body on the lawn the day of the Easter egg hunt. He was wearing your bunny suit and he'd been stabbed. Sarah was killed in the same manner less than a week ago in the gift shop at the house."

"Oh. My. God." Blinky slumped against the seat cushion and covered her face with her hands. Marla noted her fingernails looked chewed and most of her polish had flaked off.

"Can you conceive of any reason for them both to die?" Marla asked.

Blinky lowered her arms, her gaze taking on a distant look. "Paolo saw something that scared him. He asked me to give him my costume. I changed in the garage and put on some work clothes hanging there since I'd left my dress at the mansion. But before I could step outside…" Her voice cracked, and she glanced away.

"What happened? This is important, Blinky." Marla bit her lower lip in impatience.

"He found us. He tied me up and marched Paolo away at sword point."

"What? He had a sword and not a gun?"

"Well, it was a short sword of sorts. More like a long dagger, I suppose."

"Did you recognize him?"

She shook her head. "He wore one of those horrible Halloween masks. Paolo said he knew who the man was and everyone would find out. He'd spotted him through a window taking one of the Fabergé eggs from the house."

Marla gasped. "So the kidnapper *is* the thief. While you were on his boat, did you notice any other items that might have come from Tremayne Manor?"

"I was too scared to look at anything when he brought me on board. Anyway, the two men vanished. When the guy came back, he had blood on his knife. He threatened to kill me, saying he'd made sure Paolo was no longer a threat. I was afraid he'd murdered the gardener and that I would be next. I said I could help him get whatever he wanted through my business connections."

"And he believed you?"

"There's a reason why he's at Tremayne Manor. I can't explain it, but he seemed awfully familiar with the place."

Maybe he works there, Marla thought, considering their theories about Rick and Daniel.

She lifted her foot off the accelerator at a traffic delay ahead. "You have to tell Dalton all this. It isn't right to run away when so many people have been frantic about you."

"Just take me to the airport, darling. I'll catch a flight to—" Blinky patted her pockets and her complexion paled. "Oh, no. I don't have my wallet."

"You left your bag on the boat?"

"Do you think I'm that brainless? I stashed my purse at the manor after I'd dressed in the bunny costume. Can you possibly lend me a credit card?"

"Absolutely not." Once traffic started moving again, Marla got off at the next exit and did a turnaround. "I'm taking you to the police station. Dalton can have you put into protective custody. Your kids will be relieved to hear you're safe. They wanted to fly out here, but Dalton told them they should stay home in case you contacted them."

"I guess I shouldn't put them in jeopardy by going to stay with them until this man is put behind bars. So you were trying to find me, huh?"

"When you disappeared that day and I stumbled onto Paolo's body, I feared the worst. Your car was still parked at the manor. Dalton had a thought that you did the deed and ran off, but I knew you wouldn't have done it."

"Good God, he's not going to arrest me, is he?"

"Of course not, but it's his job to consider all the possibilities. We spoke to your neighbors and your colleagues, and nobody had heard from you. I was so afraid that you were another victim, and that we hadn't found your body."

"The man's name is Anton Wiley. Or at least, that's the name he had me use for the real estate deal."

"What? Why didn't you say so earlier?" Marla veered off the exit ramp toward Palm Haven. She glanced in the rearview mirror. Fortunately, nobody appeared to be following them. She hoped this Anton person had been far away when she picked up Blinky.

"I know it's a false name. I'll bet your husband finds the boat registered to this guy, too."

"You said a property sale was involved?"

"That's right. The purchase was legitimate. The odd thing was that Anton didn't list himself as the buyer. He put Daniel Tremayne's name on the deed."

Marla's heart skipped a beat. "Daniel! What does he know about this?"

"I'm not aware that he knows anything, but I didn't witness any live transactions."

Was any of this true? Marla shot her friend a suspicious glance. Could Blinky be playing her? This all seemed too convenient somehow.

"Tell me, how did you get a phone to call me? And why wouldn't you call the cops to come and rescue you?"

"I flagged down a car. The driver let me use his phone when I told him my vehicle had broken down farther up the road. I didn't want to involve the police."

Marla would let Dalton determine the truth of her words. As they both fell silent, thoughts somersaulted through her mind. While part of her was relieved Blinky was safe, the other half realized the culprit was still out there.

****

"My work is done," Marla told her husband later that night. She had dutifully delivered Blinky to the police station, related privately what she'd learned, and left to go home. Lying in bed, she pulled the sheet up to her neck. "I had planned to return to Tremayne Manor to question the cook again, but I'm satisfied now that Blinky is safe. Finding her was my main goal."

Dalton gave her an incredulous stare. He looked sexy with his hair still damp from the shower and his chest bare. "You don't care that a murderer is still out there? Hallelujah! You're finally leaving the solution to me." He poked her arm. "I appreciate your faith, sweetcakes."

"Hah. That's not the reason." She put a hand on her belly. "Our son would prefer that I don't go chasing after killers."

"Smart little man. He'll keep you busy enough very soon."

"Did you figure out who Blinky's captor might have been? It has to be somebody she'd recognize without the mask."

"Obviously. Or else he just didn't want his face to be seen. It could be the guy who has been meeting with Daniel and Rick at the estate."

Marla's brow furrowed. Something didn't add up in that scenario. "If this person is a fence, why would he buy a piece of real estate in Daniel's name?"

"Money can be laundered through property sales."

"So Daniel steals artifacts from the house, sells them, and uses the cash to buy an estate similar in size to what he should have inherited? That would be a suitable revenge on his father for cutting him out of his will."

Dalton, who'd been leaning on his side, flopped back on his pillow. "Yeah, but I still don't get it. Why would Connor Tremayne deed his family estate over to his wife? He did this before his boating accident."

"To avoid probate? He could have put the property into a trust to accomplish that purpose."

"Maybe he knew Daniel wouldn't appreciate the place's history and would sell the contents if they belonged to him."

"Lacey said as much herself," Marla reminded him. The air-conditioning cycled on, cooling her exposed skin. "But why didn't he leave Daniel his personal belongings?"

"According to Lacey's attorney, everything went to his wife when he died."

"Even his collectibles, like his stamp and sword collections? Lacey told me she'd sold his stamps. I guess that means they were included in the personal property she inherited."

"That would be correct. I imagine the same applies to his swords, although no one seems to know where he kept them."

"What happens now? Is Blinky hidden away somewhere safe? Did she notify her kids that she's all right?"

"Yes, she spoke to them from the station. We're not telling anyone else. She's staying at a safe house until this is over."

"Did you get any clues off the boat?"

"The owner is Anton Wiley. We're tracing his background. He seems to be a ghost. His trail goes only so far and then vanishes."

"He must have some connection to Tremayne Manor. Maybe it's Rick or Daniel using a false name. That would be a blow to Lacey. I was hoping our suspicions about her son would be unfounded."

"More likely this Anton Wiley is the man in the hoodie whom Daniel and Rick have been meeting on the estate grounds."

"To what purpose?" she asked, raising her hands in the air.

"I'm not sure yet. Daniel and Rick could be accessories to murder and kidnapping if they knew what this guy was doing. Daniel's involvement gives me reasonable cause to get a warrant to inspect his hard drive. We're looking for correspondence between him and Wiley. If either he or Rick Eaton is involved, it could put Lacey in danger."

Chapter Twenty-One

Lacey wouldn't be happy to hear the kidnapper bought a piece of property in Daniel's name, Marla thought on the way to work Tuesday morning. That certainly seemed to point an arrow of guilt, or at least complicity, in his direction.

Nonetheless, she managed to keep secret the fact that Blinky had turned up unharmed from her colleagues at the salon. The news eddied on her lips, but she held back the tide.

She couldn't hold back the tumultuous wave when Daniel burst into the salon. The front door crashed open as Marla was working on a client's highlights. She froze, brush in hand, and gaped at the entrance.

"What the hell do you think you're doing?" Daniel hollered as he stormed toward her with a furious expression. "This is your fault."

"I'm sorry. I don't understand. Tell me what has you so upset," Marla said in a calm voice. She put down her brush and picked up a pair of shears, the better to defend herself with should the need arise.

Daniel scraped a lock of unruly hair off his face. Stubble carpeted his jaw. Along with his rumpled clothing, it gave the impression he'd been up most of the night. "Your husband took my hard drive. He has no business taking away my means of making a living."

"Don't you have more than one computer? If that's your main source of revenue, surely you keep backups?"

"He requisitioned my laptop, too. Good luck to his team in getting past my firewalls. I know you're to blame. You told him somebody was tampering with the security feed at the house, didn't you?"

Marla gave him an oblique look, biting back the words she wanted to say. *No, you idiot, Blinky was kidnapped by a guy in a hoodie and forced to do a real estate deal with your name on the deed. Were you the abductor, or are you working with this fellow?*

"It's pretty obvious," she said instead. "The security monitors didn't pick up the thief stealing the Fabergé egg during the Easter event. You're the one with the expertise who would know how to erase that segment."

He sneered at her. "Or maybe I could recover the lost data if anyone asked me."

"Look, can we take this private?" She gestured to the interested onlookers in the salon. "I'll be finished with Esther's highlights in a minute. We can talk while she processes." Marla hadn't scheduled anyone between customers, hoping for a break. Fatigue already weighed her down, and the day had just started.

"Your husband is trying to pin things on me, and I'm innocent," Daniel said once they were alone. She'd led him out the rear exit but had left the door ajar. He stomped on a dead leaf like a petulant child. "I'm not the only person who could alter those recordings. Hasn't Detective Vail interviewed Rick? Our security chief hired those yoyos to work with him because they wouldn't notice a bee flying in front of their noses."

Marla leaned against the concrete wall. Fortunately, they faced away from the sun blazing overhead. A whiff of trash warming in the heat drifted her way from a nearby bin. Farther along the alley was the meter room where she had stumbled upon her rival's dead body. She didn't care to be reminded of that sad incident.

"You're implying that Rick Eaton stole the Fabergé egg? Why, isn't he getting paid enough by your mother?" she said.

"You think money has to be the only reason? Have you spoken to the guy? He has a big chip on his shoulder. Never was friendly toward me."

"Your window overlooks the rear lawn. You didn't see anyone sneaking by that afternoon?"

"I was working. When I'm in the zone, I don't notice anything. Cook will tell you I can forget to eat. But let's get back to Rick. He wasn't on duty that day. He'd assigned Ed to the job, and Ed is a flake. He's more interested in cars. You'll find him more often than not in the visitor parking lot checking out the models. He should have been a chauffeur, not a guard."

"He wanders outside even when he's supposed to watch the interior during tours?"

"Nah, he does his stint, but he takes a lot of breaks. Long breaks, if you get my meaning."

"How about the woman, Claire? Is she good at security?" Marla gave herself mental points for remembering the lady's name.

"She'll maintain her post, but half the time she's chatting on her cell phone to that lousy boyfriend of hers."

"How would you know this?"

"Because when she's patrolling the family quarters, which the guards do from time-to-time, I can hear her jabbering." His mouth curved into a smirk. "Also, I've rigged my own set of monitors. Who needs security when you have me? The guards are more for show."

Marla stared at him. She'd wondered if he had his own surveillance system, and he'd just answered that question. "Did you see who took the Fabergé egg? What else have you learned?"

He shook his head. "I set it up after Paolo's death. Figured I'd better keep a closer eye on things. But now that your husband has my equipment, that idea is moot. You'd better tell him to give my stuff back to me undamaged and as soon as possible."

"He's in charge of the case, not me. Why don't you buy an external hard drive in the meantime? If you use an online backup system, you can download your files and get back to work."

"I was in the middle of something. The data wasn't saved."

"That's too bad. Was this for the company that employs you?" If she recalled properly, he worked in cyber security.

Anger mingled with disappointment on his face. "No, it's something else. Now I've lost my chance, but that's nothing new where I'm concerned."

Marla had a sudden thought and had to ask. "You're not playing the races and meeting with a bookie, are you? You've been seen on the property meeting a guy wearing a hoodie."

Daniel's eyes darkened, and his body went stiff. "Who told you this?"

"I don't reveal my sources. Do you know this man's identity?"

"If I did, I wouldn't tell you."

"Were you aware Paolo served time in jail? I've been wondering if this character was someone he met there."

"If you keep making guesses like that, it'll bring you trouble."

"Is that a threat? Exactly what were you doing on the computer that you don't want anyone to know? What's so important to you?"

"Why the hell do you care? Nobody else gives a hoot what I think."

She heard the hurt in his tone. "I believe you're much more talented than people realize. I also get the impression you have an agenda you're not sharing."

Is that why you came to see me? she thought, wishing she understood him better.

The young man couldn't confide in his mother, and nobody else had faith in him. Marla's heart softened until she realized the whole thing could be an act to disarm her. Daniel knew she'd tell her husband about their conversation. This could be a ploy to misdirect his investigation.

"You wouldn't understand what I want," Daniel replied, gazing into the distance. His voice held a wistful note.

"Like your father? Were you sorry when he passed, or did you always have an estranged relationship?" Marla said.

"The old man never cared about me. He got the end he deserved."

"They say his body was never found. His boat was found drifting with no one aboard."

"It was hard on my mother. She had to wait to claim his estate. At least he'd had the foresight to deed the house over to her several years earlier."

"Why wouldn't he have left it in trust for you? You must have been highly resentful. Were you angry enough to steal the items in the house that should belong to you?"

"That crap means nothing to me, but I respect that it's important to my mother."

"Are you telling the truth? Or is the man in the hoodie a fence who's selling these goods for you? Who else could he be, and why are you meeting him?"

Daniel shoved his hands into his jeans' pockets. "It's none of your business."

"Lacey said you get an allowance. So why would you need more money? Are you saving up to afford your own place?"

"It serves my purpose to live at home for now. This conversation isn't getting anywhere for me. I should go."

"I'll tell my husband you need your computers back as soon as possible," Marla said, hastening to appease him. Although he'd come by supposedly to have her ask Dalton to return his electronics, she'd gotten the distinct feeling he needed a sympathetic ear more than anything.

"Thanks," he said in a reluctant tone. "And Marla, I appreciate you listening. One of these days, I might tell you what's on my mind, but not until I have the means to make it happen."

As he walked away, a new idea struck her. There had to be another reason why he didn't want Dalton to discover what was on his hard drives. Could he be viewing porno sites?

Maybe the man in the hoodie was blackmailing him. Was Daniel giving payouts to this guy?

Wondering if Dalton's team had made any headway in breeching Daniel's firewalls, she texted him about the man's visit.

We'll talk later, he texted back. *Forensics team is still working on devices. It may take time, but they're good at what they do.*

Marla's feet ached from standing in place for too long, so she went inside to check on her client's progress and get a drink of water from the cooler up front.

Robyn, the receptionist, gestured to her from the front desk. The brunette lived in the same neighborhood as Marla and had been looking for a job after quitting her corporate marketing position. Since coming to work at the salon, she'd updated their website, started an email newsletter, and coordinated their charity fundraisers. Marla liked her client appreciation days the best, and so did their customers. Their traffic always increased during those events. While not a mystery reader like Nicole, Robyn enjoyed hearing about Marla's escapades.

"I'm sorry. I should have stopped that man from bothering you, but he charged past me." Robyn twisted the pink candy cane streak of hair on her head. She'd taken to highlighting a strand in different colors, changing it as frequently as the men she dated.

Marla waved a hand in dismissal. "No problem. He's a person of interest in Dalton's case. The guy seems to want to talk to me, but he never gives a direct answer."

"So did you learn anything new from your conversation?"

She nodded thoughtfully. "He doesn't think much of the security staff at their mansion. Daniel mentioned the woman guard, Claire. She has a boyfriend. If he's a bad type, he might have gotten her involved in stealing goods at the estate. He could be the man in the hoodie who's been reported skulking around the property."

"Are there any security cameras on the grounds, or just in the house?" Robyn asked, her face alight with curiosity.

"The lawns and gardens aren't monitored. Where would you put the cameras, in the trees?"

"I suppose. When did the thefts start? Was Claire employed there then?"

"I'll have to ask Lacey. She's the one who noticed items missing, although some of the larger pieces may have been replaced with reproductions. Dalton needs to have an art appraiser come in to authenticate certain artifacts, like the Fabergé eggs. He's been more focused on the homicide investigations."

Marla returned to her station, checked on her client's highlights, and sent her to get shampooed. Nicole rushed in just then and shoved her purse inside a roundabout drawer.

"Hey, Marla. Sorry I'm late. Kevin and I had a meeting with the minister this morning."

"Awesome. How did it go?" she asked, readying the tools she'd need next.

"Smooth as silk, girlfriend. We're each going to say our own vows."

Marla couldn't help her broad grin. "I can't believe your wedding is in six weeks. Is your mom driving you crazy?"

Nicole chuckled, her teeth flashing white against her cinnamon skin. "It's a good thing Mama lives up north. She's planning our wedding breakfast. You know that was her idea, not mine. Kevin's mom is coordinating the guest list from the rehearsal dinner with her. They'll invite the same out-of-towners to both functions."

"It'll be a wonderful weekend. Here's your customer. We'll catch up later." Marla turned to her own station when her client returned. Work resumed, and she didn't get a break until early afternoon. Ignoring the phone messages that needed replies, she stuffed down a hummus and tomato sandwich in the rear storeroom.

Curiosity got the better of her, and she called Dalton. "How's Blinky? Does she need anything that I can bring her?" Marla asked, wondering at the location of the safe house and if any guards were stationed there.

"She has clothes and toiletries," Dalton said in his deep voice that never failed to comfort her. "After being confined for two weeks on the boat, your friend has cabin fever. She can't wait until it's safe for her to resume a normal life. It eats at her that she can't tell her work colleagues that she's okay."

"Why can't you notify them that she's alive and well?"

"The fewer people who know, the better. Her safety is our paramount concern, and we don't know who we can trust at this point. We've informed her kids, but that's all."

"I wish I could visit her. Poor thing. First she's locked in a cabin on a boat, and now she's stuck in a safe house. What's the danger at this point? The kidnapper will assume she's ratted him out to the police."

"She's still a live witness. This man is presumably the same person who killed Paolo. The gift shop manager must have learned his identity, and he stabbed her next. Blinky would have been his third victim once she finished the task set for her. Now she's free, and he'll assume she's told the cops everything. What would you do in those circumstances?"

Marla hugged the phone to her ear. "I'd cover my tracks. The police would check into the boat's ownership and search aboard for clues."

"Anton Wiley is the name on file. The guy has nothing about him that's traceable. He paid cash for the boat."

"Do you have an officer posted at the marina?" If she were this man, she'd return to wipe away any evidence of his existence.

"Yes, and our team has been through there at least once. They got some prints but so far there isn't a hit on any of the databases."

"Any hints about his personality that could be revealing?"

Dalton snorted. "The boat's salon had peanut shells all over the coffee table and floor. And the man has a taste for classical music judging from his CD collection. Otherwise, there wasn't much of a personal nature."

"How about DNA evidence?"

"We've sent samples to the lab. But we have to catch him for the results to be useful. That also means keeping your friend out of harm's way. She's a loose end he'd want to eliminate."

Marla clutched the receiver while aware that time was ticking away. "Listen, I meant to ask if you've looked into the security staff at Tremayne Manor other than Rick Eaton. When Daniel was here, he mentioned Claire, the woman guard. She spends a lot of time on the phone with her boyfriend. This man could be the guy in the hoodie."

Dalton clucked his tongue. "Then Claire would be the one meeting with him, not Rick or Daniel. We've checked out the backgrounds of the other guards. The boyfriend didn't raise any flags. He has trouble hanging onto a job for very long but seems clean otherwise. I'm guessing Claire is the breadwinner in their relationship. Did you know she did a stint in the Army in her earlier years?"

"Is that so? Good for her." Marla's respect rose for the woman. "How about Ed, the man on duty the day of the Easter egg hunt?"

"Ed has a drinking problem. He's been sober for the past

six months and goes to AA meetings. Get this—he's a veteran, too. Rick Eaton has also served in the military. I gather he's helping out by hiring other veterans for his staff."

"That's commendable." Marla glanced at her ankles, longing to put her feet up. It was harder as her pregnancy progressed to stand all day. The aroma of coffee in the staff's brewing machine tempted her to pour a cup, but she strengthened her resolve to avoid caffeine.

"Remember that Daniel needs his computer equipment returned as soon as possible so he can do his job," she told her husband. "That was the main point of his visit to me, other than having someone listen to him."

Voices sounded in the background on Dalton's end. "I have to go," he said. "Oh, there's one more thing. Regarding the café and the gift shop financial records, it appears both Sarah and Michelle had things to hide. I'll tell you more later."

"Wait, don't hang up," she called as a resounding click ended their conversation.

Chapter Twenty-Two

Marla compressed her lips as she dialed Dalton back. "Hey, you can't leave me hanging," she told him after he answered with a curt greeting. "I still want to have a chat with the cook at the estate. It would help if I had some ammunition to persuade her to talk."

"You can't reveal information I've given you, Marla. You know better than to ask."

"I won't say anything without your permission, but can't you at least tell me the scoop on Sarah and Michelle?"

He gave an exasperated sigh. "All right. Sarah's accounts for the gift shop show a steady stream of losses. It appears she was gifted in terms of acquiring items for the store but not in the business management end of things. She altered the records to make it appear the shop made a profit."

Marla narrowed her eyes. "I would have assumed the place did well. The items on sale offer a wide selection, and the stuff isn't shlock. Sarah traveled overseas to find unusual objects. Are you thinking she intentionally misled Lacey about the shop's accounts?"

"Maybe she feared for her job if Lacey discovered they were losing money. So yes, I'd say she fudged the records on purpose. Or else she was skimming the profits, which could also account for a loss. Her personal bank accounts didn't show any unusual sources of income, though."

"In other words, it appears Sarah wasn't stealing from the estate. Instead, she made poor business decisions."

"That's my opinion," Dalton stated.

"What about the reproductions for sale? Were you able to trace their origins?"

"We found one craftsman who supplies the Russian candlesticks and those nesting dolls for the gift shop. Enameled wood art seems to be his specialty."

"Lacey said a set of her dolls was missing. I thought those weren't valuable. They're a popular item in the gift shop, but I don't recall them being very expensive."

Dalton chuckled. "You got me at dolls. It's not on my radar."

"Why would the thief want something that wouldn't sell for much?" Unless it was Daniel, she thought. Lacey's son had denied stashing away items in the event his mother bequeathed the estate to the historical society.

"What makes these dolls so special, other than being made in Russia?" Dalton asked.

Marla switched to her web browser and looked them up. "Matryoshka dolls are colorfully painted wooden figures that fit inside each other," she summarized from one reference. "The first piece was designed in 1891. They represent fertility and are given as gifts for good luck. The sets can be small, with as few as two pieces, or larger with forty pieces or more. Most of the ones you see in gift shops are inexpensive, but museum quality pieces do exist."

"Why would someone want Lacey's doll if it wasn't worth much?"

"Maybe an item was hidden inside, like the surprise tucked into a Fabergé egg. If you remove some of the inner dolls, it would be possible. Have you hired an appraiser yet to authenticate the eggs? It would be helpful to know if they're real or fakes."

"Not yet. I've been following other leads."

"Okay. If I can't make it to the estate later this afternoon, I'll stop by tomorrow. In the meantime, please let me know if Blinky needs anything."

She felt a kick from inside her belly. "Our son says hello. He must have recognized your voice. Or else he's getting restless because I've been standing too long."

"Try to get off your feet. Love you." Dalton hung up.

Marla headed back into the salon where the sounds of normalcy comforted her. Splashing water, chatting customers, and whirring hair dryers competed with the popular music playing in the background. Once again, she questioned her drive to solve crimes. Didn't she have enough to do between her family and her workload to be content?

After the baby came, she'd feel a greater sense of fulfillment. But in the meantime, why shouldn't she continue her quest for justice? The answers would bring peace to Lacey and her household and allow Dalton to focus on their own family.

Her doubts erased at least for the moment, Marla focused on work for the rest of the day.

****

It wasn't until Wednesday afternoon that she finally made it back to Tremayne Manor. Marla hoped to make this a fast visit, especially since the cook was probably involved in dinner preparations. To this purpose, she knocked on the staff door at the rear kitchen entrance.

One of the cook's assistants answered. She wore a black uniform with a white apron. "How can I help you, miss?"

"You're Kristina, aren't you?" Marla asked, recognizing the blond woman. "I'd like to speak to Joan, if she has a few minutes to spare. I'm Marla Vail, the police detective's wife."

Kristina's face whitened. "Don't tell me there's been another murder."

"Oh, no. I'm actually here on behalf of my mother, who's getting married in a few months. I wanted to talk to Joan about wedding menus."

"Thank heavens. I'll go and get her. Please come inside."

Marla entered the kitchen, which appeared empty of other occupants. The aroma of roasting chicken emanated from the oven. An array of fresh vegetables sat on a wooden cutting board by the industrial-size sink.

Raised voices drifted from the direction where Kristina headed. Marla stepped closer so she could better listen.

"Not that one, you stupid girl," Joan shouted. Marla recognized the cook's commanding tone. "Really, Tammy, how can you not know a soup spoon from a ladle? And did you count these serving pieces? My best silver salad set is missing. What have you done with it?"

"I haven't been in the silver closet, ma'am. You don't allow us."

"Then what did those utensils do, walk away by themselves? Lacey will be distressed to learn more of her fancy pieces have vanished."

Kristina's reasonable tone interceded. "You and Mrs. Docket are the only other people with keys, Cook. Have you asked the housekeeper if she sent any items from the collection to the maids for polishing?"

Joan grunted. "Unlikely. Lacey has us sign in when we unlock the closet. Nobody has been here since my last visit. I wouldn't need these things today if it weren't for that last-minute breakfast meeting in the morning. I should have done as Lacey suggested and called in the caterers. These unexpected events are too much for me to handle on my own."

She walked into the kitchen, spotted Marla, and rolled her eyes. "What do you want?"

"Sorry to intrude, but I'd hoped to ask about your catering menus. My mother is getting married in September, and we need to book a venue. Didn't you say you managed smaller events yourself? Like, how many people would put you over the top in terms of hiring outside help?"

"This isn't a good time to discuss those details. You can see we're busy."

"It'll only take a few minutes." Marla gave her a coaxing smile. "Please? I told Ma I would check out this venue for her. She loves the manor and would adore having her function here."

The cook's round face softened. "Oh, all right. But it can't take long." She launched into an explanation of catering details.

Half-listening, Marla ruminated over what she'd heard. Silver serving pieces were missing? Joan hadn't mentioned Daniel as possessing any keys to their special closet. That left Lacey and Mrs. Docket. How well had Dalton's team vetted the housekeeper?

"Can you see what dates are available for that month?" Marla asked.

Joan scraped her fingers through her rust-colored hair. "You'll have to ask Lacey about scheduling. She does the bookings for special events. As for our banquet menu, you can download it from our website."

"I'll do that, thanks. It's too bad you can't get the café owner to help in the kitchen when you have a large crowd."

"Are you kidding? Michelle wouldn't lift a finger to help us." Joan took a seat on a stool by the work counter and gestured for Marla to do the same. "The woman is a good chef. I can say that about her."

Marla, relieved to be seated, tilted her head. "Wouldn't she be interested in opening a bigger place in town someday? She must have built quite a reputation by now."

"I don't see how she could afford it. Her husband doesn't earn much money as a hospital orderly, and they have two school-age kids. Unless she finds an investor, Michelle won't be going anywhere."

"Where did she get the funds to open the café?" Marla asked, hoping she wasn't coming across as overly nosy. She'd already covered some of these topics with Michelle, but she might learn something new from the cook's viewpoint. Joan seemed willing to rest her feet for a bit and exchange gossip.

Chatter from a back room led her to believe the kitchen assistants were ironing table linens, which kept them conveniently out of the way.

"The building was already there, having served a purpose in the estate's earlier days. Michelle did the remodel and was responsible for her own finances. I'm not sure what other arrangement she and Lacey have in that regard."

"Renovations must have been costly. Michelle might have saved up enough from her previous jobs to cover the expenses."

"Oh, I don't think so. They're putting their children through private schools. That costs a fortune. I figured Michelle must have taken out a loan. That's what I would have done in her circumstances. It makes me wonder if she's having trouble paying back the money. She always seems so stressed when I see her. She's happiest during tourist season when her seats are filled."

A shadow crossed the window overlooking the back lawn. Marla's gaze intensified.

"Was that the bug man I saw outside wearing a gas mask?" she asked, pointing.

Joan grunted. "My herb garden is having problems. I've asked him to spray. You'd better hold your breath if you go out that way. It wouldn't be good for you to inhale the fumes."

Was that a subtle hint of warning in the cook's voice, or was it genuine concern for the welfare of Marla's baby?

"Thanks for the heads-up. Is Karl still mooching meals from you during the day?" She remembered Joan had said the beekeeper stopped by to get extra portions.

"Nah, he grabs lunch to go, but that's all. He must be getting dinner on his own, because he hasn't asked for any handouts in that regard since Monday. Maybe he's decided to watch his weight. Karl could afford to lose a few pounds," Joan said with a snicker. "I've always thought he would make a great Santa Claus with his beard and bulky figure. We should ask him to play the part this year."

Oh yeah, like he seems the type. Scrooge is more up his alley.

"Speaking of meal planning, do you and Michelle ever exchange recipes?" Marla asked. Surely they must get together to discuss food industry topics.

Joan's mouth curved down. "Heck, no. Michelle considers my job beneath her skill level. I don't tout my training and education like she does." Joan glanced at Marla's belly. "I'm so sorry. I should have offered you a drink. Would you like a glass of chocolate milk? Daniel drinks it, so we keep a carton in stock. If you're hungry, I'll give you a slice of my upside-down pear cake."

Marla's stomach grumbled. "That sounds delightful, thanks so much. I won't keep you for much longer. I know you have dinner preparations for the family to make."

Joan rose and served Marla the snack, taking a drink of water along the way. "Lacey has leftovers from her dinner out the other evening, and she plans to reheat them herself tonight. Daniel isn't home. Lately, that boy is gone more often than here. I'm pulling together a meal for any staff that's hanging around. Then they can help themselves."

Marla took a greedy sip of the chocolate milk before downing a forkful of cake. *That's right, Marla. Eat dessert before you serve Dalton and Brianna their dinner. It's late. You need to wrap this up and leave.*

"Do many of the staff members stay after dark?" she asked.

A frown crossed Joan's face. "Sometimes Rick does a final security sweep before he leaves. Bruno always seems to have a project that keeps him around. That man is a workaholic. He finds something new to fix every day. He should tend to that shack where he stores his tools. It's becoming an eyesore."

"Where is this? I've seen Karl's workshop. And Lacey told me the gardeners stash their tools in the greenhouse."

"You'll find the maintenance shed out by the garage. It's not visible from the road or the tourist paths."

"I must have missed it. By the way, what did you mean about Daniel being gone more often than he's home these days? Is he meeting friends? I'd gotten the impression he's more of a loner." Marla enjoyed the moist texture of the cake as she chewed a bite.

"He's been going out regularly on Sunday afternoons, but now it's nearly every day. The kid never has friends visit him here, so I can't imagine what he's doing."

"Does he ever stop by the kitchen for a chat or to steal snacks?" she asked, thinking if she lived in this big house, she would mosey down here for company.

"Not really. He lives in that cave of a room." Joan shook her head. "But my mouth is running off. I should see if those girls have finished their chores yet."

"How come they're doing the ironing? Isn't that something the housemaids would do?" Marla asked, rising. She carried her dirty plate and glass to the stainless steel sink.

"Usually a cleaning service picks up the linens, but Lacey believes the staff should be versatile. We have a cross-training program so we can learn each other's skills."

Lacey strode into the kitchen. "House staff should be interchangeable to cover for each other when the need arises. Also, I believe it's important for morale to offer your employees educational opportunities. Surely this applies to your salon stylists as well."

"This is true," Marla agreed. She studied the estate owner who appeared every inch the society lady in a floral tea-length dress with pearl jewelry. She'd swept her hair into a chignon and looked ready for a garden party rather than a quiet evening at home. Maybe Lacey hadn't changed yet from her latest outing.

"Joan, if you're done for the night, you and the girls can leave," Lacey told the cook with a pointed glance.

Joan, who'd risen at her employer's entrance, gave a nod. "I'm waiting for the chicken in the oven to finish, ma'am. And I have to refrigerate those vegetables. But if you need a moment, I'll check on my assistants to hurry them along. Marla stopped by to ask about our venue for her mother's wedding. I told her to check with you on dates."

As the cook bustled from the room, Lacey glanced at Marla with quirked eyebrows. "I'd wondered why you were in here schmoozing with the cook and you hadn't come to say hello."

Marla faced her. "I wasn't sure who to ask about booking the place. Joan was telling me about the menus. We're planning a reception in September for about fifty people."

"Let me see what's available." Lacey pulled her cell phone from a hidden pocket. "Did you want to reserve a Saturday or Sunday? Lunch or dinner?"

"I'm not sure." Marla texted the available dates to her mother. "We'll have to get back to you. My mom might want to inspect the place with her fiancé. What are the extra charges besides tax and gratuity? Do we have to pay for security, or is it included?"

"We use our own security team in the reception areas. But if you want extra coverage, like in the parking lot, you'll pay an additional fee. We don't have a food minimum for any of our menus, but there is a liquor allowance depending on the number of guests. And there's a room charge. The rental fee for our smaller reception space is five hundred dollars."

"You have three people on your security team, right? I know Rick Eaton has been here for a while. How about the others?"

Lacey frowned. "Ed and Claire are fairly new hires. It's

been about six months since Claire started, and four months for Ed. I don't know why, but Rick seems to attract transients. None of them want to stay for long."

"Did Claire come on duty before or after you noticed items missing from the house?"

"She started afterwards. Why, does that matter?"

"Dalton said Claire has a boyfriend. Have you ever met the guy?"

"No, she keeps her personal life private. I don't see what this has to do with anything." Lacey's eyes flashed with irritation.

Marla decided she'd better change the subject before she got kicked out.

"Has my husband mentioned to you about having an appraiser come to authenticate your Fabergé eggs? Considering Sarah's shop sells reproductions, wouldn't you want to be sure the thief hasn't taken more than is obvious?"

Lacey gasped and drew a hand to her chest. "You mean, he might be substituting fakes for our works of art?"

"It's a possibility, although only three of you possess keys to the display cases. But you have paintings and other valuables that are not under lock and key."

"I suppose it wouldn't hurt to have some of our items validated. It's been years since we've done professional appraisals. Tell your husband he can send in an expert and that I have no objections."

"Thanks, I'll let him know. I've read up on Russian nesting dolls since you told me one was missing from your collection. Are you sure the one you lost wasn't worth more?"

Lacey's gaze chilled. "Are you questioning my word, darling?"

Just as Marla was wondering how to redeem herself, Lacey's cell phone rang. She answered it, her eyes widening as someone spoke on the other end.

"Oh. My. God. Daniel, what do you mean you've been arrested for murder?"

Chapter Twenty-Three

After listening to Daniel on the other end of the line for a few more minutes, Lacey hung up. A stunned expression froze her face. Then she awakened from her stupor and swung a venomous gaze at Marla.

"It's your fault! You told your husband I don't trust my son. I never should have confided in you."

Marla raised her hand in a stop signal. "Slow down, Lacey. Tell me what's happened."

"You heard. Daniel said he's being questioned about murdering the gardener. I have to get to the courthouse. He'll be arraigned for bail or whatever it is they do." Jerky movements betrayed the woman's state of distress.

"Shall I drive you there? You'll need someone to accompany you."

"I'll ask Bruno. He hasn't left yet. I know I can count on his support." From Lacey's dripping tone, it was clear she'd left Marla out of that category.

"I'm so sorry. The police must have some reason why they've detained your son." Perhaps they'd found damning evidence on his hard drive. The computer specialists at the station might have cracked Daniel's encryption codes.

Lacey shook her head. "Daniel might be different in some ways, but he's not a murderer. This is only going to set the poor boy back further. Like, he hasn't had enough grief in his life."

Marla glanced at her wristwatch, anxious to be on her way. "If I learn anything from Dalton that I can share, I'll let you know. Are you sure you'll be all right?"

Lacey's gaze hardened. "Don't worry about me. In fact, forget I ever asked you to investigate the thefts here. You've found squat so far. I won't be requiring your assistance any longer."

Marla's spirits fell. She'd only been trying to help. "I know you're upset right now, Lacey, and that's understandable. I'm here if you need me, okay? Good luck with Daniel. Hopefully, there's been a misunderstanding and you'll be able to take him home."

She left through the back door, holding her breath in case the exterminator's pesticide lingered in the air. Her feet dragged as she headed toward the parking lot. It seemed her presence here would no longer be welcome. *Ma had better find a different venue for her wedding. Lacey won't want to hear from me again, even if it is to book an event.*

Marla was halfway down the drive in her car when a thought recurred to her. What was it the cook had mentioned about Bruno having a tool shed by the garage? She hadn't noticed any other structures nearby at her previous visit.

She turned around and headed back, parking just off the main road before the driveway leading to the private detached garage. She emerged into the warm spring air. The days were getting longer, and it would be an hour or so yet before darkness descended. Birds twittered in the branches of a live oak, while a honking noise sounded in the distance. Could that be an alligator from a local pond? A floral scent perfumed the air, making her glad mosquito season hadn't started yet. Her skin was a magnet for the pesky insects.

Like nectar to bees?

As she stepped around the side of the garage, she glanced behind her shoulder, not wanting to be surprised by the exterminator spraying out in this direction. Wasps could nest around the eaves, so it was logical he'd come this way on his rounds. But it wasn't the beekeeper she spied in the near distance.

Lacey was rushing in this direction.

Alarmed that she'd been spotted, Marla dashed around the rear of the garage to the other side. Why else would the woman be here? Oh, wait. Lacey had been about to drive into town to see Daniel. She'd wanted Bruno to accompany her.

Marla pressed against the wall, hoping Lacey hadn't spied her. After a few seconds, she peeked around the corner. Lacey approached a prefabricated shack by a stand of palms. It blended into the background so that Marla hadn't noticed it there before.

Bruno stood in the doorway. He greeted Lacey with a quick embrace and led her inside.

Realizing she'd better escape while she could, Marla hurried to her vehicle. Thank goodness she had parked down the road instead of in the garage driveway, or Lacey would have seen her car.

During the drive home, Marla considered what she'd gained from this visit. Regarding the thefts, someone was stealing sterling silver pieces from the flatware collections. Both of the junior security guards had started after the thefts began. So most likely, they were not involved. According to Lacey, Rick's team experienced frequent turnover. Why was that? Did people not like working with Rick for some reason?

Lacey had given permission for Dalton to send an appraiser. Would this grant now be revoked? Then again, Dalton may not need permission since Daniel had been accused of a crime. What had Dalton's men found that led to his arrest? Was he being held for Sarah's death as well as the gardener's murder?

Each time she thought she had the answers, more questions came her way.

"Where have you been?" demanded Brianna, when Marla stepped through the inner garage door into their kitchen at home.

She dropped her purse on the counter. "I stopped by Tremayne Manor to ask the cook about wedding menus and available dates for my mother's event."

The teen, hair tied in a ponytail, regarded her with admonishment. "You should have let me know you'd be late."

"I know, and I'm sorry. I didn't think it would take this long."

"Did you learn anything new about the suspects while you were there?" Brianna asked with a smirk. She knew Marla would never let an opportunity like that one pass without taking advantage of it.

"Yes, but let's sit down first." Marla glanced with appreciation at the dinner table that had been set. "I presume you took the dogs out, fed them and refilled their water bowls?" She stooped to pet Spooks and Lucky who danced around her feet.

"They're set for the night. Aren't you tired? Do you want me to heat up your food? Dad said he'd be delayed and not to wait for him."

"I'll get my own, thanks." They were eating leftover shepherd's pie tonight. "Did he tell you the latest news?"

Brianna's toffee eyes rounded. "No, what's happened? Did he get a breakthrough?"

"He arrested Daniel Tremayne. I haven't heard the details yet."

"Oh, man, I hope this means his case is solved."

"We'll find out soon enough. I'll be sorry for Lacey if Daniel is the culprit, though." She washed her hands and joined Brianna at the table. While they ate, she gave the teen a brief rundown of her findings to date. She turned on the TV news and was disappointed when the television newscasters failed to mention Daniel's arrest.

Would his mother be able to afford the bail? She couldn't wait until Dalton came home to learn the details.

Brianna ran off to prepare for her next school debate.

After doing the dishes, Marla checked her email on their desktop computer and then phoned Anita with an update.

"We'll have to cross Tremayne Manor off our list," Marla concluded.

"No problem. It was kind of you to ask on our behalf. Reed and I will look at places on our own." They discussed several possible venues for her mother's nuptials. Then inevitably Anita's dialogue turned to the baby shower. "Did you look at that swing set I'd recommended to add to your registry? It has wheels, unlike the activity center you picked out."

"Yes, I've added the Jumperoo to our list. I like the one with a rainforest theme. But it's getting late. We can talk more during the daytime." She rang off and went to get ready for bed.

She didn't realize she'd fallen asleep until sounds woke her. "Dalton, is that you?"

He poked his head out of the bathroom, his hair damp and his chest bare. "Yep, I'm home. Sorry I woke you."

"I didn't mean to fall asleep." She shoved herself into a sitting position. "What happened with Daniel? I'm dying to hear the details. What made you decide to arrest him?"

Dalton finished towel-drying his hair and put on a pajama top to match his trousers. Then he came to give her a kiss and to sit on her side of the bed. "Do you really want to hear this now?"

"Yes, I won't go back to sleep otherwise."

"First of all, we didn't arrest him. We brought him in for questioning. The boys were able to access his computer files. The man was not only engaged in online gambling, but he kept records of payouts to a loan shark named Luigi Romello. It appears Daniel had borrowed money from this guy."

"Online gambling? No wonder he spent so much time in his room. That can be a true addiction. You know, the cook said he always leaves the house on Sunday afternoons. I doubt he's going to church. Maybe he belongs to one of those gambling anonymous groups and is trying to kick his habit."

"Regardless, the man needs cash. Whether it's to pay off his loan or to keep fueling his poker games, it doesn't matter. Lacey might have been right when she suspected her son of stealing their artifacts."

"This may be true, but what does it have to do with the two murders, if anything?"

"The loan kingpin, Luigi Romello, has a prior arrest record. He's served time. And get this—he was Paolo the gardener's buddy in prison."

Marla's jaw gaped. "No way! So this man connects Daniel to Paolo." She attempted to visualize the relationships in her mind. "Are you thinking Daniel might be the one who killed Paolo? I don't get it."

"I'm tending to believe him when he says he's innocent. According to his story, he stayed in his room that afternoon. Nobody saw him coming or going from the house. The surveillance recordings corroborate his alibi."

"Yes, but Daniel could have altered the files. We know the cameras didn't catch whoever stole the Fabergé egg. He's the only one who has the skills to hack into the system."

"There's also the question of motive," Dalton pointed out, wiping a droplet of water off his forehead. The clean scent of his soap wafted her way. "I could see him killing Luigi to get rid of a bad debt, but not Paolo or Sarah."

"Could Paolo have found out about his gambling through Luigi and been blackmailing Daniel? That would give Daniel a reason to knock off the gardener," Marla suggested.

"Or maybe Daniel found out about Paolo's prison record. When he needed a loan, he asked Paolo to give him a name. Later, Daniel decided to eliminate Paolo as a loose end," Dalton countered.

"What did Daniel say when you questioned him?"

"He denied murdering anyone. As for his payments to

Luigi, Daniel said he was paying off his loan with money earned from his job."

"There's another possibility," Marla said. "This Luigi person could be the culprit in the homicides."

"That would potentially make Daniel an accessory to the crimes if he knew about them."

Marla frowned at him. "But why would this loan shark murder the gardener? Because Paolo was blackmailing Daniel, and the trail might lead to him? Where would Daniel get the money to pay blackmail plus make payments to the loan shark?"

"The answer is obvious. Daniel is the thief. He's paying off his loan by selling artifacts from the house. His job can't bring in that much income if he's still living at home."

"So Paolo found out and threatened to tell the authorities?"

"He might have threatened to tell Lacey."

Marla slapped a hand to her cheek as a new idea struck her. "Omigod. Could this Luigi fellow be the man in the hoodie?"

Dalton gave her a startled glance. "You might have hit the nail on the head. It makes sense. Daniel takes out a loan to feed his gambling habit. He steals stuff from the house to pay it back. Paolo, who'd recommended Luigi to Daniel, gets wind of the thefts."

"Luigi doesn't want to lose his cash cow, so he kills Paolo." Marla shook her head. So many theories caused her mind to spin. "Wait a minute. If this Luigi person is the guy in the hoodie, how does Anton Wiley fit in? Blinky said her kidnapper wore a jacket with a hood."

Dalton plucked at the top sheet. "Maybe they're one and the same."

"Don't forget about Sarah," Marla reminded him. "What would Luigi gain by murdering the gift shop lady?"

They both must have reached the same conclusion, because they shouted in unison, "Reproductions!"

Marla stared at her husband. “Sarah must have commissioned fakes to substitute for the artifacts in the house. Daniel did the actual switchovers, paid Rick to ignore his monitor screens, altered the video feed, and gave the real items to Luigi to sell.”

“And then what? Sarah decided she wanted out, so one or both of them murdered her?” Dalton scoffed.

“Why not? Did you ask Daniel about Sarah’s death?”

“Of course I did. He denies harming the woman. Said if he’d wanted to hurt her, he would have done it years ago when his dad began seeing her. According to Daniel, Sarah and Connor had a thing for each other.”

Marla allowed this news to trickle into her brain. “This confirms what Mrs. Docket hinted at earlier. If Lacey knew, it would have given her a motive to get rid of Sarah. But why wait until now? She would have done it years ago when her husband was alive.”

“Nor does this theory connect Lacey to Paolo’s death.”

“I agree. Did you ever find the murder weapon?”

Dalton grimaced. “Not yet. If we could find the blade, that might the telling item.”

“In the meantime, I’m curious about where Daniel goes on Sundays and if he’s trying to kick his gambling habit. That would give him some brownie points in my book. We should tail him this weekend.”

Dalton snorted. “Just what you need to do in your condition. I’ll put my team on it. Daniel should be home by now, but he’s still our strongest lead as a suspect.”

“You have to locate this Luigi fellow and bring him in for questioning. He could be a key witness, or even the killer.”

“He’s probably in the wind if he’s aware of Daniel’s movements, but we’ll see.”

Marla gave a yawn. “This requires too much thinking. Let’s call it quits for tonight.”

Tomorrow was her late day at work. She’d like to track

Mrs. Docket down before the housekeeper went to work at Tremayne Manor for the day. The woman had mentioned that Sarah had been sweet on Connor. Maybe Marla could coax more information from her. Although any relationship between the pair would have happened in the past, Marla had a hunch it might be important to Dalton’s murder cases.

Chapter Twenty-Four

Marla got off to a slow start on Thursday morning. Dalton was already gone by the time she dressed and fixed her hair. Brianna rushed off to school. That left Marla to care for the dogs, prepare a meal for dinner, and respond to email before she could go anywhere. She'd never catch Mrs. Docket before the housekeeper went to work at Tremayne Manor.

She debated what excuse to create for another visit while she browned a lean beef chuck roast in a skillet. She put the seared meat into the slow cooker, then added pre-sliced mushrooms, onions, diced celery and carrots, plus halved cloves of garlic. Tomato sauce, Burgundy wine, and beef broth came next, followed by a sprinkle of thyme and a couple of bay leaves. With the lid on, she set the timer on low for eight hours. It should be done by five o'clock when Brianna came home.

Her kitchen clock read nine-thirty when the phone rang. Her mother's name popped up on caller ID. *Great, like I need another delay,* Marla thought, in a grumpy mood.

"Hi, Ma. What's up?"

"What are your plans for this morning? Do you want to meet for lunch before you head into the salon?"

A brilliant idea exploded in Marla's mind. "I have a better idea. I'd planned to make a stopover at Tremayne Manor to talk to the housekeeper, but Lacey won't be thrilled to see me. How about if you come along to check out the wedding reception rooms? We can have lunch there in the café."

"Have they reopened for tours since the murders?"

"The gift shop is closed, but Dalton said the other public areas are open."

"Who's doing ticket sales if that woman is dead?"

"You know, I have no idea. It's a good question. So are you game to accompany me? I can pick you up in fifteen minutes." What would she do when Ma moved to Boynton Beach? These casual encounters would be over.

A sense of loss weighing her shoulders, Marla grabbed her purse, waved goodbye to the dogs lounging in the family room, and exited into the garage.

Your mother deserves her own life, she told herself as she drove onto the main road. *Ma won't always be around to help babysit, nor should we rely on her. Dalton and I will have to make our own arrangements for child care. At her stage in life, Ma should have fun.*

She'd better start looking into the various options. Her friend Tally had set an example with day care, but it would be great to hire a nanny. One of her other friends had recommended an agency. A wave of guilt swept her. She should be totally focused on getting ready for their son's arrival rather than chasing suspects. Would she ever learn to do what was best for her?

Not as long as the drive for justice compelled her to seek answers.

Once at the estate, Marla and Anita split up as they'd agreed in the car. Anita rang the front doorbell, ostensibly interested in seeing the wedding venues. Marla hoped Lacey would be out for the morning. Perhaps one of the docents would be selling tour tickets. The sign pointing to the gift shop had been moved and now indicated the front entrance.

While Anita created a distraction in the foyer, Marla sneaked in through the staff entrance at the rear. Inside the kitchen, she summoned one of the assistant cooks to notify Mrs. Docket that Marla would like a word. Bacon sizzled in a pan, judging from the aroma that made her mouth water. The scent of coffee lingered in the air, tempting her palate. Man, would she be glad when she could follow a normal diet again.

Marla stood by the walk-in pantry. Her son kicked his displeasure at her lack of movement. She rubbed her belly in a soothing circular motion. “Be patient, my son. Soon the killer will be caught, and we’ll all breathe a sigh of relief. Then you’ll have our full attention.” She went through a mental roster of boy’s names beginning with an ‘R’ while waiting.

A few moments later, the housekeeper appeared looking prim in her starched black uniform and with her hair in a bun. From her sour expression, she wasn’t happy to see Marla.

“I thought Miz Lacey told you to stay away,” Mrs. Docket said as they both moved out of earshot from the kitchen staff.

“My mother wanted to come see the catering halls, so I thought I’d take this opportunity to say hello. And there is something I need to ask.”

The housekeeper gave a nervous glance over her shoulder. “Follow me,” she said, leading the way into a storeroom that wasn’t open to the public. It held more sets of china and glassware but these didn’t appear to be collectibles. The family probably used them as everyday dishes. Marla noted a locked cabinet with a glass door that housed bottles of liquor. She eyed the keys on a ring pinned to the woman’s waistband.

“Do you know what each one of your keys opens?” she asked, genuinely curious. “There’s so many of them, I would never be able to keep track.”

The housekeeper stiffened. “Of course I do. It’s part of my job.”

“I understand Lacey, Daniel, and Rick Eaton are the only people who possess master keys to the display cases around the house.”

Mrs. Docket’s face pinched. “That’s right. What’s your point?”

"Don't those things get dusty? How can you ever clean them if they're locked away and you don't have access?"

"If any items need cleaning, Rick lets me know. I'll take care of them personally."

"It doesn't bother you that Lacey trusts him to have a key and not you?"

"It's her business to decide how things are done in this house." Turning sideways, the older woman aligned a set of iced tea spoons on the countertop.

"Are any of the keys on your ring unaccounted for? Like, you don't know what they unlock?"

Mrs. Docket kept her head bent. "There may be a couple."

"You'd mentioned that Connor kept a sword collection in a private vault. Would one of your keys open this safe?"

"Possibly, but I'm not aware of its location. Rumor says Connor hid his most valued items in a secret room. Not even his wife knows where it is."

"What about Rick? Do you think he's discovered this stash?"

"He'd have notified Miz Lacey if he had found it. It would raise him a notch in her estimation. You might have noticed, but she doesn't confide in Rick like she does Bruno." The woman's face reddened. "Forget I said that."

"You're aware of something going on between Lacey and Bruno? Is it wishful thinking on his part, or is his interest returned?"

Bruno had been working there since he and Connor had been kids. Maybe his fondness for Connor's wife had deepened into something more. Their words spoken in the corridor she'd overheard certainly lent credence to this theory. So did their earlier embrace.

"It's not my place to gossip about my employer. Was there anything else you wanted? I have to get back to work." The housekeeper cast an anxious glance at the door.

"Maybe you can't tell me about a living employer, but how about a dead one? Did Connor Tremayne return Sarah's affections?"

"Why should that matter now?" Mrs. Docket glanced at the door again, while Marla noted this storeroom had no windows. It was a good place to talk without being seen.

"Because Sarah is dead. Did they have an affair when Connor was alive?"

The housekeeper lifted her nose. "I won't cast aspersions on a former employer. My loyalty to the family is paramount."

"Even when Daniel might be accused of being an accessory to murder? Don't you owe it to the family to share what you know in order to exonerate him?"

Mrs. Docket bit her lower lip as she struggled with a decision. Finally she said, "All right. Sarah and Connor were lovers when he was alive. There, are you happy now?"

"Did Lacey know? That must have been when Sarah worked as a maid in the house."

"If she was aware, she never let on. Miz Lacey always maintained her dignity. Then again, she might have been involved in own pursuits."

"You mean, with Bruno?" At the housekeeper's curt nod, Marla's elation soared. *Now they were getting somewhere.* "Was Connor aware of his wife's infidelity, or didn't he care?" It was one thing for a man to have an affair, but another when his wife cheated on him. Most men wouldn't be so tolerant.

"They were discreet, but he suspected. That's why he wasn't affectionate toward Daniel the way a father should have been."

"Did he believe Daniel might be Bruno's son? Lord save me. That would explain a lot."

A pained expression crossed the housekeeper's face. "Miz Lacey denied it, of course. To this day, I'm not even sure of the truth. Poor child. He's the one who was caught in the middle. All he ever wanted was his daddy's approval."

"It must have been hard on him." Marla shifted her feet, wishing she could sit to ease the ache in her lower back. How was her mother doing with the reception rooms? She'd like to see them for herself, even though their visit had been a ruse. But this conversation was more important.

"Daniel went through a difficult period," Mrs. Docket said, leaning against the counter. Her gaze softened, as though she was glad to unburden her heart. Or else it was her fondness for the boy showing through. "His father's disdain made it tough for him to make friends. He didn't feel worthy. Still doesn't. The man should stand up to his mother and tell her what he'd like to do with the place."

"And what's that?"

"He has plans that would bring life back to this mausoleum. Miz Lacey could still donate the contents to the historical society."

"She doesn't give her son enough credit." Marla noticed the housekeeper hadn't answered her last question. Did she know what Daniel intended?

Mrs. Docket waved a hand. "Can you blame her for not being able to rely on him? The boy shuts himself in his room all day and doesn't socialize. Or at least, he didn't used to go out much until recently."

"He works in cyber security. That's a job he can do from home." *When he's not playing online poker, that is. Did the housekeeper know about his gambling habit?* "Several people have mentioned seeing a man in a hoodie around the property," she said. "He's met with Daniel and Rick at different times. We suspect he might have a connection to Paolo. Would you know anything about this person?"

"I'm afraid not." Mrs. Docket glanced at her wristwatch. "Oh, my. I've wasted half an hour talking to you. No offense, but I have to cut this short and get back to work."

Marla noticed how she'd changed the subject. Did the housekeeper truly not know anything about the stranger on the premises? Or was she purposefully misdirecting their conversation?

"And I need to check on my mother. Thanks for the information, Mrs. Docket. I hope things get resolved soon so the household can get back to normal."

"Amen to that. Let me show you out. You'll want to head over to our catering wing."

Marla found her mother in a breezeway between the mansion and the reception rooms. Anita looked cheerful in her canary yellow pants ensemble crowned by her stark white hair. She held a folder in one hand and gazed at the gazebo in the garden.

"Hi, Ma. I'm here. What did you learn?"

Anita turned to her with a bright smile. "This place would make a lovely setting for a wedding. Or any celebration, really. The Orchid Ballroom seats up to two hundred guests. The smaller Gardenia Room holds fifty. For cocktail hour, there's a covered terrace at the far end. It's screened and has ceiling fans."

"What are the rates?" Marla imagined these special events brought in more money than tour ticket sales.

"Room rental fee for the larger ballroom is seven hundred fifty dollars. This includes the screened veranda. The smaller room is five hundred dollars as you told me. We'd have to contract with their preferred caterer, and there's a liquor allowance required as well."

"Does the rental fee include table linens?"

"Yes, and they have a variety of colors to choose from for the cloths and napkins. The caterer takes care of the table set-up. We'd also have to get liability insurance. It's about a hundred fifty dollars for the number of people we're having."

"How about security?" Marla asked.

"They provide one security guard at the venue but not in

the parking lot. That's extra. This place may be ideal, but I wouldn't book our event here. Things will be unsettled until Dalton solves his case. We have other venues we're considering."

They discussed alternate choices and wedding details as they strode toward the main path. The small event Anita had initially wanted was ballooning into a larger affair since she and Reed had decided to invite their extended relations.

"You might need a bigger space, Ma. You're closer to seventy-five guests than fifty."

"We'll see. You'll meet Reed's sons at our engagement party. They're great kids. You should get along just fine."

"I can't believe you're getting married," Marla said, trying to muster a sense of joy.

Anita halted. "Reed makes me happy, *bubeleh.* You know I'm not trying to replace your father. He'll always be at my side and in my heart. But my life isn't over, and in my remaining years, I'd like to enjoy myself. I hope we have your blessing."

She gave her mother a fond smile. "Of course you do. Dad would want you to live life to the fullest. I'm being selfish in wanting to keep you for myself."

Anita surveyed her with an air of wisdom. "I understand you're nervous about having a baby. You and Dalton are about to embark on a new adventure in life. And while it may be his second round, it's your first time. It's only natural that you'd want your mother nearby. We're not moving to the ends of the earth, angel. The drive may be longer, but I'll still be here when you need me."

Marla's eyes moistened. "Will you be available when I go into the hospital?"

"You'll be fine. You have a good doctor and are going to the best facility. Dalton will be there with you. You won't want your mothers getting in the way. I'll be eager to meet my new grandson, but only when you're ready for visitors."

"We have the closet people coming on Saturday for his room. Then we'll be able to put away all the cute stuff we've been collecting."

"You'll get a lot more gifts at the baby shower. Charlene responded that she's coming, by the way."

"That's good. Maybe things have smoothed over for her and Michael." A wave of guilt hit her. She still hadn't called her brother. Then again, he could call her once in a while to ask how she was doing. Why was it always her role to take the initiative? "We've added a few more things to the registry," she said to change the subject. "Cynthia sent us the car seat we wanted."

"That was generous of your cousin."

"Our relatives are going to get hit up twice, between my baby and your wedding."

"We should always have happy occasions to celebrate. Tell me, how did your talk go with the housekeeper? Did you learn anything new that will help Dalton with his case?"

"I'd rather not talk about it now. I'm starving."

They resumed their walk toward the café. Marla spotted the restaurant ahead with its lime green awning. The outdoor seating already had a few patrons. It was a beautiful April day to sit outside. The warm air caressed her skin and carried a hint of perfume from a cluster of roses bordering the path. Marla hoped there wouldn't be any bees among the blooms.

Speaking of bees, was that the beekeeper in the distance? She squinted through her sunglasses. Sure enough, his stocky figure in full protective gear scurried past a ridge of trees beyond the formal garden. Maybe he was going to collect the honey from his hives.

She'd just stepped onto the gravel path leading to the café when a scream pierced the air.

Chapter Twenty-Five

"You go to the café," Marla told her mother. "I'll see what's happening." She rushed off, her heart pounding. The noise was coming from the private garage area.

No, not the garage, she noted as she rounded the far side of the mansion. The maintenance shed behind it. Lacey stood outside by the open door.

Several people ran from the house at the same time as Marla reached the scene. Mrs. Docket, Bruno, and Rick clattered along the walkway.

"What's wrong?" Marla asked the shaking lady of the manor.

Lacey spoke in a choked tone, her gaze stunned. "Inside. On the counter."

Marla stepped across the threshold, at first spying nothing unusual. Tools and equipment littered the worn counters bordering the room. A bed with rumpled sheets in one corner made her wonder if Bruno slept there on occasion. Two doors in the back stood closed. What had Lacey seen that spooked her?

She scanned the work tables, looking for anything out of the ordinary. Wait, was that an antique dagger? Her breath hitched as she moved closer to the object lying among an assortment of screwdrivers. The fancy knife looked like an artifact that might be found in the house. Its carved bone handle had a dog's head at the top and a double-edged steel blade.

"What's going on?" Rick Eaton demanded from the doorway. He looked intimidating in his uniform and wore a scowl on his face.

Marla pointed to the blade. "Does this belong here?" Possibly Bruno had brought the item to his shed for cleaning. He'd need specialized tools for some of his more delicate restoration work. But that wouldn't explain Lacey's response, or why she'd been there in the first place.

As Rick glanced over her shoulder, she heard his gasp of surprise. Then he roamed the room to examine the other counters. "Hey, lookie here. I recognize this stuff from the house."

Marla hurried to where he was pointing at a set of jewelry nestled inside an open toolbox. It looked like an expensive diamond and sapphire necklace with a matching bracelet. A couple of Russian religious icons leaned against the wall, while a miniature portrait of a czarina stood beside a bejeweled figurine of a lady.

Meanwhile, raised voices sounded from outside. Lacey and Bruno were engaged in a heated argument. Bruno broke away and rushed inside.

"I don't know how this stuff got here," he cried. "It's not mine."

Lacey, who'd trailed after him, pointed an accusing finger his way. "These things didn't walk here by themselves. You weren't expecting me today. Is this what you're doing in your spare time, stealing from us? How did you get my necklace? It's not enough to take items from the house, but now you've invaded my personal space, too?"

Bruno, red-faced, clenched his fists. "I've stolen nothing. Somebody else put these here."

"The police will sort it out," Rick said, seizing Bruno's arms and placing them behind his back. "Mrs. Docket is calling the cops. I'll hold you here until they arrive." Whipping a set of restraints from his pocket, he cuffed the maintenance man.

Marla sent Dalton a quick message of what was happening. Then she texted her mother to go ahead and order lunch. Aware the scene would be off limits once the authorities arrived, she padded toward the rear of the shack and opened the door to the right. It led to a shabby bathroom.

"You can't go in there," Bruno shouted, as she entered the next room.

This appeared to be his office, judging from the dented desk, metal file cabinet, and papers strewn across every surface. But that wasn't all. Pinned on the wall were photos of Daniel growing up and of Lacey in smiling, affectionate poses. Framed pictures of Lacey and Bruno also adorned the small space. Upon close examination, she noted the resemblance between Bruno and Lacey's son. They both had the same firm jaw and slightly tilted smile. Where was Daniel this afternoon, anyway? She hadn't seen him dash over to investigate the ruckus.

Mrs. Docket had been right about Lacey and Bruno. Was this where they met for their trysts? Could it be why Lacey had come by today, to surprise her lover with a visit?

Sirens sounded and soon the police stormed onto the scene. Marla explained her role, then said they could find her at the café. She felt slightly lightheaded and realized she'd better eat. One look at her bulging belly, and the cops let her go. Besides, she told them her detective husband would soon be on his way.

Anita had ordered them each a chicken salad sandwich made with walnuts and dried cranberries, a cup of tomato bisque, and a glass of lemonade. Rolls sat in a wire basket on the cloth-covered table. They sat outdoors under an umbrella. It was pleasantly shady as Marla dropped into a chair with a weary sigh.

She gulped down half the drink and ate a bite of the sandwich before answering her mother's rapid-fire questions.

"Lacey saw something inside the maintenance man's shed that startled her," Marla explained between slurps of soup. "It looked like an antique dagger. I was thinking maybe he'd brought it in there for fixing, but then Rick found more goods from the house, including some jewelry that belongs to Lacey."

"Who's Rick?" Anita asked, polishing off half of her meal.

"The security chief. I'll be interested to hear Dalton's observations. He may want to send that dagger to his forensics team to see if it matches the type of blade the killer used."

"Ugh, this isn't a pleasant topic for lunch," Anita commented with a grimace.

Marla laughed. "You should know me by now. We usually end up discussing Dalton's latest murder case at our family dinners."

"Yes, and that's a bad habit that has to end when you have the baby. Dalton should leave his work at the police station when he comes home."

"I help him solve his cases, Ma. He needs me for a sounding board."

"That's what his team is supposed to do. I'll have a word with him that you require peace and tranquility in these final months."

"Good luck in that regard." She glanced at her watch. "Oh no, I'll be late for work." She made a frantic call to the salon that she was on her way and then jumped to her feet. "I'll get the bill from the waitress. We have to leave."

After dropping her mother off at home, Marla sped to the shopping strip that housed her salon and day spa. A half hour late, she entered through the front door and scanned the waiting customers. Her one o'clock wasn't there, but her next appointment had shown up. The woman gave her an impatient frown.

"Jackie couldn't stay," Robyn said from the front desk. "Rose is here for you, though."

"Great, thanks. Did you reschedule Jackie for another time? I'll have to call her and apologize."

"She's coming in tomorrow. Did you see the breaking news? They've caught the Tremayne Estate murderer, as they're calling him."

"What?" Marla swung toward the TV mounted on the wall by customer seating. Sure enough, a reporter was speaking from the front steps of the manor. "How could the news people show up so fast? I just left there thirty minutes ago."

"They're saying the culprit was the maintenance man. Lacey Tremayne found an incriminating dagger in his work shed along with some stolen items from the estate."

"Dalton's forensics team has yet to examine the knife. I saw it on the counter. It looked clean. Even if the killer used it, any trace evidence might be gone."

Robyn, always eager to help, jabbed a finger at her. "Maybe the edges of the wound match the knife's parameters. Didn't you say two people were stabbed in the same manner?"

Marla nodded. "The dagger has to be an antique. It had a bone handle with a dog's head on top. But I don't recall seeing anything like it in the house's collections."

****

Later that night, Dalton confirmed her observation. "It's an Imperial Russian hunting knife. We couldn't find the matching leather scabbard engraved with acorn branches and wolf heads."

"Wolves? I thought it was a dog." She lay in bed, exhausted from the day.

Dalton lowered onto his side, the mattress sagging under his weight. He wore his shorts and nothing more. Marla was too tired to get aroused. She needed to rest more often during the day to conserve her energy.

"The carved bone handle had a dog's head at top, so you're right in that regard."

"What about the blade? Does it match the configuration for the stab wounds?"

"I'm waiting for the report. It's a twelve-inch steel blade with slight damage to one edge."

"That should help determine if it was the murder weapon. Did your CSI guys get any trace evidence?"

He shook his head. "The thing was polished clean. We were unable to find an empty spot in the house where it might fit, either on a wall or in a display case."

"Is it valuable?"

"According to my research, the market value for this type of dagger is six thousand dollars."

"Holy highlights, that's a lot for a fancy knife. Did Bruno say where he'd obtained it? Did he confess to the murders?"

"He denies ever seeing the weapon before today and claims he didn't steal anything. Nor is he a murderer, but they all say that."

"Did you look in his office? He keeps pictures of Lacey and Daniel."

Dalton's mouth curved down. "Yes, I saw the photos. Bruno wouldn't admit to anything, but Lacey confessed to having a long-standing affair with the man. She evaded my questions when I asked about Daniel, though."

"Mrs. Docket led me to believe Bruno may have fathered Daniel and not Connor Tremayne. Connor might have suspected the child wasn't his, and that could be why he was always distant to the boy."

"Wouldn't he have fired Bruno then?"

"Not if Lacey objected to his dismissal. She might have brought more money into the marriage than he did. Or perhaps she knew about Connor and Sarah, and she would have done the same to the former maid if Connor let Bruno go."

"So they each had their lovers employed in the household. I don't understand one point in your scenario. Connor raised Daniel as his own son, even if he had doubts about Lacey's fidelity?" Dalton leaned on his elbow to regard her.

The air-conditioning kicked in, and Marla drew the top sheet up to her chin. "It looks that way. Connor and Lacey must have had a tense relationship. Perhaps that's what Heather, the head docent, meant when she'd said theirs was a marriage made in heaven, until it wasn't."

"I showed Blinky several profiles, including Bruno's. She didn't recognize him and said she'd thought her captor was taller. But it would make sense if Bruno was Daniel's biological father that he'd buy a piece of property for his son. The maintenance man must have saved up money his entire life working at the estate."

Marla's brow furrowed as she considered the possibilities. "Have you asked Daniel if he's signed any legal documents in recent weeks? Like, how could Blinky's captor buy property in his name without his signature? A forgery would invalidate the sale."

"That's a good point. I'd also like to assess the kid's reaction to Bruno's arrest."

"I should talk to him. He seems more relatable to me."

"Hah. You don't have any spare time to go snooping."

Marla winced as her schedule scrolled through her mind. "You're right. I'm fully booked for the next two days. Brie is staying home on Saturday to let in the closet people for the baby's room. What are we going to do when she goes to college?"

"We'll miss her terribly, especially if she gets accepted at one of the schools in Boston. Why she wants to go there with the bitter winters is beyond me."

"She'll appreciate Florida all the more after a couple of seasons with miserably cold weather," Marla reassured him.

"We'll see. It's hard enough to believe she's entering her senior year of high school in September," Dalton said, his mouth curving down. "Meanwhile, I'll try to interview Daniel tomorrow to see how much he knows about his mother's relationship to the maintenance man."

"I still want to follow Daniel on Sunday when he goes out for the afternoon. I'm hoping he's attending a gamblers anonymous meeting. The man might have a brilliant mind that he could put to better use."

Dalton quirked an eyebrow. "From what I've gathered, he makes a good salary at his job in cyber security."

"Is he saving any of it, or does he squander his income on poker games?"

"He has been stashing regular amounts into his savings account," Dalton replied. "I was surprised to see how much is in there, considering how he's been paying Luigi Romello. Plus, he's been writing checks to NSU."

"What? That's something new."

"I figured he's been making payments on an old student loan, since that's where he got his degree. Besides, it's not relevant to the case."

Marla felt a surge of sympathy for the kid. "No wonder Daniel hasn't moved out to get a place of his own. He has too many debts, which he'll never pay off if he doesn't stop gambling."

"He has to want to help himself first. Nor is it your role to intervene. Let me handle it for a change."

Marla wrinkled her nose. "First Daniel gets taken in for questioning, and then Bruno gets arrested. It's almost as though someone wanted to shift the blame from Daniel to the maintenance man."

"What are you saying?"

"Maybe Lacey didn't stumble onto those items in Bruno's shed by accident. Maybe they were placed there on purpose to incriminate him."

Dalton's gaze narrowed. "Who would do such a thing?"

"It's your job to find out. If you think about it, why would Bruno keep that stuff in plain sight when anyone could walk in and see it, especially Lacey? I'm tending to believe his story, and that means the real murderer is still out there."

Chapter Twenty-Six

Marla forgot all about the Tremayne Estate murders, as the newscasters dubbed them, during work on Friday. She fielded questions from her staff and customers about the case, saying little other than she hoped the culprit had been caught. Keeping her suspicions to herself, she couldn't wait to follow Daniel on Sunday to see where he would go.

Meanwhile, she and Dalton were receiving baby gifts with the shower only one week away. It was exciting to come home from work each day and see packages at their front door. The latest were a bedtime sound machine and a set of onesies with matching bibs sporting cute elephants. They'd decided to go with the animal theme for the nursery.

Around lunchtime, her friend Tally called. "Hey Marla, I haven't heard from you in a while. What's going on? I saw on the news that they caught the killer over at Tremayne Manor. You must be relieved. Now you and Dalton can focus on getting ready for the baby."

"I wish." Marla had a few minutes to spare before her next customer arrived, so she went outside in the delightful April air to sit on their front bench for privacy. She filled Tally in on recent events as well as her suspicion that Bruno might have been framed.

"If he's not guilty, then who is left?" Tally asked.

"The security chief. The guy in the hoodie. The beekeeper or either one of the Tremaynes. I don't think

Michelle, the café manager, is involved. She doesn't have as much access to the house. The dagger had to have come from one of the collections."

"How about the man in the hoodie, Luigi somebody? How would he get in?"

"He might be working with someone on the inside, like Rick Eaton. Or possibly Daniel. Daniel owes him money, so maybe the man coerced the boy into giving him entry."

"That makes sense. Has Dalton confirmed the dagger matches the entry wounds for the victims?"

"He's still waiting for the report. I don't see why the weapon would have been placed in Bruno's shed otherwise. It makes me wonder where this item has been hiding. Supposedly, Connor Tremayne had a sword collection, but no one seems to know where he kept it."

"Not even his wife? That's secretive of him."

"There's been mention of a private vault somewhere in the house. The security chief suggested that Lacey wouldn't want weapons displayed among her delicate artifacts."

"Did you find out who left the note on your car in the visitor parking lot?"

"No, but let's talk about happier topics. How's Luke? Is he doing well at day care?"

They discussed child care options, the upcoming baby shower, and Marla's progress with the nursery at home. Marla hung up when she spotted her next client pulling into the parking lot.

Her cell phone rang. Cripes, she didn't have time for another call now. The caller ID said unknown caller. Instinct drove her to respond. "Hello?"

"Hi, it's Blinky," said a familiar voice on the other end.

Marla's heart leapt into her throat. "What is it? Are you all right?"

"I'm sorry to bother you. Nothing's wrong. I need you to get my purse."

"What?" Her racing heart started to calm. "Whose phone are you on?"

"It belongs to my guard. The day of the Easter egg hunt, I stashed my bag inside a drawer of the roll-top desk. You know, the one in the library? Hopefully, it's still there. My cell phone is inside. I may not be able to use it yet to make calls, but I'd like to have it for my calendar and such."

"Sure, I can get it for you. How will we connect?"

"Give it to Dalton. I can't wait to go home, Marla. It's awful being cooped up here, especially after being confined to that boat. Did your husband ever trace the owner?"

"He's still looking into it. By the way, did you leave a warning note on my car in the parking lot one day at the estate?"

"No, I didn't. Dalton showed me the message. The person who kidnapped me must have left it there. Oops, I have to go. The guard is signaling me. Thanks, Marla."

One more reason to go back to Tremayne Manor, Marla thought with an inward sigh. And here she'd been hoping to ease off the case until Sunday, when they would follow Daniel. She'd like to ask him about signing any real estate papers in case Dalton forgot to follow up on that idea. In the meantime, when would she be able to retrieve Blinky's purse?

Tours would be in progress during the day at Tremayne Manor. The last one concluded at five o'clock, after which most of the staff left except for the cook, if Lacey required her. That meant Marla should go today after work rather than tomorrow. Special events took place on weekends at the estate, and from the glimpse she'd gotten of their schedule, nearly every spot was booked.

Her shoulders drooping with fatigue, she stopped home after work to let the dogs out since Brianna wouldn't be back until later. Her heart sank when she thought how empty the house would feel without the teen's presence. Then again, they'd have a baby to fill the void, although she'd miss her stepdaughter.

Late Friday at the Tremayne estate brought the scent of spring blossoms and a light, warm breeze as she parked in the visitor lot and proceeded along the familiar path. The crime scene tape was gone from the gift shop entrance, she noted. Would Heather, as head docent, manage the ticket sales until Lacey hired a new gift shop manager?

That wasn't her concern at the moment. Obtaining Blinky's handbag, without tipping anyone off about her rescue, was the priority. Marla also wanted to talk to Daniel if he was home.

She veered onto the side path that would take her to the kitchen entrance, preferring to enter without disturbing Lacey, who had dismissed her from the case.

Marla breezed through the staff entrance and waved to the startled cook. "Hi, Joan. How are you? Sorry to barge in like this, but I need something from the house that I left here yesterday. I'll just be a minute."

Without waiting for a response, she strode purposefully through the series of rooms until she reached the library. None of the guards stopped her. Had they all gone home for the day, or was Rick still here, viewing the monitors in his office? If so, he might have already noted her arrival. She wouldn't have much time.

The smell of lemon polish wafted into her nose as she stood by the roll-top desk. It really was a beautiful piece of furniture. She remembered hearing during the tour that it had been made in Germany in the 1700s. Dalton would love to own something like this. With his interest in history, he'd appreciate its intricate construction.

Her gaze roamed the bookshelves lining the walls and the decorative art objects dotting the room. A plush sofa, lamp tables, and antique armchairs made for a comfy reading center.

She moved to the shelves and perused the labels. Many of the books were classic literature, with some texts on boating and stamp collecting suitable to Connor's hobbies. Her eyebrows rose at the section on antique weaponry. Had those books belonged to his father?

A glass-encased miniature replica of Excalibur stood on one shelf. She ran her hand over the domed top. The maids must be cleaning it, because it seemed clean compared to the layer of dust on the shelves.

A gold chalice caught her attention. No doubt it was another acquisition stemming from Imperial Russia. The lid looked like an upside-down military helmet. How appropriate someone had placed it next to the books on weapons.

Her time limited, she strode to the desk and opened the top. There were numerous drawers and cubbyholes to explore. As she opened one drawer after the other, she observed old papers, ledgers, and handwritten notebooks along with ancient desk supplies. One drawer had a magnifying glass with a horn handle.

Finally, in a large drawer to her right, Blinky's camel leather purse glimmered in the light.

As Marla bent to retrieve it, the bag resisted movement. The strap had caught on something. With a guilty glance at the security camera mounted on the ceiling, Marla crouched down to free the strap. Her actions might make her look suspicious, but she had a good excuse for being there.

What the heck was the strap snagged on? She reached in and felt around, her fingers tracing the strap. It was caught on a knob in the back. As she twisted the knob to free the bag, the back fell out. Whoa, what was this?

Using the flashlight from her purse, she shone a light inside. Now on her knees, she had to bend her neck to view the compartment that had just opened. A stack of banded papers rested inside.

She drew them out, felt around to make sure she wasn't missing anything else, and shut the false backing. Wanting to leave the desk as she'd found it, she slid the drawer back into place before straightening to her full height.

Her fingers trembled as she regarded the documents in her hands. What was so important about these particular papers that Connor had kept them hidden? Or had they belonged to his father, and he never discovered them?

A glance at the doorway showed that nobody seemed interested in her presence. She'd take a minute to scan her booty.

Clutching Blinky's bag in one hand and the papers in another, she moved to a cushioned window seat out of range of the security monitors. Or so she hoped. They could have hidden cameras among the *tchotchkes*. Glad to rest her feet, she undid the rubber band that crumpled upon touch.

A musty odor rose from the stack of papers, bringing memories of another time and place when she'd peered through old letters from Aunt Polly written to her lost love. Marla had discovered them at Sugar Crest Plantation Resort, a haunted hotel on Florida's west coast, which had once belonged to her family. Those handwritten letters had brought to light her aunt's sad history. What would these documents reveal?

The first one made her heart beat faster. Marla stared at a birth certificate confirming Daniel as Bruno's son. Wait a minute. Had Lacey put this here? That would mean she knew about the secret nook. Had she provided her husband with a false document naming him as the father?

More likely, Connor knew about the secret drawer since the desk had been handed down through his family. Perhaps he'd put the birth certificate in there, meaning he'd known all along that Daniel wasn't his son. That would explain his distance from the boy and his estrangement from his wife. For society's sake, he'd raised Daniel as his own child. But when it came to an heir, he'd deeded the estate to Lacey and left Daniel nothing.

No wonder Bruno had seemed fond of the kid and protective of his mother. His affection held even to this day.

Did Daniel sense anything? He'd seemed wounded by his father's inattention. Maybe he'd understand better if he knew the truth. Likely Lacey was afraid to tell him for fear she'd alienate him further.

What other secrets did this stash contain?

She unfolded a series of receipts. The first batch related to sales of the Fabergé eggs and other artifacts to a single buyer. This person must be a private collector as his name hadn't popped up during Dalton's investigation. Even more interesting were the commissions to an overseas artist for reproductions.

The implications made Marla's blood run hot and cold. This confirmed the eggs in the house were fakes, along with certain other art pieces. Was Lacey aware? Was that why she hadn't claimed insurance for the thefts rather than being merely reluctant to report them? Then again, the items she'd mentioned had been missing, not replaced.

Hold on. This must be why the thief who'd stolen the egg the day of the hunt had left it discarded by Paolo's body. He knew it wasn't worth anything. But why take it in the first place?

Because each egg holds a surprise, she reminded herself. Perhaps the killer hadn't been after the egg but a more valuable object hidden inside. So who had stolen it? Paolo the gardener, or the person he'd seen through the window, who had hunted him down and killed him?

Nervous that each minute ticking by would bring unwanted attention her way, she quickly flipped through the rest of the papers. Nothing seemed to be of great import except for one more receipt. It was for the sale of something called an Inverted Jenny in the amount of one million dollars.

A shadow crossed the window, but when she glanced outside, she saw nothing. Perhaps a cloud had momentarily blocked the sun.

Another document appeared to be a certification for a stamp. Wait, the stamp was named an Inverted Jenny. Connor had possessed a stamp worth a million dollars? What was the date on the bill of sale?

A rustle at the other end of the room made her jerk her head up in time to see Rick Eaton slinking into the room. She froze, afraid to make a sound. Had he spotted her on the security cameras, or was he up to mischief of his own?

He didn't seem to see her. As he headed over to one of the bookshelves, she assessed her chances for getting away while his back was turned. She could scoot through the door into the next room, opposite from the route he'd entered, but he might note her movement.

The security chief went directly to the bookshelf with the section on military history. As Marla watched, wide-eyed, he slipped the gold chalice into his uniform pocket and sauntered out the same way he'd come in.

Marla let out the breath she hadn't realized she'd been holding. Holy rollers, that had been close. Stunned by what she'd seen, she didn't get up for a moment. Then she rose unsteadily to her feet. She should notify Dalton, but he'd want evidence. This confirmed that the security thief must be the one swiping objects from the house. But was he working alone, or with Daniel, to erase the security footage?

Was he also the killer? Had Paolo spotted him through a window stealing the fake Fabergé egg, which neither would have known was a reproduction? But then why would Rick have discarded the egg? Had he dropped it in his struggle with Paolo as she'd originally surmised?

Confused by the possibilities, Marla texted Dalton her news before exiting from the room. She'd accomplished her purpose in retrieving Blinky's bag.

She hadn't gone far when someone grabbed her by the arm and drew her to a halt.

Chapter Twenty-Seven

"What are you doing here?" Rick Eaton growled, his muscular forearm restraining her. The former military man's stocky build blocked her exit.

Marla shook herself free and took a step back. "Blinky—I mean, my husband—requested that I retrieve Blinky's purse. She'd left it here the day of the Easter egg hunt."

His eyes narrowed. "How did you know where to look?"

"I remembered where she had put it that morning before she'd changed into the bunny costume. Dalton thought it would be safer in police custody until Blinky, um, turns up."

"I didn't see you come in through the front door." The way he glowered at her made her think of a street hoodlum. Her free hand instinctively went to her belly.

"I entered via the kitchen. Joan let me in. Are either Lacey or Daniel at home?" she asked hurriedly, before he demanded to know where the purse had been hidden.

"Mrs. Tremayne is out for the evening. Her son is upstairs," he replied in his gruff tone.

"No, I'm not," Daniel spoke from behind. "Marla, what are you doing here?"

She spun to face him and repeated her story. The two men exchanged a glance. Could they be colluding together as she'd suspected? Rick stole the objects and Daniel handed them to Luigi to sell? Rick was sometimes seen meeting with the guy in the hoodie, too. It seemed logical that the three of them were working together. She had to ascertain Daniel's role.

"Daniel, may I speak to you in private?" she asked, hoping Rick wouldn't throw her out.

The young man shrugged. "Sure, I was going to get dinner, but it can wait a few minutes." He signaled for Marla to follow him into the study. Rick didn't look happy about it, but he let them go.

"Are we free to speak without being overheard?" she said, nodding at the security camera mounted in a corner.

He took an object from his pocket, twiddled with the dials, and set it on a table. "Now we're clear. I've jammed the frequency. Have a seat. You look tired."

"Thanks." She chose a chair nearest to an exit. He straddled a chair opposite from hers. "Have you heard of a man named Anton Wiley?" she began.

"Can't say that I have."

"Did you sign any legal documents lately relating to a piece of real estate?"

"No. What's this about?" Daniel demanded, hunching forward. His owlish eyes seemed accentuated in his round face.

"It's police business, so I can't say more. Have you signed anything that you didn't initiate in the past few weeks?"

"I told you, I haven't… well, there was one time."

Her pulse accelerated. "Go on."

"Karl needed authorization to order some new hives, and my mom wasn't home. He asked for my signature."

Karl, the beekeeper? Why would he ask Daniel to authorize his purchases? "Wasn't that unusual? I didn't realize your mother involved you in the estate's operations."

"She'll ask for my help from time-to-time, when she doesn't have a choice," he said with a bitter edge. "I can't say Karl's request was out of the ordinary."

"Do you have much interaction with him?"

"Not really. He's mostly outside, and when he comes indoors to spray, it's only in the public rooms. Besides, he likes to keep to himself. There's something about him, though…"

"Yes?"

Daniel shook his head. "Can't explain it. Is that all? Because if so, I have things to do."

She put up a hand to stop him when he half-rose. "We know about Luigi and your debt."

His face soured, and he sank back into his chair. "Figures your husband would ferret out everybody's secrets. I'm paying Luigi back. That was a mistake."

"You playing online poker or borrowing money from a loan shark? Who introduced you to Luigi in the first place? Was it Paolo?"

He lifted his eyebrows as though her question had surprised him. "No, actually it was Rick. He's in the security business. I asked him where I could get a loan other than at a bank or credit union and where people wouldn't ask questions."

"Rick put you in touch with Luigi? I presume Luigi wears a hoodie when you meet him on the grounds to make your payments?"

Daniel gave a dour nod. "He wasn't here the day Paolo was killed if that's what you're going to ask next."

"O-kay. We know your reason for meeting him. What is Rick's? He's been seen with Luigi on the property."

"How should I know? I suppose people in Rick's line of work have shady connections. Maybe the guy is an informant."

"I have an alternate explanation. Rick is the one stealing items from the house, and Luigi is acting as his fence."

"What?" Daniel nearly knocked his chair over in his haste to rise.

"Don't tell anyone, but I saw him just now lift a gold chalice from the library. He stuck it in his pocket. I'll bet he isn't taking it to the housekeeping staff for polishing."

A look of astonishment washed over the young man's face. "But he's head of our security."

"What better position to steal from you."

Daniel's eyes darkened. "From my mother, you mean. Nothing here belongs to me, so why should I care what happens to it?"

"Because it should be your legacy. And if not, this house and these treasures are valuable to the public. I can understand why your mom is considering donating them to the historical society. It would ensure people could continue to enjoy the historic property and its collections. This place is beautiful and stands as a testament to the past. Why would you want to sell it?"

"You don't understand. Nobody does."

"What is your dream, Daniel? I know you'd have another plan in mind if this place were yours. But can it be done without destroying a piece of history that so many people enjoy?"

He turned his back on her. "This conversation is over."

"Do one thing for me, will you? At least help us catch Rick in the act. Can you monitor your surveillance cameras to keep an eye on him?" She wasn't sure this would be legal in court, but it might help get a confession out of Rick when the time came.

"I'll do it for my mother's sake," he said in a grudging tone. "Maybe she'll see I have some merit after all."

Poor kid, always yearning for approval from his parents, Marla thought as she drove home. Why wouldn't he confess his hopes and dreams? Maybe he'd faced ridicule from his father in the past. Lacey didn't take him seriously, but how could she unless he stepped up to accept more responsibility?

Later that night, she described her findings to Dalton as they got ready for bed. She'd given him Blinky's handbag.

"We're still going to follow Daniel on Sunday afternoon, right?" she asked, sinking onto the mattress with a sigh of pleasure. It felt good to lie down and stretch her legs.

"That's the plan," he said, his expression thoughtful. Marla had given him a lot of information along with the documents from the desk.

"There's another angle we should investigate. That receipt for a stamp I discovered among the papers from the roll-top desk? It's possible this stamp was the surprise hidden inside the Easter egg I found on the ground beside Paolo. Look at the date of sale. It's after he was killed."

Dalton, who'd been combing his hair, stopped and glanced at her. "This whole thing was about a postage stamp?"

She nodded, excited by her theories. "The stamp was worth a million dollars. Didn't Lacey name a collector on the west coast who'd been Connor's friend?"

Dalton retrieved his notebook from the dresser top and flipped through the pages. "Lacey mentioned a fellow named Jonas Sommers. Let me see tomorrow what I can find out about him. We might want to take a trip to talk to this guy."

****

Saturday arrived, and Dalton texted her at work in the salon. Marla glanced at his message after setting the timer for her client's color process.

Jonas works at the botanical garden in Naples. We can bring Brianna and take our Sunday nature walk there.

"What about tailing Daniel?" Marla replied. "I don't want to lose that opportunity."

I can assign one of my men to the stakeout. It's more important that I speak to this man.

As Marla got through the day, she considered what questions to ask the avid stamp collector over on the west coast.

"Somebody knew the stamp was inside the fake Fabergé egg," she said on Sunday morning during their drive across Alligator Alley. Brianna sat in the back seat and fiddled with her cell phone. "Let's assume this person stole the egg to get the stamp."

"So who took it? Rick the security chief?" Brianna asked. "You've implicated him as the thief who's been stealing objects from the collections."

Marla's brow furrowed. "Nobody would know about the stamp except the person who put it there."

Dalton cast her a bemused glance. "That was likely to be Connor Tremayne. He'd already sold off the original eggs. His signature was on those receipts. He knew the ones on display were fakes, commissioned by Sarah who must have been colluding with him. Where else would he hide such a small item in a place no one would think to look?"

"How could he have sold the stamp after Paolo died?"

"That's a good question. Remember, his body was never recovered from the alleged boating accident."

"So what are you saying—he's still alive?"

Dalton shrugged and focused on the drive, while Marla stared out the window at the river of sawgrass as they cut across the Everglades.

She didn't spot any alligators sunning on the canal banks. During one season, she'd counted over twenty gators, but not since then. They tended to seek the warmth of the sun in winter.

Soon they'd entered the cypress preserve, where tall trees supplanted the earlier flat horizons. Fluffy white clouds meandered overhead in an azure sky. It was the perfect day to visit a park. A great white heron took flight, its graceful wings lifting it in the air current.

Marla was ready for a rest stop by the time they turned into the botanical garden. She rushed into the ladies' room while Dalton paid their admission fees and asked where they might find Jonas Sommers.

Brianna washed her hands next to Marla. "I hope you're not going to take too long talking to this guy. I want to explore the trails."

"It'll help if he's cooperative," Marla said. They had too many burning questions that would steal the enjoyment of the day unless they got some answers.

They obtained maps at the Visitor Center and headed out. Following a shaded concrete path, they passed the Children's Garden and Butterfly House before hesitating at a junction. As they stood, deciding which way to go, Marla admired a brightly colored swathe of red flowers in front of a ridge of tropical greenery. Palms and other tall trees dotted the expanse of grass. In the distance, a manmade waterfall made a lovely photo backdrop.

"Did you find out where Jonas is working?" she asked Dalton.

He plopped a pair of sunglasses on his nose. "Sommers should be in the Florida Garden at the far end, so we can take either path. He's not just any gardener. The man is the landscape designer for the entire place."

"That's cool," Brianna said, studying her map. "Let's go through the Brazilian and Caribbean Gardens. Then we can cross one of the bridges to the trail on the other side of the waterway."

"I'm hungry." Marla took a protein bar from her purse and gnawed on it as they walked. Not knowing if the nature center had a concession stand, they'd each brought snacks and water bottles.

They strolled past a totem pole anchoring a cluster of crotons, their vivid colors a contrast to the surrounding greenery. The only sounds were birds twittering and branches rustling in the warm breeze. Marla's cares eased away as they progressed along the winding path. She stopped at a pond to observe the water lilies. When she got stressed, she should imagine herself floating on the surface like those flowering plants.

They crossed a bridge and ended up in the Asian section. A stone statue of a slender woman highlighted a desert plant section with cacti growing from a bed of gravel. The succulent garden ended at a sandy patch. Marla veered around a Madagascar palm with sharp spines.

They played a game of identifying trees until they arrived at a Polynesian hut. This photo opportunity was one they couldn't pass up, and they took turns sitting under the thatched roof on a wicker armchair and taking pictures of each other while listening to creaking noises from a cluster of bamboo.

As they continued along, the trail led them past a two-story structure with a sloped blue tile roof. It overlooked the rock waterfall. Marla wished they could relax and enjoy the peacefulness of the place, but they had a purpose in coming. The Florida Garden was straight ahead.

A man in a safari outfit and hat sat on a bench sketching on a notepad. As he appeared to be the only person around, Dalton approached him.

"Hello, could you tell me where we can find Jonas Sommers?"

The fellow regarded the three of them standing in front of him and blocking the sun. "That would be me."

Dalton introduced them. "We want to talk to you about Connor Tremayne. I understand you knew each other through your interest in stamp collecting."

"That's correct. I was sorry to hear of Connor's passing. We attended many conventions together. And call me Jonny, please." He rose to face them, his body lean and his skin leathered from the sun. Deep lines framed his eyes, while his mouth curved into a smile.

"How did you get interested in collecting stamps?" Dalton asked.

Jonny gestured for the ladies to sit on the bench while the men stood. Marla was glad to be seated. She adjusted the sun hat she'd worn and let Dalton take the lead with questioning.

Brianna busied herself on her cell phone, probably uploading her photos to social media.

"Well now," Jonny began, tucking his hands into his pants' pockets. "It's sort of what *you* do as a detective. People have been collecting stamps ever since they were first issued. We search for highly valuable stamps based on their history and rarity."

"So their history is part of their value?" Dalton said.

Jonny gave a vehement nod. "Most definitely. Philately is the study of stamps, postal history, and related topics. You can be called a philatelist even if you don't own any stamps. For example, a philatelist might study rare stamps that have a significant historical value, like the ones you see in museums. Postage stamps reveal more than the history of a letter. They can represent the history of a nation."

"That means a stamp collector is inherently a philatelist, but a philatelist isn't necessarily a stamp collector." Dalton stroked his jaw with a thoughtful expression.

"That's one way of putting it." The landscape designer lifted his bushy eyebrows. They matched his ash gray hair. "Philately is derived from the Greek word, *phileo*, meaning 'love of' and from *ateleia*, that means 'without tax' because postage stamps replaced a cash postal charge."

"What draws people to collecting stamps?" Marla asked. "They're essentially pieces of paper."

"They're so much more, my dear. Each stamp tells a story. They're art, history, economics, and romanticism all in one. The introduction of special commemorative stamps drew even more interest to the hobby. The first stamp in this country that was issued to remember our history was in 1893 to commemorate Christopher Columbus' discovery of the New World. These stamps can be worth thousands of dollars, depending on their condition."

"Do collectors have a focus, like a particular area of interest?" she asked out of curiosity.

He nodded. "People might collect stamps from a particular country. Or they might pursue a certain topic, such as scenes with birds or famous scientists or sports. My specialty is stamps with flowering plants issued in the United States. These show our living botanicals from an American landscape perspective."

"What makes a stamp rare?" Dalton inquired, no doubt leading up to mentioning the Inverted Jenny that Connor Tremayne had possessed.

Jonny clasped his hands behind his back and began pacing. "Rare stamps may be firsts, have printing errors, or are simply old and rare because of limited printings. We evaluate them based on condition, age, rarity, and grade. The grade refers to the centering of a stamp's design. For a used stamp, the degree of cancellation is an additional factor."

Dalton adjusted the ball cap on his head and moved into a portion of shade. "I've heard of the Inverted Jenny. What can you tell us about that one?"

Jonny's mouth spread in a crooked smile. "One hundred of them were issued in 1918. With a face value of twenty-four cents, these stamps are famous because the biplane featured in the picture was unintentionally printed upside down."

"What would one of these stamps be worth?" Dalton asked.

"The latest Inverted Jenny sold this past November for one-point-three-five million dollars." Jonny regarded an anhinga taking flight at a nearby pond. "Out of the hundred issued, only sixty-five have ever surfaced."

"How do you sell them? Don't you have to find other collectors who might be interested?" Marla cut in. She couldn't help becoming interested in the topic. She'd never really thought about the different pictures or meaning of a stamp.

"We sell them to a stamp dealer or offer them to a philatelic auction house. An average collection may be worth several thousand dollars. Most of us aren't in it for the money, though. We want to learn more about the history, culture, science, and technology that the stamps illustrate. And sharing our hobby with other collectors and dealers can lead to lifelong friendships."

"My wife found a bill of sale from Connor Tremayne," Dalton said. "He'd had an Inverted Jenny that he sold. Do you recognize the buyer's signature?" He showed the landscape designer a photo of the document on his cell phone.

"Hell, yes," Jonny said after squinting at the screen. "That's one of our foremost collectors in Florida. Many of us know each other. What of it?"

"This sale took place within the past few weeks."

"That's impossible. Connor is dead. More likely, his wife sold it. See, that signature isn't definitive. You can hardly make out the first name."

Marla stood and peered at it. "He's right," she told her husband. "Maybe we misinterpreted. You can have your handwriting experts verify the signature. Besides, Lacey admitted to selling off the rest of Connor's stamps to a dealer."

"I'll look into it. We appreciate your time," Dalton told the other man. "Here's my card if you have anything to add."

During the long drive east across Alligator Alley, Marla and Dalton discussed what they'd learned.

"I'd like to visit Lacey again tomorrow," Dalton mentioned. "Was she the one who sold the stamp? Did she even know about the secret drawer in the roll-top desk?"

"If so, then she also knew her husband had sold off some of their treasures and substituted fakes," Marla reiterated.

Dalton gave her a meaningful glance. "His boating accident was convenient for her. She got rid of a cheating husband and inherited his estate at the same time."

"That would be true, except he'd already deeded the property to her," Brianna reminded them from the back seat.

"There's still something we're missing," Marla said.

"Can I come with you when you speak to her? Maybe Daniel will have caught Rick stealing items from the house by then. Have you heard from your guys who were tailing him today?"

"Not yet. I'll check in at the station after we're home."

Marla patted his arm. "We're getting closer. All we need is one break, and the pieces will fall into place. You'll see."

Chapter Twenty-Eight

"You searched through my roll-top desk without permission?" Lacey said, her lips pursing. Her gaze chilled, contrasting to the warm colors of her coral-colored blouse and cocoa pants.

"I had a hunch," Marla replied, seated next to Dalton on a sofa in Lacey's private quarters. "It paid off when I discovered these documents in a secret compartment. I'm sorry if I violated your trust, but the opportunity arose when no one was around to observe me, and I took it."

Lacey's face paled as she leafed through the papers. "I don't understand. Connor must have hidden these there."

Dalton folded his hands and leaned forward. A lock of hair flopped endearingly onto his forehead. Marla, weary from the weekend, wanted him to solve his cases so they could move on.

"The Inverted Jenny stamp was sold after Paolo's death," he noted.

"We're thinking it must have been hidden inside the Fabergé egg stolen during the Easter egg hunt," Marla said. "The thief knew about the surprise, and that's why he left the artifact behind. Plus, he might have been aware it was a reproduction and not the real thing."

Lacey's forehead creased. "It couldn't have been Connor. So who…?" Her eyes widened and she gasped. "My son. Connor must have shown him the secrets of the desk."

Marla shook her head. "If Daniel gained a million dollars

from the stamp sale, he'd have paid off his debts." That is, unless the young man had posed as Anton Wiley, bought the boat with the money, and purchased himself a piece of property with the rest. When had the boat been acquired? Wasn't it earlier, meaning her suppositions wouldn't work?

"I doubt Daniel knew about these documents or the reproductions," Dalton suggested. "You know how he goes out every Sunday afternoon? My boys tailed him yesterday. He volunteers at a children's center in town. Your son is teaching kids computer coding and other software skills. His mentor said he's passionate about his work and wants to open a summer computer camp for underprivileged children."

An expression of disbelief crossed Lacey's face. "If that's true, why does he waste time playing games in his room all day?"

"He's into online poker, not video games," Dalton explained. "Gambling is an addiction, but your son is trying to kick the habit. Meanwhile, he's been paying off a loan he took to cover his debts. His job in cyber security is legitimate and pays well. He's also using some of that income to take courses at NSU toward a master's degree in education."

"What? Daniel wants to become a teacher?" Lacey's gaze turned inward. "I wonder if that's what he meant when he said he'd use this house for a different purpose. The historical artifacts mean nothing to him. Maybe he meant to hold classes here. If only he'd said something…"

"All he's ever wanted is your approval," Marla mentioned. "Your son may not share the same interests in history and art, but perhaps you could reach a compromise."

"I would have suggested he use our catering halls for after-school activities."

"Yes, but where would the kids sleep and play for summer camp? This house isn't exactly child-proof. And they'd need computer stations. A serious remodel would be required."

Could this be why Anton Wiley had bought Daniel a separate piece of property? Had he been the person who'd sold the stamp so Daniel could fulfill his dream?

Remembered conversations floated through her mind. Rick was the one stealing artifacts. She hadn't seen Daniel on this visit to ask if he'd recorded the security chief in the act of thievery. But had it been Rick the day of the Easter egg hunt? That would mean he knew about the hidden surprise and the secret compartment in the desk. Was he the one who'd framed Bruno?

Her thoughts twirled in circles while Lacey and Dalton continued their conversation. Her husband had said he'd received the report on the dagger found in Bruno's shed. Its shape and measurements matched the stab wounds on the victims. Yet where had it been stored?

They were still missing something. *Connor's sword collection!*

Nobody knew where he'd hidden these relics, not even his wife. Apparently he hadn't felt the need to brag about his private treasures or to show them off.

The bud of an idea drifted into her brain and blossomed into full bloom. She rose and addressed the others.

"Would you excuse me? I want to check on something in the library."

"I'll meet you there," Dalton said, aiming a pointed glance her way. She recognized the warning that flashed in his gray eyes. *Stay there and wait for me.*

She scurried off, eager to test her theory. Inside the cozy room lined with books, she paused before the shelves on ancient weaponry. Most of them covered Russian and French eras when czars and kings ruled the land. So why was a glass-domed replica of Excalibur here? That legend came from Great Britain. Mythology didn't fit in with books on Imperial military weapons.

Her fingers smoothed the dome and encountered a knob

in the back. She twisted it and gasped as a latch clicked. The bookshelf section swung open. She stared into the gap, her heart thumping. Was this it, the entrance to Connor's secret vault?

Casting a glance over her shoulder to see if she was still alone, she crept through the archway. But first, she had the presence of mind to stick a book across the threshold so the panel wouldn't swing shut on her. A light inside came on automatically.

Her breath hitched at the sight within. Swords, knives, battle axes, maces with spiked heads, and other armaments of war ringed the room, mounted on the walls or displayed in glass cases. Beneath each one was an engraved plaque giving the history of the piece. She breathed in purified air, noting a thermostat at one end.

Sure enough, a blank space faced her in the section with daggers. Alongside it was a leather scabbard that must belong to the weapon found in Bruno's shed. The label identified the missing piece as a double-edged Imperial Russian Hunting Knife.

On its right was a Caucasian Dagger with a twelve-inch blade. It had a bone handle with a number, eight-four, marked in silver. A black leather scabbard accompanied this item, which was valued at three thousand dollars.

On the other side was a Cossack Kinjal Dagger. Its fourteen-inch, double-edged blade had a wave pattern and a horn grip handle. It came with a scabbard tipped by a metal ball. This item was worth a couple of thousand, so even less than the other one.

The values didn't impress her. This wasn't exactly a priceless collection. These things might add up to a big deal when taken together, but Connor may have just wanted to savor them in private.

She roamed the room, admiring the ancient weapons and reading about their history. She liked the short sword with turquoise stones embedded in silver. This one was also stamped with the number eighty-four. According to a wall plaque, this number represented the minimum silver assay standard set for silversmiths.

"Marla, are you in here?" Dalton called, his voice muted.

"I found the vault," she shouted back. "Look for the gap in the shelving."

A moment later, he'd joined her. His astonished glance took in the weaponry on display. "I can't believe the vault was hidden in the library all this time. How did you figure it out?"

"The Excalibur sword replica in the glass dome didn't seem to fit in with books on Russian and French armaments. Look, there's the empty space where the murder weapon should go."

He stepped forward, a frown on his face as he read the plaque. "You're right. Whoever stabbed the victims must have cleaned the knife and put it back until they planted it in Bruno's shack. That doesn't tell us who knew about this place to access the collection."

"What about Rick? We know he's been stealing items."

"Then this stuff would be long gone. Besides, what grudge would he have against Bruno?"

"He could have wanted to throw suspicion off himself."

"We were questioning Daniel, not him."

Marla tapped her chin. "A lot of this seems to be about protecting Daniel or providing for him. The dagger you retrieved from Bruno's shack looked as though someone had lovingly polished and waxed it. Wait, waxed… as in beeswax?"

They stared at each other.

"The boat owned by Anton Wiley was named Beethoven," Dalton said with a thoughtful frown. "Maybe it's not about the composer but about the bees. We need to talk to Karl Simmons."

"What is this?" Lacey's voice called out. "I can hear you but I can't see you."

"Over here." Marla stuck her arm out and waved.

A moment later, Lacey had joined them. "Good Lord, is this where Connor hid his swords? I never knew this space existed."

"It may have been built by his ancestors," Marla suggested. "Look, we need to talk to Karl. If he's not in, would you give us permission to look around his shed? I can't explain now, but he may be the person responsible for the murders."

Lacey put a hand to her mouth. "But why would he kill Paolo and Sarah?"

"That's what we hope to find out," Dalton said.

"This is all so confusing." Lacey's face sagged, and she regarded them with sad eyes. "Of course, you can take a look. The sheds on the property belong to me, after all. The sooner you put an end to this investigation, the sooner we can all get back to normal. What do you need me to do?"

Marla remembered the key ring pinned to Mrs. Docket's apron. "Do you have a key to his shed? If he's out on the grounds, we could let ourselves in."

"There may be one on the housekeeper's ring. I'll go borrow it from her. Meet me at the back entrance."

On their way from the vault, Marla yanked the heavy book off the floor and let the panel shut behind them. She dropped the book on an accent table as they exited.

Lacey met them in the kitchen a few minutes later and handed them the keys. "If you don't mind, I'll wait here. Karl isn't the most pleasant person on his good days."

A light breeze caressed Marla's skin as she paused on the rear terrace to appreciate the bright and sunny morning. Here's where she'd stood weeks ago with Tally, wondering what had happened to Blinky.

Now maybe they'd learn the answers. She headed across the wide expanse of lawn toward the beekeeper's shed. Dalton was already several paces ahead of her.

"If he's inside, you should wait out here for me," he told her when she'd caught up to him.

"And miss the chance to hear what he'll say? That's assuming he isn't out tending to his hives or spraying the plants with insecticide."

Unfortunately, or perhaps not, Karl wasn't inside. Marla lifted the housekeeper's key ring and methodically inserted one key after another until they found a match. She wrinkled her nose at the peanut shells littering the floor and the smell from an overflowing garbage can.

"What should we look at first? The beekeeping equipment or the papers strewn over the counters?" she asked her husband.

"Let's examine the documents. There might be something relating to Anton Wiley or the yacht where Blinky was held captive."

Suddenly, the door—which they'd closed—crashed open. Karl stood in full protective body gear in the doorway. He yanked his veiled hat off and snarled at them.

"What are you doing here?"

"Your employer gave us permission, Mr. Simmons. Or should I say, Mr. Anton Wiley." Dalton waved a document in the air. "That is your alias, isn't it? Here's a receipt for some work done on your boat. You're the man who abducted Bonnie Morris. Clever to name your vessel Beethoven. We didn't get the connection to your beekeeper hobby until just now."

Karl's eyes narrowed and his mouth thinned. "What else have you figured out?"

"You kidnapped Blinky because she knew you'd killed Paolo," Dalton stated.

"Why would I hurt the gardener?"

"I'm guessing he spotted you through the window stealing the Fabergé egg. You didn't care about the artifact. All you wanted was the surprise inside, an Inverted Jenny stamp worth a million dollars." Dalton took a step forward, pointing his finger. "What I don't get is why you used that money to buy a piece of property in Daniel's name."

"I understand," Marla spoke up, studying the bearded man in the bulky beekeeper suit. "You wanted to do what was right for your son. Isn't that so, Mr. Tremayne?"

His expression turned thunderous. "You snooping bitch. Why didn't you heed the warning I put on your car? I know you've been talking to everyone at the house. I wanted to do one good thing for my son and right the wrongs I'd done him. Why couldn't you leave things well enough alone?"

"You killed two people, Connor. Paolo was unfortunately in the wrong place at the wrong time. But why Sarah? I thought you two were lovers."

A pained look entered his eyes. "I'm sorry about Sarah, but she became a liability. She knew who I was all along. It was her idea to bring me back as a beekeeper. I could wear my mask and no one would be the wiser. But when I took Blinky, she kept nagging at me to let her go."

"Why did you keep Blinky alive?" Marla asked, needing confirmation of what her friend had told them.

"She had connections in the real estate field. I was sorry I'd cut Daniel out of my will and wanted to provide for him. The kid deserved better."

"You resented Daniel because you'd suspected he wasn't your son. Is that correct?"

"Oh, I knew it. Lacey tried to hide the birth certificate but I found it. Yet I raised him as my own. I couldn't leave him my family's legacy, though. I knew Lacey valued the estate's history, so I deeded it over to her before I staged my boating accident."

"You meant to fake your death," Marla continued, while Dalton stayed as still as a stiffly sprayed hair. Tension coiled from his taut muscles but he let Marla take the lead. He eyed his suspect, no doubt waiting for the slightest move that would put them in jeopardy.

Connor gave a glum nod. "I had built up too many debts. Maintenance of this place took its toll. I'd spent most of the assets I'd inherited, along with the funds Lacey had brought into our marriage. She's a smart woman. I figured she could manage on her own."

"Lacey had no idea you'd substituted reproductions for items in the house, including the treasured eggs. Sarah ordered the replicas for you, didn't she? How did you manage to switch the real objects with the fakes without Rick seeing you on the security cameras?"

He gave a harsh laugh. "Rick figured out who I was, but he couldn't say anything because I knew he was stealing stuff from the house. I saw him sneaking around when he didn't realize anybody was watching."

"And that didn't bother you? Those things were part of your legacy," Marla reminded him.

Connor swept his hand in a dismissive gesture. "It was small stuff. I'd sold off the more valuable pieces with no one the wiser. Considering how we're cousins, and my pa tricked his dad into selling property inherited from our grandparents, I felt it was his due. Besides, that wasn't important in my grand plan, which was to provide for my son and sail away on my new boat."

"It didn't work out too well for you."

"No, because you two came along. I'd stuck around only long enough to make sure Daniel was okay. I won't allow you to interfere with my plans."

"Was it you who planted evidence in Bruno's shack?" Dalton asked, his voice gruff.

"That's right. I couldn't let Daniel go to jail for my mistakes." Regret flickered in Connor's eyes, but then they hardened with intent.

"We only want what's best for Daniel," Marla said quickly to forestall whatever he was planning. "You can help if you give yourself up. I'm sure my husband can make you a deal."

"I doubt it." Connor yanked the lid off a swarm box on the counter. Bees flew out, zooming around in the small, enclosed area.

Marla instinctively crossed her arms in front of her face.

"I hope you're not allergic to bees," Connor said with a malicious grin. "Don't move, or they'll attack. Even now, they're picking up on your anxiety since you're breathing faster. They can sense your carbon dioxide emissions, you know. Better still, hold your breath."

He snickered, turned around, and fled through the door. With a loud slam, he shut them inside. A thud sounded from outdoors, as though he'd wedged something there, and then his footfalls faded away.

Chapter Twenty-Nine

"Keep still and don't panic," Dalton said, retrieving his cell phone. "I'll call for backup."

Marla's heart raced as the bees expanded their area of flight. How would it affect the baby if she got stung? Her nerves prickled as a buzzing hum rose in the air. They had to get out of there.

She scanned the countertops, searching for anything that would get them past the swarm. Her gaze zeroed in on a metal canister with an upside-down funnel for a lid and an attached bellows. She cried out in excitement.

"We can use the smoker," she said. "I've watched a YouTube video. I know how to do it if we can gather the components."

"What's that going to accomplish?" Dalton asked after finishing his call. "I should phone the house. Someone there could let us out of here."

Marla eyed the bees and tried to regulate her breathing. "You do that while I get the smoke going. Remember how Stuart Howard told us it fools the bees into thinking there's a wildfire? They go inside the hive to eat honey prior to making a move. It also masks their alarm pheromone and disrupts their communication."

"That's right. Smoke acts as a bee tranquilizer. Go for it."

Feeling as though she was on a desperate scavenger hunt, she scanned the countertops and corners for the items she would need. A newspaper, an automatic lighter, and a bag of pine needles would work for the method she had in mind. Karl must use them for the same purpose.

Working as fast as she could, she crumbled a piece of newspaper into a ball, lit it at one end with the lighter, and stuffed it inside the open metal canister. She pumped the mini-bellows to add air and keep the fire going.

Next she grabbed handfuls of pine needles and stuffed them inside, pumping vigorously until white smoke poured out. Then she set the conical lid on top. Still pumping the bellows, she aimed the funnel toward the bees.

They moved away from the smoke and buzzed around the swarm box.

Her throat constricted from the smoky atmosphere, making her cough. "Try the door. I'll keep the bees away."

Dalton turned the knob but the door wouldn't budge. "Connor must have blocked the exit from the other side. Let's try going through that window instead."

She followed the direction of his gaze. "It's too high to reach."

"Not if we use that cart to get a foothold." He pointed to a printer stand by a computer station and headed that way. With a grunt, he shifted the printer to a nearby counter. Then he wheeled the cart toward a spot under the window. "Get me that hammer and a rag," he told her.

Marla complied, careful to keep the smoke between herself and the bees, which were now mostly in the swarm box. Dalton climbed onto the sturdy wooden stand and smashed the window. He used the rag Marla had given him to push away any remaining shards and to cushion the window sill.

It wasn't easy for Marla to get up there in her condition. Dalton took the smoker, laid it on the counter facing outward so it aimed at the hive, and helped her climb onto the cart and out the window. The drop on the other side was manageable, and soon they both stood outdoors in the fresh spring air.

Rick and Ed sprinted their way across the grass. Sirens sounded in the distance. Marla breathed a sigh of relief. They were free at last. Connor Tremayne wouldn't be so lucky. Dalton had put in a call to detain him at his boat where he'd surely be heading.

****

The day of Marla's baby shower dawned bright and sunny. She woke up excited and happy. Gifts had been arriving daily, and now she could celebrate the joyful occasion with her family and friends. Dalton would spend the time with Reed and John. It would be good for the men to bond.

She showered, did her makeup and hair, then put on a maxi dress after breakfast. Inside the baby's room, she paused to look over the results of their labors. They'd chosen gray and white for the dominant colors. The dresser and changing table combo took up one whole wall, with the crib and a chair opposite. A lamp table stood by the window. Dalton had picked out a peel and stick tree decal with woodland animals on its branches for the wall décor.

He came up behind her and put his arms around her waist. "It won't be long now," he said, pride in his tone.

She gave a contented sigh. She'd seen the obstetrician that week for her eighth month visit. "Soon we'll have a baby in the house. That means no more crime-solving for me. I've made up my mind. I'll have enough to do between the salon and our son."

Dalton grunted. "Like, is that even possible for you? You can't seem to stop sticking your nose into other people's business." He said it in a nice way, not as though it were a bad trait.

"I promise," she said, meaning it this time.

"There's something else we need to talk about. You've had your Camry for years now. It's time for you to get a new car. We'll need an SUV to carry all the baby stuff with us whenever we go anywhere. I've been checking out the various models."

Surprised delight squeezed her heart. "I would love to have a bigger car. I haven't even thought about it, but you're right. It would be so much more convenient."

"I'll start looking into what deals are available. We'll save money if we go with a pre-owned vehicle with low mileage."

The doorbell rang. Marla eased from his embrace and hurried to answer.

Soon she was driving to the baby shower with her mother and Kate while wishing she already had a bigger car. Dalton would stop by the venue later to help haul their gifts home. Meanwhile, she helped carry in the decorations and other items her family members had brought along.

Brianna, already in the party room, clapped her hands at their arrival. She looked all grown-up in a turquoise and white sundress with matching jewelry. Marla admired her skill in curling her dark brown hair so it fell in waves to her shoulders.

A pang of wistfulness took hold. How long would it be until Brianna acquired a steady boyfriend? She'd avoided any serious relationships in high school so far, preferring to concentrate on her studies. In September, she'd enter her senior year. The goal-directed teen had already selected a college major, and it wasn't law as Dalton had hoped.

To their surprise, she'd chosen a pre-med program instead. Her mother had died from cancer. With her skills in science and math, and the detective genes inherited from her dad, Brianna meant to pursue a career in medical research. She'd found a curriculum she liked at Boston University focused on molecular biology and genetics.

"Marla, congratulations," said Tally, interrupting her thoughts. Tally rushed over after placing a gift on the designated table. She hugged Marla, then stepped away. She'd done her blond hair in a chignon and looked as model-perfect as ever in a coral and navy wrap dress.

"Thanks. I can't believe how well everything worked out with Dalton's cases," Marla said.

Tally tapped her arm. "Do tell before everyone gets here."

"I'd rather save the explanations. Other people will want to hear, and I don't care to repeat myself. Hey look, here's Blinky." She'd invited their friend, now free to resume her life.

"Oh my God, Marla. It is so good to be here. You deserve all the happiness in the world for saving me and finding the guy who killed Paolo," the woman told her, blinking rapidly.

"So do you, after what you've been through. Let's not ruin the day and talk about it now, though."

Nonetheless, while they sat around eating tea sandwiches, people started asking questions.

"Marla, you promised to tell us how you caught Blinky's kidnapper," Tally said with a remonstrative glance.

"What about Mrs. Tremayne and her son? Is it safe for us to visit Tremayne Manor?" Kate asked in her cultured tone.

"I saw on the news that the security chief was accused of stealing from the estate," Cousin Cynthia added.

"And that Connor Tremayne faked his own death!" Anita chimed in.

Marla shook her head. She wouldn't reveal all the family's secrets in public. They had a right to privacy. So she only told what most people could find in the news. Then she diverted their attention by opening gifts and serving cake. Brianna acted as photographer, recording the afternoon for posterity.

Later, when most guests had left and the men had arrived to help load the gifts into her car, Marla sat on a sofa surrounded by her closest friends and family in folding chairs.

Nicole and Robyn remained from the salon staff, along with her friends Tally and Jill, deli owner Arnie's wife. Marla had invited Susan Feinberg from down the block. Susan hadn't left yet either, staying to hear the juicy gossip. And leave it to Cynthia, her closest cousin, to linger while the rest of her extended family had left.

"Now tell us what really happened," Nicole said, her engagement ring gleaming against her cinnamon skin. She'd tied her hair into a high ponytail and looked comfortable in a palazzo pants set. As an avid mystery reader, she wouldn't let go until she'd heard all the details.

"Lacey Tremayne asked you to investigate the thefts at the estate, which she'd never reported to the police or to her insurance company?" Robyn asked to get things started.

"That's right," Marla replied. "She was afraid her son was the one stealing things. It wasn't him at all. In fact, he helped us nail Rick Eaton, the security chief. Apparently, Rick held a grudge against the family because Connor's father had swindled his dad out of some inherited property. So Rick felt it was his right to take what should have belonged to him."

"He sold the stuff through Luigi, the man in the hoodie who'd been spotted on the grounds," Brianna added, knowing the whole story. "Rick introduced Luigi to Daniel, Lacey's son, when he needed a loan."

"But this guy wasn't the killer?" Cynthia plucked at her floral skirt.

"No, he was just a bad egg," Marla said with a grin. "And speaking of bad eggs, Connor had sold all the real Fabergé eggs and substituted fakes. He did the same thing with some of the other art works, too. With the money and a new identity as Anton Wiley, he bought a boat that he named Beethoven."

"I thought he worked on the estate as Karl the beekeeper," Susan put in with a frown.

"Yes, thanks to Sarah, the gift shop manager. She was in love with Connor and helped him get the position. Sarah had a talent for finding unique items to sell in the gift shop, but she wasn't a good businesswoman. She hid the shop's financial losses from Lacey, afraid of losing her job. That would mean she couldn't be near Connor, who kept leading her on to ensure her loyalty."

"She knew about his staged death," Brianna said. She beamed at Marla as though proud of her contributions to the case. Her insights had been truly helpful.

Marla confirmed her statement with a nod. "Connor needed Sarah. She was the one who ordered the reproductions for him to swap out with art works in the house. He got rid of her when she became a liability."

"Tell them about the surprise inside the egg," Brianna prompted.

Marla complied. "Connor had hidden a valuable stamp inside the ruby egg. He stole the egg the day of the hunt when everyone was occupied. Paolo spotted him through the window. Connor glanced up and saw the gardener peering at him. Paolo got scared, realizing who the beekeeper had to be, and asked Blinky for her costume."

"Wait a minute," said Blinky, raising a hand. "How did Paolo recognize Connor with his beard?"

"Connor had a key to the display cases, remember? Paolo must have figured it out. He changed into your bunny suit in the garage but Connor intercepted you both. He tied you up and marched Paolo away to get rid of him. It was only your quick wits in offering to help him through your business connections that kept you alive."

The men had finished loading the gifts and putting the cake leftovers in her car. They stood outside chatting while waiting for the women. She'd have to end this soon.

"Didn't you suspect the café manager of needing money?" Nicole asked, tapping a painted fingernail against her chin.

"Michelle is the breadwinner for her family. She's still

paying off the loan she took to open the restaurant. Lacey has made her an offer that will help. Instead of bringing in an outside caterer for their special events, she'll use Michelle as chef. That would bring more money Michelle's way and keep the catering in-house."

"That's a great idea," Tally said. "You spoke about Heather, the head docent, at one time."

"Oh yes. She's a lovely lady who truly values the history of the house. The poor woman has the burden of medical care for her ailing husband. I don't believe Heather would ever do anything to jeopardize her position. She's too much a fan of the place and needs the income. Lacey said Heather was upset to hear about the reproductions."

Tally tilted her head. "What will happen to the estate now?"

"Daniel spoke to his mother. He admitted his dream of teaching software skills to kids and running a summer computer camp. He's been working toward a graduate degree in education. But he has no interest in Tremayne Manor, especially after learning his biological father is Bruno. He doesn't feel any sense of obligation to the estate."

"Then he gets nothing? I thought Connor had returned to make things right by him," Kate pitched in. Her mother-in-law paced the tile flooring, clearly ready to move on.

"Daniel has the property Connor bought for him. The bill of sale was legitimate, and he signed the documents making him the legal owner. He plans to move there. Lacey has discussed with him her desire to donate the house and most of its contents to the historical society. She's decided to leave Daniel her personal assets now that she knows he's on a better path."

"Will Lacey continue to live at the manor?" Nicole asked. The other stylist sat on the arm of the couch.

"She'll donate it with the stipulation that she can live there as long as she wants. I think she realizes Bruno has more to offer than his maintenance services. He was right when he thought he saw a ghost. He'd noticed Karl's profile, and it struck him as similar to Connor without the beard. Lacey urged him to report it, but he let it go."

Blinky's nervous habit reinforced her nickname. No doubt this topic brought back unpleasant memories. "I'll forever be grateful to you, Marla, for solving this case."

"Hey, are you forgetting about me?" Dalton strode inside to stand among them. "Anyway, this is the last time Marla will be involved in any crime-solving. She's promised to focus on the baby from now on. I plan to hold her to those words."

Marla stood and advanced to her husband's side. She took his arm and faced their guests. "We have a new future ahead. You're the ones most important to us. Hereafter, I'm dedicating my time to all of you and to our son. No more snooping. No more tracking down killers and other bad guys. All I want is to be a good mother, daughter, and friend to you all."

"Did you guys decide on a name for your baby?" Jill asked in her Southern drawl. Arnie's wife had pitched in with some of her other friends to get the stroller they needed.

"Yes, we did," Marla replied with a grin. "But we don't want to jinx anything by telling you now. You'll hear it when the baby is born." Her son kicked his agreement. Or was that his elbow jabbing her insides?

She regarded the assembly, her heart swelling with joy. Soon her child would take his place among them, and their world would expand. With her family and friends, there couldn't be anything else she would ever need.

Acknowledgements

With deep gratitude to the following:

Dr. Judy Melinek, forensic pathologist and co-author with T.J. Mitchell of the memoir *Working Stiff* and the novel *First Cut,* for answering my questions about autopsy results relating to details in this story.

Richard L. Cohen, avid stamp collector, for sharing his expertise regarding stamp collecting and his knowledge of postal history.

Special thanks go to my beta readers—Jan Irwin Klein, Sally Schmidt and Taryn Lee.

Your comments were invaluable in improving this book. Thank you for your diligent eye in looking the story over and suggesting ways to make it stronger.

Author's Note

Easter Hair Hunt was inspired in part by Hillwood Estate, Museum & Gardens in Washington D.C. This former residence, now a museum and botanical garden, once belonged to heiress Marjorie Merriweather Post. The house is fascinating to visit with its Imperial Russian and French decorative art collections. Not to be bypassed are the lovely grounds with manicured lawns, colorful flowers, and shady tree-lined paths. Stopping for lunch at the café is a must-do when you come for a visit. There's no handy Metro stop nearby, so you'll have to catch a ride, but this place is well worth the effort. Read more at www.HillwoodMuseum.org.

For my story, I relocated the setting to South Florida and evoked a similar atmosphere with a stately mansion and expansive grounds. I had originally intended for this story to be a novella. Since I'd already written *Haunted Hair Nights*, I thought a series of holiday novellas would make a nice bundle. However, as the number of suspects grew and the premise expanded, I realized this story had to be a full-length novel.

Soon I was researching all sorts of interesting material, such as beekeeping, health benefits of honey, love bugs, postage stamps, Russian nesting dolls, and Fabergé eggs. I hope you enjoyed learning about these unusual topics as well.

Regarding the places in the Redlands, I changed the names so I could add my own details. Craig Berry Farm is based on Knaus Berry Farm. http://www.knausberryfarm.com/. Robert's Marketplace is modeled after Robert is Here https://www.robertishere.com/. Shelley's Winery is similar to Schnebly Redland's Winery https://www.schneblywinery.com/. These are all fun sites to visit if you're in the area.

As for Marla's personal evolution, she's finally come full

circle with her character arc in that she's looking forward to motherhood. She and Dalton will have a big adjustment ahead as Brianna goes to college and they welcome a new baby into their home.

****

For updates on my new releases, giveaways, special offers and events, join my reader list at https://nancyjcohen.com/newsletter. Free Book Sampler for new subscribers.

Thank you for taking the time to read my book. If you enjoyed the story, please consider writing a review at your favorite online bookstore. Reader recommendations are critically important in helping new readers find my work.

Recipes

GARLIC CHEESE BISCUITS

Ingredients

2 cups biscuit mix
1/2 cup shredded cheddar cheese
2 cloves garlic, minced
2/3 cup low fat milk
2 Tbsp. butter, melted
1/4 tsp. garlic powder

Directions

Preheat oven to 450 degrees. Combine biscuit mix, shredded cheese, and minced garlic in a large bowl. Stir in milk until moistened. Drop by the tablespoon onto a greased cookie sheet. Bake for 10 minutes or until browned. Meanwhile, mix together melted butter and garlic powder. Brush over warm biscuits and serve. Makes 12 biscuits.

SLOW COOKER ROAST LEG OF LAMB

Ingredients

3 to 4 lb. boneless leg of lamb
4 peeled cloves garlic, cut in half
0.75 oz. package fresh rosemary
Olive oil
1 lemon, halved
1 jar mint jelly (optional)

Directions

Using a small knife, make several incisions in the lamb. Stuff a half clove of garlic and a few rosemary sprigs into each cut.

Drizzle a small amount of olive oil over lamb. Place the meat in the slow cooker. Squeeze the lemon over the lamb, and drop the lemon shells into the slow cooker. Cook the lamb on low for 8 hours or until the meat easily pulls apart. It should register at least 135 degrees on a meat thermometer.

Uncover and discard lemon shells and rosemary sprigs. Transfer meat to cutting board. Cover with foil and let rest for 15 minutes. Slice and serve warm with mint jelly on the side. Serves 6 to 8.

SLOW COOKER MUSHROOM POT ROAST

Ingredients

3 to 4 pound boneless lean beef chuck roast
2 Tbsp. canola oil
16 oz. sliced mushrooms
1 large onion, sliced
8 oz. diced celery, carrots, onion mixture
10 garlic cloves, peeled and quartered
1 ½ cups beef broth
8 oz. can tomato sauce
1 cup Burgundy wine
2 bay leaves
1 tsp. dried thyme
¼ cup cornstarch
¼ cup water

Directions

Heat oil in large skillet. Sear meat on both sides until lightly browned. Put beef into slow cooker. Add the rest of the ingredients. Cook on low for 8 hours.

Transfer meat to cutting board, cover with foil, and let rest for 15 minutes. Skim fat from pan juices. Strain juices into a separate pot. Dissolve ¼ cup cornstarch into equal amount of water and stir into gravy. Cook until thickened. Pour into gravy boat. Slice meat and serve warm with gravy on the side.

ROASTED ACORN SQUASH

Ingredients

2 Acorn Squash
Olive Oil
Paprika, Oregano, Parsley, Garlic Powder

Directions

Preheat oven to 350 degrees. Cook acorn squash in microwave on high for a few minutes until somewhat soft. Place the squash on a cutting board and slice it in half length-wise. Remove the seeds. Lay the half pieces cut-side-down on the board and slice into ¼ inch length-wise slices or along ridges.

Arrange the slices in a single layer on a greased aluminum-foil lined baking sheet. Drizzle olive oil over the top of each squash piece and sprinkle with spices. Bake for 40 to 50 minutes or until slices are fork-tender. Serves 4.

ROSEMARY RED POTATOES

Ingredients

3 lb. bag of petite red potatoes
1 Tbsp. fresh chopped garlic
1 large onion, sliced
0.75 oz. package fresh rosemary, stemmed and chopped
Olive Oil

Directions

Preheat oven to 400 degrees. Clean half of potatoes and cut into quarters. Store the rest for another use. Put the cut potatoes into a large bowl. Mix in garlic, onions and rosemary. Add enough olive oil to moisten. Spread onto greased 9x13x2 inch baking sheet. Bake on the next up-from-bottom rack for 30 to 45 minutes or until potatoes are browned and fork-tender. Serves 4.

TILAPIA DIJON

Ingredients

4 tilapia fillets
2 Tbsp. light mayonnaise
2 Tbsp. grated Parmesan cheese
1 Tbsp. lemon juice
2 tsp. Dijon mustard
1 tsp. prepared fresh grated white horseradish
1/4 cup dry bread crumbs
2 Tbsp. butter, melted

Directions

Preheat oven to 400 degrees. In a small bowl, combine the mayonnaise, 1 Tbsp. Parmesan cheese, lemon juice, mustard and horseradish. Put fillets in greased 9-inch square baking dish. Spread mixture over fish. Meanwhile, in another bowl, mix the bread crumbs, melted butter, and remaining 1 Tbsp. Parmesan cheese. Sprinkle over fish. Bake for 20 minutes or until fish is cooked through. Serves 4.

About the Author

As a former registered nurse, Nancy J. Cohen helped people with their physical aches and pains, but she longed to soothe their troubles in a different way. The siren call of storytelling lured her from nursing into the exciting world of fiction. Wishing she could wield a curling iron with the same skill as crafting a story, she created hairdresser Marla Vail as a stylist with a nose for crime and a knack for exposing people's secrets.

Titles in the Bad Hair Day Mysteries have been named Best Cozy Mystery by *Suspense Magazine*, won a Readers' Favorite gold medal and a RONE Award, earned first place in the Chanticleer International Book Awards and third place in the Arizona Literary Awards. Nancy's instructional guide, *Writing the Cozy Mystery*, was nominated for an Agatha Award, earned first place in the Royal Palm Literary Awards and the *TopShelf Magazine* Book Awards, and won a gold medal in the President's Book Awards. Her imaginative romances have proven popular with fans as well. These books have won the HOLT Medallion and Best Book in Romantic SciFi/Fantasy at *The Romance Reviews*.

A featured speaker at libraries, conferences, and community events, Nancy is listed in *Contemporary Authors, Poets & Writers*, and *Who's Who in U.S. Writers, Editors, & Poets.* She is a past president of Florida Romance Writers and Mystery Writers of America Florida Chapter. When not busy writing, she enjoys cooking, fine dining, cruising, and visiting Disney World.

Follow Nancy Online

Email – nancy@nancyjcohen.com
Website – https://nancyjcohen.com
Blog – https://nancyjcohen.com/blog
Twitter – https://www.twitter.com/nancyjcohen
Facebook – https://www.facebook.com/NancyJCohenAuthor
Goodreads – https://www.goodreads.com/nancyjcohen
Pinterest – https://pinterest.com/njcohen/
LinkedIn – https://www.linkedin.com/in/nancyjcohen
Instagram – https://instagram.com/nancyjcohen
BookBub – https://www.bookbub.com/authors/nancy-j-cohen

Books by Nancy J. Cohen

Bad Hair Day Mysteries
Permed to Death
Hair Raiser
Murder by Manicure
Body Wave
Highlights to Heaven
Died Blonde
Dead Roots
Perish by Pedicure
Killer Knots
Shear Murder
Hanging by a Hair
Peril by Ponytail
Haunted Hair Nights (Novella)
Facials Can Be Fatal
Hair Brained
Hairball Hijinks (Short Story)
Trimmed to Death
Easter Hair Hunt

Anthology
"Three Men and a Body" in Wicked Women Whodunit

The Drift Lords Series
Warrior Prince
Warrior Rogue
Warrior Lord

Science Fiction Romances
Keeper of the Rings
Silver Serenade

Nancy J. Cohen

The Light-Years Series
Circle of Light
Moonlight Rhapsody
Starlight Child

Nonfiction
Writing the Cozy Mystery
A Bad Hair Day Cookbook

For more details, go to https://nancyjcohen.com/books/

CPSIA information can be obtained
at www.ICGtesting.com
Printed in the USA
LVHW021605130121
676402LV00012B/1311

9 780999 793275